Love
Redeemed

Other books by Kelly Irvin

The Bliss Creek Amish

To Love and to Cherish
A Heart Made New
Love's Journey Home

The New Hope Amish

Love Still Stands

Love
Redeemed

KELLY IRVIN

HARVEST HOUSE PUBLISHERS
EUGENE, OREGON

Cover by Garborg Design Works, Savage, Minnesota

Cover photos © Chris Garborg; Bigstock / Copestello

LOVE REDEEMED
Copyright © 2014 by Kelly Irvin
Published by Harvest House Publishers
Eugene, Oregon 97402
www.harvesthousepublishers.com

Library of Congress Cataloging-in-Publication Data
    Irvin, Kelly.
    Love redeemed / Kelly Irvin.
        pages cm. — (The New Hope Amish ; Book 2)
    ISBN 978-0-7369-5495-2 (pbk)
    ISBN 978-0-7369-5496-9 (eBook)
    1. Amish—Fiction. 2. Life change events—Fiction. I. Title.
    PS3609.R82L65 2013
    813'.6—dc23

                                                        2013012860

Printed in the United States of America

14 15 16 17 18 19 20 21 22 / LB-JH / 10 9 8 7 6 5 4 3 2 1

For my brother, Larry Lyne, Jr.
May you rest in blessed peace.

And for my parents, Larry Sr. and Janice Lyne,
who learned to go on.

Preface

Phoebe and Michael's story wasn't an easy one to write, even though the words came more quickly than any novel I've ever written. My biggest fear is that I didn't do their story justice. I dedicate this book to my brother, Larry (always known as Little Larry to distinguish him from our dad, Big Larry). Little Larry died in a boating accident at the age of thirty in 1991. A big guy, well over six feet tall, he loved to fish and hunt deer and tell jokes. He loved his wife, Jana, and his daughter, Holly, who was five at the time. He didn't get a lot of breaks in his short life, but he always remained a good guy. As adults, our life journeys took us on very different paths and we didn't see each other much, but he remains a part of my life to this day.

I was eight months pregnant with my son when I received the news of Larry's death a thousand miles from my South Texas home. I always know exactly how long it's been since he left us as I celebrate my son's birthday each year. I hope my parents will understand how much their ability to accept and learn to go on affects the words on these pages. I also hope this story honors all parents who have lost children far too soon.

A special thanks to my editor, Kathleen Kerr, who took time from her busy schedule more than once to read early drafts and assure me everything would be fine. I believe her exact words were "Dude, stop panicking!" Thank you, Kathleen, for your abundance of patience and kind words.

As always, thanks to my husband, Tim, for his unfailing support and to my children, Erin and Nicholas, for simply being who they are. Love always.

Who is a God like you,
who pardons sin and forgives the transgression
of the remnant of his inheritance?
You do not stay angry forever
but delight to show mercy.
You will again have compassion on us;
you will tread our sins underfoot
and hurl all our iniquities into the depths of the sea.

MICAH 7:18-19

The Original New Hope Families

Luke & Leah
Shirack
William
Joseph
Esther & Martha
(twins)
Jebediah
Hazel

Elijah & Bethel
Christner

Silas & Katie
Christner
Jesse
Simon
Martin
Phoebe
Elam
Hannah
Lydia
Sarah
Ida Weaver
(Katie's sister)

Thomas & Emma
Brennaman
Eli
Rebecca
Caleb
Lilah
Mary & Lillie Shirack
(Emma's sisters)

Tobias & Edna
Daugherty
Jacob
Michael
Ephraim
Nathaniel
Margaret
Isabel

Aaron & Mary
Troyer
Matthew
Molly
Reuben
Abraham & Alexander
(twins)
Ella
Laura

Benjamin & Irene
Knepp
Hiram
Daniel
Adah
Melinda
Abram
Joanna
Jonathan

Peter & Cynthia
Daugherty
Rufus
Enos
Deborah
Rachel
John
Mark
Phillip
Ruth
Naomi

Chapter 1

Phoebe Christner longed for water. Sweet, cool water. The kind that soothed a parched throat. She should be concentrating on living water, but the blazing August heat made it almost impossible. Who had the bright idea of holding baptism classes outside in hundred-degree weather? Probably her *daed*. As if the searing heat would make the scholars more likely to choose the church and eternal salvation. She hid a smile behind her damp palm and then swiped at the sweat trickling down her forehead with the back of her sleeve.

The sound of hymns sung by the other members of her community wafted from her family's barn, a slow, steady hum that threatened to lull her to sleep. She jerked upright on the hard wooden bench. No sleeping in class. The humid air hung heavy on her shoulders, making her dress sodden under her arms. She strained to feel a tiny breeze, a hint of fresh air to dissipate the rank smell of manure and horse that hung over the corral. Her stomach rumbled like a train, threatening to drown out the sound of the blue jays chattering in the oak trees that shaded their small class.

The heat of embarrassment rolled over her, compounding her discomfort. She hazarded a glance at Michael Daugherty. He sat back straight, arms folded over his chest, on the bench across from her, next to his best friend Daniel Knepp. She tried her best not to stare, but Michael's dark blue eyes, full lips, and the hint of dimples rarely seen

12   Kelly Irvin

but surely there made it hard to look away. His gaze sideswiped hers. The skin of his tanned face grew darker. He ducked his head.

Now she'd embarrassed him too. Her face as warm as the sun that beat on them, Phoebe wiggled in her seat and leaned over to brush away a piece of dry grass from her dusty prayer service shoe. Michael's cousin Rachel elbowed her and gave her the look. The look that said *Stop it now before it's too late*. Molly Troyer, sitting at her right side, coughed into her hand, a soft, warning cough. They'd all been friends since before Phoebe could remember. They knew how easy it was for her to get off track.

Too late.

"Phoebe, are you sitting on a pile of ants, by any chance?" Despite his words, Thomas Brennaman didn't sound angry. Phoebe so wanted to possess the deacon's unending well of patience. Instead, she flitted from one thing to the next, like a hummingbird. "Forget those flights of fancy and concentrate. Baptism is one of the most important and sacred acts in your life."

Mortified, she cast a swift glance in Michael's direction. A touch of something—sympathy maybe—softened his gaze. He shook his head slightly, as if to ask, *What's going on with you?* He had no idea how hard she tried. He so rarely talked to her beyond a few mumbled words of greeting at the singings or a congratulatory whoop when she got a hit at the baseball games they'd played outside the schoolhouse in the old days. In fact, he seemed to go to great lengths to avoid talking to her. To be fair, he wasn't much of a talker with anyone. If only he could make an exception with her.

"Phoebe, do you have corn cobs in your ears?" Now Thomas did sound aggravated. "Hello?"

Daydreaming again. Her face burned. "I'm sorry. It's so warm today. And I didn't have time to eat breakfast this morning." She flapped both hands in front of her face, trying to create a breeze. "Now it's hard to concentrate because I'm so hungry. The lesson and three hours of service—well, it's a long time until we eat."

"You always have an excuse. We've been through a half dozen lessons this summer, and you're still offering excuses. You're not a child anymore." Thomas's thick eyebrows waggled over a new pair of gold-rimmed spectacles that made him look like her daed when he sat down to read *The Budget* newspaper in the evening. "After you join the church, you'll be considered an adult. *If* you finish these classes. You can't burn the candle at both ends…"

He let the sentence trail off, but his gaze wandered to the others in this group, all young, all at the tail end of their *rumspringas*. The older folks turned a blind eye to the shenanigans that went on during this period of running around, but sometimes it was hard to miss. The late hours, the *schinckt* of cigarette smoke lingering in clothes, a necklace one of them forgot to remove. Phoebe tried never to flaunt her forays into the *Englisch* world in her parents' faces, but she knew they cringed at her late hours and unexpected absences. This morning she'd over-slept and only arrived downstairs in time to clean the kitchen. She couldn't expect to eat if she didn't help prepare the meal.

"I'm sorry. I promise to do better." Her stomach growled again, like a bear threatening to claw its way out. Embarrassment made the tips of her ears hot. "I'll study hard."

"Pray hard. Look into your heart and make sure this is something you want to do. To commit to the church and to follow the *Ordnung* for the rest of your life." Thomas's gaze roved from Phoebe to Molly and Rachel on the girls' side and then, with slow deliberation, to Michael and Daniel. "If you have any doubt in your mind, wait. There'll be another opportunity in the spring."

His gaze came back to rest on Phoebe. She tried to hold it but faltered. He seemed to know of the turmoil in her head. She wanted to be baptized. She wanted to commit to the church for life. She loved her family and her community. But mostly she wanted to marry, live with her husband on their own farm, and have children. Two things had to happen first. She had to be baptized and she had to somehow get Michael's attention. Hard as the baptism classes were, the first seemed easier than the second. So here she sat outside her family's home, sweating in hundred-degree Missouri weather, hoping to take a step in the right direction on both counts.

"The second sermon is beginning. We need to go in." Thomas

stretched his long legs out in front of him, his expression somber. "You'll meet with Silas in two weeks. Be sure you keep working through the Dordrecht Confession of Faith. We'll review the seventeenth and eighteenth articles next time. The date for baptism will be set for two weeks before the fall *grossgemme*. Then it will be time for communion, which you will take as members of the church. We should have dates by the next class."

Baptism and then her first meeting as a member of the church. She would have a vote on changes in the Ordnung. Then her first communion. Phoebe swallowed against the bitter taste in the back of her throat. Her days of rumspringa would be over. Days of slipping out to hear music and watch the big-screen TV over the bar in the little tavern in New Hope would be over. So would riding with her hair down and blowing in the hot wind in their Englisch friend Dylan's convertible on the back roads that wound their way through fields full of rustling cornstalks. Time to grow up. Time to marry and have children. She hoped.

"But in two weeks we'll be at Stockton Lake." Her voice timid, Molly raised her hand as if she were still in school. "All our families will be there."

The thought of the lake and swimming and fishing and barbecuing hot dogs and marshmallows and making mountain pies and telling stories in the tent after dark made Phoebe want to stand up and shout hallelujah. She caught herself just in time. Michael's daed had announced his intention to take the whole family as well. She'd have plenty of opportunity to cross paths with Michael morning, noon, and night. To strike up a conversation. Maybe he'd ask her to take a walk in the woods some evening. Maybe. Just maybe.

A nudge from Rachel told her she'd done it again. Quickly, she fixed her gaze on Thomas, who perused the calendar book he always brought with him to the classes.

"You're right. I've lost track of the days." Frowning, he shoved his hat back on his head. "I'll talk with Luke and Silas about the dates. You'll be told with plenty of time for prayerful consideration." He stood. "Go. I don't want any of you missing the service."

No one needed to be told again. Everyone popped up from the benches like wild horses set free from a corral. Rachel and Daniel traipsed ahead of Thomas, pretending they didn't know each other from Adam when everyone in their tight circle of friends knew the two were leaving the singings together on Sunday nights. Phoebe hung back, wanting to give Michael a chance to say something—anything. Molly gave Phoebe a skeptical glance, sighed, and trudged after the others.

A band tightened around Phoebe's heart. The man her friend fancied would marry another in November. At least Phoebe still had hope. As far as she knew, Michael hadn't shone his flashlight in anyone else's window. "Molly, wait." She slipped over and gave her friend a quick hug so she could whisper in her ear. "You'll meet someone soon. Don't worry."

"All in God's time, right?" Molly sniffed and swiped at her nose. "For you too, right?"

"Right." Phoebe patted her back. "You're such a good girl. You'll see. It'll all work out."

"It always does. God has a plan." Molly managed a watery smile. "Anyway, I'd better get in there. My *mudder's* waiting. Yours too, I expect."

"Aren't you coming to the singing tonight?"

"Nee. I don't want to see…him." Molly swiped at her nose again with the back of her sleeve. Her huge brown eyes fringed with dark lashes—her best feature—were bright and wet behind her brown-rimmed glasses. "I never have a handkerchief when I need one. Anyway, behave, friend. They're watching, you know."

"I will."

Molly's funk melted away and she chuckled, a soft, sweet sound that made Phoebe smile. "No you won't, but you *will* try."

Looking like a chubby pheasant in her dark brown dress, she trudged toward the barn, her head down.

"Cheer up," Phoebe called. "Everything in its time. Isn't that what they always say?"

Molly flopped one hand in a wave, but she didn't look back.

Phoebe turned to find Michael staring at her, an odd expression on his face. She tugged at her apron, certain her *kapp* needed straightening. "Are you going in?"

What a silly thing to ask. Of course he was. She might as well have commented on the weather. *Hot, isn't it?*

Michael stood, his tall, broad frame towering over her. His eyes, the color of the sky on an early spring morning, seemed to pierce her. "Did you understand what Thomas was saying?"

"About *gelassenheit?*" She struggled to organize her thoughts. She'd heard her daed give dozens of sermons on the topic, but she hadn't given it much thought. She'd spent her whole life yielding to a higher authority—mostly Daed's. Still, she'd wanted to talk to Michael. Even if she didn't get to pick the topic. "I think so. We're supposed to yield to the will of God and be content about it."

"I wonder how we're supposed to know what His will is." Michael cocked his head, his forehead wrinkled under his Sunday service hat. Tufts of his dark—almost black—hair escaped under the brim. "Do you ever wonder that?"

Phoebe generally left the talk of religion to those who understood these things better. She only knew what she felt. She might be hotheaded and hot-blooded by her folks' standards, but she loved her Lord God and she loved her community in a speechless bigger-than-her sort of way. She was in a hurry, that was all. Her mudder said she had always been that way for the entire nineteen years of her life. Learning to walk and talk earlier than her *bruders* and *schweschders*. Learning to read sooner. Speaking English first. Always running to school instead of walking.

"Nee, not really." She traced a line in the dirt with the toe of her shoe. "I just do the best I can. I figure He'll do the rest."

Michael smiled then, a brief smile so breathtaking Phoebe forgot how to move. She forgot how to breathe. She forgot the two languages she knew how to speak. Her mudder's voice entreated her to always remember *Gott watches. Gott knows.*

Before she could say anything or do anything, Michael started toward the barn. Her opportunity slipped through her fingers once again. "Michael, wait."

His long-legged pace slowed. He glanced back. "We don't want to miss the sermon."

"Your family is going to Stockton Lake?"

"*Jah.*" He halted and turned. "Yours too?"

"Jah."

The pause lengthened. *Say something, say something.* She really wanted Michael to say the something that would lead to the next step. Whatever that next step turned out to be. She had no experience with this. Instead, he fixed her with a perplexed look as if he had no idea, either. "Then I guess we'll see each other there."

"I guess we will."

He shifted from one foot to the other. She did the same. "Maybe we—"

"We could—"

"What's going on here?" Phoebe's daed strode toward them, his tall, wiry body backlit by the sun. At first she couldn't see his expression, but she heard the surefire irk in his words. "Phoebe, get yourself into the service. Now."

"Nothing's going on—"

"Go."

"Daed—"

"Phoebe."

The command in his voice sent her scurrying toward the barn. His gaze icy, he moved aside so she could pass. She'd finally exchanged more than two words with Michael, and her father was about to break the slim thread between them. "Daed, please." She poured all the entreaty she could muster into the words. "We were just talking."

"When you should've been listening to the sermon."

She risked one last glance at Michael. He looked the same as always. Untroubled. Shoulders broad enough to bear the weight of the world. "I'm sorry. I had a question about the lesson," he said. He wrapped his fingers around his suspenders, his expression earnest. "I held up Phoebe, thinking she could help me figure it out."

Her daed's glare faded a little. "You should ask those questions of Thomas." The growl in his voice dissolved. "Or me."

"I will."

The two men seemed to size each other up.

Michael didn't know her daed all that well. If he did, he'd look a whole lot more worried.

Chapter 2

Phoebe took the dirty plate Hannah offered and dipped it in the tub of dishwater, swished it around, and applied elbow grease with the dishcloth. When her brothers and their *fraas* stayed for supper, the stack of dirty dishes on the counter certainly took its sweet time in getting clean. They'd gone on home to do evening chores, leaving the sisters to do the cleanup. She didn't mind, though. Washing dishes gave her time to think. Time to daydream. She rubbed an itchy spot on her nose with the back of her sleeve and stared out the window above the tub. The sun still hung above the horizon. She loved these long summer evenings that stretched endlessly. Full of opportunity for fun and frolic. What was Michael doing right now? Getting ready for the singing? She hoped so.

Maybe this would be the night when he finally asked her if he could walk her to the door. The disadvantage of having the singing at their house meant he wouldn't need to give her a ride home. Of course, they could take a buggy ride. The destination didn't matter. She sighed, already feeling the night air cooling her warm cheeks in a rush as the horse picked up speed at Michael's urging.

The thought of a cool breeze led her to the thought of Stockton Lake. The photographs in the brochure Daed had received in the mail danced in her mind's eye. Four whole days by the water. Four whole days with no chores other than cooking and washing dishes and taking care of the *kinner.* Plenty of time to cross paths with Michael.

The lake would be perfect. She could almost smell the hamburgers sizzling on the grill and feel the leaves under her bare feet and hear the lap of the water against the shore. She inhaled, thinking for a moment she would smell mountain pies cooking over the open fire. Instead she breathed in burned pork chops. Her contribution to Sunday supper.

"The more you daydream, girl, the colder the water gets." Mudder's brisk voice startled Phoebe. The slick, wet plate in her hand nearly ended up at the bottom of the tub. "Wake up or the job will never be done."

Mudder picked up the kettle on the stove and brought it to the tub, her round body forcing Phoebe to move aside. Steam billowed from the kettle as she poured. "Hannah, go sweep the floor around the tables. Lydia made a big mess with the bread. And take a washrag. Sarah has apple butter all over her hands and face. Wipe her down and get her out of her highchair. Then take the two of them upstairs and get them ready for bed. Your daed and I want to talk with your sister."

Phoebe swiveled. Sure enough, Daed stood in the doorway, his hands on his narrow hips. A curious look on her freckled face, Hannah dropped the towel she was using to dry the dishes, tossed a damp washrag over her shoulder, and grabbed the broom. At twelve, she knew better than to ask questions. She ducked past Daed and disappeared through the door.

Daed had laugh lines on his laugh lines. Even with his sun-beaten skin and the start of wrinkles around his blue eyes, he had a pleasing face. Even Phoebe could see that. Now, no laughter lit his blue eyes. Stern lines weighed down his mouth. She'd seen that look before. Almost always directed at her.

"I'm sorry I burned the pork chops. I got distracted when Lydia spilled the pan of green beans she was snapping." Phoebe twisted the washcloth between her hands. Apologize before he could chastise. It had served her well in the past. "The pie turned out fine even though I left it in the oven a tad too long."

Daed strode across the kitchen to the counter. He poured himself a glass of sweet tea, but he didn't take a drink. He set the glass down hard enough that the tea sloshed over the side. "Your cooking would be fine if you would pay more attention and stop mooning around all the time. You've been neglecting your chores lately."

"Silas, can we sit and talk?" Mudder squeezed into a chair at the pine prep table and folded her hands together on top. She never sat until the supper chores were done. Phoebe's stomach rocked, making her wish she hadn't eaten the tough pork chop and fried potatoes. Mudder had that disappointed look on her face she always had during these conversations. "Calmly."

"Jah, jah." Daed cleared his throat, but he remained standing a few feet from Phoebe. He towered over her, making her feel as if she was still five or six. Just like always. "It's not just the chores. You're not applying yourself to the baptism classes."

"Why? What did Thomas tell you?"

Daed's thick gray eyebrows hunched like caterpillars and his forehead wrinkled. "Thomas hasn't said anything. I have eyes in my head. I can see for myself."

"I haven't missed a class."

"What your daed means to say is we want to make sure you're…" Mudder didn't sound as sure of herself as Daed did. She seemed torn. "That you understand how important these classes are. How important it is to be baptized. To marry. And then to start a family."

What other way would there be? "I do understand. It's the only way I know."

"Sometimes, when a person reaches your age, it's hard to see the order of things in the midst of all the…feelings." Daed's red face turned redder. He picked up the tea glass and set it down again. "What I saw in the yard today—that's not the order of things. You know better. I'm certain you were taught better."

"We weren't doing anything. We only wanted to talk."

"You hung around in the yard to talk to a young man instead of getting yourself inside to hear the sermon. I won't abide by that kind of behavior."

"Michael had a question."

"So he said, but I've sat in on my share of those classes. Michael knows the answers to the questions. I'm not sure you do. That makes me wonder why he'd claim to ask you for the answers."

"How are your studies for baptism coming?" Mudder's softer tone took some of the tension from the air that hummed in Phoebe's ears. Mudder could be fair, even when Daed took a hard line for no apparent reason. "Are you keeping up?"

Keeping up with the eighteen articles of the Dordrecht. In German. She'd been a decent student in school, but this religious quagmire made little sense to her. Nor did much of what Thomas had said today. "It's hard to understand."

"I know, but you'll get it." Mudder smoothed a hand over the stained wood of the table. "It's hard for all of us. You don't have to understand every bit of it."

Could she be baptized into a faith she didn't understand? Phoebe wanted to argue, but thought better of it. After all, her puny little brain couldn't hope to understand something as big as Gott.

"In the meantime, I think you should stay here when we go to the lake." Daed crossed his arms over his chest, his face all angles like the limestone cut from hillsides along the highway. "Someone needs to keep an eye on the house and feed the livestock."

"Nee!" Phoebe touched her fingers to her lips, trying to stifle the cry. It wouldn't do to argue with her daed. A daughter didn't do that. But to not go on the trip, their first since moving from Kansas to Missouri...He couldn't be that heartless. Not Daed. "I mean, I thought Onkel Elijah and Aenti Bethel were planning to take care of things here since she's too..."

Too near the time for the baby to come. Especially for a woman who used crutches to get around. Elijah and Bethel had chosen to marry in January instead of waiting until November. Given the few chores to do in the dead of winter, it made perfect sense to Phoebe. Snow made it hard for some folks to get to the wedding, but the two hadn't wanted to wait for the traditional season at Thanksgiving.

"They have, but another pair of hands won't hurt, especially with Bethel needing help now."

She was thankful he looked over her shoulder at the window when he spoke of her aunt's condition. No girl wanted to talk with her father about these things. "I need to go to Stockton to help Mudder with the cooking and cleaning and watching the babies. Otherwise it won't be a proper vacation for her."

"Nice of you to think of your mudder, but I'm sure you're thinking of yourself and *your* vacation too." He pinched the bridge of his nose, his gaze unflinching.

"Jah, I think of myself. It's been a long, hard year for all of us, getting used to being away from Bliss Creek and living in a new place. I thought we would have a vacation as a family. Isn't that what it's supposed to be? A family vacation?"

Daed dropped into the chair next to Mudder. Finally. Phoebe's neck hurt from looking up at him. His gaze never left her face. She felt as if she were an ant under the magnifying glass her brother Elam liked to carry around to look at rocks and bits of wood he found. "It's my job to make sure everyone in this family follows the Ordnung."

"I'm following—"

"Schweschder! Aren't you going to tuck me in?" Lydia trotted into the room in her nightgown, her blonde hair half out of the braid that hung down her back, her chubby, dimpled face perturbed. "Hannah can't hear my prayers like you do."

"That's not true!" Puffing, Hannah scurried into the room, her kapp askew, face red. "I'm sorry, Daed. She got away from me. She ran down the stairs and almost took a tumble trying to outrun me."

Lydia's cheeks creased in a grin. She climbed into Daed's lap. "A story before bed, Daed."

"You're four years old now. Old enough to know better. When Hannah tells you to get in bed, you get in bed. As if it were Mudder or me or Phoebe." Daed gripped the little girl's arms and deposited her back on her bare feet. Despite his rough words, he ruffled her hair with blunt, callused fingers. "Another willful daughter. How did I end up with a house full of them?"

"I'm not willful." Hannah sounded hurt. "I do everything Mudder tells me to do. I'm not like—"

"Where's Sarah?" Mudder put both hands on Lydia's shoulders and steered the girl toward Hannah. "Now that she's crawling, you mustn't leave her alone unless you put her in the crib. She'll take that tumble down the stairs you were worrying about with this one."

"I know. She's happy as a kitten in her crib and half asleep already." Hannah shook a finger at Lydia, looking like a shorter, equally plump replica of Mudder. "Not like this one. Running all over the place."

Only twelve years old, Hannah was already better at taking care of kinner than Phoebe. Sometimes it seemed as if Mudder liked Hannah best. Phoebe couldn't help but see the way Mudder looked at her—perplexed, as if she'd found a baby giraffe among her litter of kittens. The thought hurt Phoebe's heart for a second, but then Lydia wiggled free of Mudder's grip and threw herself at Phoebe. "Come to bed with me, schweschder. It's bedtime. Daed said."

By *schweschder*, she didn't mean Hannah. An unkind thought. Phoebe squashed it. This wasn't a popularity contest and Hannah did much of the work without complaint when Phoebe slipped away on her rumspringa adventures. Hannah never said a word when Phoebe came into the bedroom late, smelling of tavern or bonfire or worse yet, the beer the Englisch boys tried to get her to drink. She didn't like the way it tasted. She couldn't even stomach the way it smelled.

No adventures tonight. Tonight she would be a good big schweschder. Time to settle down and concentrate on her baptism lessons. Phoebe grabbed Lydia's warm, sticky hand. She didn't seem the least bit fazed by Daed's words. At four years old, she already knew what they all knew. Daed might be stern, but he loved his kinner. "I'll take her. Come on, Hannah."

Looking relieved, Hannah trotted toward the door. Trying not to think of the trip to Stockton Lake that she wouldn't be taking and all the fun she'd miss—all the possibilities of time with Michael she'd miss—Phoebe followed.

"Phoebe."

She paused in the doorway and looked back. Daed smoothed his beard, his blue eyes hard as marbles. "You think you're grown-up now. With growing up comes responsibility. And the decision to join the

church and follow the Ordnung." He crossed his arms over his mus-
cled chest. "You have to choose. But you're right about the trip being a
family vacation. You will go, but I expect you to think about what I've
said tonight. And the commitment you'll make when you're baptized.
Whenever you choose to do it."

Phoebe squeezed Lydia's hand hard. The girl squealed in protest and
Phoebe loosened her grip. "I promise I'll cook and clean and watch the
kinner so Mudder can enjoy the time too."

"See that you do." His smile was slow in coming. "Behave at the
singing tonight."

"I will."

She marched toward the stairs, Lydia in tow. She would prove to
him she could be trusted. She'd finally outgrown her rumspringa. Time
to be an adult.

"Phoebe? Phoebe!" Lydia tugged free and planted her bare feet on
the wooden floor.

"What? What's the matter?"

"I don't want to go to bed yet. It's still light."

"That's so we can see our way up the stairs. The days are longer in
the summer, but we still have to go to bed early so we can get up early."

"Are you going to bed now?"

"Nee."

"Why?"

"You, little one, ask too many questions. Little girls should be seen
and not heard."

As if she'd ever paid attention to that rule. Daed said bees were silent
compared to her constant buzzing. She crooked a finger at her little sister. "Go. Now."

Her lower lip protruding, Lydia stomped up the stairs, her feet
making a *slap, slap* on the wood. Phoebe glanced out the window at the
foot of the stairs. Buggies pulled in outside the barn. She paused for a
second, one hand on the banister, and then forged ahead.

She would do the right thing. She would go to the singing and then
march herself up the path to the house at a decent hour. No hanging
around hoping Michael would approach and ask to take her for a ride

in his buggy. She couldn't chance it. If Daed decided she hadn't lived up to her end of their agreement, she wouldn't be allowed to go Stockton Lake. She had a much better chance of having a conversation with Michael there.

Patience was a virtue. One she intended to cultivate even though it seemed to go against the very grain of her character.

Chapter 3

Michael led the horse to the hitching post outside the Christners' barn, all the while keeping a lookout for Phoebe. In all likelihood she'd already gone inside. Still, he didn't want to miss her if she were walking across the long stretch of gravel road that led from her house to the barn. He liked to watch the way she sauntered along, arms swinging, head high, her gaze lifted as if searching for something just beyond the horizon. She didn't walk like a girl. She walked with an assurance that made him want to fall in step next to her and find out what she studied so intently in the clouds. Heat crept up his neck at the thought. Not that he would do it. He wasn't that forward. But he could watch for her and help her carry something if she needed it. In the gathering dusk, he couldn't see much of anything beyond the corral fence, but he would know if she approached. His heart would do that *zing-zing* thing it did and he would know.

"What are you doing standing out here? The singing is inside." Daniel hopped from a two-seater. "You are going inside, aren't you?"

Michael and Daniel had been close friends since they were old enough to catch tadpoles in the pond, but they didn't always see eye to eye. They were about as alike as an apple and a turnip. Daniel jumped feet-first into the fire without considering the consequences. Michael thought on the consequences long and hard. Doing right was better than doing first. "Nice two-seater. I like the upholstery and the headrests."

"Hiram is letting me use it while he goes to Bliss Creek for a visit." Daniel tied the reins to a hitching post close to the hay stanchions. "It's a surprise for Rachel. I bet Jacob would give you his, now that he's married. He doesn't need it anymore."

Michael made sure his horse had enough tether to feed on the hay and started toward the barn door. "He sold it. Needed the money for the new house."

"That's okay. You'll never need a two-seater if you don't actually ask a girl to take a ride with you."

"Courting is private."

"Only if you're actually courting."

Michael shrugged off the irritation his friend's insistence always caused him. He didn't have Daniel's easygoing nature. He wasn't good at talking to girls—or anyone for that matter. He didn't see much need for chatter, which made this whole courting thing painful. It had become apparent to him early on that conversation would be required. The girls liked that. He'd tried a time or two and that was enough. He'd rather get a tooth pulled or dig eighty postholes or clean the chicken coop or…The list of things he'd rather do was as long as his leg. And he was well over six feet tall.

"Hey, here comes Phoebe. Here's your chance."

Daniel slapped him on the back and disappeared through the door. Michael whirled, nearly tripping over his big feet. It was too late for him to leave without her thinking it was odd. Walking at a good clip, Phoebe was already close enough for him to see her face in the light of the kerosene lantern she carried. She wore that dark green dress that made her blue eyes bluer and her white skin whiter. At a distance she looked like a little girl, so slight was her figure. He could probably heft her over his head with one hand and sling her over his shoulder, given the need. Say there was a sudden tornado and he had to rush her to the cellar for her own safety. He stifled a smile at the thought and stowed away in his mind the image of her headlong dash toward him, along with all the others he'd collected over the years.

She glowed in the lantern's soft light as it bobbed up and down, up and down. She glowed with something he couldn't put a name to. High spirits or love of life or simple happiness. He found that glow touching. He wanted to protect it.

"Michael. Hello."

Her high voice had a slight quiver to it. It didn't have the usual happy ring it did when she chattered with the other girls about sewing frolics and canning and baking and such. They had their own foreign language. Or so it seemed to him. He turned toward his horse and checked the tether. It was fine, just as it had been a minute or two before. "Hey, Phoebe."

"Are you coming or going?"

"Coming." At least he had been, until now. Now he considered grabbing the reins and hopping on the horse. Except that would be cowardly. He was no coward. If he could break a horse to a saddle, he could talk to a girl. "I'll stay for a while, I guess."

"*Gut.*"

Gut. She thought it was *gut.* Why did she say that? He turned to look at her. The lantern in her hand cast shadows around them and made it hard to read her expression. Her daed had cause to worry, he suspected. A girl so pretty and so lively had plenty of suitors lining up. Silas was a stern taskmaster, but fair. He hadn't said much outside the barn earlier in the day. Only that Michael knew how important the prayer service was. Dallying outside instead of getting inside for the second sermon had been a mistake. One he wouldn't repeat.

"Is something wrong? Is your Daed still upset? Because if he is, I'll talk to him again."

"Nee. Well, a little, but it's not about you. It's about me. I need to learn to do better." She held up the basket she carried in her other hand. "Mudder sent pumpkin spice cookies and Rice Krispie treats. I'll go back for the lemonade in a bit."

He cast about for a response. This was what he didn't like. Conversation about nothing or anything at all. "Your mudder made them?"

Her smile faded. "Jah, I didn't have time to bake yesterday. I do bake, though. A lot. I made pecan pie for supper today. It baked a little too long and the crust was singed, but it was still—"

"I imagine it was good." He stemmed the flow by holding up his hand. "I'm still full of the supper my mudder made."

She tucked the handle of the basket in the crook of her arm. "Guess we should go in."

"Guess we should."

She didn't move. Neither did he.

Some friends squeezed past them. Samuel and Rafael called out. He nodded. Still, his feet didn't move. Neither did his mouth.

"Is that your buggy?" She sounded delighted. He followed her gaze. Daniel's buggy—Hiram's but Daniel's now. "It's nice."

"It's—"

"It has padded seats—and a radio!" Awe made her voice soft.

"It's not mine. It's Daniel's."

"Oh." A wistful look on her face, she sidled closer and put her hand on the wheel. "It's nice."

"Jah."

She looked around. "Where's your buggy then?"

He gestured at Cookie—so named by his little schweschder for some unknown reason. "I rode my horse."

"Oh." She ducked her head, no sign of a smile now. "They've started singing. Rachel's waiting for me."

She slipped past him and disappeared through the door.

For sure he'd said the wrong thing as usual. Done the wrong thing. He'd ridden his horse because Daed and Mudder were visiting at his Onkel Peter's when he left the house and the second buggy needed a new wheel. They didn't have a third. He should've stayed home. Coming on horseback served no purpose. Now she thought he wasn't interested. And he was. Very interested. Someday he'd figure out how to tell her. If he didn't figure it out soon, someone else would, of that he was certain.

❦

Katie slid her dress on the hanger, stuck it on the hook, and began to take the pins from her prayer kapp, waiting for Silas to say something.

He stood at the window, his blunt fingers gripping the curtain, his expression guarded. He'd been so quiet since their talk with Phoebe. When he didn't talk to Katie, it meant something was troubling him. He had to work it over in his mind, mull it over, until an answer presented itself. Years of marriage to the man had taught her to give him the room to do that. It made their conversations much easier when he finally broke his silence.

"She stood out there and talked to Michael a good five minutes." He let the curtain drop and faced Katie. "She didn't understand a word I said to her."

"Her brain understood. It's her heart that speaks another language." Weary, Katie sank onto the daisy chain quilt that covered their bed. Her back and her feet ached in unison. When she looked at Phoebe, she saw herself, only younger and thinner. Phoebe had her blonde hair and small build. From her father she'd inherited two things—his blue eyes and his independent nature. "She's only doing what girls and boys her age do. It's that time in their lives where they figure out who they are and who they want to be with. I trust we've done everything we can to teach her what's right."

"I thought helping out at the school would settle her down, but from the stories Hannah tells, all she does is play baseball at recess and eat everyone's cookies from the lunch boxes. I don't know how Deborah puts up with her."

"Deborah is like a big sister to her. She knows how to steer her in the right direction better than anyone."

Silas's expression said he didn't think that meant much. "I saw her talking on a cell phone out behind the barn the other day."

"I know."

"I won't abide phones in this house."

"She knows that. When she's baptized all that will stop, anyway."

The flickering light of the pole lamp cast shadows across the room, making the lines on her husband's face seem harsh. He chose a seat on the only chair in the room rather than his usual spot next to her on the bed. "How can we be sure of that?"

"We can't. You know that. Like Martin and Simon and Jesse before her, she has to make her own way. We've been through this three times already. We'll go through it four more times after her. Each time, they'll make the decision to come into the church and marry one of our kind."

"Phoebe's different."

"She's more willful, but she also feels more deeply." Katie measured her words. Silas was the fairest man she'd ever known, but he didn't see much gray, only black and white. "There's so much of you in her."

"Me?" He snorted, his beard bobbing. "You're daft, woman. She's like a tulip in a field of dandelions. I don't know how she got there or what to do with her."

"She's smart. She gets things quicker than most, but because of that she flits around from one thing to the next, all excited for something new. She'll calm down. You did." Katie stood, her knees popping, hips protesting, and went to him. She scooted between the chair and the wall so she could put her hands on his shoulders and knead the tight muscles she knew she'd find there. His head dropped and he sighed. His muscles were like stone. She kneaded harder. "Don't you remember what it was like when we were courting?"

His enormous hands, tough as leather, came up and covered hers. He squeezed in a tight grip. "Like it was yesterday."

"Do you remember how it felt?" Inhaling his man scent, Katie dropped small kisses on hair far sparser than it used to be. "How big it felt...like we were the first ones to ever feel that way?"

"That's the problem. I do remember." Silas's deep voice rasped with emotion Katie knew he would never express. He pushed her hands away and swiveled in the chair so he sat sideways and she could see the unspoken want in his eyes. He pulled her toward him. "Come here, fraa."

Laughing, she tumbled into his lap. The ache in her back and feet disappeared. "Silas! You'll want to check on the young folks in a bit. You know you will. You won't be able to stand it."

"I'll have plenty of time for that. They'll be out there half the night, you know that. I remember what it was like to be young and not need sleep."

His arms slid around her in a hug that held her tight against his warm body. She snuggled against his chest, listening to the steady *thump, thump* of a heart she knew better than her own.

"I'm worried about her," he whispered in her ear. "We had the strength or the will or the faith to do the right thing. I'm not sure she does."

"Gott will see her through." Katie lifted her face to Silas's. "Besides, I suspect she's set her sights on Michael and you and I both know he's a good young man. He'll make a good husband. The kind who can rein Phoebe in."

"She's too young to be anyone's fraa."

"In your mind she's still eight. She's grown-up now."

"She doesn't act like it."

"It's time for her to wed and start her own family."

Silas shook his head and smiled. "I remember when you were that age."

"Me too."

Silas's lips covered hers.

Thank You, Gott, that some things never change.

A creak that sounded like a shot in the deep silence of a country night brought Katie out of the chair so fast she nearly fell. Silas grabbed her arm to steady her and popped to his feet.

Lydia stood in the doorway, her eyes squinting against the light. She pushed the door wider and padded into the room, her nightgown— a hand-me-down from Hannah—dragging on the floor behind her. Another one who looked like Katie but acted like her daed.

"Mudder?" Her plaintive tone said it all. "I need you. Hannah's asleep and she won't wake up."

"What's a matter, little one?" Silas responded first, his tone stern despite the twitch in his lips that told Katie he was trying hard not to laugh. "We've had this talk already tonight. You're supposed to be in bed."

Sniffling, Lydia rubbed at her eyes with the back of her plump hands. "I had a bad dream and I need a drink of water."

"No water at this time of night. You'll only have to get up again later." Katie snatched the lantern from the small table next to the bed and took her daughter's hand. Little girls were so much easier at this age, but they still had to learn. Teach now or pay with a willful child later. "Back to bed."

"But the dream—"

"It was only a dream and it's over now. Dreams aren't real. You know that."

She led Lydia from the room without looking back, knowing that Silas's grin would only make her giggle like a girl.

She almost made it. His deep, hoarse chuckle floated on the air. "Hurry back, fraa."

Katie slapped her hand to her mouth, but the giggle escaped.

"What's so funny, Mudder?" Lydia frowned, her freckled nose wrinkling. Like Phoebe, she had Silas's brilliant blue eyes. "Am I funny?"

"Nee. It's nothing. Your daed told me a silly joke, that's all."

Thank You, Gott, that some things never change.

Phoebe sang out. She let her voice mingle with Rachel's and the other girls'. She loved the faster songs, the ones that made her breathe harder and her heart lift. Truth be told, even if she weren't at a courting age, she would love the singing anyway. Even if Michael hadn't brought his buggy, which meant he had no intention of asking her or anyone else to take a ride after the singing. She should find some bit of comfort in the fact that not only did he not have an interest in her, he didn't have an interest in anyone else.

The voices climbed and then faded away as the song ended. She sighed. Such a lovely, peaceful feeling she received in these hymns. Smoothing her apron, she rose from the pile of hay that she shared with her friends. Time to bring out the lemonade and sweet tea. "Can you help me carry out the drinks?" She included all three girls in the sweep of her glance. Might as well make one trip. It'd been a long day. "We need more cookies too."

"Sure." Rachel smoothed back a few wisps of her strawberry blond hair that had escaped her kapp and scrambled to her feet. Her gaze fluttered over Phoebe's shoulder. Phoebe glanced back. Michael's cousin Richard Bontrager stood by the barn door, one hand propped on the wall. Rachel grabbed Phoebe's arm and leaned in close to her ear, her whisper barely audible over the chatter of two dozen young folks. "I think Richard's waiting for you. Maybe you should go on ahead."

"Nee. He's not." Her gaze connected with Richard's. He grinned and ducked his head. Maybe he was. "I mean…"

"Go. We're right behind you."

Daniel squeezed through the crowd, headed their direction, and Rachel's face dimpled into a smile, her green eyes wide with anticipation. Phoebe suspected her friend would be hard-pressed to keep her word. She wiped shaking hands on her apron and threaded her way through the throngs of teenagers already clustering into little groups, chattering until the noise level reached such a pitch that surely there were a hundred people in the barn, if not more.

She had to pass Richard to get out the door. He pushed it open for her. It took only a second to realize he'd followed her out.

"Wait."

She hesitated and then kept walking.

"Come on, Phoebe." He drew up next to her and shortened his stride to match hers. He looked a lot like Michael. Tall, broad shoulders, dark hair, but his eyes were brown. She couldn't see them in the dark, but she knew. He was no Michael. "I wanted to ask you a question."

"Ask away." The fact that her voice didn't quiver in the least surprised and pleased her. "I'm all ears."

"No, you're more than ears." He laughed, a deep-pitched sound that made the hair on her arms prickle. "I wanted to know if you would take a ride with me."

"I can't. I have to serve the refreshments."

"Not now. I mean after. After the singing."

She chewed on the inside of her cheek, trying to think. Richard had moved to New Hope from Bliss Creek a few months earlier to work with Michael's daed and his uncle. He lived with Michael's Onkel Peter but worked at both of the side-by-side farms. They'd known each other since he moved to Bliss Creek when she was ten or eleven. Still, she had never spent much time with him. She didn't know him like she knew Michael.

"Just a short ride." His teeth were white in the lantern light. "I promise to hold up my end of the conversation. We've never really talked before."

"Nee, we haven't."

"Isn't that what singings are about? To get to know a person."

Maybe so, but she'd always pictured it differently. She'd pictured it with Michael.

"Richard, wait!"

There was the voice that always sounded in her head when she thought of buggy rides. Amazing how she could summon it at will.

Richard slowed and turned. Phoebe did the same. Michael strode up the gravel road behind them. He sounded out of breath. She hadn't summoned his voice after all.

"What is it, cousin?"

Michael shoved his hat back on his head. His face had a dark, ruddy hue and his forehead a sheen of perspiration. His gaze stayed on Richard as if he didn't see Phoebe. "My horse seems to have come up a little lame. I don't know what happened. I thought maybe you could give me a ride back to the house, since it's on your way to Onkel Peter's."

"I'm not—"

"It's all right if you need to help out your cousin." Lightheaded with relief, Phoebe cut Richard off. She knew it was bad form to interrupt a man, but she couldn't help herself. "I have to get the lemonade anyway, and my daed's keeping watch tonight. I expect he'll be making his rounds any minute now."

Richard didn't answer right away. He kicked a rock with his Sunday go-to-service shoe, sniffed, and then stared at the sky. "Sure, I can give you a ride. It's getting late anyway."

"Neither of you have to go right away, do you?" Phoebe cast around for words. The evening was still young. "We have more Rice Krispie treats coming out and lemonade and sweet tea—"

"Like Michael said, we all have to get up early in the morning."

Richard's gaze went from Phoebe's face to his cousin's. He shrugged and stomped past Michael. "You coming, cousin?"

Michael touched the brim of his hat with his finger and nodded at Phoebe. "Goodnight."

"Goodnight."

He turned and followed his cousin toward the buggies.

"Michael."

He looked back. Phoebe kicked herself inwardly. She was never at a loss for words. Never. According to her daed, she'd been born speaking complete sentences. "See you next week."

"See you next week." The serious lines of his face creased into a smile. Her breath whooshed from her lungs. "Maybe sooner. You never know."

From Michael, nine words were a veritable speech. These words held a promise. And Michael was the kind of man who kept his promises.

Content to wait, Phoebe smiled back. Something told her it would be worth the wait.

Chapter 4

With a gentle burp, Michael threw his long legs over the wooden bench and turned to face the lake, a cup of steaming *kaffi* in one hand. The aroma mingled with the lingering smell of bacon even though his mudder had already turned off the Coleman stove and poured the grease into a can for use in gravy later. A flash of white caught his gaze. An osprey taking off, skimming low on the water. The sun bobbed on the far edge of the lake like a bright buoy warning sailboats they'd reached the end of the earth. Despite the August heat, a steady southeast breeze cooled by the vast acres of water tantalized him, tempting him to pitch himself headfirst into the lake.

Maybe if he did the shock of the cold water would clear the cobwebs from his head. He hadn't been sleeping well. It'd never been a problem before. Now, every time he closed his eyes he saw the wistful look on Phoebe's face when she touched the wheel of the two-seater. He saw the look on her face when she realized he'd come on horseback with no intention of taking a girl for a buggy ride. Worst of all, he saw her sauntering up the road at Richard's side.

Then he saw the look on her face when he'd said he would see her next week. She looked interested. Definitely interested. Trouble was, next week had come and gone. They saw each other at baptism class, of course, but that was no place to court. He'd learned his lesson about that. Then, he stayed home from the singing that night to help his daed with a sick hog. The hog died. Not a good night at the Daugherty farm. They planned to butcher it, can the meat, and have it all winter long. It had been deep in the night before he hauled himself into bed and realized he'd missed the singing and missed Phoebe.

What she must think of him. Forget it. He'd ruined it. She thought he wasn't interested. Likely, she'd move on. Likely, next time Richard asked, she'd say yes. Maybe she already had.

His face burning at the thought, he leaned back and closed his eyes, listening to the birds in the towering oaks that shaded the campsite. Birds, cicadas, frogs…a regular concert, the best kind, better than any music he'd heard on the jukebox in New Hope during his rumspringa. A blow to his ribs brought him upright. "Hey! Watch the kaffi."

"Are you bird watching?" Daniel, his face split in his usual grin, nudged him again with a sharp elbow. His friend flopped back on the bench, his hat in his other hand. "Elam was going on and on last night about maybe seeing a bald eagle here."

"They're only here in the winter." Michael had done his own research before the trip. He liked knowing about things as much as Phoebe's little brother did. He and Elam got on better than Michael did with her older brothers. The older brothers knew about courting and were protective of their sisters. "I did see an osprey and a blue heron, though."

"I'm thinking we find our girls and take them bird watching," said Daniel.

Our girls? Daniel might have a girl, but Michael didn't. And he knew for sure Daniel had no interest in birds.

"The fun I have in mind involves a fishing pole and my new lures." Michael pushed his hat down over his face to block the sun creeping up over the trees. "I hope the crappie and walleye are biting. I read that walleyes are great fishing here. And I heard a guy talking at the marina who said he caught a huge black bass yesterday."

"We've got four days to fish. I have a plan and I need to put it into action." Daniel looked the way he always did on these trips. Like a little boy at the fair who couldn't decide whether to have cotton candy or deep-fried Oreos first. "I have to see Rachel."

"You're not supposed to announce these things to the world."

"I can't help it." Daniel had the loony grin of a crazy person. "I'm sorry, *freind*, I really can't help it."

He only spoke the truth. Michael knew that, but he still had to try to rein his friend in. Doing these things the right way gave the best results. "We came here to camp and to fish and to hunt and to swim. They're renting the fishing boat today."

"It's a good place to take walks too."

"You're crazy."

"Crazy in *lieb*."

Holding his tin mug out to keep from splashing his pants, Michael scooted down the bench to make more room for his best friend. "We're fishing today. We're renting the boat. That's the plan. That's what we came here to do."

"Yeah, Mudder thinks she's cooking up a mess of catfish for supper," added Daniel's sister Adah, who squeezed between the two men to grab their plates. "Can you two move so I can get these dishes done? I want to go fishing too."

"You're going fishing? You never stop talking. You'll scare all the fish away." Daniel whooped and ducked when his sister pretended to throw an empty cup at him. "Okay, okay, you can come, but only if you tape your mouth shut."

"*Ach*, you're mean." She trudged away, arms full of dirty dishes. "I'll catch more fish than you will. You just watch!"

"Girls fishing." Daniel's tone held disgust, but he continued to grin. "What next? They'll want to join us for cannonballs off the cliff this afternoon."

Michael doubted that, but it would be quite a sight. Not one his parents would allow, but still.

"What are you thinking about, so serious-like? You need to stop thinking deep thoughts and start figuring out how to talk to Phoebe. If you don't, Richard will beat you to it."

"It's none of your business." Never mind that Michael had had the exact same thought. He glanced over his shoulder. Mudder and Irene stood at a bucket of water on a folding table next to a spigot. They were chattering away like hens comparing notes on their broods. Daed had the fishing reels spread on a blanket while Ben and the boys discussed the pros and cons of lures versus live bait. He leaned toward Daniel. "It's private."

Daniel's eyebrows disappeared under the brim of his hat. "What is? You haven't done anything. Now's your chance. You have four days here. You'll be running into her all the time. You're not gonna get another chance like this." He smacked his hand on Michael's forehead. "You'd have to be stone cold dead not to get that."

Michael slapped Daniel's hand away. "I'm not dead. I want to do things the right way."

"This is the right way." Daniel leaned closer and lowered his voice. "I'm serious. Richard has his eye on her. I see the way he looks at her at the singings. I saw him leave the barn with her the other night."

"Nothing happened."

"Because you jumped in. That's how I know you care. You would never make something up—"

"I didn't make it up." God's providence had given him a lame horse. Did God get involved in these things? Surely He wanted to make sure folks ended up with their intended fraas, didn't He? "I really needed a ride."

"Go down to their campsite and ask her to take a walk with you."

"I'll think about it."

"Don't think too hard. Sometimes you have to stop thinking and planning and jump in. Before Richard does." Daniel stood. He was half a foot shorter than Michael and ten pounds lighter, but he made up for it with sheer willpower. "She'd rather it be you than Richard, but a girl can't wait forever."

"What makes you say that?"

Daniel shrugged. His face turned red. "Nothing."

"Come on. What did you hear?" Michael started to lift his cup to his lips, then stopped halfway. "What did Rachel say?"

Daniel threw a glance at the others. They were far too engrossed in getting ready for the day's fun to notice the conversation. "I'm not supposed to say anything, but I can tell you this much. You ask Phoebe to take a walk, she'll go. She likes you."

The thought that Phoebe might reciprocate his feelings caused something to well up inside Michael, something he couldn't identify. It was so intense it almost hurt. "Rachel said that?"

"Jah. Besides, you'd have to be blind not to see the way Phoebe looks at you." Daniel swung his legs over the bench and faced the table. "Don't you want to find out for sure?"

"Jah."

"Then take her for a walk."

"Is that what you're going to do with Rachel?"

"Jah. We're meeting at her campsite in half an hour."

"You'll get her in trouble."

"I'm not going to walk in and announce myself. I'll wait until the right moment. Her daed and bruders will go fishing too."

"They're gonna wonder why you don't go," said Michael.

"I'll figure out something. Rumspringa, remember?" Daniel grinned.

Concern for his friend lying heavy on his shoulders, Michael shrugged. "Do you really think Phoebe will say yes?"

"Are you joshing me?" Daniel watched him with obvious eagerness. "You'll do it, then? You're going to do it, aren't you?"

"I might." Once the words were out, Michael knew he would do it. He had to do it. If he didn't, his cousin would. Richard hadn't said as much, but his actions made it clear. "I am."

"*Gut.*"

"*Gut.*"

"Then we'll go fishing tomorrow morning at the crack of dawn." Daniel stood, adjusting his hat once more.

"Crack of dawn," Michael agreed.

Unless things worked out with Phoebe and he had another walk to take.

Phoebe leaned over the tub of dirty dishes. It seemed at least ten degrees cooler on the shores of this enormous blue-green lake. A steady breeze wafted from across the water. It felt exactly as she had imagined.

She inhaled the scent of fish and leaves and mud. She knew nothing of trees except that they smelled green and cool. Elam had entertained them on the ride here by pointing out elms, red oaks, hickory, sugar maple, and red bud as they drove into the park. She couldn't tell one from the other, but these things interested her little brother with his guidebook and his magnifying glass.

The sunflowers and goldenrods lifting their faces to the sun—those she recognized. She scraped the last of the bacon grease into a lard can and stuck the skillet in the tub of water she'd lugged over from the spigot. After she washed the breakfast dishes she could join Molly and Rachel and the others for a swim. She shivered at the thought. Despite the August heat, the water was cold. They'd waded in the shallow spot along the shore the night before, splashing each other and screaming with laughter as they dashed back and forth trying to avoid a dunking in their clothes. Even Daed had waded in, his pants rolled up around his knees, his hat pushed back on his head, a grin on his face.

Smiling at the memory, she shoved tendrils of hair from her forehead with the back of a wet hand and plunged back into the work of finishing the dishes. The sooner she finished her chores, the sooner she could have fun. She wished they had one of those beautiful sailboats they'd seen lined up at the marina. She'd love to take sailing lessons. They would rent a pontoon for fishing, but sailing cost too much. *Be content with what you have.* She'd heard those words so many times she could almost hear Mudder saying them aloud.

"Here's the last of it." Speaking as if she'd read Phoebe's thoughts, Mudder limped across the campground from the cluster of picnic tables where they'd gathered to eat, a stack of plastic plates and bowls in her hands. "Something about being outside makes everyone eat twice as much. I thought we'd have plenty of bread with the dozen loaves we brought, but now I'm not so sure. The kinner want to make mountain pies tonight. That takes a lot of bread."

"Why are you limping?" Phoebe laid the plate on the towel and studied her mudder's face. She'd never been able to imagine her mudder as old. She had so much bustle in her. But lately, her walk had slowed. "Did you hurt your ankle? Are you sleeping all right? You look tired."

"I'm fine, girl. Stop with the twenty questions." Mudder laughed and slid the stack of plates into the tub. "It's just the arthritis acting up again."

The doctor had given her mother the news about this disease that made her joints ache when she was still having babies. Still young. "Sleeping on the ground surely doesn't help. Didn't you bring your pills?"

"With all the last-minute rushing around, I forgot them. Besides, I thought all those foam mattresses we brought would be plenty of padding." Mudder rubbed her hip absentmindedly. "Guess I'm getting old. The other women and I will walk over to Mr. Chester's campsite and ask him to drive us back to the marina. I can pick up some aspirin and a couple more loaves of bread, just to be on the safe side. And we'll need more ice for the ice chests if they get a good mess of fish. I figure we can cook it all and then store it on ice, at least for a day or so."

Thinking of what fun they would have with a bonfire and mountain pies that evening, Phoebe grinned. "Did you remember the pie filling?"

"I did—apple and cherry." Mudder smiled back, but she had switched to rubbing her elbow. "I'm so glad we had rain this summer. There's no fire ban. Bonfires and mountain pies are half the fun." She eased onto a stool they'd brought from home and heaved a big sigh. "I wish Jesse and Nan had come. Then the entire family would've been together making mountain pies. Jesse loves the cherry pies."

"With Nan's mudder ailing in Bliss Creek, I can see why they decided to go there instead."

"Jah, it's just..." Her mudder closed her eyes. She looked so weary. "I like having my kinner all together."

Phoebe studied her face. A second later she abandoned plans to wander in the direction of the Daugherty campsite later in the morning. She'd hoped to run into Michael, but it would have to wait. She needed to help her mudder. That would be her first priority on this trip, just as she'd promised her daed. Mudder looked done-in and it wasn't even noon. "Are you sure you don't want me to go to the store? Are you sure you want to do the walking on your sore hips?"

Mudder opened her eyes, stood, and stretched. "I think the walk will do me good, working those stiff muscles and all. I want a chance to visit with the other fraas anyway." She stuck her head inside the tent she shared with Daed and pulled out her canvas bag. "We'll be back in an hour or so. You keep an eye on the little ones. The bunch that went fishing won't be back until late this afternoon—later if the catfish are biting. A fish fry for supper sounds mighty good."

Her mudder deserved this free time. She so rarely got it. The work frolics they had at home were fun, but this was an adventure in the great outdoors. "Hannah and I will watch the kinner. We can take them on a little hike if they get bored with the playground."

Which wasn't likely, with its big plastic slides and fort and swings and monkey bars. They'd chosen this site at Cedar Ridge because it had a playground, a beach for swimming, and nearby fishing. If the men got a hankering to hunt, they could do so on the nearby conservation lease. It was perfect.

Emma Brennaman strolled through the clearing with little Caleb and Lilah toddling behind her. Rachel's mother, Cynthia Daugherty, brought up the rear with her three youngest. Watching them approach, Phoebe could only think that she knew exactly what Rachel would look like in twenty years. She had the very same oval face, green eyes, fair skin, and wide mouth.

"Think you can handle these wild and wooly babies?" A hand on her baby-swollen belly, Emma nodded toward the little procession. "They slept really well last night and they're likely to run around like little heathens. The rest of my brood went fishing, lucky for you."

"Eli, I can imagine fishing, but I can't believe Mary and Lillie went— or Rebecca for that matter."

"Even Adah went. They'll spend the whole time whispering and driving the boys crazy by making noise when they should be quiet."

Phoebe laughed at the thought and wiped her hands on the towel. She swung Lilah onto her hip. The towheaded toddler squealed in delight and then stuck her thumb in her mouth as if suddenly shy. "Where are Molly and Rachel?"

"Molly will be over after she finishes the book she's reading." Cynthia held up both hands in a *what-do-you-expect?* gesture that made them all laugh. That sounded like Molly. With a big beautiful lake in front of her, she had her nose stuck in a book. "She'll drag Rachel over with her as soon as that one gets through taking a walk with Daniel."

"She's walking with Daniel?" A nasty green snake of jealousy slithered through Phoebe. She wanted to take a walk with Michael. She swatted the thought away. Her friend had been sweet on Daniel her whole life—she should be happy for her. "What does her daed say about that?"

A frown on her face, Rachel's mother shook her finger. "He'd already left for fishing and I'm not supposed to have seen them so I'm trying very hard to put the sight out of my mind."

Emma patted her friend's arm. "I'm not looking forward to Rebecca's rumspringa, either."

An awkward silence fell as the three woman glanced at Phoebe and then away. She couldn't think of a thing to say. She hadn't done anything on her rumspringa other girls didn't do. Wasn't that the point? Besides, she'd almost finished her baptism classes. Finally. It must be hard for her parents. The whole community waiting and watching to see if each daughter or son joined the church. It was as if that was how they gauged their success as parents. Her parents were good. Their oldest three sons had joined after enjoying their rumspringas to the hilt. She would join in September and everyone would stop watching the Christner family until it was Elam's turn.

"We should go so we can be back before the fishermen bring us a mess of fish to fry." Fortunately Mudder always knew what to say. "Keep the kinner away from the water." She patted Caleb's head. "And don't let them eat the dirt. You know how Sarah loves a good mud pie."

The awkwardness gone, Phoebe laughed with the women, feeling a part of this close-knit group of women who thrived on taking care of children. She didn't have her own yet, but she would. "You three go on. Hannah and I have it covered."

Hannah, hearing her name, waved from her spot on the grass in the shade of two white oaks. She'd thrown down several blankets back to back and had Sarah playing with a stack of wooden blocks in every color. The children trotted to the playground. Lilah crowed and flapped her hands so Phoebe set her on her two bare feet and released her. The girl toddled after her big brother, Caleb, as fast as her fat legs would carry her.

Laughing at how cute they all were, Phoebe waved goodbye to the women and joined her sister on the blanket, flopping back with her eyes closed. She might catch a catnap if the kinner cooperated. She let herself drift off for a few minutes, enjoying the sound of the chatter-boxes on the playground. Their giggles as they climbed on the play-scape were like music. Happy, contented music. "Ahh, this feels good, doesn't it?"

"Jah. It's restful."

The words sounded so funny coming out of the mouth of her twelve-year-old sister that a chuckle burbled up in Phoebe. The leaves rustled in the tree over her head. Sunbeams burst through now and again as the branches moved in the breeze. *Beautiful, Gott, beautiful.*

"What's so funny?" Hannah frowned over Sarah's head. "Are you laughing at me again?"

"It's just that you try so hard to be all grown-up. Lighten up."

"I'm twelve. I am grown-up. Just because you act like the kinner still doesn't mean I have to act that way."

"Give it a few years and then come talk to me about how fun it is to be grown-up."

"I thought you had a special friend."

"I don't have a special friend," Phoebe protested.

"Do to." Hannah tugged on Phoebe's apron. "It's a sin to lie."

"Courting is private."

"Then why is Michael Daugherty walking over here to talk to you in broad daylight?" Hannah tugged harder. "Sit up."

"What? Now?" Phoebe sat up and swiveled to look behind her. Sure enough, Michael was striding toward them. His hat hid his face. She'd give anything to see his expression. "I wasn't expecting…"

"No, but you were hoping." Hannah tried to look sage, but mostly she looked sly. "While the cat's away, the mice will play."

"Don't be silly. I'm no mouse." Phoebe dusted leaves and grass from her dress as she scrambled to her feet. She straightened her kapp and tried to look nonchalant. "Michael, how are you? What are you doing here? Why didn't you go fishing?"

Michael's gaze traveled to Hannah, who stared back with unabashed curiosity written across her freckled pink face. He cleared his throat. "I…I didn't feel like fishing this morning." He stopped, cleared his throat again. "I thought maybe I'd…you'd…we'd…"

Hannah giggled.

"Hannah, hush!" Phoebe tried to think. This was exactly what she'd been wanting, wasn't it? Time alone with Michael. "Keep an eye on Sarah and the others."

Ignoring Hannah's halfhearted protest, she started toward the picnic tables.

"Phoebe, push me, push me!" Lydia's high voice mingled with the chatter of two blue jays perched on the boughs of an oak tree. "I wanna go higher."

"In a little bit," she called back. "Go down the slides again."

"Push me." Lydia's whine turned into a wail. "Please, schweschder."

"Give me one minute." Phoebe smiled at Michael and pointed to the wooden bench at the table. "Have a seat."

"I can come back some other time, if this isn't a good time." He sounded almost eager. "I can see you have your hands full."

"Nee, nee, this is a good time. Just one minute." She couldn't let him get away now that he'd finally made the first move. She trotted across the grass, aware of his gaze following her. She gave Lydia's swing a big push. The girl barely weighed more than a gnat, and the push sent her sailing into the air. She shrieked her approval. "There you go. I got you started. The rest is up to you."

"Higher! Higher!" Lydia hollered. "Make me go higher!"

"Me too! Me too!" Philip scrambled toward the swing set on short, chubby legs. His little sisters, Ruthie and Naomi, who did everything he did, were right behind him. "Push me too."

"Nee." Phoebe backed away from the swing set. If she didn't get out now, she never would. "I'll be back in two shakes."

"Promise?" Lydia's legs pumped and the swing sailed higher and higher, taking her sweet voice with it. "Two shakes?"

"Promise."

Phoebe fled back to the picnic table and sat down opposite Michael. His hands lay flat on the table in front of him, and then he curled them up into balls. "Hey."

"Hey." He cleared his throat. "It's nice here."

"It is. I like it."

"The lake's…nice."

"It's beautiful." Phoebe wrapped her fingers in the soft cotton of her apron. *Come on, come on, Michael, you can do it.* "Why didn't you go fishing?"

His long, thin fingers traced a crack in the picnic table. "I was thinking…"

"Jah?"

"I was thinking we might…take a walk." His gaze went to the kinner on the playground. "A short walk. I'd like to…talk to you…about something."

Hallelujah. Phoebe pinched the skin on the back of her hand to keep from saying the word aloud. "You didn't come to the singing last week. I thought…"

"One of our hogs was sick."

That explained everything. Amazingly enough. "Did it die?"

"Jah."

"I'm sorry."

He cracked his knuckles. "Anyway, I wanted to go for a ride then, but I couldn't. A walk here would be even better."

"I think so too."

His face reddened under a deep tan. His head came up and his gaze met hers. She never thought of blue as being warm, but the color of his eyes reminded her of the flame on the gas stove when it was turned up high. Crackling with a heat that seeped into her bones. *"Gut."*

"When?"

"Now?" he asked.

Biting her lip, she tried to hide the wince. She glanced back at the playground. Hannah had Sarah in her arms, trying to get her to stand up. The little girl kept plopping on the blanket in her droopy diaper.

Caleb had a stick digging in the dirt by the monkey bars and Lilah was busy trying to catch a butterfly in her two outstretched hands.

That left Lydia, Philip, Ruthie, and Naomi taking turns on the swings. Philip, the little man, was trying to give Ruthie a push. He sat down hard on his rump and all four kinner howled with laughter.

"I guess you can't really leave right now."

She turned back to him. If she didn't do this now, he might never ask again. Everything about the way he sat, the way he spoke, the way he couldn't meet her gaze, said he found this unbearable. She didn't know why, but she couldn't take a chance he would decide it wasn't worth it. "Hannah, I'll be right back." She waggled her hand at her sister. Hannah frowned, but she waved back. "Two shakes, okay?"

"Okay." It didn't sound okay, but hadn't Hannah just been talking about how grown-up she was? "Come right back. Mudder won't be gone long."

Goose bumps ran up Phoebe's arm. She slid from her seat and tried to match her stride to Michael's. His long legs ate up the ground, forcing her to do a double step. They headed into the thick stand of trees that hugged the shore of the lake. An armadillo trundled across the path without looking up. Michael slowed, giving it safe passage and her time to catch up. "Sorry. I didn't mean to make you run."

"That's okay. Those armadillos are strange looking, aren't they?"

"We probably look odd to them too."

She laughed. "Never thought of that."

"I guess I think too much sometimes." Red crept across his damp face. The dark curls under his hat clung to his neck and forehead. "I think animals are interesting, that's all."

"They are." She rushed to assure him. "I think they are too."

"This way."

He headed into the stand of trees on the other side of the road that led from the camp grounds. Almost immediately dappled shade replaced sunshine. The air felt cooler and the leaves crackled under her feet in a thick carpet.

"Where are we going?"

"Nowhere in particular." Now that they were moving the tension seemed to leave his body. He had a loose, easy stride that spoke of a familiarity with being outdoors and trudging long distances. The corners of his mouth turned up and his breathing eased. "Just far enough that we're…alone."

Alone.

The goose bumps on her arms ran up her shoulders and traipsed across the back of her neck.

"I took a walk after breakfast and I found this place. It's a little cranny. You'll like it. There's a place to sit."

A few minutes later and they were there. The trees opened up into a tiny clearing. "See, a bench."

The bench was a fallen tree. Shyness descended on Phoebe. She never felt shy. Not in her life. Now she was alone with Michael for the first time. She'd thought of this moment, imagined this moment, so many times, that it didn't seem real now. It happened so quickly. Hoped for. Wished for. Prayed for. And now it was here in a place far from home, far from the barn and the horses and the creek that ran through their farm. Far from the familiar where she knew what the rules were. What were the rules here? She swallowed. "What now?"

He seemed to consider. "We sit. Just for a minute. I know you have to get back." He sat as if to show her how and patted the tree log. "Right here."

She sat.

They were both silent. Their breathing mingled with the sound of birds overhead and the rustling of leaves in a soft breeze. A dragonfly buzzed close by and a butterfly flitted among the bushes. Shafts of sunlight burst into the clearing as the oak and hickory branches bobbed above them. It was perfect.

"I—"

"We should—"

Michael laughed, a husky sound that sent another chill up her arm. "I wanted to ask you something."

She nodded, afraid to breathe, afraid to move for fear the moment would be lost and the question would never come.

"If I were to shine my flashlight in your window, would you let me take you for a buggy ride sometime?"

Hallelujah times ten. Or twenty. She gripped her hands in her lap to keep from grabbing his. "I would like that."

He exhaled a gusty, noisy breath.

She couldn't help it. She laughed.

"What are you laughing at?" He frowned. "This courting business—it's painful."

"It's not that bad." She giggled again. "It's a simple question. How hard can it be? You didn't have to bring me out here. You could ask anytime."

He growled like an angry bear, but he smiled, that dimpled smile that displayed white, even teeth. "A girl would say that. You don't have to do the asking."

"Nee, you have to wait to be asked. That's worse."

He picked up a leaf from the ground and smoothed its wrinkled edges. It seemed to be the most interesting thing in the world to him, so closely did he study it. He tilted his head to one side and peeked at her. "Have you been waiting for me to ask you?"

"Maybe."

"Maybe? That's the best you can do?"

"Truth be told…" Now she was the one ducking her head and studying the ground and looking for her own leaf. "Truth be told I've been waiting all my life for you to get the nerve to speak up."

"All your life? Huh." His hand touched her chin. She looked up at him. "Since you were a child? That's what you're telling me?"

"That's what I'm telling you."

His hand dropped. He leaned in and kissed her. She saw it coming, but couldn't move to meet him, even though she wanted to more than anything. The kiss was soft, tentative at first, then stronger, almost fierce. Her first kiss. It couldn't be more perfect. The shade of the trees, the smell of bark and leaves. The smell of him, light, breathless, sweet.

He wrenched away, his face the color of a radish. "I'm…I'm sorry. I'm so sorry. I shouldn't have done that. I didn't mean any disrespect."

Feeling as if she'd been dropped from the hay loft, Phoebe grabbed his hand. "I'm not sorry. I've been waiting for that forever too."

"You have?"

"You must be blind as a bat. Do you need glasses?"

He laughed, an uncertain, dumbfounded sort of laugh. "You are a firecracker, Phoebe Christner."

"Ach." She slapped her hands to her hot face. Had she sounded too forward? "Sorry. My daed says I never know when to close my mouth. I can't help it. It's just the way I am."

"I like the way you are."

"I sure hope so. You just kissed me."

"It seems you kissed me back." His gaze somber, he rubbed both big hands on his legs. "I don't think we're supposed to do that. Not yet anyway."

Phoebe ducked her head. He was right. "That's the thing about me. I do everything double-time. You'll learn that about me. That's what my mudder says. I do everything in a hurry."

"I'm a little slower on the uptake." He took her hand and caressed the soft skin along the back of her knuckles. "I like to take my time and figure things out. Is that a problem?"

"Nee. Just don't wait too long."

He kissed her again, this time short and sweet, then he let go. "I won't." He stood. "We should get back. I don't want to leave your sister alone with the kinner too long."

"We should—"

"Phoebe! Phoebe, where are you?"

Hannah's voice, high and shrill, shattered the soft quiet of the forest. It severed the bond that held them still, staring at each other, lost in those first few moments of beginning to learn just how achingly special someone could be.

"I need you! Phoebe!"

Chapter 5

Phoebe stumbled to her feet. Hannah sounded frantic, more than frantic. Hysterical. Her heart slamming against her rib cage, Phoebe jolted forward. They'd only been here a minute or two, hadn't they? Time had lost meaning the second Michael sat next to her and began to talk. She dragged herself from those thoughts. "Here, I'm here, Hannah!" Her voice sounded puny and spun away in the breeze. "I'm coming!"

Two shakes. She'd said two shakes. What could've happened in the brief time since they left the campsite? All Hannah had to do was keep watch over seven kinner. Not that hard for a Plain girl. They'd been taking care of kinner their whole lives. "Call her," she yelled at Michael, whose long strides ate up the ground ahead of her. "Your voice will carry better."

"Hannah, here. We're here."

His voice had deepened to a bass that made him sound just like his daed, Tobias. It boomed against the tall trees around them.

"Where?"

They surged around a bend in the soft dirt trail and there Hannah was, scrambling toward them, her face wet with tears, her cheeks red, little Sarah on her hip. "Where have you been? Where have you been?"

"Whoa, slow down." Michael darted forward. He lifted Sarah from the girl's arms and settled her on his chest. "What happened? What's wrong?"

"Where are the other kinner?" Phoebe slammed to a halt. "What's wrong?"

"Rachel and Molly showed up right after…right after I realized I couldn't find Lydia." Hannah sobbed over the words, painful, gasping sobs. "They helped me look. Molly watched the babies while Rachel and I looked."

"What do you mean you couldn't find Lydia?" This didn't make sense. How hard could it be to keep a four-year-old on a playground? "Where is she? You found her, didn't you?"

"Nee," Hannah wailed. "I can't find her. I can't find her anywhere. You said you'd be back. You promised. Two shakes, you said, two shakes. Come on, we have to find her."

"Come on." For a big man, Michael moved fast. He held Sarah with one arm as if she weighed nothing and headed down the trail, not looking back to see if they followed his command.

Phoebe tore after him, brambles ripping at her clothes, branches slapping in her face in his wake. Hannah's breathless sobs told her that her sister managed to keep up. Rocks and burrs bit into the soles of her bare feet. The pain barely registered. She stubbed a toe and swallowed a cry. They burst into the clearing, slowing for a brief second to make sure no cars would run them down, then slammed across the road.

Phoebe scanned the open space. The picnic tables. The playground. The open water ahead. No four-year-old in a lilac dress and bonnet. Molly huddled with the other kinner on the blanket. She shook her head at Phoebe's unasked question. "Rachel went to get help."

"What happened?" Phoebe gasped. "How did this happen?"

"How did this happen?" Her voice far higher than usual and filled with accusation, Hannah dropped to her knees on the blanket and held up her arms. Michael deposited Sarah in her lap. "You mean how in the world did you decide to go traipsing into the woods instead of staying here and watching the kinner like you told Mudder you would?"

Gasping for air, Phoebe bent over and put her hands on her knees, trying to settle the rocking of her stomach. "I mean, how long has she been gone? Where did you look?"

"I took my eyes off them for just a second. Just a second." Hannah scrubbed at her face with the back of her hand. "I went to the tent to get another diaper for Sarah so I told Lydia to make sure the others stayed put. She's the oldest. She's four; she knows better."

Hannah's tone begged Phoebe for confirmation. She'd done what Phoebe would've done. Even Mudder would've done. Lydia already had chores, gathering eggs in the chicken house, pulling weeds in the garden, snapping beans, trundling piles of laundry as tall as she was up the stairs to the bedrooms. She was old enough to make sure the babies stayed put. Phoebe nodded, sure her fear would show in her face. Four years old and lost on a lake of thousands of acres. This wasn't the farm where Lydia had been born and knew all the fun places to play hide-and-seek. Here, she would be truly lost.

"What happened?" Phoebe tried to work out in her mind what they would do next. They would find Lydia and she would be properly punished for running off. And then they would go for a swim and eat fried catfish and watermelon and catch fireflies and let them go. "When did you notice she was gone?"

"Sarah's diaper was so stinky, I couldn't stand it. I glanced toward the playground when I came back, I'm sure I did, but I changed the diaper and the baby was kicking and cooing at me and I was cooing at her." Hannah's voice wobbled. "She was so cute. I made raspberries on her fat little belly and pinched her chubby cheeks and she giggled and giggled and made me giggle right back."

Hannah's voice broke entirely then. She lifted her apron to her face and sobbed.

"It's all right, it's all right." Molly reached across the blanket and put an arm around the younger girl. "We'll find her."

"I heard one of them crying—I thought it was Caleb." Hannah's words were so muffled Phoebe could hardly understand. She tugged the apron from her sister's face. Hannah looked up at her, bewildered, the mirror image of Lydia. What Lydia would look like eight years from now. "But it was Philip. He was sitting in the dirt by the swing, fussing. He kept calling her name."

"So you went to look for her?"

"As much as I could, just right around here. I had the kinner and I couldn't take them all with me." Her voice rose. Phoebe could hear the barely contained accusation in it. If she'd been here, it wouldn't have happened—or she could've gone immediately to look for Lydia. "I was thinking of trying to walk with them to the next campsite when Rachel and Molly got here."

"Get your cell phone." Michael jerked his head toward the tents. "Do you have it in the tent?"

Phoebe hadn't even thought of the cell phone. How did he know she had one? "I don't…"

"You do. I saw you with it once. Get it. Hurry!"

She ran, stumbling, to her tent, and burrowed with shaking hands through her clothes to the bottom of the bag where she'd tucked the small, shiny rectangular phone with its pink rubber cover. She ran back to Michael. "Here, here it is."

"Call 911."

"What?"

He tugged the phone from her hand. "Let me."

"You've used one?"

"I have one, but I left it at home. I couldn't imagine using one here."

Truth be told, Phoebe couldn't imagine Michael with a cell phone anywhere. Of course, she'd never seen him at any of the Englisch parties she'd attended over her long rumspringa. She thought of him as the keeper of the rules. Until today. Until that kiss. Now a cell phone seemed right. It seemed God-sent. They could call for help. Get the park rangers. They would know what to do. They probably looked for lost children all the time.

Michael growled. "No service." He smacked the phone against his leg in exasperation. "No signal out here."

"What do you mean? What good are those things if they don't work in an emergency?"

"No towers around here."

Towers? She had no clue what he was talking about. And how did Michael know about these things?

He swung around, facing the lake, his back to her. As if he couldn't bear to look at her. Phoebe's throat went dry. Horribly dry. She tried to swallow the lump lodged there but found she might choke on it. "Michael?"

"I'll look along the shore. She can't have gone far on those short legs."

He was right. They had to think only of Lydia right now. Nothing else. Not about what they were doing when this happened. Were they being punished? Surely not. It had been an innocent kiss. She forced the lump down in her throat and sucked in a long breath. Think about Lydia. *Gott, protect her and keep her until we can find her and bring her home safe.*

"I'll go east toward the highway." She didn't want to think about Lydia in the water or on the highway. They both posed terrible threats to a little girl who didn't know about big cars or deep water. "Molly, you go west toward the other campgrounds."

Molly shook her head. "Rachel said to stay here until she returns with our daeds and bruders. She said we might get lost and then they'd have to look for us too. Besides, I'm not leaving poor Hannah alone with the kinner again."

Hannah shifted closer to Molly, who gave her another quick hug. From the look on her little sister's face, she might never accept a hug from Phoebe again. Phoebe didn't blame her.

"We can't just stand around here waiting. Every minute we wait is another minute…"

Hannah's face crumbled again. She hid her face behind Sarah's bonnet, her sob small and wet and strangled.

Phoebe fought back her own sobs. This was her fault. All her fault. The memory of Lydia, swinging higher and higher, her round face split wide with a grin, shrieking with laughter, played itself in Phoebe's mind's eye over and over again.

Higher, higher, Phoebe, higher. More, Phoebe, more.

The sound of her sweet, high-pitched voice sang in Phoebe's ears. She wanted to slap her hands over them, but it wouldn't do any good. The memory would play over and over again inside her head.

"We can pray." Molly said, her hand rubbing in a circular motion on Hannah's back. "That's what we do. Pray."

Michael didn't turn around. He seemed mesmerized by the expanse of water in front of him, with the brilliant sun bouncing across it like a light hitting a sheet of ice and reflecting at odd angles.

"We pray." Phoebe nodded.

They bowed their heads. She didn't peek to see if Michael joined them. The silence stretched, broken by Sarah's cooing and the other kinner chattering on the playground, oblivious. Safe and sound.

"Amen."

Phoebe raised her head. Fear tightened in a knot between her shoulders. If she didn't do something now, she'd be twisted like a pretzel on the ground any minute. "We have to do something. We can't just stand here, waiting, while she wanders farther and farther away." She marched toward the edge of the road and then stopped. "It could take them twenty minutes or more to get back here from where they're fishing with the time it takes Rachel to walk over there."

"She wasn't walking, she was running." Hannah's voice cracked. "Even so…"

"Michael." Phoebe whispered his name. What had they done? *Gott, please, let him be the one to find her and bring her back.* It was a selfish prayer. *Let someone, anyone, find her and lead her home safely. Lord, I pray. And forgive me. Lord, forgive me.*

"Tell them I'll take the route to the next swimming beach and then double back." Michael's voice brooked no argument. He sounded much older now. Older than her Daed even.

"Don't get lost."

"If I don't find her, it might be better if I did." The words were distinct even as they faded into the heavy, humid air between them. "For everyone."

Chapter 6

Phoebe found she couldn't sit. So she stood. Waiting at the edge
of the campsite, the lake shimmering in the distance. Waiting.
Any minute now. Who would come first? Mudder or Daed? Which
would be better? Mudder, definitely. Or maybe it was better to face
Daed's fierce sternness than Mudder's infinite disappointment. She
tried to pace but her legs wobbled, so she leaned against the closest
tree and waited. How long had it been? Five minutes? Ten minutes?
She couldn't tell. Each minute that Lydia didn't skip her way back into
view seemed like a dozen years.

*Gott, please, let her come back. Please bring her home. Show her the
way, Gott. I know she's in Your hands. I know You'll keep her safe. You'll
bring her home. You are Gott. Our Savior and Provider. All this is according to Your plan.*

According to Your plan?

She drew a long, painful breath and let the smell of earth and decaying leaves calm her.

The sound of an engine revving made her jerk upright. Mudder or
Daed? An old blue van rolled around the bend in the road and heaved
to a stop, gears grinding. Daed was in the front seat with Mr. Lewis,
their Englisch neighbor from New Hope, who loved to fish and came
here every year. Daed thrust upon the front passenger door before the

engine died. His boots thudded against the dirt, little puffs of dust rising around him.

Luke, Thomas, and Tobias piled out, followed by all the children who had been with them. No one spoke. No jokes or chatter or *my fish was bigger than your fish* stories, no stories of the big one that got away. Her daed strode directly toward Phoebe, his eyes squinting against the sun, his glare unrelenting.

"What's this I hear from Rachel?" he demanded. "Where's Lydia?"

"She wandered off." Phoebe began. Her voice quavered and she fought for control. "Michael's looking for her."

"Rachel said something about Mudder going to the marina…" He let the sentence float away, waiting for her response. "Were you in charge of the kinner?"

"I was. I was, Daed. It's my fault." Hannah tore across the open space and hurled herself into Daed's arms. He caught her against his chest with an *ooph* as if he hadn't seen her coming. Her tears stained his shirt a darker blue. "I had to change Sarah's diaper and I looked away for a minute, for only a second and then I couldn't find her—"

"Hush, Hannah, hush." Daed's arms tightened around the girl, but his gaze remained on Phoebe's face. "Is that what happened?"

"Jah." Phoebe chewed the inside of her cheek until she tasted blood. "I mean, I didn't exactly see what happened."

"Why not?"

"Michael came over—"

A look of anger, pure and white-hot, whipped across Daed's face. Her breath strangled in her throat and Phoebe took an involuntary step back, hands clasped to her cheeks and neck.

"Michael was here? He stayed at camp this morning. Said he wanted to do some hiking." Tobias, who'd been in the middle seat of the van, tromped over to stand next to Silas. "What was my boy doing here?"

"He came to…he wanted…"

Tobias's face shuttered. "Where is he?"

"Looking for Lydia."

"I hate to interrupt, folks, but the closest visitor's center is several miles from here." Mr. Lewis held up a cell phone. "I tried to call, but I can't get a signal. We'll need to drive up there and contact the Corps of Engineers. They'll work with the Park Service and the sheriff's department to put together a search."

The anger dissipated in Daed's face, leaving it white-gray with blotches of red on his cheeks. He rubbed Hannah's back for a second and then peeled her arms from around his neck. "Go help Molly and Rachel with the kinner."

Hannah hiccupped a sob. "I'm sorry, Daed."

"It's not your fault. Go on, the girls need your help. Phoebe, go with your sister."

"Daed, I'm sorry—"

"Go." He turned his back on Phoebe. "Luke, will you go with Brian to the visitor's center? Tobias, do you have the map we were looking at last night? We need to divide up the area. Everybody goes out in pairs. I don't want anyone else getting lost. Her legs are too short to have taken her very far. We'll have her back before the Corps folks can get out here."

Back in no time. He sounded so sure of it. Daed was here. He'd find Lydia. He'd find her and all would be well. All would be forgiven.

Phoebe shuffled backwards, not wanting to take her gaze from him. He would fix this. He could fix anything. He might be mad at her now, but when he found Lydia, it would be fine. He'd forgive her. He always did.

Before she could make it to the picnic tables, Mr. Chester's green van rumbled into sight and pulled in next to Mr. Lewis's. A sledgehammer beat in Phoebe's chest. It banged against her ribs in a painful *bam-bam-bam* so hard she thought it might splinter the bones.

Mudder hopped out first. Her expression puzzled, she paused, the door still open. "Silas? Why did you come back so soon? Did you get any fish? I was planning a fish fry—"

"Rachel came to get us. We came back to look for Lydia." He didn't sugarcoat the news. "She wandered off."

Mudder took a step forward. The plastic grocery bag in her hand dropped to the ground and a loaf of sandwich bread spilled out. "Wandered off?"

Leaving Hannah frozen in her tracks, Phoebe rushed to her mudder.

"It's okay. Michael is looking for her. He's been out there at least half an hour. He'll find her. She couldn't have gone far."

"Michael?" Comprehension flitted across Mudder's face. "Michael was here?"

"He came to see me. We…we took a short, short walk. Very short. A few minutes, really, only a few minutes, and Hannah was here."

A strangled sob reminded her of Hannah's presence only a few feet away. "It's my fault, I know that, and I'm sorry. We'll find her. She'll probably wander back into camp any minute."

"*Ach*, Phoebe." There it was. That disappointment she'd seen so many times in her mudder's disbelieving face. She shook her head hard. "Phoebe."

Chapter 7

Michael gritted his teeth and put one foot in front of the other. He wouldn't stop. More than eight hours of picking his way through rocks and sand and weeds in a broiling August heat that beat at his head and face and shoulders, burning him as he wound his way in and out of the trees that hugged the shore. His body had given out on him at least an hour earlier, but he'd forced himself to continue on. In and out of the trees. In and out.

Every few yards, he called her name. Again and again until his voice was hoarse and his throat ached. In between, he prayed. *Gott, let me find her. Please Gott, let me find her.* More like begging than praying. After a while, he couldn't remember what it felt like before the nightmare began. Like when he had scarlet fever as a kid. For the longest time, he couldn't remember not feeling sick and feverish and achy. Now all he could remember was the churning nausea in his gut every time he pictured the look on Hannah's face and the fear in her high-pitched voice. *Lydia's gone.* Nothing of what came before remained. Not even the memory of Phoebe's lips on his could bring back that lighthearted euphoria he'd felt earlier in the day. Every day since he realized he loved Phoebe. It was gone, covered up by this horrible mistake he'd made.

He had to fix it. Make it right. He had to find Lydia. He would never make such a mistake again. *Gott, please don't let Lydia pay for my mistake. Don't let Phoebe pay for my mistake.*

He longed for a drink of cool water. Sweat made his shirt heavy against his back and chest. It stuck to him and chafed his neck. The sun burned his face until it hurt. His chapped lips cracked and bled.

"Michael? Michael!"

The shout came from deep in a stand of oaks and spruce. A second voice joined in. "Michael!"

Against his better judgment, he stopped. If he stopped now, he might have to drop to the ground, curl up, and close his eyes. He stood, wavering, the sun to his back, eyes half closed.

Elam, Simon, and Martin Christner emerged from the trees. Like triplets in varying heights, each a little younger than the next replica of Silas. Only the oldest brother, Jesse, was missing. For that, Michael could be grateful. These three didn't look pleased to see him. "So that's where you went." Simon stuck his hand above his eyes to shield them from the glare. "It's not enough we're out here looking for Lydia, but it looked like you'd gotten yourself lost too."

He didn't say it but the implication hung in the air. Not enough that he'd caused Lydia's disappearance. "I'm looking for Lydia." He didn't recognize his own voice. It sounded bruised and distorted. "I've been all the way to the next swimming beach."

"Nothing?" Elam glanced beyond Michael as if he couldn't help himself, hoping against hope. "You didn't see anything?"

Michael would've given both arms to be able to say yes. "Nee. Nothing."

"The park ranger says there's almost three hundred miles of shoreline." Elam's voice broke. "How are we going to cover that kind of ground?"

"Lydia's legs are short. She couldn't have gone that far. We'll find her. You should go back." Despite Simon's tense, jerky tone, he held out a water bottle. "Have a drink of water. You look like you could use one. Then get back. Your daed's looking for you."

Michael took the water and drank. His thirst made it impossible for him to sip. He gulped, water running in rivulets down his face and neck into his shirt. He lowered the bottle and gasped. He wouldn't go running back to the camp. He would keep looking until he found her.

The two older men, only two and three years older than Michael, had identical looks on their face. They tried to mask it, but the grim set of their mouths and the lines between their eyes, the wrinkles across their foreheads—like younger versions of Phoebe's daed—made it obvious. They knew. They knew about Phoebe and him and what they'd being doing when Lydia slipped away from the camp. Elam simply looked baffled. At fourteen, he was still a little too young to understand.

"I'm sorry." Michael knew it sounded inadequate. "About this."

"Do you have something to be sorry for?" Simon wrinkled his nose and crossed his arms over his thick chest. "Something you want to say?"

"Nee." No, not to them. It wouldn't be to these three.

Martin kicked at a rock with a filthy boot. "Our daed knows what happened."

"Hannah told him?"

"Hannah's stopped talking." The thin veneer of politeness wore away. "Seems like she might not talk again. Not for a while. The doctor says that happens sometimes when a person is traumatized. It was Phoebe. She told Mudder and Daed."

Doctor. Was someone hurt? Phoebe? "Why a doctor?"

"The search and rescue team brings out an ambulance with…not a doctor…what they call a paramedic."

Gut. That was *gut.* Phoebe was okay. As okay as she could be, under the circumstances. Did she blame him? Had she told the whole story?

"What were you doing at our campsite?" Simon posed the question.

He pulled himself to his full height and breathed. Nothing less than the truth. That's what his daed always said. "I asked Phoebe to take a walk with me. I wanted to talk to her."

Martin's hands fisted. "We'd better get back to the camp."

Simon nodded. "It's gonna be dark soon."

They could be twins, the way they finished each other's thoughts and sentences.

"Maybe they've found her," Michael offered. "Maybe she'll be there when we get back to the campsite."

"Nee." Simon shook his head as he started along the rocky path, his back to Michael. "The Corps has boats in the water. Other campers have volunteered to go out in their boats too. They'd sound the bullhorns if she'd been found. That's what they told us."

"Plus they gave us radios." Martin held one up. "So no one else gets lost. Luke wasn't happy about it. He said only to use it in case of emergency. Like phones. Like this isn't an emergency?"

"They're battery-operated," Michael agreed. "What's the problem with that?'"

"Luke's the bishop." Simon kept walking. "He's responsible."

Michael held back a few seconds, letting the distance between him and Phoebe's brothers lengthen. He didn't want to walk into camp with them. Everyone's gazes on them, thinking, hoping, praying.

He wanted to be able to shout it out. That he'd found her. He'd been responsible for losing her, but now he'd found her. He'd be forgiven and their vacation would go on. They'd fish and hunt and make mountain pies over the fire.

But he hadn't. He hadn't seen or heard one single thing that would bring them closer to a little girl in a purple dress.

He forced himself on. *You're not a coward. Go.*

His gut churned in anticipation of what he would face. Silas. Katie. Phoebe.

Ach, Phoebe.

Mudder and Daed. They would be so ashamed. He swallowed against the bitter bile that rose in his throat.

His fault. All his fault. They couldn't blame Phoebe for this. He insisted she come with him. She would never have done it otherwise. He had to tell them that.

They would forgive him. Like Phoebe's brothers had? It was hard to tell. They hadn't said as much. Neither had they expressed blame. Not in so many words. *What were you doing at the camp?*

Nothing they hadn't done with their own girls. The girls who were now their fraas.

Only their courting hadn't ended with a little girl lost.

His throat hurt with the effort to stymie the emotions that broke like waves over him. If anything happened to that little girl, he would never forgive himself.

He picked up one foot and put it down, placed one foot in front of the other, just as he'd been doing since Hannah's headlong flight into the woods to tell them Lydia had gone missing while he wooed her sister. What had he been thinking? What was the big rush? Why did everything about Phoebe make him want to run headlong into the future with her?

Whirling lights caught the periphery of his gaze. He looked up. Red and blue lights cast crazy patterns against the trees and the water near the campground ahead. A dozen or more cars and trucks now lined the dirt road that led to the isolated spot where the Christners had pitched their cluster of tents. Police cars? Sheriff? Park rangers? Ambulances? Simon had said the Corps. The Army Corps of Engineers. They took care of the lake, the part that wasn't state park. They would be in charge of the search. They had experience. They knew what to do. A vise tightened around his head and a noose around his throat. Lydia hadn't wandered back into camp, safe and sound.

They were still searching.

Cramps tightened in his gut. He lurched to a stop, leaned over, and breathed. In and out. In and out. Elam, Simon, and Martin didn't look back.

Gott, forgive me. Give me the strength to face the consequences. I deserve whatever You dole out. I'll take whatever You give me. Please bring Lydia home.

He straightened and strode forward into the camp. Lights streamed from a dozen lanterns scattered around on the picnic tables. A man in brown pants and a matching shirt talked to a cluster of men, including Silas, Thomas, Ben, and his daed. Daed saw him approach first. He broke away from the others and strode toward Michael. He grabbed his arm in a tight, painful grip and stopped him short of the circle.

"Where have you been?" The steel in his father's voice bit into his skin. "Isn't one lost child enough?"

"I'm neither lost nor a child." He kept his own voice soft, low. Daed had every right to be angry. He didn't raise his voice—it wasn't his way—but the lines in his face shouted. "I've covered all the ground along the shore up to the next swimming cove."

"Tobias, Mr. Dover wants a word with us." Silas's voice was even. "He's waiting."

His father's hand dropped and he turned his back on Michael. Michael saw nothing in Silas's face except fierce concentration. "Silas, I—"

"Quiet, son," Tobias said, moving to stand next to Silas. "Mr. Dover is from the Army Corps of Engineers. They're coordinating search and rescue with the state park folks and the sheriff's department from the county."

The man stuffed big hands into his pants pockets. "We have to suspend the search for the night. We've covered all the ground closest to these campsites. We'll continue with a grid search further into the surrounding woods as soon as it gets light."

"We will continue to look." Silas's voice was respectful but firm. He cleared his throat. "I don't want to leave my daughter out there overnight...alone."

Thomas shook his head, one hand smoothing his beard. "Silas, Mr. Dover is right. We can't go stumbling around in the dark. Someone is bound to get hurt or lost."

"Lydia could be hurt." Silas stopped. The only signs of his distress were the pulse beating in his temple and his gritted jaw. He swallowed. His Adam's apple bobbed above the collar of his blue shirt. He glanced around as if looking for something or someone. His gaze met Michael's and then bounced away. "There's wildlife out there. Bears. Cougars. She's four years old."

"She's a smart girl, Daed." Simon slipped in between Thomas and the park ranger, Martin and Elam crowding behind him. "If any little girl can survive the night out there, she can."

"What we can do now is pray," Luke said. "We'll start out again at daybreak."

"You have to keep looking."

The high, tight voice came from behind Michael. He swiveled. The women were huddled together near the playground, some standing, some sitting on blankets, babies sleeping against their chests or at their feet. Several, including his mudder and his aenti, looked as if they were praying, hands clasped tightly in their hands, heads bowed. Katie had spoken. She took two tottering steps. "You're thinking we'll all go to bed and sleep? While my baby's out there in the dark?"

"Fraa." Silas broke away from the group. He strode past Michael without looking at him and took his wife's arm. "Come into the tent."

"You have to keep looking." She glanced around as if embarrassed at all the faces watching them. She bent her head and leaned into her husband. "I can't bear it."

She whispered the words but Michael heard every syllable—and the terrible fear in each one.

"We'll find her tomorrow." Silas leaned close to her. He put his arm around her shoulders. "She's in Gott's hands. What happens now is up to Him." His rough, hoarse voice turned to a soft whisper. "Come."

Without looking at the others, he led Katie toward the last tent, guiding her as he would a blind woman. As they passed Michael, she looked up at him. Her gaze clouded, but she didn't speak. She nodded and allowed Silas to pull her along.

Michael couldn't stand it. He couldn't stand Silas's sagging frame and Katie's tottering shuffle. He'd done this to them. "I'm sorry." He blurted the words, not thinking. "I'm sorry."

Silas halted. Without letting go of Katie, he turned back. "Your apology is accepted. We forgive you."

Katie nodded her head, up and down, but the tears that spilled down her lined cheeks told another story.

Michael's throat closed as they slipped into their tent, alone with their distress and fear and uncertainty. All caused by him. He had done this. He would accept the consequences, come what may.

"Michael."

He forced himself to look up at the small whisper. It came from the shadows on the other side of the playground. It didn't matter how soft or how far, he would've heard it and recognized it.

Phoebe.

He strode toward the sound of his name.

"Phoebe, I'm so sorry."

She seemed to fold into herself, tiny and scared. She sat cross-legged on the grass. "We did this."

"I know."

She gazed up at him. "If she doesn't come home…"

"I know." He dropped to his knees and laid a hand on her shoulder.

Her expression horrified, she shrank from his touch. "Don't."

"It's not your fault."

"While you were…kissing me, Lydia was…"

"We didn't know."

"We should've known."

"Tomorrow we'll find her and we'll bring her home. I'll do everything I can to bring her home. I promise. It'll be fine," Michael said.

The words must've sounded as empty and hollow to her as they did to him.

She scooted back beyond his reach. "Nothing will ever be fine again."

※₰₰₰

Phoebe shambled to the tent, her arms wrapped around her middle, head down. She didn't want to see the men seated around the picnic tables, their conversation a low rumble across the campsite. She felt their gazes, sharp, accusing, judging. Except for Elam. He looked confused, his face white in the light of the kerosene lamp. They would all be seated around campfires, burning marshmallows and making s'mores and mountain pies if it weren't for Michael and her. Hot tears streaked her face, mixing with sweat. No tears. Tears did no good. She wiped at them with her sleeve, inhaled the cool night air, and forced herself to pick up her feet. If Lydia could be brave out there in the dark, she could be brave here, surrounded by family.

"We're staying with you tonight."

She dragged her gaze from the rocky ground. Molly and Rachel huddled together at the entrance to the tent Phoebe had been sharing with Hannah…and Lydia. Molly took her arm. "Hannah is staying in your parents' tent tonight. They thought it best for her. My mudder took Sarah. She was already asleep—she won't know the difference."

Phoebe allowed herself to be drawn into the tent she'd shared the previous evening with her giggling sisters. Hannah and Lydia couldn't seem to settle down. Sleeping in a tent under the stars, water lapping the shores in the distance, was such an adventure for the little girls. For her too, but she tried to be more grown-up about it. A little more. "You don't need to stay. I'm fine." To her chagrin, her voice cracked. "Really, I'm fine. I'm not going to sleep anyway."

"You need to sleep. You look frayed at the edges." Rachel put her hands on Phoebe's shoulders. She looked so calm, with her pale white skin, her serene green eyes, and her strawberry blonde hair still perfectly smooth around her kapp. She'd walked with Daniel today and nothing had happened to her family. Why Lydia? Why Phoebe's family? "Sit and I'll do your hair."

Unable to answer the questions smacking into each other inside her head, Phoebe sank onto her sleeping bag, the nylon material soft and silky under her outspread hands. She closed her eyes and let her best friends remove the pins that held her prayer kapp in place. Rachel undid the bun and began to brush her hair in long, rhythmic strokes. "It'll be fine, you'll see," she murmured in a low, reassuring voice. "They'll find her in the morning and she'll be here safe and sound with you when you go to sleep tomorrow night."

Molly's voice mingled with Rachel's. She was praying softly but steadily, never ceasing. "Gott, we ask your guidance and protection for our lost little sister and friend. She's alone out there in a place she doesn't know. Please put your arms around her and keep her safe until morning and then bring her home. If it is Your will. Thy will be done."

Nee. Nee. Not Thy will. Phoebe jerked away from Rachel. "What if His will is that she not come home?"

"What?" Molly pushed her glasses up her nose and regarded Phoebe. "I don't know. That's what Luke always says. That we should pray that God's will be done, not ours. It's selfish to pray for our own wants and needs."

"I thought God provided for our every need."

Confusion settled on Molly's plain round face. "I don't know much. All I know is God is in control." She removed her glasses and rubbed her eyes, already red with fatigue. "We don't control anything so there's no use worrying about it."

"Right."

As if by mutual, silent agreement, they laid down, still fully clothed, on top of the sleeping bags that filled most of the tent. The murmur of voices outside the tent told Phoebe the men still sat around the picnic tables planning for tomorrow's search. Night sounds filled the air. Crickets, frogs, the lapping of the water. These would be the same sounds Lydia could hear, wherever she was. Maybe they would comfort her as they did Phoebe. God sounds. Maybe she wouldn't be so afraid.

The sound of deep breathing filled the tent. Molly. Phoebe could tell by the half snore, half snort. Molly could sleep through anything. Trying to ignore the sound, Phoebe rolled onto her side, her hands under her cheek. She didn't dare close her eyes. If she did, she was certain she would see Lydia out there, wandering around, lost and confused and scared. Stumbling in the dark. Crying out for Mudder and Daed. Crying out for Phoebe. All because Phoebe had been selfish and stupid.

She sniffed and willed herself to squash the emotions that welled up in her. She wouldn't be a whiny baby about it on top of everything. *I'm so sorry, Gott. Please forgive me. Please don't use this to teach me a lesson.*

What harm could there have been in one kiss? She could hear her daed's voice in her ears. "It's a slippery slope. Start down it and you'll end up on your behind at the bottom. It won't be pretty."

I promise it won't happen again. Never. Just bring her home, please Lord, bring her home.

Her eyes burned. She tried closing them, but the blackness unnerved her. She wiggled, trying to get comfortable. "Rachel, are you awake?" she whispered.

"Jah."

"You went for a walk today with Daniel?"

Her friend stirred and rolled closer. "Why?"

"I know courting…you don't talk about it…but I need to know."

Rachel sat up. Phoebe did the same. "Jah, we walked," her friend whispered.

Phoebe couldn't see Rachel's face in the dark. She crossed her legs and leaned her elbows on her skirt. "What did you do…besides walk?"

"What do you mean?"

"I mean, did you stop anywhere? Did you bird watch? What did you do?"

"We picked up pretty rocks and leaves." Rachel's voice sounded like a smile. "I want to take them home as souvenirs—you know, to remember this time by." She stopped. "I'm sorry. I didn't mean this time—"

"I know what you mean. Has Daniel…has he ever…do you ever…"

"Do we what?"

"Have you ever kissed?"

Rachel's sharp intake of air answered the question. "Nee. Daniel's not like that."

"Not like what?" Michael and Daniel were as different as a horse and a steer. It always struck Phoebe as funny they could be such good friends. Daniel, so lighthearted, such a big talker, so easygoing. Michael was wound tight like a roll of barbed wire, all prickly and ready to stand guard against unwanted intruders. Daniel seemed much more likely to kiss a girl. Michael could barely find a way to talk to one.

"Daniel is like his daed. Plain as plain can be." Rachel's voice got closer as if she'd leaned forward. "He talks a big talk, but when it comes down to it, he would never do anything to taint what we have. He wants to marry me. Why do you ask?"

"I always thought Michael was like that. Always doing the right thing. He seems so serious in his quietness."

"I don't know. He never talks. Who knows what he thinks about anything?" Rachel paused, the silence filled with crickets chirping in the distance. "I always thought he was a little…a little big for his *galluses*."

"What?" The word came out a screech. Molly mumbled in her sleep, the words indistinguishable. Phoebe struggled to bring her voice back to a whisper. "Michael's suspenders fit him fine. He doesn't think he's a big deal, either. He's just not much of a talker. He's more of a thinker. What did he do that was so bad?"

"You asked me if Daniel and I had ever kissed. I reckon you want to know because you and Michael did. You've been wanting him to shine his flashlight in your window for a very long time and first time he takes you for a walk, he kisses you. It's not done that way."

Rachel was smart and wise. Phoebe nodded in the dark, as if the other girl could see her. "I don't know what happened. I think...I think we've wanted to be together for so long that when it finally happened, we just burst with the joy of it."

"Burst with the joy of it?" Skepticism soaked Rachel's words. "That's what Thomas would call a flight of fancy. It's just silly."

She was right. Phoebe couldn't explain it. Still, she had to try. A fierce need to defend Michael roared through her. "Nee. It was like we were pulled together by an invisible thread that kept getting shorter and shorter until we touched."

"Flights of fancy."

"It's true. I don't know how else to explain it."

Rachel didn't speak for a long moment. Her breathing sounded loud and uneven. "But that's all, just a kiss."

"Only a kiss." A beautiful, sweet kiss, gone now, lost in the ugly aftermath of a day Phoebe wanted to forget but knew she never would.

Rachel's sigh filled the tent. "Is it...would it be unseemly for me to ask...did you like it?"

"It was wonderful. So wonderful." Phoebe let her head drop into her hands. They were warm and sticky in spite of the cool night air that wafted through the flaps of the tent. "And now it's gone. We'll never have it again."

"You will. If not you and Michael, then the man God has in His plan for you."

"I wanted it to be Michael. I thought it was Michael."

"I gathered that, or you wouldn't have let him kiss you." Rachel's voice had gone dry and prickly. "At least, that's what I figure."

"I didn't let him kiss me. I kissed him back."

"I'm glad we got that straightened out."

Sweet Rachel could be sarcastic when she put her mind to it. Phoebe ignored it so she could ask the question that weighed her down like a fifty-pound sack of feed. "What if God punishes us for it?"

"I don't think God's like that."

"How do you know?"

"Mudder and Daed love God and they wouldn't worship a God who punished a boy and a girl for one kiss. He wouldn't take the girl's little sister to punish her. If Lydia dies, it's because it is her time to go. God has always known when He would call her home. What you do doesn't matter."

"I hope you're right. It would be unjust for Him to take Lydia because of what I did." Molly rolled over to her other side and squirmed. Phoebe fought to keep her voice down. "And I couldn't be baptized and join a church that worships that God."

Rachel scooted closer and put her arm around Phoebe's shoulder. "It'll be fine. They'll find Lydia tomorrow and everything will be fine."

"What if they don't?"

"You have to have faith."

"Pray for me. I don't have the words."

"All right."

Rachel prayed and prayed. The words poured over Phoebe like clean, fresh water. She laid down again and Rachel did the same. "I'll always be your friend, no matter what," she whispered. "Go to sleep. God is watching over us."

Phoebe would rather He watched over Lydia.

Chapter 8

The park ranger—Katie couldn't remember his name, she couldn't remember any of these men's names, she could barely remember her own—used his thick body to block the trail. He stood with his back to Silas and her, talking to one of the men from the Army Corps of Engineers. Their voices were soft but the whispered, unintelligible words picked at her like barbed wire.

The park ranger looked back. She would never forget the expression on his young face, made haggard by two days and nights without sleep or rest, days of tramping through the wooded parkland looking for a tiny slip of a girl. Like he wished he were far, far away. His gaze fled from Katie to Silas and back as if he didn't know where to look.

He couldn't be more than twenty-six or twenty-seven, the age of their oldest son, Jesse. He probably hadn't done this before. Told parents news that would rip their hearts out as surely as if he'd taken a knife and cut open their chests. He probably didn't know what words to use. He took off his hat, revealing tousled yellow curls damp with sweat. They made him look even younger. Less official. Like a little boy playing at a grown-up game. His voice cracked, filled with so much sympathy. She wanted to push him away, push away his sympathy. She didn't need it. It wasn't her Lydia down there on the shores of this lake she'd once thought so beautiful. It couldn't be.

"You folks should wait back at the van. You don't want to be down here." He started forward as if to lead the way. "I don't know why they didn't tell you that up at base."

Because Silas hadn't waited for their instructions. When he'd seen the volunteer rush into the search and rescue base set up near their camping site, he'd nodded to Mr. Chester, and they'd hurried, Luke and Thomas close behind, to the van to follow the white truck to this secluded, tree-covered spot less than two miles from their campsite.

Less than two miles.

The young man was right. Katie didn't want to go down to the edge of the water. It must be mid-afternoon now, but it seemed dark to her. It seemed dark, like mud and decaying leaves and rotting fish. Forty-eight hours. Forty-eight hours. Two days now since her Lydia had skipped out of the campsite in search of her big schweschder. Katie had this image in her head. She knew for certain Lydia had skipped. Because she always did. She skipped and hopped and ran. She never walked.

Katie shivered. The sun should feel warm on her face. It might even be burning her skin now, but she shivered with cold.

A flash of color. A tiny swatch of purple shone in that same sun. Light purple. Lilac.

Silas's hand gripped hers so hard she feared the bones in her fingers might be crushed. She bit her tongue to keep from crying out.

"Nee."

He uttered the one syllable in a low, guttural sound barely distinguishable as language. It came from same deep place she held inside herself. A place where pieces of her heart ripped apart and were swallowed up in a sickening swirl of fear, disbelief, and horror.

"Is it…" She managed those two syllables. Stopped. Her mouth couldn't form the words.

"We have to wait for the medical examiner." A muscle in the park ranger's cheek twitched. His breathing hiccupped on the word *examiner*. "He's on his way."

"I would like to know." Silas's voice held steady. Katie clung to that. Silas would lead the way through this. "Is it a little girl?"

The park ranger nodded. "Blonde. Blue eyes." His jaw twitched. "Purple dress. No shoes. About four or five."

To her surprise, Katie's knees buckled. She intended to stand tall next to her husband. If God had taken Lydia home, it was her time to go. Katie's arms flailed. She fought to right herself, but her bones had turned to water and no longer held her upright. Silas's hand jerked from hers and caught her arm in an iron grip.

"Nee."

The man from the Corps sidled closer to the park ranger. He leaned toward the other man. "Let him ID her." His voice was low and urgent. "This is insane. They're here. Don't torture them like this."

The park ranger nodded. Any emotion in his face slid away and his features became shuttered, neutral. "Sir, if you would follow me. Don't touch anything. You won't be able to touch her. You understand?"

His expression wooden, Silas nodded. He let go of Katie. The world tilted and she went into a free fall, falling, falling, falling. Yet, she still stood on trembling knees, muscles so weak she swayed from side to side to keep her balance.

"Stay here."

Katie nodded, no more capable of walking than a newborn. She heard rather than saw Thomas and Luke drawing closer. Their boots thudded on the grass, dry and crackling in the August heat. They didn't speak, but their breathing sounded loud in her ears. They probably thought she should've stayed in the van. That this was the business of men. She disagreed. This was the business of a mother. Still, she took solace in their presence. They would know what to do next. She only had to be here now, present.

She watched through the trees as Silas and the two other men marched single file down the path, weaving in and out of the oak and hickory trees. She kept her gaze on Silas's blue shirt as he halted on the rocky shoreline. She heard no sound. He didn't cry out or scream. Still, she knew. His broad shoulders sagged. His knees bent as if he would kneel, but the park ranger laid his hand on his chest, stopping him. Silas thrust both his hands out, but the other man stepped between

Silas and the purple swatch of material that lay on the banks, water lapping around it.

Her husband turned and trudged up the path, his boots slipping and sliding on the carpet of leaves. The closer he came, the harder it became for Katie to breathe. Darkness seeped in, blotting out the sun. The humid air stifled her. No birds sang. No cicadas buzzed. The frogs stopped talking, as if their silence honored the dead. The stillness lay so heavy on her she thought it might bury her.

Every step brought him closer. Every step brought the sure knowledge their little Lydia had gone on home ahead of them.

Katie lifted her chin and met Silas's gaze. His red-rimmed eyes were dim with grief. He nodded.

"What happened? Did she…what happened to her?"

"It looks like she fell in somewhere along the shore where the bank was too steep for her to climb back out. The current eventually carried her here." The park ranger spoke before Silas could. "It probably happened not long after she disappeared from the campgrounds. Otherwise, she would've heard the rescue teams calling for her."

"I want to see her." Katie bit her lip, fighting to keep the anguish from boiling up and out in a scream that would go on and on. *Be still, and know that I am God.* The soft words came to her, calming her still beating heart. How could her heart continue to beat when her child's did not? "Can I see her?"

His lips pressed together so tightly white lines formed around his mouth, Silas shook his head and held out his hand. "Nee. It's best you don't. We'll go back to the camp now."

"I'll not leave her down there alone."

Silas's grip tightened. "She's not here anymore. You know that."

She did know that. If she could only wrap her mind around the notion that her little Lydia, with the giggle in her voice and the skip in her walk, had gone on to be with the Lord. God had given them the gift of this child for only a short while.

Silas knew best. Emma and Thomas would go to the funeral home for them. Katie would sew a nice white dress for her. And a fresh prayer kapp. Emma and Leah would braid her hair and wind it around her small head. Luke and Thomas would see to the arrangements for Lydia to be brought to the house after the funeral home was done. Arrangements would be made.

Katie took her husband's hand and together they started toward the van. First, the kinner had to be told.

Phoebe had to be told.

Silas halted when they reached the black asphalt. He cleared his throat. Cleared it again. His mouth opened but no words came out. Katie stopped and waited, her heart beating in her throat, gagging her, her stomach threatening a revolt. She wanted to keep walking, but Silas's grip held her. She wanted to keep walking and walking, never stop. Keep walking until they were home in New Hope where there were no lakes and Lydia would be pulling weeds in the garden or gathering eggs in the chicken coop like the good little girl she had been. Katie forced back the heaves and waited.

The park ranger waited too, his face lined with exhaustion and the knowledge that his best efforts hadn't brought their little girl back alive.

Luke stepped forward, shoulder to shoulder with Silas. Thomas joined them. "We'll want to bury her body in New Hope." Thomas gave voice to Silas's thoughts. "How soon can we have her?"

The park ranger's eyes were wet. "The coroner will need a day or so, sir. We'll get her home to her family as soon as we can. That's a promise."

"She's already home," Katie whispered. "The Lord took her home."

The park ranger nodded. "Yes, ma'am."

He turned as if to go.

"Mr. ...I'm sorry. I don't remember your name."

"Lee. Lee Grissom."

"Mr. Grissom, thank you."

Surprise washed across his face. "I'm sorry I couldn't...that we didn't...I'm sorry, ma'am."

She swallowed against a wave of nausea. "You did your best. We thank you for that."

He nodded.

Lydia had gone home. Praise Gott. She's home.

The words pinged around in Katie's head, all sharp, painful points like knives that inflicted raw wounds wherever they landed.

Praise Gott.

Chapter 9

Aware of his father's height and breadth behind him, Michael stood in the Christner living room, his hat clutched in his hands. Silas rose and stood next to Katie in front of the dark, empty fireplace. Hannah sat curled in a hickory rocking chair, her sunburned face still and listless. Elam occupied the other rocking chair, his expression watchful, as if Michael might be there to cause some further damage of some kind. The baby fussed in the playpen in the corner, but none of them seemed to notice. A pole lantern flickered, the light casting shadows against their still faces.

Nothing about the Christner house had changed. It looked the same as his own, as every Plain home in New Hope, with their unadorned walls, dark furniture, and simple wooden floors covered with homemade rugs. It smelled the same. Fried chicken. Apple pie. The remnants of supper scarcely eaten. He'd been inside their home many times for Sunday socializing, holiday gatherings, and work frolics of all sorts. He'd sat at their table and eaten their food, all the while watching Phoebe's face as she served, ate, laughed, and chattered with her sisters and brothers. It was a house filled with family and faith and love and contentment. Now, everything seemed different. As if something had seeped out, leaving behind a growing black hole that threatened to engulf everything. He'd done this. He'd caused this fracture in their world.

From the noise emanating from the kitchen a gaggle of women were cleaning up after supper. Thomas stared out the window, one hand on the wooden frame. Luke sat at a table going over a list with some of the other men. Probably the death list—everyone who needed to be notified so they could come to the funeral. They'd call Bliss Creek in the morning. Word would go out and a load of family and friends would come to New Hope.

Might as well get this over with. He couldn't stand here forever, looking at all of them, not looking at him, contemplating in their heads the repercussions of an irresponsible, selfish man.

"I came to tell you..." The words came out in a croak. He gritted his teeth and cleared his throat. "I came to tell you how sorry I am. None of this would've happened if it weren't for me. I should never have come to the campsite while you were gone."

Katie's dishwater-red hands plucked at the ribbons on her kapp, but her face remained serene. "The Lord gives and He takes away. It was Lydia's time to go home."

She took a careful step forward, slowly, as if she needed to balance herself or she would fall. Then another. Before he could grasp what she intended to do, she squeezed his hand, once, and then let it drop. "Still, you are forgiven."

Michael looked over Katie's shoulder at Silas. The man's gaze didn't waver, but Michael could see the battle waging in his eyes. Silas knew what he must do. It might be the hardest thing that had ever been asked of him. Michael couldn't have done it himself.

Silas opened his mouth and then closed it. His nostrils flared as he breathed, the sound harsh and low in the silence. Even baby Sarah's wails had ceased. "I forgive you."

Michael willed himself to stifle the tears. *Take it like a man.* He nodded. Silas nodded back, but he sank into a straight-back chair next to Hannah's rocker as if his legs no longer supported him. The girl's expression didn't change. She seemed unaware of the conversation going on around her.

Michael edged toward her. "Hannah, I'm sorry. I shouldn't have asked Phoebe to leave you alone with the kinner. It's my fault. Can you forgive me?"

Nothing in her face indicated she'd heard him. Her eyes were glassy and distant, her mouth parted. She didn't look up. She didn't seem to look anywhere.

"Hannah's…It'll take some time." This time Katie's voice quivered. "You understand."

He crushed his hat between his hands and then tried to smooth it. He had dared to hope—a hope he shared with no one, but nurtured in the quiet times late at night when no one was around—that these folks might one day be his in-laws. Family. Now they would forever look at him and see a man responsible for the death of their child. They would forgive, but how could they ever forget?

The question twisted like a hunting knife in his gut. They couldn't. He couldn't. He could never forgive himself, and he could never forgive God. What kind of God let this happen? What kind of God gave him these feelings for a girl he'd known all his life, but let this wedge be driven forever between them?

The decision had been all his. Not God's. All his. God had allowed him to make decisions and he'd made the wrong choices. Now he had to live with them.

Phoebe. How must she be handling all this? Were they looking at her the same way? With a mixture of judgment and pity they probably didn't even realize they felt, so deep were they in their own misery. The thought of facing Phoebe after what he'd done to her, the position he'd put her in, was almost unbearable, but he owed her the same apology. *Take it like a man.* "I'd like to…to see Phoebe."

His daed's boots made a scraping sound on the floor as he shifted his weight. Michael could almost hear his disapproval in the roughness of sole against wood. Simon and Martin both looked up from where they sat at the table. Jesse rose to his feet. Hannah's head jerked at the mention of her sister's name. Elam went to the bottom of the staircase and stopped as if standing guard. As if Michael might try to sneak past him. Katie retreated to a spot next to her husband's chair.

Silas's voice sank so low the words came out a grunt. "She's in her room. Gone to bed I expect."

Supper barely done. The sun still hovering above the horizon. It seemed unlikely. "But I wanted…I just—"

"We'll leave you to rest." Tobias intervened, a restraining hand on his son's shoulder. "Have you had word from the medical examiner yet?"

"Lydia…the body will arrive at the funeral home tomorrow." Silas's voice sounded stronger now. This he knew how to do. "The boys will deliver the notices to everyone tomorrow as well. The funeral will be the day following."

Tobias nodded. "We'll let folks down our way know. Don't get up, Silas. We know the way out."

He guided Michael to the door with an iron grip. No one accompanied them to bid farewell. In the buggy, Daed snapped the reins without speaking. They jolted forward. Heat still billowed from the road in front of them and lightning crackled across the sky in the distance, its brief light revealing dark, low-hanging clouds. The smell of rain and damp dirt wafted in air heavy on Michael's shoulders.

"It'll be fine, with time." Daed didn't take his gaze from the road. "Silas and Katie are good people."

"Their words say one thing, their faces another."

"The grief is fresh. They've lost a child." His daed's voice lost some of its assurance. "We all face death, sooner or later. Even though we know God has written down the day and time each child is to return to Him, we don't expect our children to go first. Mind you, it's something to think about. You'd better finish up your baptism classes. A person doesn't know when his day of reckoning will come."

"Lydia is with Gott now." Michael gripped the railing in front of him so hard his fingers ached. The things he'd learned in baptism class seemed foreign now. He couldn't make heads or tails out of any of it. He couldn't commit himself to that which he couldn't fathom. No point in going back. "Are we to be glad of that? Joyful?"

He risked a quick sideways glance. Emotion carved lines in his daed's face. "Strong in the knowledge. Glad might be a bit much to ask right now. Give them time, son. It'll take time to heal their wounds."

He snapped the reins hard and the buggy jolted forward, as if he were in a hurry to get home. Or to end this conversation. "It'll take time for yours as well."

An acknowledgment that his father knew he suffered.

"You'll learn from this. It'll make you a better man. A better husband and father."

Knowing the depth of his own pain—like a gaping wound in his chest where his heart had been—Michael couldn't conceive of a time when Silas and Katie would be healed of their wounds. Or he of his. The time might never come. They might never truly forgive, as often as they said the words. He understood this. It didn't seem possible he would ever forgive himself.

He raised his face to the rain-swollen sky. The wind picked up and carried fat rain drops into the buggy, cooling his face. Still, it burned. He would have no chance to be husband and father. He would have no place in the lives of the Christners—in Phoebe's life—until the family could look at him and not ache with this awful loss. Everything he'd dreamed of and hoped for had been lost in the minutes that it took a little girl to lose herself in the trees.

It seemed only just.

Lydia lost her life. He lost his.

And God?

The God who hadn't answered his prayers for Lydia's safe return. Did that God forgive him? Or was this his punishment?

Was God gone from his life too?

⁂

The buggy had long since disappeared from sight. Phoebe stared at nothing. With a start, she let the curtain drop and sank to the floor, turning so she could lean her back on the wall. Outside the wind picked up and whistled through the eaves of her room. The sound formed words that echoed in her head.

Be good. Be good. Be good.

The curtain rose and fell as if touched by an unseen hand. Her head lolled to one side, too heavy for her to hold up. She should put on her nightgown and get in bed. But the thought of the material lying on her skin unnerved her. It would be too much, too heavy, like the night air, like the curtain under her fingers, like her head. She inhaled the scent of the room she'd slept in her entire life. It smelled of dust and her own sweat. Nothing about it seemed familiar. The corners were dark and empty. As if no one lived there anymore.

Why had Michael come to the house and not spoken with her? He couldn't face her? He couldn't bear to look at the face of a girl who'd led him down the path of temptation to a place from which neither could return?

Be good. Be good. Be good.

Wanting to escape the thoughts that tormented her from the time she awoke to the time she slept—and even then as she dreamed in fits and starts—she crawled onto the bed and closed her eyes. Lydia's face swam in front of her. Giggling. Then scared and lost and lonely. Falling. Struggling to breathe. Then floating, floating, motionless.

Phoebe jerked her eyes open. She stared at the ceiling in the gathering dusk. The shadows crowded her. She rolled over and curled up into a ball, clutching a pillow to her chest. She wanted her mudder. Like a child. But she couldn't ask Mudder for comfort. She, who had caused this pain for Mudder and Daed, couldn't turn to them. They would look at her the way they'd been looking at her for the last two days. Like they were seeing someone they didn't recognize. A stranger they'd invited into their home, only to have that person abuse their hospitality. More than that, steal from them. Steal their serenity and security and peace.

She hugged the pillow to her face to stifle the sobs. The sound of footsteps in the hallway brought her upright. Mudder had come to check on her? She dragged her sleeve across her face to erase the tears and smoothed her kapp. A door opened. Not her door.

Hannah.

Swallowing her tears, Phoebe bolted from the bed and tugged open her own door. Hannah stood in the hallway, poised to enter her bedroom. She looked up at Phoebe. Her vacant expression didn't change.

"Hannah, are you all right?"

No response. Phoebe slipped closer. Hannah backed up. As if she were afraid. Afraid of Phoebe.

"Hannah, I'm so sorry. I know I keep saying that, but you never answer me. I should never have left you. It's all my fault." She gripped her hands in front of her to keep from reaching for her sister. Hannah would bolt as she had done the last time Phoebe attempted to talk to her. "I'm truly sorry. Please forgive me."

Hannah blinked. She stepped back into the room she shared with Lydia—had shared with Lydia—and Sarah. Without a word she shut the door, making no sound.

Phoebe stood in the hallway for a long moment, hands dangling at her sides. No sounds came from the other side of the door. Suddenly chilled to the bone despite the stifling heat, she scurried back into her room, shut the door, and lunged onto her bed where she pulled the quilt up to her chin. She couldn't stop shivering.

Gott, Gott, where are you?

Was what she had done so terrible that even God had forsaken her? *I'm sorry. I'm sorry.*

She laid there for what seemed like hours, staring at the ceiling, begging for an answer. The farewells of people leaving drifted through her open window. Luke's voice, deep, Leah's higher. Thomas and Emma. Elijah and Bethel. Her brothers and their fraas. Their voices were replaced by the sound of thunder rolling and rolling until it seemed to roll right through her window. Then the rain came. Softly at first, then harder. The wind hustled drops through the window and splattered them on the chair and floor. Phoebe thought to close the window, but instead leaned out, her face lifted to the lightning-illuminated clouds. Their first rain in months. Cleansing rain. Clear, cool water. She wanted to be cleansed of her sin. Was it even possible?

What does it take to prove it to You? I'm so sorry. I'll never do anything like this again. I'll be good. I promise I'll be good.

She darted across the room and opened the cedar chest at the foot of her bed. She scooped up the cell phone and the fake pearl necklace she'd bought at the discount store in town. She dropped them both into her apron, along with an iPod and two country music CDs she and Rachel and Daniel played when they rode in Dylan's car. She wrapped her apron around them and slipped through the door. At the top of the staircase, she paused. Everyone except Mudder had gone to bed. Mudder sat in the rocking chair, little Sarah in her lap, rocking.

She looked up when Phoebe arrived at the bottom of the stairs and started toward the door. "Where are you going?"

She didn't sound truly interested, more as if she felt obligated to ask.

"To get a breath of fresh air."

"It's raining."

"I know. The first rain in months. I only want—"

"Go."

It almost sounded like a command. Go. And never come back? "Mudder?"

"Get a breath of fresh air on the porch. It'll be good for you."

Phoebe scurried out the door before Mudder changed her mind. She had no intention of staying on the porch. She ducked her head against the driving rain and scurried, slipping and sliding in the mud, past the corral, past the barn, and into the trees. The branches dipped and shimmied in the rain. The lightning lit up the sky, creating huge tangles of shadows that danced in unison. The rain pelted her face. Her prayer kapp came loose and slid down her back, taking her bun with it.

Gott, are You here?

Lightning crackled. Thunder boomed. She ducked and blocked her face with her free arm, silly as it was, as if to ward off a blow. The tree boughs dipped and the branches danced around her, leaves brushing her hair and her face. She stumbled deeper into the stand of trees until the darkness enveloped her and she could go no farther. If she did, she'd never find her way out of the black night that surrounded her.

There, in the almost continuous flare of lightning that snaked across the sky, dividing itself over and over as if multiplying, she fell to her knees under a massive oak, bending and waving in a strange, distorted dance in the wind. She let the phone and the iPod and the CDs and the necklace slide into the mud. She began to dig with her bare hands.

No more. No more. I'll be good. I promise. I'll be good.

She said the words over and over in her head as the slick mud caked her hands and coated her dress and her apron.

I'll be good. No more. No more.

When the hole was deep enough she pushed the phone, the CDs, the iPod, the necklace—the things that had soiled her life—into it and began to cover them with mud.

"I'll be good now, Gott, I'll be good," she yelled over crashing thunder. Pounding rain battered her face, mixing with hot tears. "I'm so sorry."

She sank back on her haunches and wiped futilely at her face with a sodden sleeve. She couldn't see beyond the blinding rain or hear more than the continuous rumble of thunder. "I'm so, so sorry."

Nothing. Only rain and thunder and lightning. She dropped her head into her muddy hands and began to rock.

"I'll do better. I'll be good. I promise. Gott, I promise!"

~~~~~~

Katie drew a finger along the line of Sarah's plump, round face. The baby cooed in her sleep, a contented sound. Katie inhaled the scent of baby powder and diaper ointment and dried milk. Baby smells. Like a balm for her scraped, raw soul. Everyone had gone home, leaving a quiet behind that unnerved her. In the daylight, with the house filled with their family and friends, she could stave off the remorse and the despair. Simon's fraa had made the new dress of white cotton for Lydia to wear. Martin's fraa brought a new prayer kapp. Jesse's fraa brought an enormous pot of chili. Bethel, Emma, and Josie baked loaves of bread and pies for the meals between now and the funeral. The scent filled the house, giving it all the trappings of a home where everything went on as usual.

Their friends and family filled the place up like a warm hug that went on and on, easing her sore heart. Now, they had gone home until tomorrow. Quiet descended and there was no doubt that something had changed. She feared getting up. Her sense of equilibrium eluded her. The sense that all would be well, all would be good…that had fled as well. The secure knowledge that her children were safe, wherever they might be—she had been robbed of that. For years she'd floated from one day to the next, certain everything was as it should be in her world. Now she jumped and started at every noise, fearful of another loss. Even for her older sons, married and living on their own, she ached with a paralyzing fear.

Earlier in the day she'd wandered restlessly from room to room until Silas begged her to settle down. The worst of it hit her at dusk, knowing the day would finally end. All this was her fault. She should've reined in Phoebe's flighty ways. She had encouraged Silas to let their oldest daughter find her own way. She'd turned a blind eye to the depth and width of her running around.

It wasn't Phoebe who needed to be forgiven.

Gott, forgive me. I've not been a good mudder. I thought I was doing right, but look what happened. I turned my back for a second and look what happened.

Gott, please forgive me.

"You should've had Hannah put Sarah to bed when she went up." Silas stood at the top of the stairs, one hand resting on the banister. He looked like his daed now, face lined, eyes hooded with fatigue, years older than he'd been only a few days ago. "Give her to me to carry and come along. You're tired."

Katie tried to get up but her body wouldn't cooperate. She was too tired to move. Too tired to think. Too tired to mince words. "Hannah hasn't touched the baby since…" Had it only been two days? Katie couldn't remember exactly. "She hasn't held Sarah since they found Lydia."

Silas put one foot on the stairs with a thud. His face creased as if each laborious movement took all his concentration. "She's hurting. She'll get over it."

"Get over it?" Katie whispered the words. Like they would all get over it. "I suppose you're right."

He gripped the banister and took another step toward her. "Come to bed, fraa."

"A few more minutes."

Despite the weariness in his face, he came to her. "A few more minutes." His blue eyes liquid with emotion, he bent and brushed her cheek with a kiss. "Tomorrow will be a long day."

Every day from now on would be a long one.

"I'll be right there."

Katie waited until he climbed the stairs again. She waited until she heard the bedroom door close. She laid the sleeping baby in the playpen. Sarah stretched and sighed a contented, soft breath in her sleep, her round face a miniature of Lydia's.

The pain of that thought spiraled through Katie, leaving her woozy and breathless. She breathed in and out, in and out, until the darkness receded.

She lifted her apron to her mouth to muffle the sound. Quietly, carefully, she knelt on the floor, the wood hard under her aching knees. She grasped the edge of the playpen with one hand to steady herself, to anchor herself to something real, something solid, something sure.

Only then did she weep.

Chapter 10

Phoebe hazarded a glance at her mudder. She sat ramrod straight on the bench, her gaze forward, her head slightly bent to the side as if she concentrated on Luke's sermon, which had picked up steam at the one-hour mark and now seemed to be winding down at the two-hour mark. His second funeral as bishop of this New Hope community and he was doing it up right. Exhorting them to remember the moment of reckoning could come at any time. They should all be ready. Be right with God. They should live their lives as a short journey through this world into God's kingdom.

Nothing in Mudder's face or her demeanor spoke of being a member of the bereaved family. With Hannah at her side and Sarah in her lap, she looked the picture of serenity. She hadn't shed a single tear. Phoebe sought to follow her example, but her throat ached so fiercely with the unshed tears that she couldn't swallow. She rubbed at it with both hands, but nothing would abate the pain. She tried to breathe, feeling faint from lack of air. If this went on much longer she would keel over in front of everyone, embarrassing Mudder and Daed.

As if they didn't already feel enough shame.

Wiggling to relieve the pain of sitting so long on the hard wooden bench, Phoebe tried to calm herself. She let her gaze rove the room, searching for relief of some kind, anything. It collided with Emily Glick. The girl stared at her with unabashed interest. So did Adah and

Rebecca and Mary and Lillie. They all knew. They knew what Phoebe had been doing when Lydia disappeared. *I'm going to do better. You'll see. All of you will see. I've changed. I'll be good.* She clamped her mouth shut tight, fearful she might have uttered the words aloud. Her sojourn into the storm had helped her see her way toward a new beginning, but no one around her recognized the change. They still saw the girl who'd lost her little sister.

Phoebe returned her gaze to where it belonged—to the front of the room and to Luke. To return to her parents' good graces, she must do what was proper. Listen to the sermon. Believe it. Live it. She tried to comprehend Luke's words, but they didn't mean anything to her. She couldn't understand them. Words from the Gospel of John about ever-lasting life. The word *reckoning*. Reckoning. What did that mean? All she understood was this: Lydia was dead. Lydia, whose body lay in a small, pine box in the next room, was dead. Dead. Not coming back. Not laughing. Not playing. Not learning to make a daisy stitch or a French knot or how to hem a dress or how to make friendship bread. Daed said she was with God, happy, safe, and loved.

Lydia had been happy and loved right here on earth.

She hadn't been safe here on earth and that was Phoebe's fault. At this time of reckoning, if it were to come now, would God ask her how she'd come to be in the woods while her little sister wandered away and drowned?

Phoebe sucked in air drenched with the odor of sweat, fearing she truly would fall over. She wanted to get out of this room so packed with family and friends. She needed cool air and cool water. She couldn't be cooped up here anymore with Lydia's small, still body. Mudder had insisted she help her and Emma with the dress and the hair and the prayer kapp. Until Phoebe had run to the kitchen and vomited in the dish tub. Then she'd been allowed to retreat to her room.

Sudden movement brought her from her reverie. Everyone knelt. Hastily, she joined them. The wood felt solid under her knees and the swaying in her head subsided. A tiny breeze wafted through the open windows, touching her burning face with a welcome breath of air. The scent of honeysuckle floated in the air. The breath of God. She leaned into it. *Gott?*

People began to scramble to their feet around her. She struggled to do the same. Her legs didn't want to hold her. Mudder's hand gripped her arm, her fingers warm and tight, and helped her up. Phoebe glanced at her face. Calm. Serene. At peace. How did she manage?

Luke began the benediction. Phoebe jerked her gaze to the front of the room. Luke's somber gaze fell on her. Phoebe wanted to look away. She didn't. She couldn't.

"Lydia Christner was four years old. She was the daughter of Silas and Katie Christner."

That was it. The summing up of Lydia's life.

People began to mill about. "Take Sarah." Her mudder handed the baby to Phoebe. She didn't hesitate, something that surprised Phoebe. Her mudder still trusted her to care for her baby sister. "Hannah and I will arrange food while your bruders move the benches. Don't go far. You're expected to be there for the viewing."

Move the benches for the viewing. Phoebe's stomach lurched. She was glad Mudder didn't expect her to handle food. Not with Lydia's body on display for everyone to see. Besides, her brothers' fraas would be in the kitchen, and Bethel and Emma, all looking at her, watching her. She shifted Sarah's weight onto her hip and squeezed past a group of women who stood talking softly in the corner, their eyes red-rimmed.

She needed to get out. Frantic, she squeezed past another cluster of women and made a beeline for the front door. She couldn't face that pine box. So small and light. Daed and Jesse could carry it by themselves. She was almost to the door. Her hand reached for the knob.

"Phoebe."

She closed her eyes. Sarah let out a surprised, unhappy squawk, reminding Phoebe to loosen her grip on her sister.

"Phoebe." A bare whisper this time. "I need to talk to you."

Phoebe opened her eyes and looked into Michael's face. His eyes were red and sunken into dark circles. "Could I talk to you for a minute?"

She glanced over her shoulder and then shook her head. "I can't. My daed…"

"I know. Mine too." He slapped the hat on his head. "For one minute."

"Whatever you have to say to me, say it to me here, in plain view." She kept her voice to a whisper as she adjusted Sarah's weight on her hip, solid and warm, reminding Phoebe of her responsibilities and how sorely she'd failed in them because of this man. "Mudder asked me to take care of Sarah while she…while they…they get ready for the viewing. I'll not make this mistake again. Nor should you want to make it."

"I don't." He drew a shuddering breath and took a step toward her. Phoebe backed away. He looked as if she'd hit him with a horse whip. "I just wanted to make sure you're all right."

"I'll be all right. I'll be fine." If she said it enough, it might become so. Aware of the dozens of people crammed into the nearby room, she ducked past him, willing herself not to look back at his face etched with grief. The face she'd loved since she was a girl. "You need to stay away from me. I can't be…I can't, Michael."

"I just wanted you to know how sorry I am." His voice, low and hoarse and full of emotion, followed her toward the stairs. "I would do anything to make it right."

She glanced back. "You can't make it right. Neither of us can. I have to take Sarah upstairs."

His face filled with a despair she knew mirrored her own. She forced herself to turn her back on him. She would never forgive herself for that moment of weakness. Of selfishness. She wanted something so much she'd been willing to sacrifice others for it. She couldn't blame Michael for that. But she could learn from her mistakes and not make them again. After her excursion into the stormy night, she'd dragged herself, sodden and splattered with mud, into the house and up the stairs to her bed, vowing she would do everything she could to earn back her parents' and Hannah's trust. She couldn't trust herself with Michael. He made her weak in the knees and silly in the head.

She would start over. She would be good. She would follow the rules. She would be the daughter her parents wanted her to be. She ran up the stairs and slipped into the room Lydia had once shared with her sisters. "Naptime, sweet thing." She lowered Sarah into the crib and stood looking down at her. "I'll never let anything happen to you. I promise. I'll look out for you."

Her voice cracked.

Sarah nestled into her favorite brown- and tan-checked blanket and closed her eyes, her thumb in her mouth. She fell asleep with the quick, easy way of an infant not yet troubled by the world around her.

Phoebe stood for a long time, watching the rise and fall of the little girl's chest. Peaceful, sweet slumber.

She had a second chance. She wouldn't squander it. If that meant being alone, so be it. She didn't deserve any more than that.

≈≀≀≀

Greedily inhaling the fresh, clean scent of cut grass, Michael shoved his hat on his head and closed the door behind him, being careful not to slam it. He didn't want anything to impinge on the soft, respectful murmurings inside. On legs that felt as if they would buckle under him he trudged down the steps, intent on getting away from this. All of this. The staring eyes. The pitying glances. The judgment. If Phoebe could forgive him he could've dealt with it. But that was too much to ask. He'd figured as much, but he had to try. She looked so scared and so sad. All he wanted to do was stand between her and the brunt of the storm, but she didn't want that. Didn't want him. She blamed him. And rightly so.

Headed toward the buggies and the horses, he wound his way through the men who stood in small clusters, talking in low voices, waiting. The viewing wouldn't take long. Then the procession to the small cemetery. Lydia would join Daniel's *groossdaadi*, the only member of their community to pass since they'd arrived in New Hope. After the funeral, a meal would be served back at the house. His own mudder had been cooking since before dawn. She wanted to make sure there was enough food for the families who had traveled from Bliss Creek.

The thought of food made his stomach turn. He lurched forward.

"Leaving already?"

The sound of Thomas's voice staved off Michael's determined, head-long flight. Thomas leaned both elbows on the corral fence. He had a strand of hay between his long fingers, rolling it back and forth, his face pensive under his black prayer service hat.

"Nee." Michael had come with his parents. He couldn't leave, much as he would've liked to do so. He'd thought to sit in the buggy and be alone, if only for a few precious moments. "Just stretching my legs and checking on the horse. Best be ready for the trip to the cemetery."

"Me too." Thomas turned around and leaned his back against the fence. "Warm in there. Not a breath of air."

"Jah."

Thomas straightened. "I thought I'd check on my horse too. He was favoring a leg this morning."

"Ours seems to be in a bad mood, jumping and starting at every-thing on the road." Michael worked to keep his tone as neutral as the other man's. "'Bout threw Mudder into the ditch yesterday when she went to the phone shack to see what time the women were coming to do the cooking."

They walked side by side toward the road lined with buggies, black against the noonday sun. Their orange triangles glowed in the light, a series of warnings to slow down. Michael had never noticed how bright they were against the dark, gloomy black. *Slow down. Slow down.* "The horse is getting older. Daed will want to start looking at the auctions soon."

"I'm getting older too. Glad my fraa isn't looking to replace me." Thomas gave a dry chuckle and tossed aside the piece of hay. "Silas and Katie are good people."

No one knew that better than Michael. "Jah."

"If they say they've forgiven you, they have." Thomas had never been one to talk much, but since he started giving the baptism lessons, his ways had changed—at least with the men and women in the class. At the moment, Michael would've preferred the old Thomas, the closed-lips one. "They don't lie."

"I know."

"Sometimes the hardest part is to forgive yourself as Gott forgives you."

Michael picked up his pace. "Maybe I don't deserve forgiveness. Lydia is dead and it's my fault."

"Lydia chose to wander away from camp. Jah, she was a little girl, but old enough to know better. We all make choices."

"We do." He'd made the choice to convince Phoebe to slip away from the campsite. He'd made the choice to push the boundaries. Simple boundaries meant to keep them on the one true road. "Some choices are harder to forgive than others."

"God sacrificed His only Son for our sins. He gave everything and forgave us the unforgiveable. You have to do the same within yourself."

Michael squeezed between two buggies and approached the Morgan. He ran a hand over the horse's warm haunches. The horse whinnied as if in greeting, his somber brown eyes watchful. "What I can't understand is why He didn't answer our prayers. All of us prayed for Lydia's safe return, and He ignored us."

"It goes back to those choices we were talking about."

"What?"

"Free will."

"You're saying a little girl chooses to wander from camp and God doesn't step in to do anything about it."

"I'm only a man, not even a very smart man." Sadness lined Thomas's face. "I only know that we can't have it both ways. If God took care of everything for us, fixed all our mistakes, babysat us every step of the way, how would we ever know what faith is? How would we ever have a shred of character? How would we ever learn from our mistakes?"

Michael rested his head on the horse's neck for a moment and then raised it so he could see the sky. "Like my parents."

"Like your parents. I'm thinking they'd like to be able to fix this mistake for you. It probably breaks their hearts that they can't."

Michael swallowed against the pain in his throat. "I have to learn."

"You do."

Why did his lesson have to involve the life of a little girl? And the woman he loved. It was too much. God expected too much.

"I don't like this lesson."

"I suspect no one does." Thomas kicked at a rock with the toe of his dusty boot. "I'm headed back inside. Why don't you walk with me?"

Michael tugged his hat down to shield his eyes from the brilliant sun. His throat closed around his response. He didn't want to see Lydia in her little wooden casket. Thomas waited, not moving, his hands loose at his side. Everything about his still silence said the choice was Michael's. Just as it had been before.

His hand shaking, he patted the horse's back and started up the road.

Thomas fell in step next to him. "These folks are your family. Take one step at a time."

Michael's feet felt as if they weighed a thousand pounds each.

Chapter 11

Katie picked up the dirty plates from the table, stacking two more on top of a stack of eight. The plain white china weighed her down. The smell of cold, congealing roast and gravy caused her stomach to roil. She chose to ignore it, instead reaching for another plate.

"That's enough. Let me get those for you." Her voice gentle, Irene Knepp leaned in front of Katie and snatched the plate. "Sit down and rest a spell. You have plenty of women around to take care of this today."

"I've got them." She needed to work. "There's plenty to go around."

Irene tugged the plates from Katie's arms. "I mean it. Sit." She whirled and trotted into the kitchen, her long black skirt swishing around her ankles. "I don't want to see you back in the kitchen. You have company."

Katie didn't want to sit. As long as she kept moving, she felt useful. Feeling useful beat feeling sad any day. And it beat thinking about the time they'd spent standing in the broiling sun, watching the tiny coffin as her boys lowered it into the ground and covered it with dirt, the clods thudding against the wood. It hadn't taken long. Such a small hole for such a small coffin.

The now-familiar pain shot through her chest. Her arm and her jaw ached. Unceasing nausea roiled in her stomach. She rubbed at her arm with her shaky hand, dodged Josie and Emma, and headed toward the kitchen. She would not sit. Sitting led to thinking. They had so much company crammed into their house, she couldn't see the door from where she stood. They'd eaten in shifts. Under any other circumstance she would've reveled in company. Her brother Thaddeus and his fraa. Helen and her new husband, Gabriel. All the nieces and nephews. Their friends from Bliss Creek. Even Micah Kelp and his fraa had made the trip.

Any other circumstance but this. Loads of friends and family making the trek for the funeral of her child. Her gaze met Silas's. He stood near the kitchen door, Luke and Elijah flanking him on either side. Along with Thomas, they were a blessing to him in this, his hour of need. Her husband had a fierce faith. Battered as he was, he stood tall, his back straight, his expression as stoic as it had been from the moment he walked up the path at Stockton Lake to tell her their child was gone.

Each night since, in the darkness, she'd clung to his faith when her own teetered and threatened to crash around her. She didn't voice her certainty that had she been a better mudder, Lydia would still be alive. If Silas blamed her, he didn't let on. She wanted his forgiveness, but the thought of voicing her failing made her throat close each time she tried. Instead, she listened to his even breathing and made it her own, in and out, in and out. Men were different, she surmised. They hadn't given birth from their own bodies. Hadn't felt a child quicken in the womb. Hadn't felt the pain of the birth. No doubt they suffered horribly at the death of a child, but she couldn't believe it was quite the same.

The lines on her husband's face told a different story. He'd aged in the last four days. The easy smile had disappeared and dark circles gave his eyes a sunken look.

He felt the loss in ways she, as a mother, couldn't understand. He saw himself as the provider and protector. He'd been unable to protect Lydia from this. Now he sought forgiveness from God and from her. She had none to give. She couldn't forgive herself for leaving Lydia in the care of her other daughters. She couldn't forgive herself for raising a daughter who chose to skip out on her responsibilities simply because of a boy.

She glanced around, for the first time wondering where Hannah was. Phoebe had taken Sarah upstairs, most likely to avoid talking to their friends and family. She hadn't seen Hannah since she jumped from the buggy after it returned from the cemetery. She hadn't eaten or helped with the serving.

"Have you seen Hannah?" Her chest tight with worry, she squeezed past Simon's fraa and directed the question to Helen, who trotted toward the kitchen with more dirty dishes stacked in her arms. "I lost track of her after the funeral. I didn't see her eat."

"Naomi and Betsy made some sandwiches and took her for a walk down by the pond." Helen's round face filled with a kind smile. "They're good girls. They'll keep her company."

The pain in Katie's chest subsided to a throbbing ache. She trailed after Helen into the kitchen. "She spoke to them about...all this?"

"She allowed herself to be led." Helen set the plates on the counter and wiped her hands on her apron. "Kinner are sometimes the best ones for this. They don't talk so much. They listen or they play. Sometimes they just need to play and not think so much."

Wise words. "You're right."

Helen ducked her head and disappeared back into the front room.

At a loss for what to do next, Katie glanced around. Surely there was something she could do here. Emma had her hands deep in the sudsy water of the dish tub. Bethel, despite being heavy with child and leaning on her crutches, had a dish towel in her hand. Annie was busy sticking food in an already crammed refrigerator. She turned and saw Katie.

"What are you doing in here?" She nestled a bowl of creamed corn between a chicken casserole and a container of mashed potatoes. "We'll take care of this."

Katie opened her mouth. No words came out. To her horror, a sob threatened to escape. She clamped her mouth shut and whirled to leave.

"Wait." Annie's voice followed her. A moment later her hand touched Katie's arm. "Let's find a quiet spot and visit."

Annie slipped in front of her and led the way—away from the people squeezed into every inch of their home. They climbed the stairs and Annie tugged open the door to the bedroom where Sarah slept, tuckered out from having been passed from relative to relative in a bounty of hugs and kisses and exclamations over how much she'd grown. Too young to know what was going on, she gurgled and giggled and returned the kisses with air kisses of her own.

"How are you doing?" Annie finally asked as she dropped onto the foot of the bed and folded her hands in her lap. "We haven't had a chance to visit. Helen said you had been having some chest pains. Did you see a doctor about it?"

"No need." Ignoring the fleeting question of where Phoebe had gone after depositing Sarah in her room, Katie leaned over the crib railing and touched the baby's rosy cheek. She wiggled and stuck her thumb in her mouth. Katie backed away, not wanting to interrupt her peaceful sleep. "I'm sure it'll pass as soon as we get back to our regular routine. It's just…all this."

Annie nodded, but the concern in her face didn't abate. She hesitated, chewing on her lip for a few seconds, her gaze on her hands. Finally, she looked up. "I know everyone is saying it's Gott's will, Gott's plan, Gott's time. Gott has your little one in His arms, and I know those words are true. I know we are to find comfort in them and we do." She kept her voice soft, barely above a whisper. "When David died, those words were just words. It took a long time for me to find the comfort in them. I didn't tell anyone that because I didn't want people to think I was weak or unfaithful. David wanted me to be strong so I tried very hard to be strong."

She twisted her fingers together. The knuckles were white. "I had people all around me who loved me and wanted me to feel better. So I tried hard to feel better. But mostly I felt alone."

Katie breathed. Annie had lost her first husband long before his time. A young man felled by disease at twenty-two. God's plan? Katie tiptoed to the window and lifted the curtain. Still daylight. How could it still be light? She'd thought yesterday had been the longest day of her life. This one had already been longer. She faced Annie. "I appreciate you telling me that. I'm older than you are. I've seen more. I choose to find the comfort in God's plan." She had no choice. How could she accept God's blessings without accepting this cross that was hers to bear? "Lydia was His gift to us. He chooses the time and the place for her return home."

Annie nodded. "Every day I got up and reminded myself that I was blessed with a son and the bakery and my family."

"And now Isaac." A new husband barely two years after David's death. And from the looks of her, another child on the way. "Gott is good."

"Jah, Gott is good." Annie smiled. "I never thought I would love again, yet here I am."

"I can't replace Lydia."

"Nor did I replace David."

"I meant no disrespect or judgment. I'm glad you found Isaac. It's meant to be. Our families are meant to be whole."

"I didn't replace David." Annie's hands rubbed her belly in a protective gesture. "I could never. I hold him in my heart, but I do go on with my life and I'm content. Because that is Gott's will for me. It gives me great comfort to know he doesn't suffer anymore."

"I know."

"I only wanted to say…I wanted to tell you that no matter what people say about Gott's will and Gott's plan, the truth is we're only human." She rose and came to Katie's side. "We are only human. Gott made us fraas and mudders. I'm just a woman, but I know He understands the terrible loss of a child. He understands if it takes time to learn to live with it."

Katie gripped the railing and stared down at sweet Sarah sucking on her thumb, her skin so white and thin that the tiny veins in her eyelids shone blue. Her lips were perfect rosebuds that puckered and then smoothed as she gave herself comfort with her thumb.

Annie patted Katie's back, her hand soft and warm. "I'm just a woman, but I think Gott understands."

Katie nodded. She touched the blonde curls that framed Sarah's head. "I hope so, because I can't begin to understand." Her throat closed. She waited until she could breathe again. "Try as I might, I don't understand. I feel as if I'm being punished for not being a better mudder."

"You are a good mudder. Your older sons have all joined the church. They've married. They're good parents. They follow your example."

"But Phoebe—"

"Is young and made a mistake. A mistake with terrible consequences, but not one for which you can take the blame."

"One she'll have to live with the rest of her life. I don't want that for her. I want her to have the life and the love and the joy that I've had with Silas. Everything I did, everything I've said all these years has been with the intent that my children be faithful followers and members of their community." Katie wiped at her face with the back of her sleeve. "I thought I taught her better. Maybe if I'd been stricter. Maybe if I'd let Silas take a firmer hand with her."

"I don't have your experience with my own children, but I know what we went through with my brother Josiah during his rumspringa. We almost lost him. No one blamed my parents. They did their best. That's all parents can do. You did your best. Phoebe is a good girl learning a terrible lesson."

"How do I know I did my best?" She really wanted an answer to that question. If she had done better, maybe Lydia would still be here. "How can it be my best when the actions of one of my daughters led to the death of another daughter?"

"You can't blame yourself for this. It's making yourself more important than you are. No matter what happens, Gott is in control."

The words were like a bucket of icy water poured over her. She hadn't seen that about herself, so *grossfelich*, so proud. "You're right."

Annie touched her arm. "I'm so sorry, Katie, so sorry."

Katie turned and accepted her friend's hug. Sometimes there were no words that could fix a broken heart, but Annie's attempt to offer her comfort touched her. The pain in Katie's chest lessened a fraction and she felt the stitches working their way in and out, in and out, sewing the wound that was her heart back together one agonizing stitch at a time.

Chapter 12

Michael fumbled with his ticket, wishing he had pockets. All the money he had to his name was in an envelope stuffed inside his shirt. He didn't want to put it in his duffel bag. What if something happened to the bag? He dropped onto a bench in the small, nearly empty building that passed for New Hope's bus station and looked up at the clock hanging on the drab green wall. Twenty minutes until the bus would pull in and stop for a few minutes before heading on to Springfield. His stomach did a strange little flip-flop. He'd never traveled anywhere alone before and never on a bus like this. He closed his eyes, gritted his teeth, and took a long breath through his nose, breathing in the smell of dust and bleach cleanser, and let it out. It would be a time of learning. That's how he tried to think of this self-imposed journey. Time to figure out how he'd gone so wrong. Time to let Phoebe's family heal without seeing him at every turn.

Whatever awaited him in Springfield, it had to be better than the judging glances, the looks of profound disappointment, the conversations that ceased when he walked into a room. Anything would be better.

"Michael!" He opened his eyes. Daniel strode toward him, his expression relieved. "You haven't left yet."

"Nee."

Daniel plopped onto the bench next to him. "What do you think you're doing? I stopped by your house to see why you didn't come to the service or class yesterday. Your mudder said you were gone. She'd been crying—"

"I'm going away." He held up his hand to stem the flow of Daniel's words. "I don't know when I'll be back."

"But you're coming back? You'll be baptized, right?"

He wanted to reassure his friend, but he couldn't. "I don't know."

"Running away won't solve anything."

"I'm not running away. I'm taking a different path." He didn't want to tell Daniel how empty he felt. How empty the world seemed. He no longer had that assurance God was with him and would take care of things. He hadn't taken care of Lydia. He hadn't answered all those prayers. "I'm getting a fresh start and giving the Christners room to have theirs."

"You need your family and your friends." Daniel tugged at his suspenders, his brown eyes troubled. "When times are hard, we need our community. We need to stick together."

"Sometimes we can't. We shouldn't."

"They've forgiven you." Daniel leaned forward, elbows on knees, his expression earnest. "You know they have. They've told you so."

"It's one thing to forgive. It's another to constantly be reminded of a loss. They need time to heal a little. As much as they can."

"Things will get better."

Michael snorted. He gazed around the bus station with its echoing, empty corners. "Not for Lydia they won't."

"So that's it." Daniel rubbed at the faint stubble on his cheeks with both hands, his expression twisted in deep concentration as if trying to figure out an arithmetic problem. "You haven't forgiven yourself."

"If it were you, would you?"

Daniel chewed at his lip, his gaze following an elderly couple, each pulling a bright green suitcase on wheels. "I'm as much to blame as you are. I encouraged you to talk to her that day."

"I made the decision to do it. I take responsibility."

"Then ask Gott to forgive you. He'll do it. That's what Thomas says. He says God's forgiveness is all we need. I asked to be forgiven for what I did that day and I have."

"I'm glad for you." He *was* glad for Daniel. He harbored no ill will toward his friend. The decision to approach Phoebe that day had been his and his alone. "If Gott answered prayers, I wouldn't be in this predicament."

Shock made Daniel's mouth hang open for a moment. "You're blaming God?" He stuttered the words. "You're in this predicament because of what you did, not what He did."

On that point, Michael remained abundantly clear. "What are you doing here?"

"Trying to help a friend back into the fold."

"The friend needs to leave the fold for a while."

Daniel was silent for a moment. "What about Phoebe?"

"What about her?" His heart lurched at hearing the name spoken aloud. He bowed his head, hoping his hat would hide the change in his expression. "Is she all right?"

"Rachel says she's grieving and that's natural, but she hasn't come to prayer service or class either. She won't talk to Rachel or Molly about it. Rachel says her heart is broken. You'll abandon her in her time of need and grief?"

He waited a beat, two beats, three, waiting until he was sure his voice wouldn't betray him. "It's for the best. She'll never be able to heal with me around to remind her of what we did."

"I thought you…" Daniel's face turned beet red. "I thought you two…you cared for her."

Always. He would always care. But that couldn't be allowed to matter. Michael stood and grabbed his duffel bag. "That's between her and me."

"I know." Daniel scrambled to his feet. "If you feel this bad, imagine how bad she must feel. Her sister. Her responsibility."

"My fault."

"She feels no less responsible and you're leaving her to face everyone on her own."

"She's better off."

"Did you ask her if that's what she wants?"

"Nee."

"You're being a coward then." Daniel's voice hardened. "You're running away and leaving her to fend for herself. You really don't care about her."

"I'm leaving because I do care about her." A voice blared over their heads much louder than necessary, considering there were only a half dozen people in the room, telling Michael his bus was now loading. "I have to go."

"Don't leave."

"Goodbye, Daniel."

Daniel didn't move to follow him, for which Michael was grateful. He led a straggling group of four or five folks heading to the parking lot where the buses loaded.

"Lydia is safe now. She's in Gott's arms." Daniel's voice carried over the murmur of people saying their goodbyes. "You're the one in danger."

"Take care."

"Write me," Daniel called. "Send me your address so I can write you."

Michael didn't acknowledge the commands. He didn't look back until he reached his bus. Daniel had disappeared from sight. His throat tight, eyes burning, Michael sucked in air and tried to regain the sense that he was doing the right thing. Phoebe didn't attend church service. She didn't go to baptism class. She suffered from a broken heart. He'd broken it.

The bus driver, a tall man with muscles that bulged under the short sleeves of his uniform, held out a hand, beckoning for the duffel bag so he could put it in the luggage alcove under the bus. Michael shook his head and held it close. The few things he owned were in the threadbare bag that had belonged to his daed. He'd hold it close. The guy shrugged and Michael shuffled forward to the open door.

Phoebe wasn't talking to anyone. She needed to move on. He wanted her to move on. He wanted her to be okay.

Michael slipped a cell phone from the pocket on the side of his bag. Swallowing against the acrid taste on his tongue, he found the number Daniel had given him several months ago. Daniel had urged Michael to call Phoebe. Talk to her. He never had. If he'd taken Daniel's advice, maybe things would've turned out differently. There would have been no need to steal her away at the lake.

The dial tone sounded in his ears.

It rang once, twice, three times, four times. Nothing. Not even a voice offering voicemail. He hadn't gone so far as to record a message himself and somehow, it relieved him that she hadn't either. He'd bought a phone in a fit of pique because he really hadn't done anything during his rumspringa that he wouldn't normally do. Then he'd never used it. His hard-earned money from the New Hope Nursery down the drain.

Even if she had the cell phone where she could see it and feel its vibration—none of them had musical ring tones for fear their daeds would hear it—she most likely wouldn't answer. And what would he say if she did? *Sorry. I'm running away and leaving you to face what we did because it's best for you.* She might try to convince him to stay. Phoebe, for all her whimsical ways, believed. She had faith in their community and their ways. He'd never heard her say anything that told him she didn't want to worship in the traditional ways, marry, have children, and live out her life as a Plain woman. She'd want that for him as a friend, if not a special friend destined for more. Her character was one of the things he most liked about her. It shone through in everything she did. He didn't have to talk to her to know.

It didn't matter. She should be free of him and the memory of what they'd done. With time, the pain and the shame of it would fade and she would find someone new. Someone who knew how to contain himself until the right moment, the proper moment.

He closed his eyes against the tidal wave of nausea. She wasn't going to answer. He didn't really expect an answer. As he walked past a trash can he let the phone slip from his hand and disappear into the mound of empty soda cans, water bottles, and dirty tissues. Those days were over. Today he moved forward as a man, independent, striking out on his own. He climbed the steps to the cool, dark interior of the bus.

He dragged the duffel bag—which now seemed to weigh a hundred pounds—behind him through the bus's narrow aisle and looked for an empty seat. Passengers were crammed into almost every row.

He'd rather have a row to himself, but he didn't see any. He gauged the people sitting in the adjacent seats, debating. The trip would take an hour. He would sit next to a stranger for an hour. Would there be conversation? Did a person talk to his neighbor when thrown together by sheer happenstance? About what? He didn't know. He'd never ridden on a bus before. Blank faces greeted him on either side of the aisle. A skinny woman with bad skin and bleached hair let her gaze collide with his and then skitter away. Hugging bony arms to her chest, she turned to look out the window even though the bus hadn't left the station. He moved on.

"Catch a seat anywhere, buddy."

Michael looked back.

The driver gave him a toothy grin in the enormous rearview mirror over his head. He had gold lining on two of his front teeth and an enormous gold crucifix dangling around his neck over a gray uniform shirt. "I need you to sit down so we can get going. I've got a schedule to keep. They don't bite—most of them, anyway."

Aware of dull thudding in his temples and heat that scorched his cheeks and neck, Michael shoved the duffel bag into the rack overhead and sank into the first open seat. His neighbor turned out to be an elderly lady wearing a funny little box hat on her head and holding a large picnic basket in her lap. She smelled like lilacs and mothballs. A wide smile on her wrinkled, powdered face, she scooted closer to the window, her arms clutching the basket. Michael wiggled into the seat, trying to figure out where to put his long legs and arms without touching her.

"Pack us in like cattle." She had the high, quavering voice of his *groossmammi*. "Like the airlines. The more people they pack in the planes, the more money they make. Don't even serve peanuts anymore without charging."

"They serve peanuts on buses?" The question flew from his mouth before he could stop it. He sounded like a hick. He should know they served peanuts. "I mean—"

"No, honey, they serve peanuts on the airplanes." She giggled, a strange sound coming from a lady who looked to be pushing eighty.

To his amazement, she patted his hand. Her fingers felt dry and crinkly, like tissue paper. "You're a silly one, aren't you? You look just like my grandson Matthew. A fine boy. A fine boy. Well, not really a boy, anymore. Goodness, he's married and has two children now. My great-grandchildren…"

So that's how it was on buses. People did talk. And talk. And talk. He rested his head on the seat and closed his eyes for a second. His hat slid forward. His hat. He grabbed it and settled it onto his lap without opening his eyes to see if anyone noticed. He should've left the hat at home. He should've left the suspenders and pants with no zippers and all the other stuff that marked him as different.

Home. It wasn't home anymore. He didn't live there. Officially, he didn't live anywhere. The thought loomed like a huge trapdoor opening under his feet. But no, he was only homeless until he arrived in Springfield. His hand went to his chest. The packet he'd slipped inside his shirt was still there. All the money he'd saved from working at the nursery in Bliss Creek and then the one in New Hope this past year rested in that envelope. The money that would give him this new start.

He squeezed his eyes shut, trying not to think. He just wanted a few minutes' rest. He'd done nothing but think as he worked with the plants for the last three weeks. Think and think until he was sick of thinking. He wanted his mind to be a big, fat blank for a few minutes, an hour, long enough to sleep.

"My daughter, Bertha, now she has four kids. All girls. I think they were trying for a boy and just kept having girls." The lady's voice continued to bathe him in babble. Soft, kind, sing-song babble. Michael liked her voice. There was no censure there, no pity. Only the need to have someone listen. "Their names are Autumn, Winter, Summer, and Spring. Doesn't that beat all? I always knew my daughter would get even with me for naming her Bertha. It was my mother's name. She swore she would change it when she grew up, but she never did. She just made everyone call her Bert like she was some boy or something…"

The bus's engine growled and the brakes squeaked as they lurched forward. Michael rubbed his forehead, trying to abate the ache that accompanied him everywhere. *New start. New start.* The rumble of the engine sang the words inside his head. *New start. New start.*

Lydia wouldn't receive a new start.

The lyrics of the song changed. *Lydia's dead. Your fault. Your fault. Your fault.*

He opened his eyes.

"Would you like a peanut butter sandwich?" The lady popped open the basket lid. "I made a bunch in case the bus breaks down or we get lost. I like to be prepared. I'd rather have chicken salad, but you can't have chicken salad unless you have a cooler and a cooler is too bulky to lug around. I'm going to Denver and it's a long ride. I have to change buses in two or three places. I can't be lugging an ice chest around."

His stomach rocked. "No, thank you. Maybe later."

She patted his hand again. "That's fine. That's just fine. You take a little nap. You look tuckered out. I won't let anyone bother you, and I'll wake you if there's anything interesting to see."

Somehow, he thought she would. He settled in and closed his eyes. The rumble of the engine and the rocking motion soothed him. He sank into the darkness.

The hot sun burned his face. Sweat trickled down his cheeks, creating rivulets like tears on his chin and his neck. No, no, it wasn't sweat. It was water. The smell of mud and rotting fish filled his nostrils. He was in the water, swimming, swimming. Trying to reach her. Yellow hair floated on the water, the purple dress spread out behind her, floating. He swam harder, but she floated away, further and further away.

He tried to inhale and water filled his nose. Sputtering, he opened his mouth, struggling for air. Water poured in, gagging him. He flailed his arms, beating against the water, bent on making it to the surface. His arms were weak. His legs flapped, useless against the current. Come on, come on. His lungs were bursting but still he fought against the waves.

"Hey, hey!" The voice quavered with alarm. "Son, wake up! You're having a nightmare. It's just a bad dream. Come on back, sweetie, come on back."

Michael bolted upright, gasping for air. Even the stale air of the bus, stinking of bodies in close quarters, was better than nothing, better than the horrible strangling thirst for oxygen when none came. The woman's dry, papery hand covered his clammy fingers and squeezed. He opened his eyes. The lady let go, but her sagging cheeks shook with concern.

"Sorry, sorry." He tried to rein in his breathing, but it continued to come out in huffs as if he'd been running up a hill. "I...it was..."

"A bad dream. There, there." The woman whipped a bottle of water from her basket and held it out with a slight flourish. "Take this. I wish I had lemonade. You're so flushed, you might have a fever."

"No, I'm fine." He took the bottle of water anyway. His mouth was so dry that his tongue stuck to the roof of his mouth, a fact that seemed infinitely unreasonable considering the amount of water his nightmare self had consumed in the terrible fight to claw his way out of the lake. "Thank you for the water."

"No need to thank me. I have more." She inclined her head toward the window. "We're almost to the first stop."

"First stop?"

He leaned forward to see around her. The countryside had disappeared into the city. Streets clogged with cars. Buildings so close you couldn't see daylight between them. Signs. Huge signs, small signs, signs on top of signs. And concrete. Lots of concrete. Everywhere he looked he saw people. "This is Springfield?"

"It is." She smiled airily. "It's a lovely town. My cousin Doris lives here. I'm not stopping to see her, though. I sent her a Christmas card and she didn't send me one back so I figure I don't owe her a visit. I—"

"I've been asleep an hour?"

She glanced at a slim silver watch on an arm covered with wrinkles and brown age spots. "Just about. Poor thing, you were exhausted. And it's no wonder, the way you toss and turn and mumble in your sleep. Who's Lydia? And who's Phoebe?"

He drank from the water bottle. He'd slept the entire time instead of spending these precious moments figuring out what to do next. When he made the plan to leave home, it only encompassed the packing of the bag, the walk to the barn, the short talk with his daed, and hitching a ride to the bus station in New Hope. His daed hadn't even tried to stop him. He said he saw it coming. His tone said he welcomed it. *Come back when you've got it all figured out. Your room will be waiting.*

When he had it all figured out.

The bus took the next corner wide and pulled into an enormous parking lot filled with buses. "Springfield. Springfield," the driver bellowed. The airbrakes honked, the engine belched, and the bus came to a halt. He pushed on the lever and the door popped open. He stood. "Springfield, folks. Those of you who are getting off for good, thanks for riding with us. The rest of y'all take twenty. Be back here at ten-thirty on the dot or get left behind. I suggest you eat and use the facilities."

The passengers began to file off.

"Isn't this your stop?" The woman rested both hands on her basket. She didn't seem to be in any hurry. "You said Springfield."

Fear paralyzed his legs, but he nodded. "It is."

"Anybody waiting out there for you?" He shook his head. "I didn't think so."

She opened her basket and doled out a sandwich made with white bread and wrapped in plastic along with a shiny red apple. "It's easier to think with food. Take it."

He took it.

"No one may be waiting out there for you, son." She smiled, showing off a set of dentures. "But you're never alone. I suspect you have folks waiting back in New Hope. I don't know what you're looking for, but you won't find it in the big city." She touched one bony finger to his chest. "It's in there, honey. It's in there."

Then she stood. "May I pass?"

With haste, he stood and scrambled out of her way. "May I carry your basket for you?"

"No need. I might find another wayward soul who needs a sandwich." She waved with her free hand. "Remember, sweetie, look in your heart for what you need and you'll always find God waiting there for you."

He grabbed his duffel bag and followed her. He wanted to believe her. Oh, how he wanted to believe her.

Chapter 13

Phoebe pulled her chair closer to the window, leaned her arms on the frame, and stared at the brown stubble where the corn had been. Despite the open window, the air in the room stifled her. Fall should arrive any day now. She lowered her head and leaned her forehead against the wood, wishing it were covered with snow blown in by a gusty northern winter wind. Anything to make the time pass, to blur the memories, to tap down the hurt.

"Phoebe? Phoebe!"

Rachel's voice called to her. Reluctantly, Phoebe leaned out the window and looked down at her friend. "Hey."

Smiling, Rachel shielded her eyes with one hand and waved with the other. "Can I come up?"

"It's too hot up here."

"Come down then. There's a nice breeze down by the creek. We'll take a walk."

"Why?"

If Rachel thought the question rude, she gave no sign. "Because I don't like to shout." No doubt. Rachel was almost as soft-spoken as Molly. When they were younger, the two could hardly get a word in edgewise when Phoebe hogged the conversation. "And I want to talk to you."

Feeling as if she had five-pound stones strapped to her feet, Phoebe clomped down the stairs and out to the yard. "I'm not really in the mood to talk."

Rachel grabbed her arm and hung on. "Then just walk with me. Like we used to do."

They used to take long walks after the chores were done, exploring this new farm so far from Bliss Creek and Kansas and everything familiar. They'd find new places to sit and daydream about boys and marriage and having babies of their own.

"I don't feel very good." Phoebe swallowed against the ever-present knot in her throat and the bitter taste it left in her mouth. "I should go back upstairs."

"Come on, we haven't visited in ages." Rachel tugged at Phoebe's elbow. "It'll do you good to get out of the house. All this moping around isn't good for you."

Phoebe allowed herself to be drawn toward the path that led to the pond. Truth be told, she was sick of her room and sick of the view from the window, sick of feeling sick. "You sound like Mudder."

"She's right." Rachel set a brisk pace as if she were eager to get somewhere. "Exercise clears the mind."

"Who told you that?" Phoebe scrambled to keep up with her long-legged friend. "You sound like a doctor or something."

"Deborah read it in a book."

The sisters had been talking about her. "Of course she did. Is she mad at me?"

"Mad at you? Whatever for?"

"Because I haven't been helping her get ready for school. You had the work frolic and I didn't even go." Phoebe wrapped her arms around her middle. "I know she thinks I'll be the new teacher when she leaves and I don't want to do it."

"She's not mad." Rachel shrugged. "Of course, she still believes you'll come around. She's so excited about Abel and getting married, she believes everything will work out in the end."

"That's Deborah."

"She's right, though. You would be a good teacher."

Maybe, but she couldn't be trusted, not with children. "I shouldn't be given that kind of responsibility."

Rachel wrinkled her nose and shook a finger at Phoebe. "Because you made one mistake."

"One terrible mistake."

"Everyone deserves a second chance."

"Not when kinner are involved."

"Molly and I were talking about…well, we were talking about you after the prayer service this morning. How we missed your funny face keeping us awake. We missed you in baptism class too." Rachel gave her a sheepish look. "Why didn't you come to class?"

Because her sin was so great, she was no longer sure she had a right to be baptized. It didn't matter that people kept saying she'd been forgiven. She didn't feel forgiven. She saw the way they looked at her when their paths crossed in town. She saw the way Mudder looked at her when she thought Phoebe wouldn't notice. She saw the way Hannah pushed food around on her plate but never actually took a bite. Her once round little sister now looked like a starving kitten. "I told you. I don't feel very good."

Rachel halted in the shade of an oak tree. She scooped up a fallen leaf from a pile that heralded the coming of winter somewhere beyond the horizon and twirled it by its stem. "No one blames you."

"They try very hard not to blame me. There's a difference."

"They're good people." Rachel studied the leaf in her hand as if it might do a trick any minute. "Why can't you come to the baptism class?"

"Because Lydia's dead and it's my fault."

"Gott forgives you. Lydia is with Him now. She's happy. She's not suffering. She'll never feel pain or want for anything."

"She'll never grow up or marry or have children either." Phoebe had heard all these words before. "I prayed to Him for hours and hours and hours that day."

"We all did."

"She died. He didn't answer our prayers."

Rachel let the leaf go. It plummeted to the ground. Phoebe trod on it. It crackled under her bare foot.

"My daed says Gott answers all prayers. Only we don't always get the answer we want. Gott knows better than we do what we need. Lydia is happy and safe and loved in His arms."

That answer, spoken a hundred times in the days following Lydia's death, gave Phoebe the same cold comfort it did every time she heard it. "Instead of in Mudder's arms. Mudder suffers instead. Daed suffers. Hannah suffers."

"They'll heal. So will you if you forgive yourself." Rachel leaned her hand on the tree, her kind face troubled. "I'm just a girl. I don't know about these things, but I know someone who does. I want to take you to talk to her. Today. Now."

"Who?"

"Irene."

Daniel's mother. Phoebe couldn't remember any conversation she'd ever had with the quiet woman. A woman almost as soft-spoken as Rachel. "Your future mother-in-law? Why?"

"As a favor to me because I'm a worrywart and I worry about you."

"I don't feel like visiting." Why couldn't anyone understand this? "I told you, I don't feel good."

"And you never will if you don't get out of the house and get back to living." Once again Rachel grabbed Phoebe's arm and tugged, this time in the direction from which they'd just traveled. "We'll take my buggy."

Half an hour later they pulled into the Knepps' neat-as-a-pin front yard. Relief filled Phoebe when she saw that no other buggies were parked there. No other visitors with whom she'd have to make small talk, knowing all the while they were thinking about what she'd done and wondering how she could live with her guilt. If their eyes weren't full of judgment or condemnation, they contained pity. Everywhere she looked, she saw pity. "I don't know if I can stomach company right now."

"Irene's not company, she's Irene." Rachel inclined her head toward the house. "Go on, then. I'll be back in an hour for you."

"Back in an hour? You're not coming in?" Phoebe had met Daniel's mother many times, but she'd never carried on a conversation with her, not once. She'd been to work frolics here, cannings, quiltings, and the like, but never to visit with Daniel's mother alone. "I'm not staying if you're not."

"Go on. She's expecting you."

"How can she be expecting me when I only just agreed to come?"

"We talked about it and we prayed about it and she said to go fetch you."

"You talked about me? *Fetch* me?"

"As a favor to me, your friend, please just hear her out."

Filled with that same awful, resentful, stubborn feeling that had weighed her down for weeks, Phoebe climbed from the buggy. "Where will you go?"

"For a nice ride. I might stop by and see Molly for a bit. She misses you, you know."

"I don't want—"

"There you are! Phoebe, I'm so glad you could come for a visit." Irene propped the screen door open with one hand and stuck her head out. "Come on in. I have a fresh pitcher of peppermint tea ready to be iced."

Glowering at Rachel one last time, Phoebe pasted what she hoped passed for a smile on her face and tromped up the steps into Daniel's house.

"Let's go in the kitchen. I've got all the windows and the doors open, plus peppermint tea. Peppermint tea makes you feel cooler, doesn't it, when it's iced? Something about the mint." Irene bustled through the house, the same bundle of energy Phoebe was used to seeing in Daniel. "The baby's asleep and the older boys went fishing with my husband. I'm hoping for catfish for supper. Adah's working. The little girls are playing with their dolls outside while Abram practices harnessing the Shetland. He's sure Ben will let him drive the buggy any day now. He's seven, so I guess it won't be long. Anyway, we'll have a few minutes to ourselves."

Phoebe couldn't imagine why they needed a few minutes to themselves, but she accepted the glass of tea, thankful for the chunks of ice

Irene broke off with an ice pick and deposited in the tall glass. She settled into a wooden chair at the pine prep table and waited to see why
she was here in this woman's kitchen.

Irene didn't seem to be in any hurry. As she laid chocolate chip
cookies on a plate of thick white china and brought them to the table,
she chatted on about the drought and her garden and the critters that
kept running off with her chickens. Phoebe sipped the tea and let the
words roll over her. Irene Knepp had the same soft brown eyes as Daniel and skin that tanned brown, never turning red with sunburn. She
talked with her hands, almost spilling her tea, such was her animation.
She seemed as nervous as Phoebe felt. She tried to relax and picked up
a cookie. Her stomach settled. Irene didn't seem to have any interest in
talking about the recent events. Whatever reason Rachel had for thinking Phoebe should visit with Irene, she couldn't see it.

"Did you know I had a baby who died?"

Phoebe inhaled too soon and the bite of cookie in her mouth
lodged in her throat. She coughed and sputtered.

"Oh, dear." Irene popped out of her chair, rushed around behind
Phoebe, and began to smack her on the back. "Are you all right?"

Phoebe grabbed her glass and gulped down tea. Tears in her eyes,
she coughed and cleared her throat. "I'm fine. I'm fine."

Irene returned to her chair. Her somber gaze studied Phoebe. "Did
you know I lost a baby?"

"Nee." The word came out hoarse. She didn't want to know more.
She didn't need to know more. "I never heard."

"It was before you were born. Before Daniel. It was my fault." Irene
dipped her finger in the condensation pooling at the base of her glass.
She drew circles around and around the glass. "I tried to save her, but
she died."

She. A baby girl. Phoebe laid the cookie on her napkin and swallowed, concentrating all her effort on not running from the house.
"How?"

"Fire." Irene met her gaze head on. Phoebe saw old scars in her eyes,
but she saw something else too. Peace. How did one find that peace?
"A fire I set."

"I don't understand."

"Neither do I." Irene broke her cookie in half and raised the smaller piece to her mouth. Then she set it back on the plate. Her gaze lifted over Phoebe as if she were looking into some other, faraway place. "I'll never know exactly what happened."

Her gaze came back to Phoebe. "Ruthie was six weeks old. She had been sick. She had a terrible cough. We both did. I don't know if I caught her cold or she caught mine. I'd been up with her two or three nights running. I couldn't remember the last time I'd slept. All those hours of boiling water and making steam so she could breathe and sleep. She'd try to nurse but she couldn't because her nose was stopped up. Then she'd cry because she was hungry, which made the congestion worse. I didn't know what to do. I was new at being a mudder and I was tuckered out. Completely tuckered out."

Her fingers brushed the cookie crumbs into small piles. "It was cold that morning. Ben went out to do his chores. Menno Weaver came by and said the wind had blown some of the roof off their shed and could Ben come help him fix it. So he went.

"We'd only been married a year. I wanted him to go. I wanted him to know I could hold up my end as his fraa, but I felt like I was sleep-walking. Ruthie fussed and fussed and fussed. I laid her in the cradle and started a fire in the fireplace. It was late November and it was cold. I remember being so cold."

Her voice, never loud to begin with, softened. Despite herself, Phoebe leaned in, straining to hear. She didn't want to know this story, but she couldn't help herself. What had been started had to be finished. She knew how it would end. What it would feel like. She let Irene continue toward an end that couldn't be avoided, no matter how hard either of them tried.

Irene shivered despite the humid, heavy air in the kitchen. She ran her hands over her arms as if she could still feel the cold of that long-ago day. "I went into the kitchen to start the stew. I remember sitting down at the table to chop the vegetables. I remember thinking I would just lay my head down for a minute. Just a minute or two. The next thing I know I feel heat and smell wood burning and smoke is billowing into the kitchen from the front room. I jumped up from the table, but I couldn't think, I couldn't think. What had I done? What had I done?"

She breathed, a ragged hiccup, paused, breathed again.

"I ran toward the front room, but flames were everywhere. Smoke. Black, ugly smoke filled the room. Somehow, when I started the fire, I didn't stack the wood right. A log must've fallen out and caught the rug on fire." Irene stared at Phoebe as if she needed her confirmation as to what had happened in that house all those years ago. "I tried to smother the flames with a towel, but it was too late. It had spread to the curtains and the pillows and my sewing and the piles of laundry I hadn't taken up the stairs yet. I grabbed Ruthie from her cradle. Her little arms and legs were limp. She didn't fuss anymore. She didn't cough. She didn't cry."

Irene swallowed and leaned back from the table. Her fingers trembled as she withdrew them into her lap where she clasped them, stilling their trembling. "I'm sorry. I haven't talked about this in a long, long time."

"Why are you..." Phoebe cleared her throat. She didn't want to know about this. She didn't need to know about this. "Why are you telling me now?"

"The flames never touched her. She was still herself with her little round face and chubby fingers. The doctor said it was the smoke. He said her lungs were compromised—that's the word he used—by her sickness. She had pneumonia. And we didn't even know it. I thought it was a cold, just a bad cold."

"How did you..." Phoebe couldn't put words to it. How did she live with herself? How did she sit here now with Daniel's little brothers and sisters playing in the backyard? How could there even be a Daniel or the other Knepp children after what happened with the first one? "How could you..."

"Grace." Irene gave her a tremulous smile. "God's grace and Ben's grace. My husband carried me through it. We lost everything. By the time the volunteer fire trucks got there, the house was gone. Ben arrived home to find me sitting on the ground in front of the smoldering ashes of our home, our daughter dead in my arms."

"And he forgave you?"

"He dropped to his knees and thanked God his fraa had survived." Irene sounded amazed at this fact even after all these years. "Right there in front of me. Then he took our baby daughter in his arms and he cried. It's the only time I've ever seen him cry."

"And then he forgave you."

"Jah. He said our gift from God was back with her Heavenly Father where she belonged." Irene stood. Her joints cracked and for the first time, she looked old. She swayed and steadied herself with one hand on the table. "Together we rebuilt our home with the help of our friends and family. Jah, there were plenty who looked at me like I was a bad mudder, a bad person. I saw it in their eyes at the prayer services and when I went into town to buy supplies. I saw it in my own relatives' eyes, but I learned to accept the words of our bishop, who told me God forgives and gives each of us second and third and fourth chances because He loves us so much and He wants us to be with Him. He's not looking for a reason to shut us out, He's looking for a reason to let us into His kingdom."

"How long did it take you to get over it?"

"You never get over losing a child, Phoebe. You only learn to go on. But you *do* go on." Irene gazed out the kitchen windows, lost in the memories that still had the power to hurt. "Your parents will learn. They will learn to appreciate the gift of the years God gave them with Lydia. They'll learn to think of the joy she gave them in those short years. They'll learn to think of her when the sun is shining and when the first snowflakes of winter fall and they'll learn to think of her when they see a newborn foal with its mother."

Would they learn to look at Phoebe without seeing her terrible mistake? "Weren't you afraid of having more children?"

"Terrified." Irene's smile held no mirth. "I didn't want more. I fought it. I kept Ben at arm's length until I realized how much it hurt him. He needed the comfort of his fraa. I couldn't withhold that from him."

"I don't think I could have a baby after that." Or having caused the death of a sister, however accidental. "I'd be too afraid."

She was too afraid now. *Be good. Be good.*

"That's what I thought until I held Hiram in my arms. God's gift to me of a new start. It's true I watched over him like a hawk. I was afraid to sleep at night for fear something would happen to him." She pointed to the ceiling and the smoke alarm in one corner. "We have smoke alarms in every room. Some folks might say that shows a lack of faith in God's plan for our kinner, but I think God wants us to be good stewards of the blessings He gives us, including the kinner. The alarms are battery operated. Some man came around trying to sell the Plain folks fire alarms that don't take batteries, but Ben just waved him off. The fire had to melt the metal before the clapper went off. Battery-operated smoke alarms are just fine."

The same salesman had visited Phoebe's house and gotten the same response, but Irene went on before Phoebe could speak. "Day by day I learned to trust in God, to have faith that whatever happened, I would be fine in the arms of God."

"You'd be fine if something happened to one of your other kinner?"

"I would mourn and grieve, just as you're doing now, but I would have God to cling to." She touched Phoebe's hand, a brief, warm touch. "Like Luke said at the funeral, life comes with an end. We don't know when that will be. Only God does. The day of reckoning could be a second or two away for any one of us. So we have to be ready now and make our peace now. "

Make peace. Phoebe tried to imagine her parents asking her forgiveness for leaving that day. Daed to go fishing. Mudder to fetch medicine for her arthritis. They owed her nothing. Michael? Jah, he'd convinced her to go into the woods, but she'd gone of her own free will, knowing she had a responsibility at the campground. She and Michael shared equally in the blame.

"God gave us free will, knowing full well, sometimes we would choose wrong." It was as if Irene knew the welter of emotion and confusion that reigned in Phoebe's head. "All He wants is for us to choose Him, knowing what we know. Choosing Him in the middle of the messes we make—that's faith."

"I don't know." Phoebe bit the inside of her cheek, trying to ward off the tears that lived on the edge, ready to fall, every waking minute of her day. She couldn't tell Irene what she really feared. She feared God had abandoned her. Fed up, irritated, irked, at His wit's end, He'd finally given up on her. "I don't know how I can."

"All you have to do is choose Him and then hang on for dear life." Irene brought the pitcher to the table and poured them each some more tea. "Eat your cookie. You're skinnier than a stray cat."

"What happened to me is different from what happened to you."

"It didn't happen to you. It happened to your sister." Irene's face was kind despite the sting in her words. "I know it feels like it happened to you, but it didn't. You get to go on with your life. You have this life to offer up. What you do with it is up to you. My Ruthie didn't get to grow up, but I had a chance to make a family and raise other children to love their Lord God. Lydia won't grow up, but you will. My advice? Don't squander the chance to live a godly life."

"What chance? The man I…the man I thought…the man who… he…I turned him away at the funeral and I haven't seen him since. My little sister doesn't talk, she doesn't eat, she won't play with the baby, she's barely breathing. My mudder and daed are hardly any better. As much as they say it's all right, as much as they try to forgive me, it's killing them."

"It only seems like it."

"You've had years to get over it."

"True. I used to walk down the street in Bliss Creek sure every person I passed was looking at me with accusing eyes, thinking I was a baby murderer at worst, a terrible, careless mudder at best. I'm just hoping you won't spend as much time feeling sorry for yourself as I did."

"Feeling sorry?" Anger coursed through Phoebe, jolting her upright in her chair. For the first time in days she felt a spurt of energy. "Don't I have a right? I've lost my sister and my other sister hates me and my parents are sick with grief—"

"But you're alive. And God loves you. He cares for you. He's right there with you."

"I'm not sure I believe that."

"So you'll believe in Him in the good times and scorn Him in the bad?"

"Nee. I don't know. Jah." She scrubbed her eyes with the back of her hand. "I can't feel Him like I did before. Even when it's hot, it's so cold and so dark."

Irene moved. A second later she wrapped her arms around Phoebe in a hug. "I know," she whispered. "I know, but God is all the light you'll ever need in your life. Stop feeling sorry for yourself and start living the life He wants for you. He gave us free will. We mess up and He forgives us. He forgives us. That's the most important thing to remember. He forgives us."

Phoebe broke away from Irene's grasp. She laid her head on the table, just as Irene had done all those years ago. She needed to rest, just for a few seconds. She closed her eyes, embarrassed to let herself go in front of this woman whom she barely knew.

The sound of pots and pans clattering told her Irene had gone about her business. A hum filled the room. A sing-song hum that Phoebe recognized. *Jesus Loves the Little Children.*

She lifted her head. "I have to go now."

A high, pain-laced cry wafted through the backdoor. "Mudder! Mudder!"

"That doesn't sound good. It's Melinda. I'll be right back." Irene wiped her hands on her apron and trotted away. "What is it, little one?"

Phoebe stood, unsure what to do. She wanted to go, but she couldn't leave Irene in the lurch if something had happened. What if the child was really hurt? The question knocked her back in her chair. She would be no good to Irene. Not anymore. *Gott, help me.*

Despite all that had happened, she wasn't a coward. Phoebe forced herself to stand on weak legs and march through the open door. She found Irene examining little Melinda's skinned knees and tear-stained face while Joanna, her older sister, sat on the edge of a trampoline, short legs swinging and a concerned look on her sun-kissed face.

"I fell off the trampoline." Melinda, who looked to be about five, announced with a sniff. "It hurts."

"I told them they were jumping too high, but they didn't listen." Abram patted the thick haunches of a Shetland pony that wasn't much taller than he was. He had the self-satisfied look of an older brother who had proven himself right about something. "They were trying to fly."

"Were not," Joanna shot back. "We were trying to do back flips."

"Silly girls. You may have broken your fingers." Irene touched the girl's dirty hand, then inspected her face. "Your nose looks fine. You'll survive. Serves you right for not listening to your bruder."

"He's too bossy." The girl's tears subsided, but she still looked miffed at the situation. "My nose feels like it's flat. My knees and my elbows hurt."

"That's going to be a nasty bruise on your cheek." Irene rose. "Phoebe, could you stay with her while I get my doctoring things?"

"I don't think—"

"You'll do fine."

Irene sped away, leaving Phoebe to face Melinda, Abram, and Joanna. They all looked at her expectantly, as if she could fix things. She couldn't fix anything.

"You're Lydia's big sister, right?" Abram slapped the reins on the Shetland. The pony began to trot around the yard, making a circle around the trampoline. "The girl who died."

Kinner always got right to the bottom of things. Not like adults, who pussyfooted around.

"Jah."

"That was sad." Joanna said. "We're real sorry."

"I appreciate that."

"I didn't know little girls could die." Melinda's forehead wrinkled like she was thinking hard on something. "My daed explained it to me."

Phoebe wished someone could explain it to her.

"Girls don't know nothing," Abram informed them as he rounded the bend behind his pony.

"Do too," Joanna argued. "Stop pretending you're driving a buggy. Daed isn't gonna let you drive anytime soon."

"Will too."

"Will not."

Phoebe held up a hand. "Stop it, you two. Neither of you know what your Daed will do because he hasn't done it yet." She couldn't help but smile at their glowering faces. "He'll do what he thinks is right, won't he?"

"Jah." Abram went back to his pony, but he gave Joanna one last dark look. "He knows I'm big and strong. I helped him put up hay last week."

"My daed is smart about a lot of stuff. He says we will go to be with the Father in heaven when we die." Melinda smiled up at Phoebe, bits of grass and dirt sprinkled across her bruised and battered face. She held out her uninjured hand. Without thinking, Phoebe took it. "I think it's like sitting on my groossdaadi's lap."

"I think you're right." Phoebe managed to keep the quiver from her voice. She smoothed a finger across the back of the little girl's hand. Her skin was soft as a baby kitten's fur. "That's a nice way of thinking about it."

Irene strode back into view, the handle of a basket over one arm. "I know I have some bandages in here and splints from when Abram fell off the horse."

"You fell off the horse?" Phoebe couldn't help herself. "And you made fun of your sisters?"

"I was a lot littler then." Abram's face flamed red, but he lifted his chin. "I got right back on."

"After I splinted your fingers and taped your ribs."

"I'm tough."

"That you are." Irene favored her three children with a smile. "You all are."

The picture of this kind women with her flock of kinner around her warmed Phoebe's hurt heart. She wanted this. She wanted it more than anything. "I have to go."

Irene looked up from taping the splints—a little too long from the looks of them—to Melinda's small fingers. "Rachel's not back to drive you home."

"I'll walk. I need to think."

"Wait. I want to send some cookies with you."

"That's not necessary."

"Yes, it is. I never send a guest home without some of my cookies."

Irene patted Melinda's head. "Stay put. Don't be running around. You're done for the day."

Phoebe followed her into the house where Irene picked up a brown cloth napkin and dropped half a dozen snickerdoodles and gingersnaps in it, tying the napkin around them. She presented them to Phoebe with a shy smile. "Share them with your special friend."

"I don't have one."

"I think you do."

"We'll see." On an impulse she didn't recognize, Phoebe hugged the woman. "Thank you for telling me your story. I know it must be hard to dredge it all up again."

"I'm starting a new quilt on Friday." Irene trailed after her to the front door. "Why don't you come to town with me tomorrow and help me pick up some notions? I need thread and material."

A new calm lay on Phoebe's shoulders like a spring shawl, light, but enough to ward off a pervasive chill. She could face the people of the town if she had Irene on her side. "I'd like that."

"I'll pick you up on my way."

Chapter 14

Despite the lazy spin of a ceiling fan overhead, the air in the fabric store seemed stuffy to Phoebe. It smelled of furniture wax and enough dust to make her want to sneeze. At first she'd dreaded this foray into town, sure that everyone would stare and point. *There's the girl who ran off to kiss a man and left a little girl to drown. There's the girl who let her parents and family down. There's the girl who was selfish and irresponsible. There she is.* She should wear a big sign that read SINNER. Now that she was here, she felt a curious lifting of her heart. It might be stuffy and it might smell a little, but the fabric store was one of her favorite places.

Right up there with the bakery. She let her rapturous gaze encompass the rainbow of colors around her. Rack upon rack displayed every kind of fabric available in all colors and patterns. She could spend all day here. All week if she had money in her canvas bag. She might not be much of a cook, but she was handy with the sewing machine. Time to get back to it. Time to stop feeling sorry for herself and be of some use to Mudder.

She trotted after Irene. The woman's lips were pursed and her forehead wrinkled in concentration as she fingered bolts of sturdy cotton in blues, greens, blacks, and purples, keeping up a running commentary on the quality and price. The process of buying material could be a lengthy one because Plain women spent so much time and effort making clothes. The material had to be a good quality that would last, but not so expensive as to eat up their household budget.

"Isn't this pretty?" Phoebe ran her hand over a piece of pale pink, silky fabric. It felt soft under her fingers, like baby's skin, but she would never wear this color, even if she could. Prone to spilling kaffi and tea or soup, she always had stains on her clothes as it was. No sense in wearing a dress that showed everyone how *doplich* she really was. "So shiny."

"And so pink." Irene shook her head, her disdain tempered by her sweet smile. "All I see are little handprints."

Phoebe grinned. Irene was right. Best stick to dark colors. Sarah liked to grab ahold of her dress and hang on for dear life. Lydia always had dirty hands.

Her gut wrenched and her lungs deflated as if she'd taken a kickball to the stomach. When would this stop happening? This thinking of Lydia as if she were still here. Being caught off guard and remembering all over again the horror of her death. It happened to her every morning when she first opened her eyes and dragged herself through the blessed haziness of sleep to wakefulness. Lydia died. The thought hit her again and again.

"You gonna buy that material?" Lois Mattox, the owner of All Your Needles and Notions, had that puckered-up look that always graced her face. Like she'd drunk a pint of vinegar. "If not, you best keep your mitts off it. Stains real easy."

How did she know? Phoebe turned her back and caught Bertha Weaver staring at her. Bertha had come to New Hope in a second wave of families from Bliss Creek. However, she'd been the first young woman to get a job in the small, tightly knit town. Phoebe had observed—to herself only—that the two women, one Englisch and the other Plain, really could've been twins born under other circumstances. Dour faced. Always watching as if they thought a customer might steal something. Plain folks didn't steal, but New Hope folks had to learn that for themselves. New Hope hadn't been much interested in having Plain folks around—too much tourist nonsense, according to the local sheriff, but things had thawed out after Bethel and Elijah's wedding. Even the mayor had come by the celebration afterwards.

Bertha didn't look like she was celebrating now. Sniffing as if she needed a handkerchief, she sidestepped a toddler following after Ben Knepp's fraa, who was headed for the cash register. Bertha stopped on the other side of a long row of flannel that would make lovely, warm nightgowns once winter made an appearance.

"I'm surprised to see you out and about so soon." She sniffed again. Maybe she had allergies. "I heard you were a bit down and out after all that went on."

In other words, Phoebe should be ashamed to show her face. "I'm helping Irene prepare for the quilting frolic later this week and she's getting some fabric for school clothes."

"Making yourself useful." Her words suggested otherwise.

"I try."

"That's not what I heard."

Phoebe eyed the door. Maybe she should wait in the buggy. "How much is this plum-colored material here? It's a nice color. Mudder would like it."

"How is your mudder?" Bertha had never been one to take a hint. For someone so young, she really did look like a dried apple with wrinkles around her mouth from frowning so much. "I haven't seen her in the store since…in ages."

"She's working hard, as always." Working hard and growing thinner and frailer by the day. "She'll be at the frolic on Friday. You should come, if you don't have to work. Of course, since you spend all day with material and notions and whatnot, quiltings probably aren't as much fun for you as they used to be."

"And Hannah?" Bertha was like those sharks Phoebe had seen photos of in magazines. They got ahold of a person's leg or arm and wouldn't let go until they tore it off. "Will she be at the frolic too?"

"Hannah's fine."

"I heard she hasn't said a word since before the funeral."

The women in their district had plenty of work to do, yet they still found time to chitchat about other peoples' business. It was the downside of living in such a small community. Hannah said words. Not many. Not any to Phoebe, but she did say words. "That's not true—"

"I think I have what I need." Irene bustled down the aisle that separated Phoebe from Bertha. "I'll get eight yards of the black, eight yards of the blue, six yards of the dark green, and six yards of the lilac. The girls need new dresses for school. What about you, Phoebe? Did your mudder ask you to bring home anything?"

Grateful for Irene's perception, Phoebe hurried after her, avoiding Bertha's accusing gaze. "No, she said she had everything she needed. What about thread? Do you need thread?"

"I do. I go through it like I do flour in the kitchen. I never have enough."

"That's what Mudder says."

"Bertha, are you doing the cutting today or is Lois?" Irene heaved the bolts of fabric onto the enormous counter in the middle of the store. "Did you hear my list or do you need me to repeat it?"

At that moment, she didn't sound nearly as sweet as she normally did.

"I may have missed one or two." Bertha picked up a pair of orange shears. "If you want it done right, you probably should hand me a written list."

"I figured as much." Her expression serene, Irene handed a semi-crumpled piece of paper to the other woman. "People busy minding other people's business tend to miss their own."

Phoebe smiled a real smile, the first one in many days. Irene nodded at her. "Phoebe, why don't you go get me a big spool of each color of thread. Do you mind? I can take care of business here."

Indeed she could. Phoebe thanked God for putting a good woman in her path. One who understood what she had gone through—was still going through. It was the first prayer she'd offered in many days that didn't involve begging or whining or seeking forgiveness.

Simply, *thank you.*

Chapter 15

Tuesday morning dawned with clear skies and a cool, fresh breeze that Phoebe knew would dissipate by afternoon, allowing the warmth of September to linger a little longer. She thought of the children in school. She should be there with them. She had a responsibility to help Deborah, at least until they hired a new teacher. She wasn't a coward. She would follow Irene's lead and learn to take each day one at a time until she could learn to live with what she'd done. But today, she had a fence to mend. If it could be mended.

The walk to Michael's house took more than hour, but she didn't mind. She kept a steady pace, the bag of cookies she'd made the night before tucked under one arm. She'd given Irene's cookies to her brothers—she wanted to bake her own for Michael. Fresh and made with her loving touch. It gave her time to think about what she would say to him. Each step on the dusty road kicked up plumes of dirt that layered the top of her feet until they looked gray. She counted the steps for a while to avoid thinking about anything else. Then she began to count the ways she was blessed. Doing as Irene had done. Letting go of the bad things and hanging on to the good.

Like Michael. Michael was good. He'd made a mistake and so had she. She needed to mend the rift with him. If they were meant to be together the death of her sister should bring them closer together, not rip them apart. They should lean on each other and learn from their mistakes. Learn to slow down and step together, following the path laid out for them by their parents and the bishop. One step at a time.

For the first time in a long time, she could breathe. She saw a future for herself. She saw Michael in it. If Irene could survive the loss of her baby and her home through her own clumsiness, Phoebe could survive Lydia's death through her own selfish, thoughtless act. At the steps that led to the Daughertys' front porch, she paused. She inhaled air scented with honeysuckle that trailed its way along the railing. *Gott, help me.* Since her talk with Irene, she'd attempted a prayer or two. They sounded feeble in her inner ear. She couldn't get past a few words without feeling like a wayward child trying to justify her behavior in the eyes of her daed.

Gott, help me.

"Phoebe! Oh, Phoebe, I'm so glad you came." Edna Daugherty pushed open the screen door and trotted out on to the porch. A short woman shaped like a plump pear, she had given Michael his dark blue eyes and dimpled smile. Everything else came from his daed. "Come in, come in."

Phoebe tried to smile in return. She held up the bag. "I brought Michael some cookies."

Edna's smile slid from her face. She wiped her hands on her apron. "I'm baking pies. Why don't you come in and sit a spell in the kitchen? I could use the company."

"Is Michael gone already? I hoped if I came early enough I'd catch him before he took off into the fields."

"Tobias is planting the last of the winter wheat." Edna smoothed her peach-stained apron with both hands. "Seth and Robert are helping him."

"But not Michael?"

"Not Michael." Edna picked up a tabby cat that wound itself around her feet. She eased onto the porch step and plopped the cat on her lap. "Sit."

Something in Edna's expression made Phoebe want to turn and run. Instead, she did as she was told. "Where's Michael?"

Edna ran her water-wrinkled hands along the tabby's back. He purred with a vengeance. His warm, wet nose pushed at Phoebe's arm as if encouraging her to join in. "Where's Michael? Is he all right?"

"I thought Daniel would tell you—or Rachel. Michael left." Edna sighed. "I can't believe they didn't tell you."

Phoebe couldn't believe it either. Rachel had seen Daniel at the prayer service and in class. She'd never said a word. It couldn't be. "Left?"

The word didn't make sense to Phoebe. The Michael who'd kissed her that day at Stockton Lake wouldn't go without saying goodbye. He'd finally made the first move because he saw something in her. Saw something for them. Maybe he went to Bliss Creek to visit his cousins. A visit to help heal. To get away for a bit until he could face his future here.

"I'm sorry." Edna's voice caught in her throat. "You've been through so much already. I hate to be the one to tell you. He's been gone a few days now."

"Gone?"

"He packed a bag and hopped a bus in town. He told Tobias he had to leave. He needed a fresh start."

"A fresh start." She couldn't help herself. She kept parroting Edna's words, unable to form her own. "Packed a bag."

"He said he'd write when he got settled in Springfield."

Springfield. An hour's drive away by car.

"Come inside. Let me get you a glass of water." Edna dumped the cat onto the grass with an unceremonious plop. He gave her a reproachful look and stalked away, his tail swishing. She stood. "You look parched from the walk over here. It may be cooler, but it's still humid."

"I should go." Phoebe stood. She swayed, and Edna grabbed her arm. "I need to get back."

"Nee, you're not walking back. You look green. You look like you haven't eaten in a week. You sit down and I'll bring you a glass of water and a sandwich. Richard can give you a ride home."

Phoebe sat with a thump and asked the only question her mind could pop out. "Richard's here?"

"Jah. He came over from Peter's early to help cut some hay. He just went into the barn a few minutes ago."

Richard had shown an interest in her. His move to ask her to take a ride with him might very well have been the nudge Michael needed to get moving himself. Before it was too late.

For all the good it had done Michael and her.

Edna pattered up the steps and swept into the house. She reappeared with a tall glass of water and a plate with a ham and cheese sandwich on it. She offered them to Phoebe, but Phoebe couldn't raise her arms to accept the food. After a moment, Edna deposited the glass and plate on the step next to Phoebe, shooed the cat away, and disappeared again, this time toward the barn. She returned a few minutes later with Richard in tow.

Richard shoved his hat back on a sweaty forehead and nodded. "Phoebe. It's been a while."

Edna brushed her hands together as if ridding herself of the entire situation. "Richard will take you home. After you eat the sandwich."

"Nee, nee. It's not necessary." She picked up the plate and held it out. "I'm afraid I can't eat this. Maybe Richard…"

"You've gone from green to white as the sheets on my clothesline, girl, and you look so skinny you're practically a skeleton." Edna cocked her head toward Richard, who examined her like a man about to approach a wild horse. "Bring the buggy up here. Take her home. I'd do it myself but I have the grandbabies today. I'll square it with your onkel—you'll be back in two shakes."

Phoebe's vision blurred. Her stomach heaved. The plate clattered from her hands and the sandwich tumbled into the grass at her feet. The cat pounced on a piece of ham and trotted away, tail high in the air as if it had captured a trophy. *Two shakes. I'll be back in two shakes.* The exact words she'd used with Hannah. What had she been thinking coming here? As if all could be made right. Michael knew. He knew. That's why he left. Nothing would be the same again.

She leaned her head forward, trying to catch her breath, and closed her eyes. *In and out. In and out.*

A hand rubbed her back in a soothing circular motion. "It's all right. Richard will take you home so you can rest."

"I don't want to rest." She looked up at Edna. "I want to talk to Michael."

Her face lined with sadness, Edna sank onto the steps as if her legs no longer held her. "Michael wanted to talk to you too, but he couldn't bring himself to do it. But he will, I know he will. He'll come back and he'll talk to you and you'll be baptized, both of you."

"He tried to talk to me and I turned him away. Now he's gone."

"He'll be back. He just needs a little time."

She sounded as if she were trying to convince herself more than Phoebe. Baptism. Of course, that would be Michael's parents' first concern. His salvation was at stake. Not just their life together. Their happiness. She should see that.

Phoebe did see that. She swallowed against the hard knot in her throat and stood. To her relief, her legs didn't betray her. They held. "You're right. I should go."

"We'll pray for God's will." Edna stood as well. "God's will be done."

As far as Phoebe could tell, God's will involved her being miserable and alone. Her own fault, she saw that clearly. What she couldn't divine was what God expected her to do about it.

The clip-clop of horse hooves and the squeak of buggy wheels forced her to turn. She squinted against the sun and Richard's tanned face bobbed in front of her.

"You all right? Let me help you up."

He held out a mammoth hand with a long scar across the back. He had dirt under his fingernails and calluses on his palms. A hard worker. She shook her head. "I'm fine."

She tottered around him and climbed into the buggy.

To her relief, he said nothing more. He simply climbed back aboard, pushed his hat back on his head, and called "giddy-up" to the horse.

The silence stretched until they reached the narrow road that led home.

"What's that in your lap?" His voice had the soft tone of a man trying to calm a child.

She looked down, surprised to discover she still clutched the bag of cookies she carried.

"Cookies."

"I like cookies." His voice softened some more. "Are you thinking about sharing with a poor hungry man who's fixing to miss the noon-day meal giving a girl a ride home?"

"Share?"

He smiled, his teeth white and even against the dark tan of his face, glistening with sweat. He had that smell of fresh dirt and sweat and sun that she associated with all the men in the community. Familiar, comfortable. He held the reins loosely, his burly frame relaxed against the seat, the picture of calm. "It seems like it's been an awful long time since breakfast."

"Jah." Glad to have someplace else to look, she worked at the knots with numb fingers that didn't seem to want to do her bidding. Aware of his sidelong glances, she managed to open the bag. Some of the cookies had broken into two or three chunks. "They're a little worse for wear."

"I don't mind. They don't have to look pretty to taste good." He plucked a chunk of gingersnap from the bag and popped it in his mouth. "*Gut*. That tastes *gut*. Did you make them?"

"Jah."

"You do make a good gingersnap. Just the right amount of ginger and snap."

He had one of those deep, hearty laughs that shook everyone around him—just like her daed. The buggy rocked along, its creaking wheels the only sound for several minutes.

"You don't talk much, I guess."

Anyone who knew her at all would argue she never let anyone else get a word in edgewise. "Not anymore."

"You came to talk to Edna, I guess."

"Nee."

"Come on, throw me a bone." He laughed again. "I'm just trying to make polite conversation to pass the time."

"Eat another cookie."

"You don't have to ask me twice." He plucked another big chunk from the bag, this time peanut butter, and deposited the entire piece in his mouth. A satisfied look on his face, he chewed in silence for another good half mile. "Now what?"

"What?"

"You just gonna keep stuffing my mouth with cookies to keep from talking to me?"

"Will that work?"

He pulled up on the reins so the buggy stopped in the middle of the road. Phoebe looked around. Nothing. "What are you doing? We're stopped in the middle of the road."

"I know you're sad. It might help to talk to me."

"It won't help."

"Then let's talk about something else."

"Are you always this forward?"

"Only when I'm asked to do someone a favor in the middle of my workday, the day I committed to helping my onkel by bringing in hay. Only when the object of that favor doesn't seem to appreciate it or me."

"You shouldn't do favors because you expect something in return. You should do them because it's the right thing to do."

"Now we're talking." He snapped the reins and the buggy jolted forward. "So are things any better? Starting to get back to normal?"

"They'll never get back to normal."

"They will. One of these days you'll stop staring out at those empty fields like you're drowning in a sea of sorrow."

Drowning in a sea of sorrow. She shook her head. "It's nice of you to ask, but I'm fine." Maybe not fine, but talking with Irene had helped. For the first time since Lydia's death, she'd opened her eyes in the morning without experiencing that dreadful sinking sensation that came with the slow surfacing of the memories. The shuddering, sick feeling as she thought of filling the hours of this day until she could lie down again and sink into the oblivion of sleep. That new optimism had been premature. She saw that now in light of what Edna had told her. Michael, with all his show of interest, his declaration, his kiss, had fled and left her to trudge into this new, dark future alone.

"You don't look fine." A red blush crept up the neck of the man next to her, darkening an already dark tan. "What I mean to say is, something is ailing you. There's not a thing wrong with the way you look."

He'd gone from sure of himself to a stuttering mass of embarrassment in a few seconds. Somehow Phoebe found that endearing. It had

been a long time since she'd really looked at the men who crossed her
path. Her gaze had been for Michael only. The void in her chest where
her heart had once resided twisted in a sudden, violent spasm. Michael
might be gone, but he still had a fierce grip on her heart. "It's hard to
imagine feeling better."

"Before my family moved back from Indiana to Bliss Creek, my
little brother's horse spooked and he fell off and broke his neck. He
was twelve."

He said it so matter of factly, Phoebe had to review the words in her
head to make sure she'd understood. "How old were you?"

"Fourteen."

"Does it still hurt?"

"I figure it always will. It's one of the reasons I came out to New
Hope. Still looking for a fresh start, I guess."

She'd figured that. How could it be any other way? "I'm sorry."

"I'm glad it still hurts."

"Why?"

"For the one thing, I never want to forget Liam. Also, it helps me
remember my blessings. Every day is a blessing. Every day."

She wouldn't have guessed from looking at his smiling face that
Richard had ever experienced anything remotely like what she had
been through with Lydia.

Or that Irene had, for that matter.

Gott, what are You telling me?

Richard took the drive in front of their house and kept going until
he rounded the corner and pulled up along the clotheslines. Mudder
was pinning Elam's pants to the line, a huge wicker basket at her feet.
She pulled a clothespin from her mouth. "*Gudemariye.*"

Richard nodded in return and scrambled down from the buggy. He
strode around to Phoebe's side before she could slip out on her own.
"Down you go." He held out his hand.

"I can get down myself."

"You were a little unsteady back at the house." He wiggled his fingers
as if to say *take them.* "Edna told me to get you home safe and sound
and that's what I plan to do."

She swallowed, aware of her mother's gaze on them. "I'm fine."

"You are." Something in his gaze communicated to her a thought so different from her intent that she felt a burning blush start at the base of her neck and leap like wildfire across her face. With reluctance she allowed him to take her hand and settle her to the ground.

"You think you'll come back to the singings any time soon?"

She shook her head. "Nee."

He doffed his hat in a gallant motion and headed back to the other side of the wagon. "Might be a good time to think about moving on."

"Moving on?"

"Getting on with your life." He hopped aboard the buggy and picked up the reins. "God's timing is everything."

She watched as the buggy rolled away, leaving a cloud of dust behind it.

She didn't want to move on. She wanted Michael.

If her mother hadn't been standing in the yard, a pair of Daed's pants in her hands, Phoebe might have considered falling to her knees in that very spot where she stood. Instead she held herself still, her back to Mudder, listening. Trying to hear something, anything, in the air, now bereft of the slightest breeze. *Gott?*

Nothing.

Chapter 16

Michael quickened his pace on the crowded, dirty sidewalk, dodging a couple holding hands and sharing a stinking cigarette. The old man behind him who smelled like beer and licorice seemed to be doing the same. Like a dark, skinny shadow, he'd been behind Michael ever since he left the motel room. When Michael turned left at the corner, the man turned left, his sneakers making a now familiar squeaking sound. *Following, following, following*, the noise said.

He couldn't be following Michael. Why would he do that? To ask him for money. To demand money. Michael didn't have much and he needed to make it stretch until he found a job. A good chunk had gone toward putting down two weeks' rent on his room. It seemed like a small fortune for a tiny room with a bed, a chair, a desk, a bathroom, and a tiny kitchenette. He wanted the kitchenette. If he continued to eat in restaurants as he had for the past few days while job hunting, he'd have no funds left in very short order.

All the job interviews had been the same. After taking a gander at his clothes and his haircut, the man or woman—it had surprised him that sometimes women did the hiring—had asked two questions. What experience did he have? Did he have a high school diploma? He'd worked in a nursery growing plants. He also knew how to harvest wheat and cut hay and saddle a horse and drive a buggy. He'd planted vegetable gardens with his mudder from the time he was three and learned to ride a horse not long after. He'd helped deliver foals and regularly milked cows before breakfast so the milk would be fresh. Not job skills anyone seemed to need in the city. He didn't have a high school diploma. Never before had that been a problem.

"Hey, man, you got a cigarette I can bum?" The old man had gained on him. He was a big greasy hairball. He wore a gray T-shirt and gray sweatpants. His white hair had been caught back in a skinny, greasy ponytail. He grinned, exposing teeth yellow with age and tobacco. "I got a light if you've got the cigarette."

"I don't smoke." Michael stepped off the curb. A horn blared and he stumbled back, nearly falling. He kept doing that. When would he learn? The old man gripped his arm and Michael jerked away. "I don't have anything you want."

"How do you know? Maybe I can be your guide. You're new in town; I can show you around." His grin widened, revealing gaps where teeth should have been. "Maybe I can show you a good time. I have some lady friends."

As if on cue, a woman in a dark pink blouse and a skirt that molded to her thick body waved from across the street. "You looking for a date, honey?" She sashayed back and forth on the sidewalk in shiny black high heels. "I'll show you a real good time, baby. Step right over here to my office."

"I don't need a guide." Michael looked up and down the street for oncoming cars, careful not to make eye contact with the woman again. "I'm not looking for anything."

"Sure you are. Why else would someone like you come to the city?" The man chuckled and then coughed and spit on the sidewalk. He leaned closer to Michael, his breath a cloud of alcohol and the stink of onions. "You're a country boy, ain't you? Come to the big city looking for a good time."

Michael shrank back. He needed to get away from this stranger with his false friendliness. A green and yellow neon diner sign blinked up ahead. A large handwritten HELP WANTED sign had been posted in the diner's window. Michael veered toward it and the old man followed. Michael picked up his pace until he was almost running.

"Hey, man, slow down. I ain't gonna hurt you. I'm just looking to make a quarter. Fifty cents to buy me a cup of coffee."

Michael slowed long enough to dig a dollar bill from the pocket of material he'd pinned inside his shirt. "Here, take it."

His black eyes bright with surprise and satisfaction, the old man snatched the bill with grimy fingers, whirled, and shot in the opposite direction.

"You can't be giving them money." A lady who sat on a nearby bench shook her finger at him. "They beg all morning and then they use the money to get drunk all afternoon. We always give them granola bars or breakfast bars—better for them."

Michael nodded to acknowledge her advice, but didn't speak. Maybe he shouldn't have given the man money. It had seemed like the right thing to do. Or maybe it had been the easy way out of a situation. Just like running away from home.

He shook off the feeling he'd let down God again and pushed through the glass door of the diner. Inside a crush of people sat in booths and filled every stool that ran along a gray Formica counter. Everyone seemed to be talking at once. Everyone knew someone. He hadn't had a real conversation with anyone since he got off the bus and left behind the kind lady who dispensed advice and sandwiches from a basket. The room had a phone, but he had no one to call. The only person he wanted to call didn't answer her cell phone.

The diner reminded him of Cooney's Restaurant back home, except the customers didn't look like farmers in town to buy a part at the hardware store or shoe a horse at the blacksmith shop. Cool refrigerated air mixed with steamy heat from the kitchen. A cook shoved plates of scrambled eggs, bacon, and pancakes through a long rectangular window toward a skinny red-haired waitress who blew bubbles with her gum as she worked. Her nametag read *Crystal*.

The food smelled wonderful. The aroma of frying hamburger mixed with bacon and sausage. His mouth watered and his stomach rumbled. He'd been trying to get by on two meals a day. He didn't really need breakfast. He usually woke up feeling sick to his stomach, anyway.

"There's a seat open at the end." A second waitress, this one with long blonde hair in a ponytail that swung when she walked, squeezed past him with plates of bacon and eggs in one hand and waffles held high in the other. "I'll be with you in a sec."

"I wanted to see about the job."

"Oscar, there's a guy here about the job." She kept moving as she yelled, the muscles in her thin arms bulging with the weight of the thick white china plates.

Oscar, a mammoth man with a shiny bald head, was dressed in a red shirt and a huge red apron. He looked up from the register long enough to eyeball Michael. His shaggy gray eyebrows did pushups. He slapped some bills into the register, speared the ticket on a spindle next to it, and slammed the drawer shut. "In the back. We're swamped. Let's make it fast."

Michael's heart began to slam in his chest. He'd applied at fourteen businesses in three days—why was he nervous now? He followed Oscar through the swinging doors.

Sizzling heat hit him in the face and knocked him back a step. Despite the sweat that soaked the back of his shirt, Oscar didn't seem to notice. Nor did the two cooks who slung hamburger patties onto a grill next to heaps of onions and a pile of hash browns that sizzled in butter. French fries crackled in baskets sunk into vats of oil that spit and spattered.

"You know how to work an industrial-sized dishwasher?" Oscar cocked his head toward a enormous machine that sat silent, plastic gray tubs filled with dirty dishes stacked all around it. "My dishwasher was a no show this morning. Ain't had a busboy in two weeks. I need both. Now." He glanced at the open window. "I got customers trying to pay. You wash dishes? You get paid three bucks an hour plus your share of tips."

"You don't want to know if I have experience?" Michael wanted the job—he'd take any job at this point—but he wouldn't do it under false pretences. "I mean, I don't actually know how to run the machine."

"It ain't rocket science, kid. Everybody's washed dishes now and again."

Truth be told, Michael had never washed a dish a day in his life. A Plain man with sisters didn't wash dishes. His stomach rumbled. "I can learn. I'm willing to figure it out."

"Great. Can you start now?" Oscar gave him the once-over and cracked a smile for the first time. He had silver caps on his front teeth. "You might want to find something cooler to wear. T-shirt is fine. You'll fit in better too."

"I don't have anything else." His clothes had been a dead giveaway at every job interview, but he didn't dare spend his precious reserve of money on new ones until he actually had a job. "But I'll get some right away."

"There's a pile of T-shirts in a box in the back. Grab a couple. They're on the house—good publicity for the restaurant. We'll do the paper-work during the afternoon lull before the supper rush." Oscar shoved open the door, then looked back again. "Food's fifty percent off for employees. Gotta pay up front, though—no charging to a paycheck you ain't got yet. Food's not bad." His deep belly laugh wafted through air thick with food smells and steam. "If I do say so myself."

The man hadn't even asked for his name. Somehow that made his trust that Michael could do the job all the more terrifying. Or comforting. Michael couldn't be sure which. He had a job. All he had to do was figure out how to run a dishwasher.

Aware of sweat running down his back between his shoulder blades and soaking his shirt, Michael rooted through the boxes until he found the t-shirts. Red. He'd never worn red before. Blowing out air, he shoved open the door marked EMPLOYEE RESTROOM and changed. He expected there would be many firsts in his life from now on. Clothes were only the start.

Next came the mammoth machine. He confronted it in the middle of the kitchen. A strange looking contraption. He gritted his teeth and examined the label on the side with its tiny print. A diagram. Power button. There it was. He touched it. Soap first?

The waitress with the blonde ponytail trotted into the kitchen, an irritated look on her face. Her nametag read Lana. She looked to be about his age. "Oscar says to not put too much soap in the machine. It leaves a film on the dishes and the folks get mad if they can taste soap in their eggs." She slapped her hands on her hips. "Why are you standing there? We're gonna be out of forks like any minute now."

"I don't know where the soap goes." He would get some kind of award for holding a job the shortest amount of time. Two minutes and counting. "I'm not sure how to turn it on."

"Leave it to Oscar. Always a softy for sad faces." She rolled her eyes under eyelids covered with shiny copper eye shadow. "It's like a conveyor belt. You stack the dishes in the rack and shove it in. It goes from left to right."

She demonstrated, adding chemicals and turning knobs. "Keep an eye on this doohickey right here. It tells you if you have dirty water. Also keep an eye on the temperature gauge. The health department will shut us down if we don't use hot enough water. Then no one gets paid. I got kids to feed."

"Got it." More or less. "Thank you."

"I got customers waiting." She whirled and headed for the door. "And you got dirty dishes on ten tables out there. Better get cracking."

He had a job. Relief poured through his veins like a warm cup of kaffi. He had a job.

"Hurry up!" Lana shouted as the door slammed. "Clean forks would be good any time now."

He grabbed a tub and followed her. She hadn't been exaggerating about the number of dirty dishes. He began to stack plates in the tub, then glasses, silverware on the side. Trash on the other side.

"You'll never get through doing it that way." Red-headed Crystal dashed by, a plate of meatloaf in each hand. "Throw them in there. You don't have to organize them. You can do that when you put them in the racks. Move!"

He moved. Time sailed past him. His back ached first, then his feet. The skin on his hands burned from the chemicals and the heat. His shirt and pants were soaked with sweat. Every time he thought he had caught up, more customers threw down their napkins and strolled to the cash register, leaving him with more dishes to bus and wash.

It was backbreaking work. One his mother had done for years without complaining. With a family of eight—and only three girls counting herself—it was like she ran a small restaurant. Except she did all the cooking and made everything from scratch with no electricity and no air conditioning and no fans, except the nice God-made breeze that occasionally flowed through open kitchen windows. Michael had new respect for his mother's hard work.

Even with the air conditioning on and fans blowing in the kitchen, the heat was sweltering. Sweat burned his eyes and every breath hurt his lungs.

"Ice water?" The cook, who'd introduced himself as Mack somewhere in the third hour of the shift, held up a glass. "You might want to pace yourself. You get dehydrated and you'll pass out."

"You're not hot?"

"I'm a cook. I do this for a living. I'm used to it."

Michael gratefully slugged down the water and went back to work. They seemed like decent people. Everyone looked him up and down real good, taking in his clothes, he suspected, but not one of them had said anything about them. Now that he had a job, he would go to a discount store and get some clothes. He would fit in better then. He only wanted to blend in, to be anonymous. Not one person here knew what he'd done and he wanted to keep it that way.

"We're closing the doors." Oscar leaned on the counter with both hairy hands, his head bobbing in the window. "Finish up. Make sure all the pots and pans get washed and wipe down the countertops. The cooks clean the grill and the stoves. Then come out here and fill out the paperwork."

It took yet another hour to complete those orders. By then, Michael's legs wobbled. He hadn't eaten since the previous day. His head throbbed and the people around him seemed to weave in and out. The lights flickered. Or was it his eyes closing?

He pushed through the double doors and swayed. Oscar, standing at the register counting bills, didn't notice, but the other waitress, the red-headed bubble blower named Crystal, did. "Hey, new guy, sit."

She tugged him into the booth. "A little heatstroke?"

"I don't know."

She studied him with concern in blue-gray eyes made bigger by a thick black line she'd painted along the bottom of each one. She tugged on a rubber band and her curly red hair tumbled down on her shoulders. She eyed him like he was a cornered animal that might bolt. "You didn't get a lunch or a supper break, did you?"

"Was I supposed to?"

"You're not supposed to work a ten-hour shift with no breaks. Oscar should've told you."

"I figured he knew." Oscar scratched his bald head and kept counting. "Anybody who's ever had a job knows that."

"Right."

Funny way to talk to a boss. "He's my uncle." Crystal grinned as if reading Michael's mind. "His bark is worse than his bite. I'm bringing you a hamburger and fries. On the house. Consider it a celebration for your new job."

"Don't be giving away the food." Oscar licked the tip of his index finger and went back to counting one-dollar bills.

"It's leftovers. You're gonna give them to the homeless guys out in the alley anyway." Crystal waved away the objection. "Drink this water and I'll be right back. Don't move."

He couldn't have moved if he tried. In a moment Crystal brought him a glass of lemonade and a plate heaping with French fries and a massive hamburger loaded with lettuce, tomato, onion, and pickle. She proceeded to sit down across from him and watch him with great interest while he ate.

"So you're Amish, right?"

He nodded, his mouth full of the best hamburger he'd ever eaten. A little pink in the middle, its juice ran onto his hands. He grabbed a paper napkin and sopped it up.

"My mom and I went to Lancaster once before she wigged out and left me and my daddy in a trailer park on the south side. Are you like those Amish?"

"I don't know. I don't know anyone from Pennsylvania."

"You're Missouri Amish?"

"Kansas originally, but now, yes." Where was this going? "I live—lived—up by New Hope."

"I think the little girls in the long dresses and bonnets are so cute."

"Prayer kapps. They're called prayer kapps." Lydia had been cute in her purple dress and small prayer kapp. The hamburger caught in his throat. He swallowed hard. "They look okay."

"Why are you working in a diner?"

She asked a lot of questions. So much for being anonymous. He would go to Kmart and buy clothes. He stuffed two more fries drenched in ketchup in his mouth and followed that with a huge bite of burger. Maybe if she could see he was busy chewing, she'd lose interest.

"I mean, you're using electricity and everything. I thought you guys didn't do that."

He swallowed. "I have to go now."

"No, no, you haven't finished your burger and you still need to fill out the paperwork. You want to get paid, don't you?" As if to punctuate that statement, she pulled a small wad of folded bills from her apron pocket and plopped it down on the table in front of him. "These are your tips from today. We split everything with the kitchen staff. It was a very good day. Tomorrow is Friday, so it'll probably be better. People get their paychecks on Friday."

He fingered the pile of bills. These were the tips only. He would also get an hourly wage for his efforts. "I'll take the paperwork with me."

"But you're coming back, right?" Her blue-gray eyes looked worried as her lips turned down. "We really need a hard worker and you definitely qualify as a hard worker. You never even took a break. Isn't that right, Uncle Oscar?"

Oscar nodded, but he didn't look up from the computer screen that sat next to the cash register.

"I'll be back. What time do I start?"

At that, Oscar's head came up. "Be here by five. You can help stock the tables and prep food before we open at six. We get a good breakfast crowd from the guys working at the furniture factory. Don't be late."

"No, sir."

He pocketed the bills, grabbed up the stack of forms, and slid from the booth. "Thank you."

Oscar nodded, as distracted as ever.

"We'll see you tomorrow, bright and early." Crystal sounded thrilled at the idea. "Maybe you can show me how to make shoo-fly pie or those whoopie pie things. Our customers would love that. I'd like to increase our dessert offerings—"

"Crystal, let the poor kid go in peace. Can't you see he's dragging his tail?"

Relieved at Oscar's intervention, Michael hustled through the double doors and headed for the motel. The door thunked behind him and he glanced back to see Crystal waving at him as she locked it and turned off the flashing neon light. The help wanted sign was gone.

He managed to raise his arm and wave back.

Shoo-fly pie. She really thought he knew how to bake a pie? He chuckled. Then slammed to a stop. It was the first time he'd laughed in a long time.

Despite his exhaustion he enjoyed the walk back to the motel. The air felt cool on his damp face. A smattering of clouds floated in the sky just beyond the buildings that shot up on both sides of the street. The sun disappeared behind those buildings, on its way home to the horizon. The earth was still out there, even in this city.

He had a job. That's what counted.

Washing dishes.

He had a job.

He could still look for another job, but at least he could eat cheap. And the daily tips would help with groceries and clothes until that first paycheck came in.

He opened the door and stepped inside his motel room. The wheezing air conditioning unit in the wall under a long window spewed tepid air. He sat in the green padded chair. The sun peeking through the dusty blinds began to disappear.

The room darkened. He remained seated, staring at his hands on his knees. The bed was a few feet away, but he was too tired to get up. Not just physically tired, although every muscle in his body screamed with exhaustion. His mind had been racing for days on end, trying to figure out what to do next, how to keep going, where to go, and what to say. And now it had finally stopped. He thought of nothing, felt nothing.

Getting a job had been his goal. Now he had one.

What came next?

A clock on the wall over the TV set *ticked, ticked, ticked.* He could hear his own breathing in tandem. In and out. In and out. Finally, after a while, he tottered to his feet and trudged across the room in the dark. He fumbled until his fingers felt the plastic plate near the door. With a flip of the switch, his life plunged in a new direction in the glaring artificial light.

Chapter 17

Katie tugged the dress from the hook in the little girls' bedroom where Lydia had left it the morning they'd rushed from the house to pile into the van, anxious for their vacation at the lake to begin. She held it up and examined the creases to make sure it didn't bear any stains. Lydia always had grubby hands. Katie couldn't give a stained dress away. This one appeared pristine. Surprising. Nothing about Lydia had been pristine. She liked to play in the dirt and chase the cats and climb trees to play with the squirrels and the birds. A child who never sat still. Like Phoebe. Katie swallowed the lump in her throat and folded the dress in half and then again before she handed it to Emma, who added it to the scant pile of clothes.

Emma smoothed the small stack of blue, green, and lilac dresses on the double bed squeezed in next to the crib where Sarah lay on her back batting her fat hands at a plastic pig that had belonged to Elam instead of napping as she should be. "Are you sure you don't want to keep these dresses? One day they'll fit Sarah."

Katie turned back to the hooks, not wanting her friend to see her face. She leaned toward the open window, inhaling the scent of cut grass. The sound of the mower being pushed by Elam in the front yard calmed her. Ordinary sounds of life going on. She didn't want to admit she couldn't bear to think of putting these clothes, once belonging to her dead daughter, on the very much alive and breathing roly-poly

163

body of her youngest child. She turned back and faced Emma. "Too long. They'll be eaten by moths by then."

Emma nodded and winced. Her hand went to her swollen middle. "*Ach*, this one is using my stomach for a trampoline."

"A boy, you think?" Katie tried to smile. "Strong legs?"

"Maybe. Or a girl practicing somersaults." Emma sat on the edge of the bed. "Is it too soon to think of having another? For you, I mean."

Katie moved to the window, seeking a breath of cooler air. "I hadn't thought of more. Truth be told, I thought Sarah would be the last. I don't know why. There's nothing to keep me from…"

Emma's cheeks turned pink, but she didn't look away. "Maybe you felt your time for childbearing done. Eight is a nice number."

Now seven.

"But Gott might think differently." Katie had no idea what Gott thought. He'd welcomed home her Lydia. It didn't make sense He'd send another in her place. How could she know or fathom His plan? "It's just that with my arthritis, childbearing is made more difficult."

"Carrying the extra weight is hard on the joints."

And carrying the responsibility of rearing another child was almost more than she could bear to think about. "You better get these home to Thomas. I know he wants to make a trip to Clark soon." A Plain family there had lost all their belongings in a fire. They had four-year-old twin girls. "And don't forget the shoes."

She ran her hand over the black leather. They were like new, having only been worn to prayer services the previous winter. Outgrown now. Lydia wouldn't need new ones.

Resolute, Katie strode toward the door.

"Katie, how are Hannah and Phoebe?"

Katie gripped the door jam and lowered her head. After a second, she forced herself to turn. "The same."

"We don't know what Gott's plan is." Emma eased from the bed, her hand on her hip, and crossed the room. She hugged Katie tight, despite the enormous belly between them. "But rest easy in the thought that He does have one. We don't know how this story ends, only that He will be there when it does."

"I know." Katie whispered. "I try."

"Fraa, where are you?"

Silas's voice boomed from below.

"Coming." She trudged down the hallway to the stairs and began the descent. "What's going on? Why aren't you cutting the hay?"

Silas's gaze went to Emma. "Scratched my hand on a nail. I came up to get a bandage. I saw the buggy in front and wondered…"

"Emma stopped to pick up some clothing." She hadn't told Silas that today would be the day when their daughter's few belongings would be given to others. She saw no need to speak of it. It was expected. Others could use them. She had a lock of Lydia's hair and she didn't even need that. Lydia's face was imprinted on her heart. She saw it in Phoebe, Hannah, and Sarah every day. "We're done up here. I'll get the bandages."

Silas's lips tightened. He cleared his throat. "How are you, Emma?"

"Fine, thank you."

Lydia's church shoes dangling from one hand, Katie trotted down the stairs. Emma followed behind her, the pile of clothing in her arms. As she squeezed past Silas, he grabbed a dress from the top of the pile. His big hands, dirty, the back side spotted with dried blood, crushed the material against his chest. Katie stopped in the middle of the room. She didn't want to look at his face.

Emma spoke first, her voice gentle, respectful. "Would you like to keep that one?"

"Nee." Silas shook his head. His voice sounded hoarse, like he was coming down with a cold. "I don't know what I was thinking."

He thrust the dress, now stained with dirt and blood, at Emma. "Best put it to use." He whirled and stomped from the room.

"The bandage—"

The screen door slammed.

Emma smoothed the dress with her free hand. "Don't worry about it. I'll wash it. I have plenty of laundry to do."

"I don't know what's gotten into him." Katie dropped into the rocking chair. "That's the third time this week he's scratched or cut himself while working. He's never been a clumsy man."

"He's distracted." Emma settled into the other rocking chair, the clothes in her lap. "Have you talked to him at all about how you're feeling?"

"What do you mean?"

"You feel guilty. I'm sure he does too. It's only natural when something like this happens to want to blame someone. You blame yourself for not being stricter with Phoebe. I'm sure he blames himself for not protecting his child."

"He wanted to rein Phoebe in. I told him to trust in Gott and let her go. It was her rumspringa. She hadn't really done anything the rest of them didn't do. She's so smart. I thought she would do the right thing. I was complacent. Arrogant. I thought my daughter was better than she was…"

"We walk a thin line. We turn a blind eye during the rumspringa because we want our young folks to know what they'll be missing—if you can call it that—when they commit to our way of life. Where do we draw that line?"

Katie had been trying to answer that question for weeks. "When they endanger themselves or someone else?"

"Josiah almost killed himself, but when I look back on it, I'm not sure there was anything we could've done differently. He had to see for himself. He had to make the decision to commit to the Ordnung and be baptized. No one can do it for them. You know that."

"The difference is Lydia didn't almost die. She did die." Katie heard the wobble in her voice and shut her mouth. She had to stop doing this. All this talking did no good. What was done was done. She stood. "I best get the oven going. The bread dough will have risen by now."

Emma rose as well. "You did everything you could."

Katie nodded, but she didn't speak. She didn't dare. If she opened her mouth, she would embarrass them both by wailing.

Chapter 18

Phoebe trudged up the dirt road that led to the schoolhouse. She couldn't put it off any longer. She needed to earn money. She needed to contribute at home. But the closer she came to the building, the slower her step. She'd begun the walk with all the enthusiasm of a prisoner on her way to execution. Last year, she'd thoroughly enjoyed being Deborah Daugherty's aide. Getting to spend all day with her best friend's older sister, telling kinner what to do, and playing games at recess. It couldn't really be called working. It was too much fun. And parents paid her to do it. Now the sight of Lillie, Mary, William, Eli, Joseph, Abram, Joanna, and all the other kinner engaged in an impromptu game of kickball set her legs trembling. She slowed some more, breathing in the smell of leaves decaying on a cool day. Fall had finally made an appearance.

Today is the first day of your new life. A life dedicated to helping kinner be good scholars. To following the rules. To being good. To making Mudder and Daed and God happy.

She'd been repeating these maxims over and over with each step that brought her closer to the school. Her new life. Dedicated to helping with the teaching of kinner. Her way of making up for what she'd done. She would be a good helper. She would be responsible and careful and a good example for each child.

"Hey, Phoebe, wanna play?" Joseph darted across the road, a dirty white ball clutched in his arms. "Come on, we got room for one more."

167

The thought of smacking a ball around with her foot sounded delightful. Pounding around, pulse racing, laughing, tumbling to the ground in the grass. Fun. It would be fun. She couldn't really remember what fun felt like.

"Oh, come on, you like kickball. You're the best. You kick hard." Joseph tossed the ball her direction and she caught it automatically. For a second, she was twelve and dashing from the home plate to first base, her legs pumping, Molly and Rachel shouting from the sidelines, Michael laughing and chasing the ball rolling past him in the grass.

She swallowed and tossed the ball back to Joseph. "No, but thanks. I want to help Deborah get things ready for the day."

"We already did all that." Luke's son's expression was scornful. "We got here early. What's with you and Hannah? She doesn't want to play either."

He jerked his head toward the steps that led to the small porch in front of the squat, rectangular school, glowing with a fresh coat of paint applied by the men a few weeks earlier. Hannah sat, her lunchbox in her lap and her hands resting on top of it. She didn't move. She didn't even seem to breathe. She had been long gone by the time Phoebe trotted into the kitchen for a quick bite of breakfast. According to Mudder, she hadn't said a word before picking up the lunchbox and closing the back door behind her.

"I'd better see if she's all right." Phoebe smiled at Joseph. He really did look like his daed, only much shorter. "She's having a hard time."

"Because of Lydia?" Joseph's tone held curiosity. "My daed says she's with Gott."

Phoebe could only nod.

"My daed says the Lord gives and the Lord takes away." Joseph's freckled nose wrinkled. "So be prepared. That's what he says. I figure it must be awful nice up there in heaven with God so why be sad?"

"Your daed is right." Phoebe chose her words with the same care she gave to threading a needle, least they prick her. "And so are you. It's just hard sometimes when you miss a person."

"I guess I would miss William." Joseph looked thoughtful—as thoughtful as an eight-year-old with a soccer ball in his hands could look. "But I don't know about the twins—they're always bugging us."

"You'd be surprised." Phoebe almost smiled at his earnest attempt to be honest. "Little sisters are special."

She had to stop then. The lump in her throat reappeared at the most inopportune moments.

"Joseph, come on, we wanna play before the bell rings!" Lillie yelled from the open field. Phoebe could've hugged the little girl for interrupting this painful conversation. "You have the ball, come on."

His concern over death and little sisters and heaven gone in a split second, he grinned and sped away. Phoebe forced herself to move on, to march to the front door, blocked by her sister. She paused in front of her. When Hannah didn't look up, she sank onto the step and perched next to her. "Are you all right?"

Hannah's eyes, blue as the morning sky overhead, didn't blink. She seemed to be studying the trees beyond the field where the other kinner played. Phoebe touched her arm. "Hannah?"

The girl shrugged away from her touch, but she didn't speak.

Her sister had never been a silly, happy-go-lucky kind of girl, but she'd been easy to be around, quick with a smile, a good girl. Now she had folded into herself and disappeared into a dark room where no one was allowed entry. "Please talk to me. Say something. Tell me you're mad at me. Tell me you can't forgive me. Just say something."

Hannah's expression didn't change. Her eyes remained distant and vacant.

The vacant part—that was the part that broke Phoebe's heart. She had done this. Hannah had lost her joy, her sense of serenity, her peace, because of Phoebe. Stricken with the knowledge that Hannah might never be the same, she stood. "I'm going inside to help Deborah." Her voice quivered and she breathed to steady it. "If you need anything, I'll be right inside."

Feeling like an old woman, she climbed the steps. Inside, the air was warm and stifling. Deborah, a taller, older version of her sister Rachel, stood at a window, both hands on the frame, her face red with exertion and frustration. "I think they painted these windows shut. I can't get them open."

"Let me try. Maybe we could use a knife to loosen the paint."

"Good idea." Deborah scurried to the cabinet next to the stove they would use to heat the room this winter. "I think I have one I brought to peel my orange."

Sure enough. She began to pry at the frame again, sweat trickling down her temples. "Guess what? Abel's here."

"Abel? He made it!" Phoebe tried to hustle up some enthusiasm. Deborah deserved that. She had so longed to see her beau, who'd remained in Bliss Creek when their families made the move to New Hope. "For how long?"

"A week or two. Can you keep a secret?"

"You know I can."

"He's asked Thomas to talk to my parents."

"He's asking to marry you?"

"He wants us to get married in November and move me back to Bliss Creek." She wiped at her face with her sleeve, a broad grin stretched across her face. "And I'm recommending to Luke that you take over teaching here."

The ringing in her ears made Deborah's voice sound muffled and far away in Phoebe's ears. She strained to hear. To understand. "Me, the teacher?"

"You're a great teacher. You're smart. You're energetic. The kinner like you and they obey you. You're just right for the job."

Leave her in charge of twenty or more kinner after what she'd done? It would never work. Luke would never allow it. And she wouldn't take the chance.

"I can't. I just can't." She whirled, tripped over a chair leg, righted herself, and dashed through the door.

"Phoebe, wait!"

She pounded down the steps past Hannah, who still hadn't moved, past the kinner playing kickball, and down the dirt road. She could hear Deborah calling her name but she kept going. The thought of being solely responsible for those children sent a feverish chill through her. Her body ached down to the marrow in her bones. She couldn't take a chance. No one should ever take a chance like that.

Not on her.

Chapter 19

The sound of her mudder's voice filtered through the quiet and Phoebe sat up on her bed. Mudder didn't usually yell from the bottom of the stairs. Her joints must be aching. She'd looked tired at the noonday meal. Phoebe swung her legs over the side of the bed and straightened her kapp. A cool breeze wafted through the curtains in her window. The shadows of tree branches and leaves danced against them. She didn't want to leave her room. She felt cozy. She'd done all her chores, swept and mopped the floors, washed the dishes, dusted, mowed the grass—which was more dirt than grass now—and swept the porch. It was at least another hour before they started supper.

"Phoebe, come down here."

The insistence in Mudder's voice propelled Phoebe out the door and to the top of the stairs. She paused, staring down at the men who stood in the front room. Luke, Thomas, and her daed. Had the officials of their church convened to pass judgment on her? Had they come to censure her after all this time? Would she be punished? She might feel better if they did. Maybe her sense of guilt would diminish if she had a punishment. Her chest tight with dread, she trod down the stairs. Finally, she arrived at the bottom. "What is it?"

"We want to talk with you about some things. Sit." As bishop, Luke took the lead. "Let's have a seat."

Mudder had arranged some of the chairs from the table across from the rocking chairs. She didn't sit, however, but disappeared into the kitchen. Phoebe's pulse jumped. She wanted her mudder to stay with her, but she knew better than to say anything. *Just do what you're told. Be good. Be good. Be good.*

When everyone had settled in, Luke began. "You haven't been attending the baptism classes. Nor the prayer service. Have you changed your mind about being baptized this year?"

Phoebe avoided her daed's gaze. He asked her each Sunday if she were ready to go. Each time she said no. He didn't force her. He didn't even look disappointed in her. She didn't know what that meant, only that it was better not to ask.

"I...I hadn't...I'm not sure...I'm not..." She struggled for the right word and finally settled on the only one that seemed right. "Worthy."

"No one is worthy." Luke stroked a beard that had two or three threads of silver in it now. Phoebe hadn't noticed them before. Luke wasn't that much older than her oldest brother Jesse. Yet here he sat dispensing wisdom. "I would think recent events would make you all the more determined to complete this important step in your spiritual life."

"It's been a lot to sort out."

"There's nothing to sort out." His gruff voice held no sympathy, but still, it was kind. "You are God's child. You must claim your place at His feet. Make sure you are ready, should your time come."

Her daed's mouth tightened and his eyes reddened, but still he didn't speak.

"I don't mean to cause you more pain," Luke added. "Nor you, Silas, but you know I speak the truth. No one knows better how suddenly these things can come to pass. God gives and He takes away on His time." Luke rocked for a second. "So it's important to be ready. Your rumspringa has been lengthy."

"Jah."

"And that is your choice. I wouldn't interfere except for there is something you should know."

What? What was it? Had something happened to Michael? Was that what Luke was taking his sweet time telling her?

"You should know that Deborah has asked to be replaced as teacher."

"Now?"

"Not now, but soon." Luke wouldn't tell her more. He couldn't until the banns were announced. "We have spoken with the other parents and we all agree. We'd like to offer you the position of teacher at New Hope Parochial School."

"Me?"

The word came out in a screech. She tried to bring her voice down to a reasonable level. "Me? How could you even think of letting me—"

"You are good with children. Deborah says they obey you and they like you. You did well in school yourself."

"But I'm irresponsible. You know I am." She couldn't keep from looking at Daed. He gave her a tiny fraction of a nod, but his eyes were bleak and sad. That hadn't changed. "There are others who would be better suited."

"Nee, you aren't irresponsible and there aren't any others. You're the only one judging and finding yourself wanting. You have asked for forgiveness and received it. Your parents agree with this choice. Deborah recommended you. The one barrier is that you haven't been baptized. We will not have a teacher in charge of our scholars who hasn't committed her life to the church and to this community. Will you finish the classes and take this job, knowing it is an honor to be asked?"

She wavered, looking first at Daed and then at Thomas before returning to Luke. Their faces said she didn't have a choice. "I will," she whispered. "I'll do better. I'll be good."

"Fine." He stood. "You need to make up the classes. Thomas will sit with you. You must catch up. The service is coming."

"Jah." She swallowed. "I'll be there."

"*Gut.* See you there."

"See you there."

After he left, the screen door slamming behind him, Thomas turned to her. "The lessons you missed concerned the state of matrimony."

Of course they did.

Chapter 20

Michael's legs and back ached from eight hours of standing in the diner kitchen, loading dirty dishes into a steaming dishwasher under fluorescent lights that blinked and buzzed. Shoving aside a newspaper and an empty Styrofoam coffee cup someone had left at the bus stop, he plopped onto the hard wooden bench to wait for his bus. His muscles groaned their approval. He'd worked hard in the fields at home and never had he felt this tired. The skin on his fingertips had started to peel from the detergent and a rash on his arms itched. He didn't care. He had his first paycheck in his pocket. Lana, who turned out to be another one of Oscar's nieces, and Crystal had urged him to get a checking account ASAP. That's the way Lana said it. ASAP. It seemed his boss had a soft heart for down-on-their luck relatives who needed jobs. And refugees from small Amish communities.

The two girls got an obvious kick out of educating Michael about all sorts of things. How to use the TV remote to change the channels when Oscar wanted to watch the football game on Saturday afternoon. How to find Oscar's favorite country music station on the radio when his team lost and he didn't want to have the TV on anymore. How to eat standing up along the back wall of the kitchen so Oscar wouldn't dock their pay for taking time for lunch or supper.

They were funny, those two. Always cracking jokes. Mostly he didn't

175

understand them, except to realize they weren't very nice. Not jokes he could repeat to his little sisters. He struck that thought. Rule number one of his new existence: No thinking about his sisters or his brothers or Mudder or Daed. Or Phoebe. Especially not Phoebe. No thinking about home period. He worked hard enough that he fell into bed at night and slept a deep dreamless sleep. That was fine with him.

He'd go to the bank tomorrow so he could pay for the next week at the motel. Crystal and Lana might think he needed a checking account, but he'd just as soon pay cash. He'd buy a few groceries to stock the kitchenette. It would be cheaper than eating out when he didn't eat at the diner, even if eating out consisted of soggy hot dogs from a vendor in the park across from the diner. And then there wouldn't be much left. No need for a bank.

He had about twenty minutes to wait for the bus. He could've walked home in that time. Most days he did to save the bus fare, but today dark clouds hung low in the sky, glowering at him, promising a deluge any minute. Then the sun broke through a crack in the clouds and mixed heat with the dampness. He bent over and planted his elbows on his knees, head down. His new sneakers had turned a dirty gray by the end of the first week at the diner. Next time maybe he should get black.

Today would be a good day for a hat. Hat. No. No thinking about hats. No thinking about anything that would remind him of home. With a stubborn ferocity, he leaned back and stuck his hands in the pockets of his jeans, the rough material dragging on his red, raw skin.

"Hey."

A soft twang of a voice. He didn't look up. He didn't know anyone here so the greeting—if that's what it was—couldn't be directed at him.

"Hey, you."

Curious at the hint of insistence in the soft voice, he hazarded a look. A girl wearing a white kapp and a long dress covered in tiny yellow and pale pink flowers gave him a diffident smile from the other side of a screaming pink motor scooter. She jingled a set of keys in one hand and studied him. "You need a ride somewhere?"

He surveyed the area. No one else waited for a bus. Just him. He hadn't lived in the city long, but he knew enough to know what she was doing wasn't smart. "Do you always talk to men you don't know?"

"No, sometimes I talk to women I don't know."

"You shouldn't talk to strange men."

"Are you strange?" She had a sweet smile that reminded him of Phoebe. He gritted his teeth and looked beyond the girl to the street. He should've walked to the motel. "'Cause you look more like a boy than a man."

He bristled in spite of himself. After everything that had happened, after what he'd done, he was a man. Or maybe not. Maybe a man would've stayed and faced the community. "Why are you talking to me?"

"How long you been in town? Are you from Jamesport or LaPlata? You don't look like you're from Seymour."

"New Hope." He rubbed his hands over his jeans and contemplated his dirty sneakers. "How did you know?"

"We see a lot of you B on B guys up this way. Our neighborhood's not so far from the bus station." She strolled around the motor scooter, revealing a pair of blue Converse sneakers. "Besides, I recognize the haircut and you don't look like you feel quite right in your clothes."

He'd bought the T-shirt and jeans, along with two other pair, at the Kmart. He had to go to the coin-operated laundry mat every three days. Next paycheck he would get more so he didn't have to go so often. "B on B?"

"Bailed on baptism."

"I didn't bail." He stopped. It was none of her business.

"It's gonna pour any minute."

"You're not Plain, are you?"

"Mennonite. You're gonna get wet."

"So?"

"So these things are dicey on wet roads." She gestured to the motor scooter. "Where are you going?"

"Landry Motel over on Olive."

Her eyes widened.

"I live there."

"'Course you do." She sank onto the seat of her scooter. "You coming or what?"

Michael considered the black clouds overhead and the prospect of sitting there another fifteen minutes. He'd never been on a motor scooter, let alone one driven by a girl who barely looked old enough to be driving. A fat drop of rain splattered on his nose and dripped onto his upper lip. "How old are you?"

"Older than I look. How old are you?"

"Old enough."

"Why do you want to know?"

"You don't look old enough to be driving that thing."

"You're not a very good judge of age." She grinned. "I'll show you. Slide in behind me. There's plenty of room."

Plenty of room, but what did he do with his hands? She gunned the motor and took off with a jolt. Michael grabbed her waist and held on from sheer necessity. After a few minutes of mind-numbing fear as she hugged the curb, then weaved in and out of slower-moving traffic, he managed to relax his grip. The wind whistled around him and his eyes teared, but it was fun. The first thing he'd done in Springfield that qualified as fun.

He leaned in close to her ear. "I don't know your name."

"Sophie," she called over the sputtering chug-chug of the engine.

"Michael."

"Pleased to meet you, Michael."

After that he kept his mouth shut in order to make sure he didn't eat bugs for supper. A few minutes later she jerked to a halt in the parking lot of the motel.

"Safe and sound."

He didn't know about sound. "Thanks."

"You should come by and see us on Sunday at the prayer service. We got a bunch of your kind who attend."

"My kind?"

"B on B, I told you."

"Thank you for the ride."

"I mean it for real. This can be a weird town." The engine on her scooter sputtered as if it would die. She revved it. "Lots of people, but nobody to talk to."

A sudden lump appeared in his throat.

"Thanks, but I don't do services anymore." He didn't do anything that might bring him within spitting distance of a God who let little girls fall into lakes and drown.

"You don't do services anymore or you're not into God anymore."

For a girl he'd just met, she saw an awful lot.

"Thanks anyway."

"Then we'll see you, Michael."

Probably not. Yet he found himself standing at his door, key card in his hand, watching her drive away. A few wisps of black exhaust fumes followed the pink motor scooter that stood out against the darkening sky and drab gray of the motel. Life seemed more interesting than it had the hour before.

Stop it. He turned and opened the door and went into his new home.

Chapter 21

Phoebe almost missed the nod from Thomas. She had her attention fixed on her daed, who delivered the second of two sermons with an aplomb he'd gained after more than a year as the district's minister. His bass boomed loud enough in the Shirack barn to keep them all awake. The gist of the sermon escaped her, such were the fluttering of the butterflies in her stomach and the caterwauling of questions in her head, demanding to know if she really thought this was the right thing to do. She'd longed to be baptized. She'd studied and worked hard for this. But sitting here on this cool October day, she could admit to herself—to no one else—that it wasn't the day she'd imagined. Daniel sat alone on the front bench across the aisle from where she, Molly, and Rachel sat.

No Michael. No future as a fraa and mother.

So be it. She had God and family. There was no turning back. She'd agreed to finish the classes and be baptized so she could take Deborah's place as teacher. She would make up for her sinful past with a future wedded to the church, community, and Ordnung.

Catching Molly's gaze, she jerked her head. The four of them rose together and followed Thomas from the barn. Her heart beating in her throat, Phoebe fell in line behind her friends. This was it. The first step toward the point of no return. She stumbled as they approached the porch of Luke's house. Molly glanced back, her plain face rigid with nerves. "You okay?"

"Jah." Her voice quivered. She shut her mouth and concentrated on putting one foot in front of the other. "Okay."

Calm. Be calm.

Thomas climbed the steps and held the door open. "Phoebe, you first." Why her first? His eyes were kind and his tone firm. If he had any concerns about her decision to be baptized they didn't show in his face. "Go on. Luke is waiting."

Her hands wrapped in the fabric of the new blue dress she'd finished stitching the night before, Phoebe moved past Thomas and into the front room. It took a second for her vision to adjust after the bright sunlight of the October morning. The beating had moved from her heart to her ears. She couldn't hear anymore, but she saw Luke's mouth moving and his hand gesturing toward a wooden chair placed across from where he sat.

She sank into the chair, grateful for its sturdiness, like an island in the middle of raging waters. *Calm the waters. Gott, please calm the waters. Soothe my soul.*

"Do you understand why you're here?"

Luke's voice sounded muffled and far, far away. As if he were talking underwater.

No, not the water. Gott, please not the water.

She nodded, afraid her head would simply fall off with the effort it took to remember how to make it move up and down.

"You need to speak up. This is, in fact, your last chance to speak up." His tone matched Thomas's. Kind, but firm. "Is there anything about your rumspringa you'd like to tell me? Anything you feel the need to share before committing your life to the Ordnung and your God and Savior."

She swallowed against the lump in her throat. Michael should be here. He should be standing in that line outside, waiting and sweating with nerves. "Nee," she whispered.

"Speak up, girl, I can't hear you."

"I said no." She didn't recognize her own voice. She sounded like another woman, someone soft-spoken and unsure of herself. He would never believe her. "Nothing. I'm ready."

Luke studied her, his forehead furrowed. "You've had a rough patch of late. Are you sure you've nothing in your heart that stands in the way of this commitment to our faith? A commitment that is for the rest of your life?"

"There's nothing." She managed to sound stronger. She had to move on. Michael was gone. She only had faith and family left. If she told Luke that he would tell her those were the most important things in this life. She was blessed, even if she felt an empty void inside her that no sermon seemed to fill, no matter how long it lasted or how deep it delved into matters of faith. "Nothing."

Nothing. What she felt was nothing.

"Are you of a mind to go ahead with your baptism?"

"I am."

Luke nodded, but he didn't rise. His gaze continued to search her face. Phoebe held herself rigid, determined not to look away. His gaze connected with hers and held. She saw kindness and concern there, but also a tiny smattering of something like disbelief.

He leaned back in his chair and tapped the table with his fingertips. "Go then. Wait outside with the others. Together, we'll return and we'll finish this, the most important thing you'll ever do."

Phoebe waited outside while her friends took their turns. Each entered looking sick and petrified and returned with faces white with relief. Once again they traipsed back to the barn. Phoebe kept her gaze glued to the ground, determined not to stumble again. Inside, cool gave way to the heat of so many bodies crammed together on row after row of benches. The smell of sweat mingled with that of horses, hay, and manure. She'd barely relaxed on the front row bench when Luke called them forward.

Rachel went first, her head down, hands clasped in front of her. Molly glanced Phoebe's way, her expression saying *Here we go*. Phoebe forced a smile. Molly trembled.

Together they knelt, Daniel off to the other side.

"These young women and this young man have made a decision," Luke began. "Today they will make a promise to Gott."

Time stood still even as Phoebe's breath picked up speed. Luke asked her if she renounced the devil. Of course she did. The world. Jah. Did she commit to Christ? Again, jah. Did she accept the Ordnung? The words buzzed in her ears. She needed the Ordnung. She needed the rules. She clung to them when all else failed her. She couldn't be sure she'd opened her mouth and responded, but she must've, because Luke nodded and moved on.

Michael, Michael, why aren't you here? She shut the question back in its box. Michael had left. She must go on alone. God demanded that. Teaching would give her a place in this community, a reason to go on, a way to give back. A way to make up for what she'd done. She would be good and God would forgive.

Eventually, so would Hannah and the others.

Lost in the moment, she started when her daed touched her shoulder. She bowed her head and he removed her prayer kapp with a soft touch that surprised her. His fingers didn't fumble with the pins. She glanced up at him as tears brightened the blue of his eyes. She wanted to say something. Thomas stepped forward, a wooden bucket in his hands. A tin cup floated on top.

Luke picked up the cup, and Phoebe closed her eyes and bowed her head. *God, give me this new beginning. Forgive me, Lord, forgive me.* The water poured over her head, trickled down her face like tears, soaking her front. Water. More water. Everywhere water.

"In the name of the Father"—another cup of water poured over her—"and the Son and the Holy Spirit." A third cup of water.

She sank back on her haunches and rocked.

God. God. God.

A hand gripped her arm and she looked up into Luke's face. His eyes somber, he nodded and helped her to her feet.

"In the name of the Lord and the church, we extend to you the hand of fellowship. Rise up and be a faithful member of the church."

She would. She would do everything she could to start anew.

Luke's fraa, Leah, came forward and delivered the holy kiss on Phoebe's cheek. "Welcome, sister." She smiled and handed Phoebe her kapp. "Welcome."

Phoebe didn't know where to turn first. Her legs trembled. In fact, her whole body trembled. She tried to identify the feelings running through her. Was this peace? It felt more like resignation. She'd done what she needed to do. What her parents needed her to do. She'd done the right thing. This was good. Her new start.

She shambled down the aisle, seeking the closest door. She needed air and sunlight so she could breathe and see clearly again.

"Phoebe." Mudder stepped into her path. She didn't smile as she drew Phoebe into a hug. "I'm so glad for you. So glad."

"I'm sorry, Mudder, for everything."

"It's forgiven. This is your new start." Mudder sniffed and dabbed at her nose with a handkerchief wadded in one hand. "Go on. You're excused from serving food today. Enjoy a moment with the others. I want to say a word to Molly and Rachel. I'm sure they'll be right behind you, once everyone finishes offering them welcome to the church."

Lightheaded with relief at being released, Phoebe squeezed past folks immersed in conversation and stumbled into the brilliant October sun. It blinded her as it had done before. A dark figure stepped into her path. She almost ran into it—a man. Her heart wrenched. He'd come. Michael had come. She put her hand to her forehead to shield her eyes from the sun. "Michael?"

"Nee. Sorry. It's only me." Richard Bontrager smiled down at her, a smile that held a sheepishness, as if he held himself responsible for her disappointment. He had a nice smile and his Sunday clothes fit him well. He smelled of soap instead of the dirt and sweat she recalled from their buggy ride. "I know it's been at least a month and a half since I gave you a ride a home, but surely you haven't forgotten me. I'm not all that memorable, but we did go to school together back in Bliss Creek."

Her throat parched, Phoebe managed a nod. "I remember all of it. I'm a little distracted is all."

"*Gut.*" He ducked his head. "I'd hate to think I'm that forgettable."

"I don't...I'm just..."

"Overwhelmed? I remember feeling overwhelmed after my baptism." He glanced around. "I could take you for a ride, give you time to collect yourself."

The gentleness of his tone and the kindness in his face nearly undid her. Here was a man she'd been acquainted with for several years but never really gotten to know. He hadn't been part of their small circle. Why, she couldn't really say. His family's farm in Bliss Creek had been farther down the road, too far to walk. Her gaze had been for Michael only. Always. Even when he didn't seem to know she was alive.

Richard liked her when so few did. Fear ballooned in her stomach and then twisted itself into a knot in her throat. *Be good. Be good.* "Nee. I can't do that."

"With all the hullabaloo going on here with three other people being baptized and the families and all, no one will miss you." He nodded toward the field beyond the barn. "My buggy is close by. We'll keep it short. You probably couldn't eat beforehand. You'll be starving once you get your nerves calmed down."

Just one minute. Just one minute. Back in two shakes. I'll be back in two shakes.

"Nee, I can't."

"Some other time, then." He smiled that seemingly ever-present smile. He had such an even temperament, such an easy way about him. His bottom teeth were a little crooked, which matched the lopsidedness of the tentative smile. He wasn't as good-looking as Michael, but Phoebe suspected few girls had rejected his invitations in the past. "I have a flashlight with new batteries."

"I can't. I'm sorry. You're a nice man." Tears pressed against Phoebe's throat. "But I can't. Never. Never."

She pushed past him, trying to ignore the startled, hurt look on his face.

"I'm sorry, I thought..."

He thought wrong. She would never do something so thoughtless and selfish again.

Never.

"I'm the one who's sorry." She threw the words over her shoulder as she scrambled up the path that led to the house. She glanced back. "It's my fault. It's nothing to do with you."

He stood there, hands at his side, head cocked, his expression puzzled. "It's all right. I'll wait until you're ready."

He didn't get it. She scurried faster and faster, but she could still feel his gaze on her, wondering, waiting.

She might never be ready. Not for anyone whose name wasn't Michael.

Chapter 22

No doubt the latest quilting frolic at Irene's would be in full swing by the time Phoebe, Mudder, and Hannah arrived. Phoebe sighed and crossed her arms. After her trip to the fabric store and Bertha's snippy comments, she'd decided to stay close to home, not accepting Irene's invitations to quilt even though she wanted to go. No sense in inviting more snippiness. Today, however, it was time to get on with things. She'd been baptized. She'd showed her commitment to the church and the community. Now she wanted a chance to talk to Irene if she could sneak a moment or two at the frolic. Nothing seemed different and she needed to know if Irene could tell her how to find her joy again.

Now Hannah refused to cooperate. Mudder insisted they all go together. Hannah thought otherwise. For someone who used to never question her parents' word, Hannah had become silently willful in a way Phoebe had never attempted.

She stood in the doorway watching as Mudder tried, kindly at first, to convince Hannah to stop sewing dresses for Sarah—the little girl had more than plenty—and come to the frolic. Hannah didn't want to come. Not that she'd said as much. She simply continued to pump the treadle on the sewing machine. Phoebe didn't move or speak, knowing Hannah didn't want her to do either. She'd made it clear in the time since Lydia's death that she had no intention of letting Phoebe get close to her. To be fair, she didn't say much to the others either. She spoke when spoken to, did her chores, and went to school. Beyond that, no one could say what went on in her mind.

"Hannah. Stop." Mudder slapped a hand on the wheel that turned the thread. "Save your energy for sewing at the quilting frolic. Irene is expecting us. It'll be fun."

Her face pinched in a sour expression, Hannah stood and stomped across the room without a word.

"After you." Mudder smiled a weak smile "She'll be better once we get there."

By the time they made their way down the stairs and out the door, Hannah had climbed into the backseat of the buggy and had Sarah on her lap. She looked away when Phoebe climbed into the driver's side in front. Phoebe sighed and picked up the reins. It had been two weeks since the baptism and still nothing was different. Nothing felt different.

No, that wasn't true. Instead of feeling that nothing would ever happen to her again, she'd felt on edge, as if waiting. For what she didn't know. She simply waited. The uneasiness of not knowing what that *something* was filled her every waking moment as she fed the chickens, grubbed the last of the potatoes from the garden, shucked the corn, snapped the beans, baked the cookies, did the laundry, and mowed the yard. Something would happen. Something had to happen.

She focused on the road ahead. Autumn had arrived in all its cool, breezy glory. She raised her face to the sun and inhaled. Soon the smell of smoky fireplaces would waft in the air. Then flakes of snow would tickle her cheeks and wet the end of her nose. Time had a way of moving on. Soon Deborah would marry and Phoebe would take over as teacher. The thought didn't scare her as it had done a few weeks earlier. Anything would be better than this terrible waiting.

"I thought we should finish up the quilt we're working on and give it to Deborah and Abel after the wedding." As if reading her mind, Mudder's determinedly cheerful noise cut through a silence that had mostly been filled with the clip-clop of the horse's hooves. "Wouldn't that be nice? She'll love the Irish chain pattern. The greens and blues are very nice in this one."

The banns would be announced at the prayer service tomorrow. The thought made Phoebe's heart hurt. She flung away the arrows of jealousy. "Deborah would definitely like that. It will look nice on the... on their..."

Chuckling, Mudder patted Phoebe's knee. "You can say it. Bed. On their bed."

Heat burned Phoebe's neck and crept toward her checks. "She'll like it."

"You know you'll marry too."

Mudder framed the words as a statement, not a question. It was her first reference to Phoebe's future in a long time.

Phoebe shrugged. "It seems unlikely."

"Have you talked to Michael?"

"Nee." Phoebe flopped the reins, wanting the horse to pick up his pace. He nickered and bobbed his head as if in reproach. "How can I when I don't even have an address?"

"Edna says Daniel knows where he is. He received a letter from him and he's written Michael back." Mudder's voice lost some of its confidence. "You might do the same."

"You would want me to do that?" Surprised, Phoebe flicked a glance at her mudder. She seemed to be studying the rambling bushes and weeds growing along side the road. "You would want Michael around?"

"When I said I forgave him, I meant it."

A strangled sound from the backseat reminded Phoebe that Hannah rode with them. She closed her eyes for a brief moment. "I don't think there's any going back to the way it was before."

"Of course there's no going back. There's only the road in front of you. You were baptized and made new. Michael needs that same new start. As his friend, you should encourage him to focus on his church and not lose his faith."

"You're worried about his faith?" The good in her mudder never ceased to amaze Phoebe. The light shone in her with an intensity that made Phoebe feel all the more dingy with fear and uncertainty. "You want him to come home to be baptized?"

"To be with his own kind and to live out his life in the Plain faith? Of course I do, as does every member of this community."

Hannah snorted again. Mudder turned in her seat. "Do you have something to say?"

No response came.

"I know you're hurting, Hannah, but you cannot heal if you don't first forgive." Mudder's stern tone didn't allow for argument. "You only hurt yourself with the bitterness you hold in your heart."

"Stop! Stop the buggy!"

Hannah's shriek hurt Phoebe's ears and startled the horse, who shot from a canter to a gallop. Phoebe wrapped the reins around her hands and pulled with all her might. The buggy swayed and veered toward the side of the road and then back to the middle. "Whoa, whoa!"

The horse slowed, but his high-pitched whinny registered his fear. Phoebe gripped the reins and pulled harder. "Stop! Whoa!"

The horse whinnied, but slowed until they resumed their more sedate pace. Phoebe breathed and waited for her heart to begin beating again. "What was that? You could've—"

"Hush." Mudder twisted in the seat. "That will be enough, Hannah. You nearly caused an accident. At least think of the baby."

"Phoebe didn't think of Lydia."

Mudder faced forward, but not before Phoebe saw her face crumple. "And she pays every day for that mistake. I've forgiven her." Her tone gave away none of the emotion Phoebe had seen in her face. She spoke the words, but her heart didn't beat in step with the sentiment. "So has your daed. It's time for you to do the same."

"I want to get down." A stubborn note of insistence rang in the words. "I want to walk to Irene's."

"That sounds like a good idea." Mudder touched Phoebe's arm. Her fingers were icy. "I think a walk will do your schweschder good. Stop and let her down. Hannah, I want you to think about what you did and what might have happened if Phoebe couldn't get the horse calmed down."

"She should think about what she's done too."

Phoebe knew exactly what her sister meant. "Do you think I haven't?"

"Not enough. I saw you talking to Richard Bontrager after the baptism. Another man so soon…"

"Richard? He talked to me." Phoebe pulled to the side of the road and stopped. "He wanted to take me for a ride. I told him no. I've changed. I really have. I'm going to be good. I'm going to be good from now on."

Hannah thrust Sarah at their mudder and hopped from the buggy, trudging in the direction of Irene and Ben's farm.

"Let her walk. It'll do her good." Mudder settled back in the seat. "She needs time, that's all."

"She's right. I'm trying so hard to be good, but it's not my nature. I feel like I'm just bad."

"You don't understand, child." Mudder held Sarah against her chest and leaned toward Phoebe, her face damp with sweat—or maybe tears. "You have to understand. You can never be good enough. No one can. We are saved through God's grace despite our sins. You ask to be forgiven and He will forgive you. It's not about being good."

Phoebe let her hands sink into her lap, reins still wrapped around them. "You mean nothing I do will make a difference?"

"I didn't say that. You don't get into heaven by good works. I thought you knew that. You get into heaven because God decides to pour down His grace over you. You have to be willing to bow down and accept that grace and live your life trying to be worthy of it."

For the first time in weeks, Phoebe felt herself relax. A suffocating burden rolled from her shoulders. She'd always known she couldn't be good enough. Now she didn't have to keep trying, knowing she would only fail.

"If we don't start moving, we'll miss the quilting altogether." Mudder grimaced and rubbed her fingers across her chest. "I hope Irene has some stomach medicine. I can't seem to get rid of this indigestion, no matter what I do."

"I think Irene has something for everything that ails a person."

Kindness. Discernment. Patience. Forgiveness. The ability to forgive herself. Phoebe had seen all those things in Irene's face and her mudder's. How did these women get to that place? Phoebe wanted to go there herself.

Her arms curiously light, she snapped the reins and the buggy jolted forward. The view ahead cleared. She could see where she was going.

Chapter 23

Phoebe pulled the buggy alongside half a dozen others in front of the Knepp house and tugged on the reins until they came to a halt near the corral. She glanced back at the dirt road where dust still whirled in the air. No Hannah in the distance. An uneasy feeling wiggled in her stomach. "You sure we shouldn't go back and pick her up?"

Mudder used one hand to steady herself as she hopped from the wagon, Sarah asleep on her shoulder. "Hannah's twelve and she knows the way. She chose to get out of the buggy and walk. It's a nice day. It's no farther than she walks to school. She'll be fine."

How Mudder could be so matter-of-fact about having a daughter out on the road like that baffled Phoebe. She started to argue. Mudder held up a hand. "I made mistakes before. Mistakes that had terrible consequences. I won't make those mistakes again. Hannah has to learn to be respectful. She's hurting, but she's determined to be willful. That has to stop. Letting it continue will only compound my earlier mistakes."

Mudder thought she had made mistakes? She felt responsible for Lydia's death. Phoebe tried to wrap her arms around such a silly notion. "You didn't make the mistakes. I did." It felt right, a relief really, to say those words aloud. "I'm the one who made a bad choice."

"I let you."

"You couldn't have known."

"Your daed didn't want you to go to the lake. He knew you were

195

getting carried away. I told him to trust in God and let you have your rumspringa. That you would do the right thing."

"And then I didn't."

"Nee, you didn't."

"I'm so sorry." Sorry. What an inadequate word. It couldn't begin to convey her feelings. "If I could do it over…"

"I'm the one who's sorry. I should've done better by you. I'm the mudder. I have experience. I was blinded by…by my…"

Mudder's face pinched and she turned away.

"Blinded by what?" Phoebe scampered after her. "By what?"

"By my love for you." Mudder's voice choked.

Phoebe followed Mudder up the path and up the steps to the front door, still digesting her words. Her mudder was a good mudder. Fair. Firm. Loving. Kind. Now she questioned herself. Another thing for which Phoebe must take responsibility. Another cross to lay at Phoebe's feet.

They entered Irene and Ben's front door without knocking. The enticing aroma of baking brownies floated in the air, welcoming them. Women crowded the front room, their sewing goods scattered among them, an enormous frame set up in the middle of the room with the partially completed quilt hanging from it. Instead of the usual hum of chatter and busy stitching, however, everyone had stopped moving or talking. Irene stood, one hand on Aenti Bethel's shoulder. Irene smiled at Phoebe. "Welcome. We thought you might have changed your mind about coming."

"What's going on?" Mudder shifted Sarah to her other hip. "Is everything all right?"

"It seems I'm having a baby today." Bethel announced. She grabbed her crutches from the floor next to her chair and stood. "I should go home."

"Now? You're having a baby now?" Phoebe grabbed the door and opened it.

Bethel winced. "Soon." The word slipped between her gritted teeth and she started forward. "I'm new at this, but it seems soon."

"Maybe you should go to the hospital." Phoebe looked to her

mudder for a cue. Mudder had all her babies at home, but she didn't have Bethel's disability. "Is Ben close by, Irene?"

"Ben's at the Troyers. I can drive Bethel home." Irene bustled forward. "Rebecca, run and tell Daniel to ride over to Marcy Cullen's. We'll want her midwife skills today at Elijah and Bethel's place. Katie, can you stay with my kinner?"

"Jah, I have to wait for my girl anyway. She's walking up the road. Phoebe can go home and get supper started."

"If you don't mind, I'd like Phoebe to drive me." Bethel's panting had eased. She slid forward on her crutches. "We'll pick up Hannah and take her too. It's a drive. We better get going."

"Me?" Phoebe scurried after Bethel, who made good time despite the size of her belly and the use of the crutches. "You want me and Hannah?"

"Keep me company. We haven't had a chance to talk in forever and I want to give you the advantage of my experiences as a teacher. I hear you're taking over when Deborah marries."

Phoebe remembered to shut her mouth as she caught the screen door before it slammed in her face. "Don't you think you'll be too busy to talk?"

"It takes a while to have a baby. You know that." Bethel hobbled across the yard, her breathing ragged. "Let's go, girl. I'd rather not do this in the back of a buggy."

Phoebe caught up with Bethel and helped her heave herself into the buggy. Breathless, she raced around to the other side and climbed in. "You don't want Irene to go with you?"

"She'll catch up. Let's go."

Phoebe did as she was told. Life had this strange way of leaping out at her in the least expected moments. They turned back out onto the road just as Hannah came into view.

"Why did Hannah get out of the buggy?" Bethel began to pant again. "I imagine it wasn't for the exercise."

"She chose to get down."

"She isn't doing well with everything that's happened?"

"She isn't doing well with me."

"You're not over it. How can you expect her to be over it?"

She and Bethel hadn't seen each other since the funeral and then, they'd barely spoken. "How do you know I'm not doing well?"

"I have eyes. Your dress hangs on you like clothes on a skeleton. Your skin's white like you haven't been going outside to enjoy the day." Bethel rubbed both hands over her belly. "Fact is, you look like you've been sick for a good while. You might want to go a bit faster."

"I'm fine. And you will not have this baby in the buggy!" Phoebe slapped the reins hard. "I can't deliver a baby."

"Most of the time, babies come out just fine on their own."

"Most of the time?" Phoebe started to sweat in spite of the cool air. She tried to remember what she'd learned when she helped the midwife deliver Sarah. Hot water. Scissors. Thread. Towels. Would Bethel's back and leg problems affect her ability to have this baby? "What about the rest of the time?"

Bethel laughed, a half laugh, half groan. "All the time, it's in God's hands. Stop for your sister."

As much as she'd like to leave her stubborn little sister in the road, Phoebe knew enough not to argue with a woman about to give birth. She tugged on the reins and brought the buggy to a stop a few yards from where Hannah trudged, her head down.

"Get in." Phoebe didn't have time to be gentle. "Hannah, get in!"

Her sister didn't look up. She kept plodding along.

"Hannah Christner, I'm about to have a baby and unless you want to help deliver it here in the road, I'd suggest you get in the buggy." Bethel groaned—this time loud enough that the horse tossed his head and did a two-step. "Now."

Her mouth open, eyes huge, Hannah scrambled into the buggy. "Why is Phoebe driving?"

"Because I asked her to." Bethel breathed. "Could we not talk for a minute?"

They were silent for several minutes as Phoebe urged the horse into a trot. They were about twenty minutes from Bethel and Onkel Elijah's house, built on a swell of land a few miles from Phoebe and Hannah's home. Land that her daed had given his brother to start his new life with his fraa.

"Bethel?" Hannah's timid voice sounded completely different from the one she'd used to accuse Phoebe on the ride to the quilting frolic. "Why did you pick me up? I would rather go on to stay with Mudder."

"Sometimes God puts situations in front of a person." Bethel leaned back in the seat with a sigh. Her hands rubbed her belly in big circles. "I figure this is one. I'm having a baby and you're both going to help me."

A knot the size of a boulder rose in Phoebe's throat. She hazarded a quick glance back. Hannah's face had turned white under the red from the exertion of her walk. She kept shaking her head. "I can't."

"You both helped your mudder with little Sarah, didn't you?"

Hannah's head bobbed up and down. "That was different. That was before."

"When it comes to babies being born, nothing has changed in all the time since God made this earth and gave Eve the pain of childbirth."

It seemed Hannah didn't have an answer to that assertion. Neither did Phoebe. Women had been having children since the beginning of time. Some of those children grew up. Some didn't.

Phoebe snapped the reins hard, concentrating on keeping the buggy in the smooth ruts so Bethel didn't have to endure more pain from being tossed about in the buggy. No one spoke again, not even when they turned on the road that led to the small, neat house that Elijah had built with his own hands, anticipating this day.

As if reading Phoebe's thoughts, her onkel strode across the yard, a saddle over one shoulder. He looked up when they crossed through the gate and his free hand went to his forehead. He stared. Then he dropped the saddle and started toward them. His speed picked up until the trot became a run. She'd never seen him move so fast.

He met them at the corral. "Is it time?" Panting in a manner much the same as the one his fraa had been using, Elijah thrust his arms around Bethel and picked her up. "Is it time for the baby?"

"It is." Bethel leaned into his grip and put her arms around his neck. "Irene sent Daniel to get Marcy. They'll both be along in a bit."

"*Gut.* That's *gut.*" Elijah didn't bother with the crutches. He swept Bethel into his arms and started toward the house. "Phoebe, Hannah, come on. Get in the house. Start boiling water. We'll need towels—"

"I know, Onkel." Phoebe scampered ahead of him, caught up in the moment. She would help bring a new life into this world. She slammed to a halt. A new life. *Gott, help me.*

"*Ach*, get out of the way." Elijah danced around her and plowed up the steps. "Coming through. We have a baby to get born here."

Phoebe glanced back. Hannah still sat in the buggy, motionless. Phoebe chewed the inside of her cheek. *Come on, Hannah, come on.* Her sister didn't move. "I'll be right there. I'm right behind you."

She ran back to the buggy. "Hannah, come on. Bethel needs us. Onkel needs us."

"Lydia needed you. She needed me. She needed us."

Tears streamed down Hannah's small, freckled face. Phoebe couldn't bear it. She clamored into the buggy and squeezed on the backseat next to her sister. "I know. I know. If there were some way to change what I did, I would do it. I can't. I'm so, so sorry."

"I don't want to be around any more babies."

"You're afraid they'll die."

"Jah."

"Don't you trust in Gott?"

"He took Lydia."

"And she's sitting on His lap right now."

Hannah scrubbed at her face. "Right now?"

"Right now."

Irene's buggy pulled into the yard next to theirs. Phoebe heaved a sigh of relief. The midwife might not get here soon enough, but Irene would know what to do. "See, there's Irene."

The screen door slammed. "You coming?" called Elijah.

"We're coming," Phoebe yelled back. "Aren't we?"

In response, Hannah stepped over Phoebe and jumped from the buggy. "Hurry up!"

"Hurry up? You're the one holding things up!"

Leaving Irene to follow at a much more sedate pace, they raced to the house. Together they followed Irene's directions, collecting towels and boiling water in big pots on the stove. By the time Marcy arrived, Bethel was in full labor, her groans almost more than Phoebe could bear. Trying to close her ears, she followed directions.

Towels. Water. More towels. Cool water to drink. Fresh sheets.

All the same things they'd done when Sarah came into the world. Working next to Hannah and Irene, she didn't have time to think. Instead, she prayed. *Gott, bring this little one into the world healthy and whole. Please, Gott, if it is Your will, give Onkel Elijah and Aenti Bethel the chance to be parents of one of Your children. Gott, thank You for Marcy and what she knows about birthing babies.*

Instead of moving quickly then, everything seemed to slow down. Minutes turned into hours. Bethel's cries became less frequent. Elijah walked a pattern in the hallway that ran from the front room past the bedrooms, back and forth, back and forth, until Phoebe wanted to scream with Bethel.

She leaned against the wall outside the door, waiting to see if Marcy needed anything else. She wanted to help. *Anything, Gott, anything I can do.*

Irene, who'd been traipsing back and forth into the room as needed with cool drinks and a pan of cracked ice and then food for Marcy, finally plopped down in a rocking chair and leaned back. She looked exhausted.

Phoebe eased into the chair across from her. "How's it going in there?"

"It's going fine. Her labor has slowed down. Sometimes that happens with a first baby." Irene brushed wisps of hair from her forehead. Tiny beads of sweat dotted her hairline. "It's harder for Bethel, too, because she has weak back muscles. She's having back spasms, which means she's suffering more pain than most. She's tired."

Phoebe shivered despite the stuffiness of the room. "It really is hard to have a baby, isn't it? Makes you wonder why anyone would do it more than once!"

Irene chuckled. "When you hold that baby in your arms, you forget all about the pain of childbirth." She rocked for a moment, her gaze on something beyond Phoebe, something she couldn't see. "We have this capacity to bear pain and to let it go."

"It's a good thing." Phoebe wasn't sure they were talking about childbirth anymore. "Otherwise, we'd never have children."

"Or love or get married." Irene sighed. "All the really wonderful things in life may cause us pain, but they're worth it, and that's why we chance it and why we survive it, because we know there's joy beyond the pain."

"I hope so." Phoebe whispered the words. "I hope so."

"Gott's plan."

"I know."

The door popped open. His face white as a pillow, Elijah stopped in his tracks. Marcy's head popped out. "Phoebe, she wants you. You too, Hannah."

Phoebe exchanged glances with her little sister. Hannah's face was full of trepidation. "Me?"

"What about me?" Elijah folded his arms across his broad chest. "Doesn't she want me?"

"She does, just not yet." Marcy jerked her head. "Let's go, girls."

They traipsed single file into the room. Despite the open windows, the air hung warm and damp around them. Bethel's head lay against a mound of pillow, her face pale except for pinpoints of red on her cheeks. She shifted, pulled herself upright, and moaned. "There you are."

"How are you doing?" Phoebe picked up a washcloth and dampened it in a pan of water. She wiped Bethel's forehead and cheeks. "You look tuckered out."

"This little one is determined to stay inside. Can you blame him? Nothing but eating, sleeping and playing?" She smiled. Despite the dark circles around her eyes, she looked happy. "I wanted my two nieces with me when he comes into the world."

"Is it…is it now?"

Bethel grabbed Phoebe's hand and squeezed so hard she almost cried out. "It's now," she panted. "It's now!"

And she was right. A minute or two later, Bethel and Elijah's first-born made his appearance. A big, strapping boy with lungs to match. Red-faced, fists waving, he began to squall his disapproval at the situation as soon as Marcy wiped him down and lifted him onto his mudder's stomach.

"A boy!" Phoebe clapped her hands together. She couldn't help herself. "He's beautiful. He looks like Elijah, doesn't he, Hannah?"

Her sister took a step back from the bed, her hands to her face. "He's so pretty."

"He is, isn't he?" Bethel tugged the blanket around the baby and shifted him into the crook of her arm. "Would you like to hold him?"

Hannah shook her head and took another step back.

A smile on his face so broad it was a wonder it didn't crack, Elijah strode into the room. "A boy? Marcy says a boy."

Bethel grinned back. "A boy."

Elijah gently scooped his new son into his arms. "John."

"John." Phoebe repeated. "It suits him."

Elijah nodded, but his gaze didn't leave Bethel's. They shared the moment as if they were alone in the room. They seemed to communicate even though no words were said aloud. Phoebe backed away from the bed. She grabbed Hannah's arm and propelled her toward the door.

"What?"

"We'll start supper. The new mudder and daed will be hungry after all this hard work."

At the door, she glanced back. Elijah had eased onto the bed. He and Bethel held baby John between them. Bethel's face was wet with tears. She caught Phoebe's gaze. "Have faith."

Have faith. A simple admonition. Her aenti meant well, but Phoebe needed her to explain how to do that. Michael had gone and might never come back. He had disappeared into the Englisch world. Who knew what he was doing now?

Daniel knew. Daniel knew how to reach Michael. He'd known all along. Her throat tight with tears, Phoebe nodded. She wanted what Bethel and Elijah had. She wanted it with Michael.

Chapter 24

Michael untied his sodden apron, wadded it up in a ball, and tossed it into the basket Oscar left in the corner of the kitchen for that purpose. Finally. He liked working the early shift better, because he got off while there was still sunlight. He'd never been in the habit of sleeping late so he didn't mind coming in early to mop floors, fill salt and pepper shakers, and set ketchup and Tabasco sauce on the tables. Rubbing gritty eyes with both hands, he used his shoulder to push through the double doors from the kitchen into the dining room.

"Heading out?" Crystal called over the din of several dozen customers, all of whom seemed to be eating and talking at the same time. Michael never actually saw anyone talk with his mouth full, but the noise indicated otherwise. "You lucky dog, getting off early. How'd you swing that?"

"You didn't come in until noon." Michael squeezed past her. Crystal tended to forget these things when it suited her. "I had to be here before dawn, remember, to get ready to open while you were sleeping."

"I'll put your tips in an envelope on the shelf under the register." She poured coffee for a man at the counter without looking at the cup. How she managed that Michael would never know. "Got big plans for the evening?"

"No." He'd learned how to operate the microwave in his kitchenette.

He had his choice of a frozen tuna-noodle casserole that wasn't half bad or vegetable beef soup from a can. With such an abundance of choices, he'd wait to see what caught his fancy. "Finishing the book I started last night."

Crystal wrote down an order with a flourish, stuck the pen behind her ear, and slapped the ticket on the spinning hanger. Her long finger-nails were a bright red today to match her hair. They were rarely the same color two days in a row. "Order up, Mac." She stuck the pad into her apron pocket. "You know what your problem is? You need a girl."

Heat washed over him. *I have a girl.* To his relief, he didn't say the words aloud. *I had a girl.* For a minute or two. One brief flash of inde-scribable joy lost the next second in abject misery. The dinging of the bell over the double doors saved him. More customers. That would keep the busybody from digging into business that had nothing to do with her.

"There you are."

He turned at the now familiar voice. "Sophie. What are you doing here?"

"Nice." Crystal chortled behind him before Sophie could answer. "Look Lana, Mikey's got a girl. And one of his kind too."

Lana, busy cutting a huge wedge of lemon meringue pie, looked up, her eyes wide with curiosity. "She's cute. And his kind. Sort of. Nice!"

"That's enough, girls. Give the guy a break." Oscar's bass reverber-ated the way it always did when he was feeling the stress of a big crowd and dwindling food supplies. "Lana, get out there and wait on table six before that guy gets up and leaves. He's been waiting at least five minutes."

Lana scuttled away and Crystal grabbed the half-full, steaming coffeepot and began making her rounds. Thankful for his boss's surly attitude toward interruptions in the workflow, Michael focused on the girl ambling toward him.

Over the past few weeks Sophie had continued to appear at his bus stop on many occasions, giving him rides to the bank, to the grocery store, to the library, and to the motel. She always acted as if it were a chance meeting, something he knew couldn't be further from the truth. Still, he couldn't complain about it. He had no one else to talk to outside work. He didn't know why she did it and if he were truthful with himself, he didn't care. He'd begun to listen for the *put-put* of the scooter and look for its pink glare as he sat alone on the bus bench, waiting for a bus to take him back to the room that served as his home.

She'd never come to the diner before. Michael used the distraction to move toward the door. "Is everything all right?"

"Everything is great." She stayed where she was. "I've never eaten here and I thought it would be cool to see where you work. My papa says the food is good. I have my house cleaning and my ironing money. I thought I'd treat you to supper and then we could go to the store."

"I already ate here once today." Michael reeled in his irritation, aware of a trio of people watching his every move. Sophie couldn't know how uncomfortable this made him. He'd let her be his friend out there in the world where no one knew him. Why not here?

He blew out air. "Sorry. I'm tired."

"Yeah, it was stupid of me. It was just sort of spontaneous."

"It was nice that you came."

"We can eat supper another time."

"No. Let's eat." He pushed open the door. "But not here."

Once outside he looked around, surprised. "Where's the scooter?"

"Tune-up."

"Ah."

"It'll be ready in about an hour. Have you ever eaten Mexican food?"

"An enchilada casserole once. Does that count?"

"Time to try something new."

She smiled, but she didn't seem her usual contagiously enthusiastic self.

"I'm sorry if I was rude before. Inside. I've lost my manners here." He waved his hand at their surroundings. "People are always bumping into me, and they spit on the sidewalk and yell dirty words for no reason and the customers in the diner complain about everything and they want refunds or free food if there's a spot on their spoon. I'm just—"

"Homesick. You're homesick."

"No. No."

"What did the waitress say to you as I was walking in?"

"What do you mean?"

"She said something that embarrassed you or made you mad. Your face was red."

"It was nothing."

"Come on." She hopped a little skip and he realized he'd increased his pace and it was hard for her to keep up. He slowed down. "We're friends, right, and friends talk to each other."

Aside from work, she was as close to a friend as he had in this town. Still, they hadn't known each other long. Not like Daniel and Molly and Rachel. And Phoebe. "She said…she said I needed a girl."

"Ah ha!" Sophie giggled. "And then I walked in."

"And then you walked in." He smacked the button at the crosswalk, hoping to get the light to change and the pedestrian walk sign to come on. "She was just being Crystal. She's like that. She jokes around."

"It made you uncomfortable because I'm not like your girlfriend or anything. I'm just a friend."

"You're a friend." For some reason it became important for her to understand he considered her a friend. If she decided to not spontaneously appear now and then, his life would be the less for it. The realization surprised him. "A friend I value."

"Thank you. That's nice of you to say. I feel the same way." She perked up considerably. "You know what, I'm not really that hungry. Let's go buy you some clothes first."

"I've got clothes."

She raised her eyebrows at him, her expression full of only partially concealed distaste. "You're wearing carpenters pants that are a size too big and a little bit too short. Who taught you to shop?"

"No one. Mudder made my pants." He gritted his teeth. No matter how he tried, his family butted into his thoughts. "I never shopped for clothes before."

"I never would've guessed." She grabbed his arm and tugged at it. Something in his face must have shown his discomfort, and she let go and put up both hands palms out as if in surrender. "There's a Goodwill store not far from here that has secondhand jeans that are really great. I have friends who shop there all the time. You need a jacket too. Come on."

"I don't like shopping very much."

"Figured as much." She raised her head as if studying the sky for rain. "We could go to a movie."

He caught her sideways glance. She was up to something. "I don't think so."

"You've never been to a movie?"

"No." The light changed and he looked both ways. Around here, a green light was no guarantee that someone wouldn't decide to barrel through the intersection. Together, they started forward. "Why?"

"Do you turn on the TV when you're in your room at night?"

"No."

"You don't belong here."

She liked to do that. Make these definitive statements as if he would know what she meant by them. He made the obligatory response. "What do you mean?"

"You still belong to your community. You try to follow the Ordnung where it's possible. You do it out of respect for God."

He'd tried the TV once, when he first arrived. The incessant babble made him want to put his hands over his ears. The irony of how he'd so wanted to watch TV when he was younger—before his rumspringa kicked in—wasn't lost on him now. *Careful what you wish for.* His mudder used to say that. *You might get it.* "I don't have any interest in watching TV, that's all."

"You won't be happy until you go home."

"You're wrong." He could never be happy at home. He'd seen to that.

"Don't be sad. We'll get in a little retail therapy."

There she went again. Sounding like the Englisch women who chitter-chattered all day long in the restaurant, talking about their hair color and the shoe sale at Payless and TV reality shows. "What?"

"That's what my English friends call shopping."

"I don't much like shopping."

"You said that already."

"I did."

She grinned. "So we'll get it over quickly. And on Saturday I'm going to take you home to meet my papa and mama and my brothers. I call them the bothers. Because they really bother me."

He slowed. One step forward, two steps back. "Why would you take me home? Do you take all your friends home to meet your parents?"

"Only the ones who need a good home-cooked meal."

"I eat fine."

"It's not the food you need; it's the company."

Something in her tone warned him. "Did you tell your parents something about me?"

"I always tell my parents about everyone I come across. It's part of my…it's what I do."

"What you do?"

"Have you ever heard of friend evangelism?"

"No. We don't do evangelism."

"I know you don't, but do you know what it means?"

"Jah. Yes."

"That's what I do. It's my calling."

"You're eighteen and you have a calling?"

"Yeah, I do, and so does my papa. He helps runaways find their way home. He helps people who are lost."

"I'm not lost."

"Not physically. But something happened to you. Something bad. You don't want to tell me about it and I get that. It's fine. But my papa is a real good listener."

"I'm really tired. I should go home."

"Look, you don't have to meet them until Saturday. We'll just buy some pants for you and then we'll eat tacos, okay?"

He wavered. He did look pretty funny in his baggy, too short pants. He'd wanted to get it over with that day—his first foray into clothes shopping. The dressing room had been bright with a fluorescent light and warped mirrors that made him look like a patient suffering from a bad disease. He didn't like seeing himself in a mirror. He didn't like taking his pants off in a public place. He didn't like putting them back on to go back out through the aisles to find something that fit. So he'd said *close enough* and bought these pants and raced for the door, vowing never to shop again.

"Fine. If we can leave the visit with your family for another time."

"Fine. As long as you sincerely mean that."

"That I'll visit?"

"Yes."

"I sincerely mean it."

She looked so happy he had to hide his guilt. He hadn't said when. And it wouldn't be any time soon.

Chapter 25

Phoebe trudged up the new dirt road the men had graded before building the house a few weeks earlier. Rachel and Daniel's fathers stood next to a sawhorse looking at a rough, hand-drawn plan of the house they were helping to build for their children. It was late afternoon, nearly suppertime, but they were still hard at work. It didn't surprise her. Even though the days were short now and daylight precious, they were hardworking men. Rachel's father looked up first. He didn't seem surprised to see her. "Looking for Daniel?"

Ben Knepp swiveled and looked back. He frowned. He showed no surprise either, but a flash of displeasure darkened his face. He wasn't happy to see her. Irene might practice forgiving and forgetting, but it seemed Daniel's daed had a longer memory.

"I need to speak with Daniel, jah."

"He's working." Ben went back to the plan.

"It'll only be a minute."

Peter Daugherty jerked his head toward the half-finished wood frame structure and bowed his head close to Ben's. He understood grace a little more. Feeling dismissed, Phoebe lingered for a second. What was going on in Peter's head? His daughters, Deborah and Rachel, would marry one right after the other in the next month. Deborah would move back to Bliss Creek with Abel. Rachel would make her home here with Daniel. Peter's house would be a little emptier, a little quieter. He still had four more children, four more times to help a son or daughter move on to the next stage of life. He might feel relief. Or a touch of pride—one he would never admit to. If it were her, she'd feel a little sad. If she ever had the chance to find out.

She found Daniel hanging drywall in the house he and Rachel would share come spring. They would spend the first few months of their marriage living with Daniel's parents until the house could be finished. A frolic a few weeks earlier had ended with the cellar dug, the frame up, and the roof completed. The interior they would complete over time. Phoebe found herself imagining what the rooms would look like after Rachel made the house a home. Her friends would be happy in this house.

A nail was stuck between Daniel's lips and his attention was centered on the drywall. He didn't look up when Phoebe slipped in the doorway.

"Daniel?"

He swung the hammer, missed the nail between his fingers, and hit his hand. *"Ach!"* He dropped the hammer and danced around, one hand cradled in the other. "Phoebe! What are you doing here?"

"I'm sorry! I didn't mean to scare you."

"Don't be sneaking up on a man like that!"

"I said I was sorry."

"What are you doing here?"

It had taken her over an hour to walk up to this house and now that she had arrived, Phoebe found her courage had made itself scarce. "This will be a nice home for you and Rachel."

He shook his hand hard and rubbed the fingers. He had dirt under his nails. Despite the crisp October air, his shirt was drenched in sweat. He looked like the hard worker he was. "You saw it the day of the build."

"I did."

"So you thought you'd take another look?"

"I wanted to talk to you."

He picked up the hammer and then laid it on a sawhorse next to the stack of drywall. "Me? Is this about Rachel?"

"Nee."

He rummaged in a can of nails, his face suddenly pensive. "Is it about Michael?"

"It is."

"It's about time."

"What?"

"I kept thinking you'd give some sign you wanted him to come home."

Phoebe turned to stare out the space that would eventually be a window. Right now it looked out over a meadow. They would need a barn and a corral. They had so much work ahead of them. Rachel couldn't wait to get started furnishing her new home. Every time they visited she talked about that part. Phoebe wanted to ask her what it was like to be this close to her dream. They'd dreamed of getting married, being fraas, and having babies since they were little girls. Now Rachel would have that.

"It's not that easy." She faced Daniel. "He needs to come home, but not for me."

"I know."

"Do you?"

"I know what he's going through."

"So you've talked to him."

Daniel stooped and picked up another sheet of drywall. He grunted and shoved it against the wood frame. "Not recently. Before. The day he left."

"But not since. I thought you exchanged letters."

"We have."

"When?"

"I got another one last week."

"And you didn't tell me."

Daniel scrubbed his face with the back of his sleeve. "I didn't know if you wanted to know."

Of course she wanted to know. "How is he? Where he is? What's he doing?"

"Maybe you should just read the letter." Daniel bent over and scooped up a handful of nails. "Better than me trying to explain."

"You have it with you?"

He shook his head. "Not at the moment. He's living and working in Springfield."

A big town where a person could get lost. A town full of dangers and temptations. "Springfield."

"Jah. He got a job."

"What kind of job?"

"Washing dishes in a diner." Daniel frowned, his opinion of this job evident in the wrinkle of his nose. "He's living in a motel."

Washing dishes and living in a motel. They had no one to blame but themselves, but still, dismay burrowed itself between her shoulders, making her neck ache. "He can't be happy living like that."

"Nobody said he was happy. Wasn't that the point of him going—to punish himself?"

"Or me."

"Michael doesn't blame you. He blames himself." Daniel wiped at his forehead with the sleeve of his shirt. A pulse beat in his temple as he gritted his teeth. He met Phoebe's gaze squarely. "Truth be told, you should both blame me."

"What are you talking about?"

He straightened and faced her. "I'm the one who egged Michael on that day. Instead of going fishing, I wanted to take a walk with Rachel. I convinced him to do the same with you. I guess I thought I wouldn't feel so guilty if we both did it."

"And now you blame yourself."

Misery darkened his face. "Jah."

"Michael had a choice. I had a choice." Even as she said the words, Phoebe recognized the truth in them. Everyone wanted to blame themselves. Each one of them had to take responsibility for their actions. Hard as it seemed. "You might be slick with words, but no one made Michael do something he didn't want to do or thought was wrong. You're his best friend. You know that. If he came to me, it's because he wanted to do it."

Her words rang in her ears. Because he wanted to do it. Michael wanted to see her enough to skip fishing, enough to break the rules, enough to incur his father's wrath. Her father's wrath. Michael cared for her.

Daniel's fingers gripped the hammer, his knuckles white. He cleared his throat. "You're right."

Phoebe wished for a chair. Her legs didn't want to hold her anymore. "He has to come home."

"Has something changed?"

"What do you mean?"

"He left because you couldn't stand to look at him. It reminded you of…what happened."

"I never said that." Nor had she told him she wanted him to stay. She'd distanced herself from him at the funeral. He hadn't tried again. With the passage of time, the hurt eased, the grief ebbed. With time, they could overcome this. "I never wanted him to leave his family or his community. He needs to be baptized. Even if we never…"

She couldn't say it. Not even to Daniel. It was private, between Michael and her, whatever it was.

"It's his choice." Daniel shoved his hat back on his forehead and contemplated the hammer in his hand. "It sounds like he's doing all right. He's made friends with a Mennonite girl and the man who owns the diner is good to him. They're helping him…get right with things."

A Mennonite girl. Jealousy stung Phoebe with the force of a horde of wasps. "What things? How can a Mennonite girl help Michael?"

"Michael had a lot of bitterness. He didn't just blame himself."

"He blamed me."

"No, he blamed God for not saving her."

"And he's better?"

"He seems to be."

Those folks in Springfield weren't family. They weren't Plain. They wouldn't understand his faith and his path. Still, they were trying to help him. He needed the help. He needed his faith back. Phoebe gathered up her courage and asked the question she'd come to ask. "Can you go talk to him? Convince him to come home?"

Daniel dropped the hammer again. This time it hit his boot. "Ouch!" He hopped around, his face scrunched up in pain. "Me? Why me? Why not you?"

She had prepared for that question. "Because I'm a girl and I can't go chasing after a man." Her parents had been through enough. She wouldn't shame them more. "It wouldn't be right. My parents wouldn't want it."

"I have work to do." Daniel stooped and picked up the hammer again, looking as if he wanted to do that work now instead of talking to her. "Rachel and I get married in less than two weeks."

"Michael's your friend."

"And I tried to convince him to stay." Daniel pounded a nail, the noise a solid *smack, smack, smack*. He could work out a lot of frustration nailing. Would it work for her? She tried to focus on his words. "Which is more than you did."

Maybe she didn't want to hear his words after all. She hung her head and studied her dusty feet.

Daniel's growl echoed in the half-finished room. "All right. All right. I'll do it."

Phoebe clapped her hands in the sheer relief of the moment. "Danki. You are a good friend."

"I'm not doing it for you. I'm doing it for Michael. He needs to come home and be baptized." Daniel's face turned candy apple red. "I'm doing it because Rachel will never let me hear the end of it if I don't."

"She's so happy. You're making her happy."

The red deepened. "We'll see."

"When can you go?"

He groaned. "Don't nag. I have to talk to my daed first. I'll go when I can. And there's no guarantee it'll do any good. I tried to stop him before he left and he wouldn't stay."

"Time has passed."

Daniel's dark brown eyes studied her. She saw a sudden kindness— a kind of pity almost—that hadn't been there a second before. "And it's helped? You're better?"

She had Irene, Bethel, Molly, and Rachel. Mudder. She had people who lifted her up. Michael could have had that here, if he'd given people a chance. "I'm getting there."

"That's *gut*."

"I'm happy for you and Rachel."

"I'm sorry for whatever I did in all this. You can't know how sorry."

She offered him her best smile—a little weak around the edges—and trudged to the doorway.

"I hope things work out."

She almost missed those last words in the banging of the hammer against nail.

She bowed her head. *Me too.*

Those two words became her silent prayer. If Daniel could persuade Michael to come home, they could both begin the next leg of the journey. Together or each on their own road. She couldn't be sure which it would be.

Michael needed God more than he needed her. If necessary, she would learn to live with that too.

Chapter 26

Michael arrived back at the motel after ten thirty. He didn't like Sophie going home so late. If she were his daughter, he wouldn't allow it.

What a stupid thought. Why had his mind gone there? Shaking his head, he lugged his shopping bag across the parking lot. It was filled with the used jeans and shirts Sophie had picked out. She'd been right about the Goodwill store. The clothes looked almost like new and she'd seemed to know which ones he should try on. He wouldn't have to do that again for a while. And they were even cheaper than the discount store.

He avoided the shadows thrown by the buildings and hugged the bright spots cast by the overhead street lights. A cool evening breeze buffeted trash across the parking lot. He zigzagged to avoid a half-eaten hamburger still wrapped in an orange paper and then a dirty disposable diaper, both only a few feet from the dumpster. The first row of spaces was filled with old, broken-down cars. It looked like an old junk lot.

Exhaustion weighed down his limbs, but he felt a certain contentment. The time he'd spent with Sophie had been almost fun. She'd tried on hats in front of a mirror and asked his opinion about silly-looking sneakers. Mostly, she'd made him parade in and out of the dressing room so she could inspect the clothes for a good fit. Finally, after what seemed like days, she'd pronounced the last three pairs as "decent." It hadn't been his normal idea of fun—not like fishing or baseball or bow hunting—but all things considered, it hadn't been half bad.

He juggled the bag and dug in his pocket for the room key. Really a room card. Apparently hotels didn't have keys. It took a second for him to realize he didn't need the card. The door stood ajar, and the curtain in the window that ran the length of the room fluttered where the glass had been broken.

Michael froze, trying to wrap his mind around what he saw. Why would someone break into his room? He didn't have much, but what he had he needed in order to get by. He should do something. But what? He'd never worried about this sort of thing back home. No one did. They were willing to share with the other families, but they did expect a *by your leave*. Should he go in? Or stay out?

He settled the bag on the ground and pushed the door with one finger. It swung open. He stuck his head in and took a quick glance around. With the parking lot lights casting a spotlight, he could see a little. He pushed the door wider and ran his hand down the inside of the wall until he encountered the switch. Light flooded the room. Squinting, he held his hand to his forehead to shield his eyes.

Someone had ransacked the room, shoving the bed spread, blanket, and sheets to the floor, overturning the lamp, and knocking over the chair that set at the small desk. An empty spot smudged with dust stood where the TV had been. The microwave no longer occupied a spot in the kitchenette and the refrigerator door stood open, his meager supplies gone.

He sank into the chair by the window. After a second he thrust his head between his legs, trying to fight the lightheaded sensation. *Breathe. Breathe.* He rose, stumbled to the dresser, and ran a shaking hand along the back side. The envelope he'd taped there was gone. His savings were gone.

His hands tightened into fists of their own accord. He loosened them. He'd worked hard for that money. He'd labored for it. For someone to take it just wasn't right.

Maybe somebody needed it more than he did. Maybe. But stealing was wrong. If a person asked, it would be different. He leaned his head back and struggled for calm. A grown man dealt with problems peacefully. A grown man knew anger solved nothing. Got nothing done. A man made a plan and carried it out.

When he was certain he could stand, he trudged back across the parking lot to the office. One dingy light illuminated the small room. The overnight clerk appeared to be napping, head down on the counter. Michael pounded on the door. The poor man popped up with a start, then hustled to unlock the door. "Can't leave the door unlocked at night. Sorry."

Michael described the scene he had found in his room. The man, whose name tag identified him as Bob Murdoch, returned to the other side of the narrow fake wood counter, a martyred look on his pimply face. "It ain't the first time and it won't be the last. Druggies, usually, looking for something they can sell." He ran a hand through greasy black hair, smoothing it to his knobby head. "Sorry about the money, but the sign says we're not responsible for valuables left in rooms. Like they told you when you moved in, we got a safe here. 'Sides, that's what banks are for. No one leaves money taped to the back of a dresser—lessen they're survivalists. You don't look like no survivalist."

Michael held up his hand to stem the flow of words. "It's fine. I'm not asking you to cover the loss. I just want to know what I'm supposed to do now. The door is broken and so is the window. The microwave is gone."

Bob Murdock looked relieved Michael wasn't making a fuss. "Tell you what, I'm just gonna give you another room." He studied something on the computer in front of him. "Yep. Here we go. We got 108 open, just a few doors down from where you are now. You can move in a jiffy. No hurry to call the cops. They ain't gonna find who did it. They never do. You can move your stuff now or in the morning—it's up to you."

"Now." Not that he had much, but what he did have couldn't be secured in a room with a broken window.

It took almost an hour, but finally he found himself alone in a room three doors down. Exact same layout, exact same brown, flowered bedspread, same drab, meadow landscapes hanging on the walls. Yet it felt different. Almost three months in the other room had made it seem a little like a home. At least that's what he'd been telling himself. This room smelled of cleansers, like they'd just cleaned the carpet in preparation for a new occupant. The toilet didn't have a ring, nor did the bathtub, and there was a new bar of soap lying in its holder on the sink.

It didn't matter. All he wanted to do now was sleep. He'd deal with the break-in tomorrow…later today. After checking the lock on the door for the third time and making sure the curtain was completely closed, he laid down fully clothed on top of the bedspread. The room was bathed in light from the parking lot. He missed the darkness of a country night. Darkness made it easier to sleep. He tried to breathe evenly. After a while the pounding in his head became more of a tapping and then faded away.

He saw a flash of her purple dress a few yards ahead of him. "Lydia? Lydia! Stop. Wait."

She ignored him as if she couldn't hear his voice. She trotted along, her arms up, reaching, as if chasing something—a butterfly maybe, or a hummingbird. He couldn't see. "Lydia, wait. Come back here. You're too close to the water."

She didn't seem to hear him. She giggled and clapped her hands together. The sound was infectious. He wanted to smile, but his side hurt from trying to keep up. He couldn't keep up. His boots kept slipping and sliding on the rocks. He tripped over the gnarly roots of a tree. Fell. Scrambled to his knees again. She disappeared from sight.

"Lydia, come on. Come back. Your daed isn't mad. He just wants you home."

She didn't answer. He couldn't see her anymore. "Lydia? Where are you?"

The light dimmed until it grew dark and the tree branches took on a looming, sinister presence. Wet leaves brushed against his face and he shuddered.

A splash. A faint splash. He stopped, not sure he'd heard it. "Lydia? Lydia!" He began to run, then—running, running, running. His lungs hurt. They might burst. He couldn't get enough air.

He saw her then, floating on the lake.

No. No. No.

He dove in. The water hit him with an icy shock that made his heart stop and then start. His lungs ached for air. Down, down, he went. It was dark. So dark. He couldn't see her. Where was she? He floundered, forced himself up until his head broke through the surface. He gasped for air and swallowed water, went down again, and then struggled back to the top. Finally, a sweet breath of air filled his lungs. He flailed about, looking, seeking, calling.

Nothing. No Lydia.

He stroked in a circle, still gasping. Nothing. No shoreline. He was in the middle of the lake, no shore in sight.

Nothing. No one. No sound.

Only his own breathing. Something grabbed at his legs and jerked him down. He struggled to stay afloat, but the force of the grip carried him down and down and down. Air gone again.

Gott, Gott. Lydia's face floated in front of him.

No, no. It was Phoebe. Her mouth gaped open, her eyes wide.

Sightless, staring beyond him, not seeing.

No. No. Gott. No.

He fought with all his strength to get to her. He couldn't move. The water had turned to mud—thick, dark mud. Clay. His arms and limbs were caught in it, immobilized. He couldn't move.

Phoebe floated away with her sister, farther and farther away, while he struggled to move, struggled for air. His lungs didn't have room to fill with air. He needed air where there was none. He needed help where there was none. He needed saving when no one was there to save him.

No one.

Michael bolted upright on the bed, gasping for air. Both hands clutched the blankets. *Gott, why, why, why?* He wanted to scream the words, but nothing came out. The ceiling fan blew cool air on his sweating face. His heart began to slow.

He couldn't take it anymore. He couldn't take the silence.

He stumbled from the bed and threw himself into the chair next to the end table where the phone sat. Three months and he hadn't touched the phone once. With a shaking hand, he punched the buttons. To his surprise he knew the number she'd given him by heart even though he had never called it.

Sophie picked up after four rings, her voice soft, drowsy. "Hello?"

The greeting sounded like a question. "I woke you. I'm sorry. I shouldn't have called."

"Michael? What is it?" She still sounded sleepy, but more interested. "What's wrong?"

"Somebody broke into my room."

"Are you hurt?" Now she sounded wide awake. "You weren't there, were you?"

"No. I was with you."

"That's good. Silver lining."

Silver lining? "They took my savings." Saving up for a real apartment. Maybe to take some classes. To learn to do something besides wash dishes and bus tables.

"Don't tell me you kept money under the mattress."

"No, behind the dresser."

"Didn't I tell you to open a savings account?" Her sigh floated over the telephone line. "What am I going to do with you, Michael Daugherty?"

"Nothing." He was a grownup. He had to figure out what to do for himself, not a young girl. "I don't need you to do anything."

"Why did you call me?" The question wasn't accusatory or querulous, more wondering.

Why had he called her? Because her voice gave him comfort. Because he needed human contact. He ached for human contact. He ached for someone to hold his hand. He ached to be crushed in a hug and to hug back. Not something he could tell her. To even think such things seemed unmanly. "I don't know."

"Come on. Don't back down now. What's wrong?"

"I had a bad dream." Now he sounded like a four-year-old. "It…I just…it was…"

"You wanted to hear a familiar voice."

"Yes."

"And you couldn't call home."

"No."

"I'm glad you called me."

He relaxed his grip on the receiver.

"Tell me what the dream was about."

His grip tightened again, making his fingers ache. "It was just a dream."

"Then why did you call?"

He lowered himself onto the carpet and leaned against the bed frame. Her even breathing lulled him. His heartbeat slowed. His breathing slowed. His head felt too heavy to hold up. The furniture seemed blurry around the edges. Unreal. His whole life seemed unreal. How had he arrived at this moment? One minute he'd been courting a girl and the next he lived in a motel and washed dishes in a town where a person could go a whole week without seeing someone he knew or talking—really talking—to a single soul. He was awake. Sophie's voice told him that, but his entire life was a continuation of the dream. Only now in the aftermath, blessedly, he could breathe again and his heart seemed to stay in his chest where it belonged. No water threatened to close over his head—for the moment.

Until he closed his eyes again.

He started talking and didn't stop until she'd heard the entire story. She didn't interrupt, but her breathing quickened over the line and once, she sighed.

Spent, he leaned his head back and covered his eyes with his free hand.

He waited for her judgment.

"Michael, are you still there?" Her voice had a breathy quality now, as if she'd been running. "Stay with me, Michael."

"I'm still here."

"Come to supper on Saturday."

Again with her family. Didn't she see? It would only make it worse. And they would want to know what he was doing so far from his own family. Plain families stayed together. "I can't."

"Come to supper."

"Aren't you going to say something about what happened?"

"Come to supper."

He closed his eyes. Be alone or be among folks who were so similar to his own. It would hurt. But it hurt more to sit alone in this motel room that seemed so Godforsaken. "Okay," he whispered.

"Good. I'll see you tomorrow."

She said it like a promise. It was the first time she'd given him advance notice that she was coming. He breathed, trying to think what it meant. "Okay."

"It'll be all right, Michael."

"Jah."

He placed the receiver in its place, crawled back onto the bed, and slept.

Chapter 27

Michael reached for his hat and then remembered. He didn't wear a hat anymore. Not that kind of hat, anyway. At the diner, he wore a red baseball cap Oscar had given him with the name of the diner embroidered across the front. The Park Corner Diner. An original name, given that the diner sat on a corner across from the park. He ran a hand through his hair to make sure it lay flat, took a breath, and knocked on the door of the one-story house where Sophie Weaver lived. At least he could be thankful that November had brought downright chilly weather and he didn't stink of sweat after his walk. He glanced at the black numbers. Two-zero-two-eight. This was the place. As if the pink scooter in the driveway didn't tell him that. He knocked again.

The door opened. "You're here. You made it." Sophie, clad in one of her usual dresses with a little flower print and a kapp that didn't quite cover her hair, clapped her hands together as if applauding his performance.

"I'm here." He shifted from sneaker to sneaker, wishing it weren't so. "You said to come so I came."

"Come in, come in. Papa and Mama are in the kitchen. The boys went to get some ice cream for after supper." She grabbed his arm and ushered him in with an enthusiasm that made him regret his own lack of it. "Did you take the bus like I told you?"

"I walked. I needed the exercise." It sounded like a silly thing to say, but he'd heard a woman say it to a man as she slid into the booth next to the one he was cleaning one day at the diner. She'd been a big woman and she'd ordered a mammoth plate of chicken fried steak and mashed potatoes drowning in gravy. "I felt like walking, I guess."

"You were afraid of getting lost again on the bus." She laughed, a tinkling sound like bells. "I'm telling you, get yourself a smartphone and you can map everything as you go. You'll never get lost again."

As if he had the money for a smartphone. He'd started saving all over again after the robbery. The police had come and filed a report, but the officer had given him no hope that anyone would be caught and punished for the theft. Anyway, leaving his community didn't mean he'd given up completely on the Ordnung. He might go back...someday. They might welcome him back...someday. He swallowed against the familiar ache in his chest. It felt like an old friend who visited regularly, staying for days at a time.

He followed Sophie and the aroma of frying chicken that made his mouth water. The Weavers' living room wasn't much different from the one he'd left behind at the farm. Nothing on the walls, simple wooden furniture. A stack of books adorned a coffee table, a Bible on top. The windows were open and green curtains ruffled in the occasional cool breeze. There was one big difference, though. A TV set claimed the central spot in the room. A huge TV on a long wooden stand. Not like the one in his hotel room that barely took up a corner of the dresser. He tried not to stare, but Sophie noticed.

"What did you think? We were Old Order? I ride a motorcycle."

"A scooter."

"And my papa has a car."

"I know."

In the kitchen James Weaver stood at the refrigerator, door open, his head ducked down as if studying the contents. Betty Weaver chopped carrots at the counter and hummed along with a country tune that emanated from a clock radio sitting on the table.

"Mama, Papa, he's here. Michael's here."

Betty dropped the knife and turned. James disengaged from the refrigerator, a jar of pickles in one hand. "So he is." James spoke first. "I've heard so much about you, young man, I decided it was time to meet you."

What exactly had Sophie been telling them about him? Michael was afraid to ask. He had no idea why Sophie had latched on to him. None whatsoever. She chattered on about books he should read when they browsed the shelves at the library and forced him to eat tacos from a street vendor because he needed "to broaden his horizons" and then she sang the praises of her brothers and her mother and her dad, telling him all about the funny things they said at the supper table or the games they played in the backyard after a barbecue. James built houses for a living and her mom took care of the family. Sophie had three brothers and an older sister, who was already married.

Michael shook James's hand and nodded at Betty.

"Well, don't just stand there, James. Take Michael out to the living room." Betty made shooing motions with her hands. Looking at her, Michael knew what Sophie would look like twenty or twenty-five years from now. Betty was a little rounder and grayer than her daughter, but just as pretty. "Supper will be ready in about fifteen minutes. Sophie, you set the table."

Frowning, Sophie opened her mouth. "I want to—"

"Don't forget to wash your hands."

That put an end to the discussion. This had been a bad idea. He didn't know these people. He barely knew Sophie. His stomach knotted, Michael trailed after James, who snatched a bowl of peanuts from the counter and led the way.

"Have a seat, have a seat." James positioned the bowl on a round table between two recliners and lowered himself into one of them. Sophie's dad was a tall, wiry man whose time in the sun had left its mark on his lined face. His hair was sparse but still dark brown, with only an occasional whisper of the silver that threaded through his beard. "I grabbed the peanuts to hold us over until supper's ready. I don't know about you, but I'm starved."

"Thank you." He took a handful of the peanuts more out of politeness than hunger. With the knots in his stomach, there was no way peanuts or anything else would stay down. "You have a nice home."

"It'll do." James settled back in his chair. "Sophie tells me you're from New Hope."

"Jah—yes."

"You leave before or after you were baptized?"

Michael opened his mouth, closed it. This guy didn't mess around. They'd barely known each other two minutes. Now he knew where Sophie got it.

"Sorry. I know it's not any of my business. I don't know if Sophie told you, but we're pretty active in our community."

"The Mennonite community."

"Jah."

"And you thought I might want to turn Mennonite?"

His face somber, James shook his head. "That's the last thing I'm trying to do. Sophie said you seemed lost and I thought maybe we could help. If nothing else, I'm a good listener."

Sophie hadn't told her dad the story of how Michael had come to be in Springfield. He was thankful for that. He regretted telling her, letting her know of his weakness and his failings. He'd wanted to leave it behind, get a fresh start. Instead, he'd let it follow him here. "You do this a lot?"

"Help people?"

"Take in Plain men and women who've left home."

"A few. All men, though. We've yet to have a young woman come our way."

"I'm not looking for a new church."

"How about a few new friends who'll stand in the gap for you until you can find your way back to your own church?"

"Why would you help me?"

"Because I hate to see young folks come to this town and get so lost that they can't find their way home."

"Do you think it's safe for Sophie to drive around on a scooter talking to strange men?" Said aloud the questions sounded hostile and accusatory. "Sorry, I didn't mean it that way. It just seems…dangerous."

"Talking to the likes of you?" He chuckled. "At first I tried to stop her. But there's no stopping Sophie. It would be like keeping a hummingbird from flapping its wings or a bee from buzzing, a cat from purring. She's wired for it. God called her to it."

James snagged another handful of peanuts and shook them absently in his big hand. He had calluses and a little dirt under his thumbnail. "God put my Sophie in your path for a reason. It may sound naïve, but Sophie is simply following the example set by Jesus. We want to be friends to the lost."

"And you think I'm lost?"

"Sophie thinks you're lost. You're not the first Plain boy she's befriended. Or her brothers, either. We've had more than a few share our supper table."

His discomfort growing, Michael shifted in the chair and eyed the front door longingly. "I'm not a boy."

"I didn't mean to offend." James tossed the peanuts into his mouth and chewed with an enthusiasm that would've been amusing had Michael not been so tense, waiting for him to continue. "Sophie has a soft heart. She only wants to offer you a second chance."

"A second chance?"

"You're a Plain man. You left your community. We may be New Order Mennonite, but we understand what that means. Something powerful happened to you. Something that cut you off not only from your community, but from your church. Some kind of blow to your faith."

A blow. A powerful blow. Michael stood. "I should go. I'm sorry. Tell Sophie I'm sorry."

James popped up from his chair. "Don't go. At least eat with us. It can't hurt you to break bread with my family. I promise. No questions."

Michael edged toward the door. He didn't want to keep reliving this. He wanted a new start. He'd come for a new start. "I can't."

His whiskered face filled with concern, James opened the door. "Don't be a stranger, Michael. You're always welcome in our home. Until you decide to go home to yours. We'll pray for you."

Michael wanted to thank him, but his throat closed. He had to get out. He brushed past Sophie's father and escaped on to the porch.

"You can trust us."

He looked back. James held the door open as if giving Michael an opportunity to return. He looked a lot like Michael's own daed. Plain, stern, but kind.

"It's only fried chicken."

"I can't."

"Have you ever noticed God places people in your path when you most need them?"

The image of the lady on the bus with her basket of sandwiches and her words of advice about his heart floated in front of him. "I've noticed."

"Don't be a stranger then."

Don't be a stranger. He lived in a big city full of strangers. They were everywhere. And he liked it that way. Michael strode down the stairs and angled across the sidewalk to the street. He didn't look back. He didn't need a new community. Did he? Did he like going home alone every night to a single room that was never quite dark enough to sleep in because of the neon lights that flashed across the parking lot? Did he like lying on the bed listening to the garbage trucks hoist the huge bins and dump the contents at five in the morning? Did he like eating cold sandwiches and soup out of a can?

He didn't need Sophie's friendship. So why did the thought of not seeing her anymore sear his heart with such painful intensity? Were his feelings more than that? He slammed to a halt, examining the feelings that welled up at the thought. No. Sophie didn't evoke the feelings he'd once had for Phoebe. She reminded him of his sisters. She was...comfortable. They could joke and banter and tease each other. Her presence in his life for the past several weeks had meant someone with whom he could talk and laugh. Be himself. A friend.

No one could replace Phoebe. The thought gave him no comfort. Phoebe might as well be in another country, another world, such was the distance between them. Come to think of it, she was in another world. He'd traveled to a distant alien place. She was right where she'd always been.

Was she waiting for him? Did she ever think of that one moment they'd shared before chaos had descended and death had ripped them apart? Did she ever think of that kiss?

Try as he might he couldn't forget that kiss. Or her sweet voice. The way she cocked her head when she thought about something. The way she looked at him as if she'd been waiting for him her whole life.

They'd shared one brief moment and it had meant everything to him. Had been everything he'd imagined it would be.

And somehow, it had all been wrong.

Pursued by his thoughts, Michael started walking again, this time faster. Faster and faster. An old green car with rust on the passenger side door pulled up next to the curb in front of the Weaver house. He stuck his hands in his pockets and kept walking. Four teenage boys tumbled out, laughing and talking, carrying bags from the convenience store Michael had passed on his way to the house. He glanced their way and ducked his head. Three were made from the same mold as Sophie. The same hair, eyes, fair skin. The Weaver kinner took after their mother. Except they had their daed's height and wiry frame.

Something about the fourth boy reminded him of someone he knew. Daniel, or maybe his brother Hiram. The haircut spoke volumes. Another Plain man.

"Hey, are you Michael?" the oldest boy called out to him. "Are you Sophie's friend?"

He slowed. Much as he wanted to, he couldn't ignore Sophie's brother. He'd been brought up better than that. He stopped. "I am."

"Did Pops scare you away already?"

"I'm not scared. I...I just remembered something I needed to do."

"Come on, man, don't let him freak you out." He laughed. He sounded a lot like Sophie. "I'm Leo and that's my dufus little brother Robert—we call him Bobby—and my other brother John, and this other guy with the goofy grin on his face is our friend Tim."

"Nice to meet you."

"Sophie talks about you all the time." Leo bent over and crawled into the backseat of the car, then reemerged, a baseball mitt and ball in his hand. "After dinner we're headed over to the park across the way for a pickup game. You should come."

Michael hunched his shoulders. A baseball. The most normal thing he'd seen in the months he'd been here. Without thinking, he yanked one hand from his pocket and took the glove Leo held out to him. "It's been a while. I probably stink at it."

"It's like riding a bike."

He wouldn't know. His district didn't ride bikes. He smoothed the leather. It smelled like long Sunday afternoons outdoors in the summer heat and sweet tea and sneakers and sweat and his mudder's brownies. He tried to return it to Leo, but the other man held up both hands. "It's yours for the day."

"I don't know."

"Come on. A bunch of guys from the high school are gonna be there. With you we'll have enough for our side." Bobby held up two bags. "But first we have to eat. We brought the ice cream. Rocky Road for Pops and strawberry for Mama. Knowing Sophie, she'll have some of both."

The four started toward the house as if he'd agreed to the whole thing. Michael tucked the glove under one arm and rubbed the ball with his thumbs. Leo looked back. "Mom's mashed potatoes and gravy are out of this world. You snooze you lose around here. We can demolish a plate of fried chicken in about one point eight seconds."

Michael hastened to catch up. Homemade fried chicken. Homemade gravy. His stomach rumbled. It couldn't hurt. With the whole bunch of them there, James Weaver couldn't focus on Michael and his problems. He'd have his own sons and their company to consider.

"I'm Timothy Shrock." The friend paused and held the screen door for Michael to enter. "I'm from LaPlata. What about you?"

"Mostly Bliss Creek, Kansas. Moved down by New Hope about a year or so ago."

"I heard about the new district." Timothy followed Michael in. "I guess it didn't work out for you."

"I don't know yet."

The other man nodded. "I know what you mean."

James Weaver's perpetual smile broadened when he saw Michael pause in the doorway to the dining room. "Come on in, son. He who hesitates goes to bed hungry around here."

Michael let out his breath. He hadn't realized he'd been holding it. "So I've heard."

The Weavers took their places at the table with much chattering and shoving of chairs. Michael ended up between Sophie and her mother. He sneaked a glance around. No one touched their forks. No bowls passed. Sophie held out her hand just as her mother did the same. Everyone joined hands.

Sophie's hand was warm and soft. She gripped his fingers with a surprising force. He closed his eyes and tried to think of nothing but his Heavenly Father.

I'm sorry. I'm sorry.

The same refrain as always. The words seemed to drown any others he might offer.

"Heavenly Father, thank You so much for the blessings You bestow on us." James surprised Michael by praying aloud, his voice deep and steady. "Thank You for this bountiful feast and for the women who prepared it for us. Lord, I thank You for each one of my children. I thank You for our guests. And Lord, I ask You to give our guest Michael the comfort he seeks, the forgiveness he seeks, and the answers he needs."

Heat burned Michael's face. His throat ached. Sophie's grip increased. So did her mother's. Sitting between them was like having the sweet, warm aroma of bread baking wafting around him in the dead of winter. He kept his eyes closed and his head down. If the others did the same they wouldn't see the blush of emotion and embarrassment on his face.

"Lord, we ask that Your will be done in all that we do. Show us, guide us, direct us on the path You would have us take. Thy will be done in all things. Guide Timothy and Michael in their travels and help them to find their way home, wherever that place is.

"All this we pray in the name of our Lord and Savior Jesus Christ."

A chorus of *amens* joined James's. Michael could only whisper his. *Let it be so, Gott. Let it be so.*

Chapter 28

Phoebe shook out another pair of Elam's pants and hung them on the line, shoving clothespins into the waistband. Pants and shirts covered most of the line, yet her basket seemed to be a bottomless pit. The sun's angle told her she'd better get the rest of the laundry hung up or it wouldn't be dry before the day's warmth dissipated. The fall days were so much shorter now. Elam was working in the fields with her other brothers, leaving her alone with the girls, but Mudder and Daed should be back from the doctor's appointment anytime now. Mudder hadn't said why they were going. Something about the look on her face kept Phoebe from asking.

Trying to ignore the queasy worry in her stomach, she focused on throwing the last pair of Daed's pants over the line. She needed to check on the ham in the oven and peel the potatoes and carrots. Hannah should help with that.

Leaving the flapping clothes behind, she trudged around the corner of the house to the front yard. Hannah knelt in Mudder's flower garden, pulling weeds as Sarah played in the dirt next to her. She looked almost content among the autumn blooming asters with their blue and purple petals, the sweet fragrance floating around her. The pink, yellow, and purple mums Mudder had planted were still blooming too. They seemed to like the shorter October days with the brisk, cool breeze in the evening. Plum, crab apple, and cherry trees guarded the flowers, their rainbow of colors waiting for spring to bloom. Her family was so blessed to have chosen this farm as their new home.

"How's it going?" Phoebe swung the empty basket, thinking she would love to stay out here instead of going back inside to work on supper and get the last of the laundry from the laundry room. "Need any help?"

A smudge of dirt on her pale cheek, Hannah looked up. It took her a minute to respond as if she'd been deep in thought far away. "Nee."

Since sharing in the birth of Elijah and Bethel's son, Hannah had been less morose, but she still didn't talk much and she hadn't returned to her former good-natured self. They'd all been changed, Phoebe reminded herself. She didn't laugh as much as she used to. She didn't rush from the house for the Sunday night singings either. Nee. Don't. No thinking of Michael.

She'd not heard a word from Daniel about her proposal that he go to Springfield to talk to Michael. Not a word. Maybe his daed had forbidden him to go. Tomorrow she'd try to talk to him again. Or maybe she should go herself, if she could convince Daed to let her. Or simply go on her own.

Nee. What if something happened while she was off chasing her dream? She would continue to try to get through each day without making another mistake and leave the rest up to Daniel and God.

"I can take Sarah in with me, if you'd rather."

"Nee." She spoke with more force this time. Hannah scooted on her knees closer to the toddler. "She's fine with me."

"I'll start supper then."

"I'll be in to help as soon as I finish this row." She brushed dirt from her hands. "I want it to look nice when Mudder and Daed get back."

"It will."

Hannah went back to her work as if no longer interested in speaking to Phoebe. Containing a sigh, Phoebe ran up the steps and into the house, intent on getting that last load of laundry.

A scream cut through the air before she reached the laundry room off the kitchen. Hannah? Sarah!

She whirled and dashed back outside, down the steps, and hurtled toward the garden. "Hannah!"

Hannah lifted a screaming, writhing Sarah to her chest. "Help me! Help!"

"What is it? What happened?" Phoebe dashed across the grass to the garden. "What's the matter with her?"

"Bee sting!" Hannah yelled. "It got her on the leg, I think. She won't stop thrashing around. I can't see."

The possibilities and the remedies raced through Phoebe's head as she grabbed the little girl's bare leg, struggling to avoid getting kicked in the face. "Let me see!"

A huge red welt covered Sarah's small, chubby thigh. The leg had begun to swell in only seconds. So had her toes. "Stop crying, sweet pea. It's okay; it's all right," she cooed. "It's okay. It's just a sting."

"Look, look at her face!" The horror in Hannah's voice brought Phoebe's gaze to the smaller girl's face. "It's swelling!"

Indeed it was. The lips were already twice their normal size and her blue eyes sank behind swollen red eyelids. Even her ears were swelling. Phoebe had seen this before—her Onkel John had had a reaction to a bee sting. He'd nearly died before the ambulance arrived and gave him a shot of something that had caused the swelling to disappear. "Take her." Phoebe laid Sarah in Hannah's arms. "Run to the house. Get the medicine Mudder gave you for your head cold. Not the pills—the wet stuff. I'll get the buggy."

"Are we going to town?"

"No time. Phone shack. Run!"

Hannah ran, Sarah still screaming, bouncing on her hip.

By the time she returned, Phoebe had Roscoe harnessed to the buggy. The screaming had subsided into wheezing, a realization that made Phoebe's heart rock, then sink. "Did you get it?" She boosted Hannah into the seat and climbed over her. "Did you give her the medicine?"

"I don't think she swallowed it. Most of it ran out because she was screaming."

"Tip her back in your lap." Phoebe grabbed the bottle of Benadryl and poured a trickle into the baby's open mouth. Her hand shook so badly that most of the pink liquid ended up on the girl's neck and dress, but some made its way into her mouth. Sarah gurgled, huffed, and wheezed, but she swallowed. She stared up at Phoebe, her eyes almost completely obscured by her swollen eyelids.

Phoebe thrust the bottle at Hannah and grabbed the reins. "Hang on."

"Why not town?"

"Phone shack's closer. They can get to us faster than we can get to them."

"Who?"

"The ambulance."

Within minutes they were at the entrance to the Shirack farm where the squat, white shack stood on the side of the road. Phoebe heaved a breath and tried to think as she climbed down. 9-1-1. 9-1-1. What to say? The address. Would they know where to come? Her fingers shook so hard she kept missing the buttons. Finally, she connected. The operator's calm voice, so far away yet so near, assured her the ambulance driver would know just where to go.

Sure enough. It seemed to take hours—maybe even days—but the sirens wailed in the distance.

Gott, not her too. Please not Sarah too. Take me. Take me. I'm no good, but take me. Please Gott, take me instead. Phoebe lowered her head into her hands. *I understand it's Your will, not mine, but please, please don't take her. For Hannah's sake, save Sarah. For Mudder and Daed's sake, leave her and take me. Mudder couldn't bear it. Hannah couldn't survive it. Take me. They'd rather it be me and so would I.*

She prayed against the backdrop of Sarah's wheezing. Her attempts to breathe seemed to get weaker and more strangled—or maybe they were drowned by Hannah's steady hiccupping sobs.

The ambulance careened to a stop, sirens still shrieking, on the other side of the road. Roscoe whinnied and reared. "Whoa, whoa. Nee, not now, Roscoe, not now." Phoebe clamored from the buggy and ran as the paramedics opened the double doors in the back.

"Help her. A bee stung her and she can't breathe."

The paramedic had to wrench Sarah from Hannah's grip. The little one didn't want to let go. Phoebe peeled her fingers from Sarah's arms. "It's okay, Hannah. They'll help her. She'll be fine."

She would be fine, wouldn't she? Phoebe had prayed for a little girl's life before and not received the answer she so desperately wanted. *Gott, please.*

The paramedics laid Sarah on a stretcher. They moved in concert. Measured, unhurried, but with no movement wasted. In seconds Sarah had a mask over her tiny face and the first paramedic injected her with medicine. "It's epinephrine to combat the anaphylactic shock," he said. "Your little sister is allergic to bees."

That part they had figured out. The individual words meant nothing to Phoebe, but she understood their import. Sarah would live. She could only nod while Hannah continued to sob.

"We have her stabilized. The swelling in her throat will go down now and she'll start to breathe more easily." The man nodded to the other paramedic and they picked up the stretcher and shoved it into the ambulance. "We need to transport her to the hospital where we can keep her under observation. Are you her mother?"

"Nee—no. Our parents are in town at a doctor's appointment."

Before the paramedic could say more, Luke Shirack rode into sight along the dirt road that led from his farm. "We heard the sirens. What's going on?" He pulled up on the reins and stopped next to the ambulance. "Everyone all right?"

"It's Sarah." Would he be upset she'd used the phone without asking anyone's permission? She hadn't given it any thought at the time, but there'd been no one to ask. She raced through the highlights. "She has to go to the hospital."

"Quick thinking." He sounded pleased with her. His gaze flickered toward the back of the ambulance, then to Hannah. "You two go with her. Stay together. I'll call Doctor Glatt's office and get word to your parents. And I'll make sure your buggy gets back home." He turned to the paramedic. "Is that all right with you?"

The paramedic nodded. "We don't want to traumatize the little girl any more than necessary. She'll need her family on the ride in. If you can get a hold of her parents and have them meet us at the hospital, that would be good. We'll need their signature on a bunch of paperwork."

Luke tipped his hat at the man and then dismounted, already focused on making the necessary phone call.

Thankful to have someone else in charge of making these decisions, Phoebe hauled Hannah into the ambulance and climbed in after her. Their first time in an ambulance. She hoped it would be the last. She clasped Sarah's hand in hers, but the little girl seemed to be drifting in and out of sleep, worn out from her ordeal. The swelling began to recede as they drove into town and the sweet baby face began to reappear.

Phoebe bowed her head. *Thank You, Gott.*

Thank You.

Chapter 29

Katie scanned the crowd in the New Hope Medical Center emergency room. Most had their gazes glued to a television set on a shelf hanging on the wall overhead. A boy moaned and vomited into a trash can. A woman sat with a girl who had a bloody bite on her face. Two men argued about a basketball game while one held his arm to his chest.

There was Hannah. Her head was downcast—she knew better than to watch the TV. Her eyes were swollen and red with tears. Poor girl. She'd been through so much. She was only beginning to get a little better since Lydia's death. Now this. She would blame herself. A simple bee sting. No one could've predicted. Sarah had been stung before and nothing like this had occurred. A little welt, a few tears. That was it. Katie sighed.

Silas strode ahead of her. Nothing about his demeanor revealed the hard words the doctor had delivered to them earlier in the day. The indigestion, the pain, the ache in her arm and her jaw. The nausea. She had been sure it was a combination of her arthritis and the flu, compounded by the pain of Lydia's death. She wouldn't even have gone to the doctor if Silas hadn't insisted. According to Doctor Glatt, she'd had something he called a "cardiac event." He also said if she didn't change her ways, there would be more to come.

As it was, he had her scheduled for all sorts of tests beginning next week. He'd wanted to begin that day, but she'd put her foot down. She'd already missed most of the day and she would be at home for supper with her kinner.

So he'd given her three prescriptions to fill. They were in her bag, waiting.

She needed to relax, he said. She needed to take it easy. No prescriptions existed for either of those orders. She wanted to yell at him. *I'm young. I have children. I'm a Plain woman. We don't relax. We don't take it easy.*

Instead she'd nodded and smiled and promised to do as he asked. For her family's sake. They'd been through so much. She didn't want to make them suffer because of her own stubbornness.

From the doctor's office to the ER. So much for relaxing. So much for taking it easy. How did one do that, exactly?

Hannah saw them coming and stood. "They would only let one of us in with her so I told Phoebe she should go. She's the one who knew what to do. She did everything. She knew just what to do."

The words poured from the girl as if she'd been waiting for them to arrive so she could release the burden from her shoulders. "See, she knew what medicine to give her. She knew to go to the phone shack instead of coming to town. She knew just what to do. She saved her. She saved Sarah."

Hannah sounded surprised and chagrinned.

"That's *gut*. Where is Sarah now?" Silas patted Hannah on the back in a hard, awkward motion that made her take a step forward. "Is she all right?"

"The paramedic said she was fine. They just wanted to keep an eye on her for a few hours, make sure the medicine worked. She's over there in one of those little rooms behind the double doors."

Silas wheeled and headed to the desk. After a brief conversation with a nurse, he returned with a stack of papers. "You go in," he said to Katie. "Sarah will want you." He nodded to the chairs. "Hannah and I will sit here and wait for you while I fill out all these papers and pay the hospital."

Silas's free hand shot out and gripped Katie's wrist for one brief second, then dropped. She couldn't have been more surprised if he'd kissed her. He never touched her in public. "The nurse says she's fine. The medicine helped. She'll be released in an hour or two."

"That's *gut*."

His gaze held hers for a few seconds. All the words he couldn't say were written on his weather-beaten face. He loved her. He was scared for her. He was scared for himself. He was scared for Sarah and Hannah and Phoebe and the boys. But he also had faith. He had the strength of his convictions. Faith overcame all fear.

She nodded. He nodded back.

Relax.

She followed the nurse through the double doors and down the long, slick, shiny hallway to a tiny cubicle at the end. It smelled of antiseptic and bleach. A man moaned behind a curtain. People talked in soft murmurs that sounded like humming. Machines beeped. Nurses trotted to and fro, their rubber soles squeaking on the tile. She felt as if she'd stepped into another world. What a strange thought for a grown woman. It had been a strange day. She slipped through the curtain that covered the doorway and found Phoebe with her head down on the edge of the bed. Sarah slumbered, her face still swollen, mouth open, lips puffy. She snored a tiny, squeaky little snore.

"Phoebe?"

Phoebe raised her head. "I want to go to Springfield."

"What?" *Relax. Relax.*

"I want to go with Daniel to bring Michael home," Phoebe whispered. "He needs to come home."

Relax. Relax. She tucked Sarah's blanket up around her shoulders, touched her satiny soft cheek, and then sank into the chair next to Phoebe's. "Hannah said you saved Sarah." Katie wanted to say more, but the words stuck in her throat. She was unaccustomed to giving praise. It wasn't their way. But with all that had happened, it should be said. Phoebe needed back her sense of self as a woman who would care for own children some day. "You knew what to do. That's *gut*."

She was proud of her daughter, but wouldn't go so far as to say so. *Pride goes before a fall. A kind word brings healing.* The two sentiments squared off inside her head. The loving mudder in her sparred with the disciplinarian. The mudder who had been too lenient and paid a terrible price for it. She pressed her lips together and closed her eyes.

"Mudder, did you hear me?" The urgency in Phoebe's voice forced Katie to open them again. "I need to talk to Michael."

"Why do *you* need to go? Why can't Daniel do it?"

"Michael needs to know he's forgiven. I've forgiven him."

"Have you?"

"Jah. I have." Phoebe's voice sounded stronger than it had in weeks. "But I need to know...Have you?"

Katie leaned back in the chair. Her pulse pounded in her ears. *Relax.*

"Are you all right? You look peaked."

"I'm just tired."

"You didn't answer me."

"I've forgiven him. I told you that before. It's myself I have trouble forgiving, but that's not your problem." Katie faced Phoebe. Her daughter's bun hung halfway out of her kapp. Dark smudges under her eyes looked like bruises. She looked as if she hadn't slept in weeks. Still, she seemed more animated than she had since the funeral.

"I'm not asking him to come back to...to be what we were trying to be before. That's not important." Phoebe popped from her chair and leaned over the railing to touch Sarah's cheek as if to reassure herself that the child was simply sleeping. "What's important is that he be baptized and return to his faith. There's more at stake than our lives together."

"You're growing up, daughter." Tiny steps forward. They would all take those tiny steps forward until they became easier, and they would one day walk with a confident stride toward their future. "It soothes my heart."

"Will you talk to Daed?"

"I will. You know you're an adult now. You've been baptized." The words came slowly. Katie couldn't believe she was saying them, but they were the truth. "You could choose to go to Springfield without your daed's permission. You don't necessarily need it."

"The last time I sneaked around to do something, the consequences were terrible." Phoebe rubbed her eyes with fisted hands like a little girl who needed a nap. "I don't ever want to do that again."

Her daughter had grown up. Katie wouldn't wish the events of the past few months on anyone in the world, but in this moment, in this quiet moment in a strange white hospital world, she could concede one thing. She could see God's hand moving in her daughter's life. With each passing day He honed Phoebe's character, turning her into the woman she needed to be. The flighty, silly girl of the past no longer existed. "No promises, but I'll talk to your daed."

"Danki."

"There's something else you should know." Katie clutched the canvas bag on her lap—the bag with the prescriptions tucked inside it. "You need to know something I learned today."

Phoebe stiffened beside her. "You went to the doctor."

"I did."

"What did he say?" Her already pale face whitened and her voice quivered. "Is everything all right?"

"Everything's fine. I'm going to start taking some medicine to help with my heart."

"Your heart?" The words came out in a squeak. "What's wrong with your heart?"

"It seems it's a little clogged up." Katie waved her hand in the air. She'd only half-listened to the doctor's explanation. What difference did it make what started the problem? The good food she cooked and ate. Silas ate the same foods and his heart was fine. She only wanted to know how to fix her problem. How to cure it. But it seemed a cure didn't exist. "I'll take some medicines for high blood pressure and cholesterol and some such other things I don't even understand."

"And the medicine will fix the problem?"

"It'll help." She patted Phoebe's hand. "The reason I'm telling you this is because you're the oldest daughter. If I have to go to the hospital or if something happens, you'll be the one to take care of our family."

"But I'm…I'm not…"

"You are. You showed me today I can depend on you. Daed can depend on you. If I'm not around, he will be lost. Men are. They don't know anything about baking the bread or canning the corn or teaching Sarah to use the potty. They don't know about laundry."

"My judgment—"

"Your judgment is fine. Gott led you on a path today that saved Sarah's life. He guided you and kept you and Sarah and Hannah safe. Because of that you were able to save her."

"He did." Her voice filled with wonder. "I did."

"It's nothing to get a big head over, but it's something to remember." Katie leaned back and closed her eyes for a few seconds "It's something for us all to remember. We'll be all right. We'll be all right."

Gott, I'm ready. You've shown me the way. Thy will be done.

Chapter 30

Inhaling the cool evening air, Michael stepped up to the plate, dug his heels into the dirt, and took a gentle practice swing. These guys brought aluminum bats. They felt different from the old wooden ones he'd learned to use on the field by the school in Bliss Creek. That seemed like a hundred years ago. They didn't have bases so they used old tin cans. Most of them didn't even have mitts. He'd received a glove for Christmas the year he turned ten. He still had it in his room at home.

If they hadn't given away his things.

Having a glove didn't matter. Even the teacher had played. So had Phoebe. She'd hitch up her skirt and run like a little jackrabbit whenever she got a hit—which was most of the time. She loved to play baseball and she was good at it. Every time he heard the ping of the ball against bat or the slap of a fist against a mitt or smelled the leather, he thought of her. So why did he keep coming back for more? This was his third game in the last two weeks. He winced, expecting the usual sharp pain these memories always brought. Not this time. This time, all he could feel was longing. A longing so deep if he inhaled he would drown in it.

He came because the exercise felt good and he liked the company. Sophie's brothers were good folks. So were their other teammates. Everyone had made him feel welcome. For the first time in months, he could relax. The smell of dirt and sweat and old leather made him feel at home…almost home. He waggled the bat and stared at the pitcher, a skinny guy wearing a St. Louis Cardinals T-shirt and a red cap. He had red hair and freckles to match. Time to forget the past and focus on bringing Robert, who was dancing back and forth off second base, home.

The other team picked up their chatter, baiting him. "Here batter, batter, batter, here batter. Swing, batter, swing!"

He ignored them and took another practice swing. The sun would be down soon and the field they commandeered in the park not far from Sophie's house had no lights. Already dusk made seeing the ball harder, but with two previous games under his belt, Michael had grown used to the less-than-ideal playing conditions. The pitch came. He swung and connected, a solid hit that made the bat reverberate in his hands. He tossed it aside and sped toward first base. The ball sailed into the gap between centerfield and leftfield. He rounded first and chugged into second while Robert slid into home plate despite the fact that the ball was still in the outfield. He just liked sliding. He liked the dirt on his pants.

"Way to go, Michael!" Sophie's high voice carried from the sideline. She sat alone on the top row of bleachers in her flowered skirt and white blouse, looking like a flower herself. "Good hit!"

He'd never seen her with friends, girls her own age. Did she have friends? It was Thursday night. A school night, but she didn't seem worried about studying or the time. She didn't seem worried about anything.

At home plate, Leo went down in three straight swinging strikes. The guy needed eyeglasses. Two of the pitches were wide. Three outs and the game ended. Michael hadn't been keeping track of the score, but the combined whooping and hollering of the other team told the story.

"Good game. We'll get them next time." Timothy shoved bats and balls into a large bag. "That was a good catch you made in the third inning."

"Thanks. You didn't do so bad yourself."

"We used to play almost every night in the summer when I was younger."

"We did too."

Timothy's hand went to his head. Looking for his hat. Michael had done that a few times before he'd broken himself of the habit.

"You taking the bus home again?" Timothy lived in an apartment he shared with a couple of guys who worked for the same construction company. He didn't have a car either. "I'm headed that direction."

"Yes. I have to open the diner in the morning."

"How is that—working at a restaurant?"

Michael shrugged. He couldn't quite explain it. He'd never seen himself doing this kind of work, what he'd once considered women's work. Washing dishes and clearing tables. But the day he'd started working for Oscar had been a good day. A day when someone took a chance on him. "It's a job. I didn't have much when I got here and my boss is a nice man."

"Jah, but it's not something you want to do forever, is it?" Timothy examined a red spot on his index finger. Looked like a splinter, maybe. "Reason I ask is the foreman on my crew said today that they'll be hiring another carpenter after the holidays. We'll finish out a lot of interiors during the winter months. You interested?"

Swinging a hammer. Michael knew how to do that. He'd gone to barn raisings and such since he was old enough to walk. Good, hard work. No steam, no detergent, no dried egg yolks or sticky syrup.

No Oscar or Crystal or Lana.

The construction company hired Plain men because they were hard workers and they knew what they were doing. He'd be with his own kind.

Which had its drawbacks. Coming to Springfield was intended to be his new start. Working with a bunch of Plain men would only lead to the same old questions, the same old discussions.

"Look, it was just a thought." Timothy nibbled at the spot on his finger and grimaced. "It probably pays more and you could move out of that motel you're staying in."

"You should probably use a needle to get that splinter out." Michael tucked the mitt Leo had loaned him under his arm and started toward the sidewalk. "You think you'll be staying?"

"At the construction job you mean?"

"In Springfield."

Timothy stuck his fist in his pocket as if to keep from messing with the splinter. "I expect I will. I'm not going back."

"You don't miss it?"

"I like my pockets."

"Your pockets?"

"I like deciding whether I can have pockets on my pants. I like microwaving popcorn." He smiled as if it were a joke, but it wasn't. "And I don't think any of those things will keep me out of heaven."

What Timothy meant to say was he didn't agree with the Ordnung and couldn't abide by it. Which meant he couldn't be baptized. He couldn't go home. He didn't belong there.

He and Michael were different. "I think I'll stick to the diner. Right now, I best get home and get some sleep."

"No, no, you guys can't go yet!" Sophie called as she rushed across the field toward them, looking like a child about to throw a tantrum. "They're having an ice cream social for the youth group at the church this evening and I just know there's still ice cream. And Mama took her homemade brownies."

"Okay, okay." Michael couldn't resist Mrs. Weaver's brownies. They were so like his own mudder's. "But I have to make it quick."

Every game ended with some kind of invitation to a youth group occasion at the church. He knew what Sophie was doing and he didn't blame her. It was her way. Besides, he liked the group. He liked the baseball. Even though they were Mennonites, they were so much like his own folks, given to plain talk, hard work and kindness, and good cooking and simple fun.

"Good." Sophie clapped her hands and crowed. "You too, Timothy, you too."

"Me too." The big guy grinned. He sidled closer to Sophie, his skin turning a darker red. "I'm not passing up ice cream. Especially free ice cream and brownies. I can't buy groceries until payday."

Laughing and talking, they strolled the three blocks to the church. Most of the crowd had dissipated already, but Sophie was right. Plenty of ice cream remained, and Mrs. Weaver had saved them a plate of her brownies. "Especially for you, Michael. I hear it's your birthday."

His face burning, Michael groaned and waved a finger at Sophie. "I told you that in confidence."

"If you think we're gonna let your birthday pass without marking it, you've got rocks in your head." Sophie wielded an ice cream scoop with the deftness of much practice, dumping a scoop each of chocolate, vanilla, and cookie dough into a bowl. She topped it with a brownie and added chocolate syrup and a sprinkle of nuts. "Happy birthday, Michael!"

He accepted her offering and shoveled a big bite into his mouth.

"And I have something else for you." She wiped her hands on a towel. "A little, small something."

He laid the bowl on the table and took the rectangular package. As soon as he felt its weight and substance in his hand, he knew. A book. The book. "Sophie."

"Open it later." Her cheeks turned pink.

Despite his best intentions, he stayed another hour, watching Sophie and her brothers clown around and chat with their friends from the youth group. They reminded him so much of Daniel and Rachel and Molly and…Phoebe. Of course, Phoebe. His nineteenth birthday and he was hundreds of miles from home. It might as well have been millions. He wondered what she was doing tonight. Did she remember that today was his birthday?

Last year her family had come to the house for supper the night of his birthday. He hadn't had the guts to speak to her directly, even though she'd been nice enough to bring him a present. A new hat. She insisted his old one smelled like horse. Everyone laughed and she grinned, looking pleased with herself. He smiled at the memory of her insistence that he throw the old hat away, hands on her hips, feet planted, a frown she could barely keep on her face. He managed to say *danki*, sure his face had turned the color of bricks. So much lost time. If he'd been able to tell her how he felt then, would things have been different?

They might have been married by the time their families took the trip to Stockton Lake. No sneaking around. No terrible, terrible consequences.

He closed his eyes, suddenly too tired to think, let alone walk to the bus stop. Better get going before the last bus or he'd be hoofing it all the way to the motel. He forced himself to stand. "Thanks, Mrs. Weaver. For everything."

She smiled. "Don't be a stranger."

She always said that. *Don't be a stranger.* The Weaver family never met a stranger they couldn't turn into a friend.

He wound his way through the chairs and tables in the fellowship hall and made it to the door before Sophie noticed. "Hey, aren't you at least going to say goodbye?"

"Sorry. I don't want to miss my bus and walk all the way to the motel."

"You forgot this." She followed him through the door and out into the parking lot, the package clutched in one hand. "It's rude not to accept a present."

"We don't do Bible study."

"But you do read the Bible, don't you?"

"What if I already have one?" He did. His groosmammi had given him her German Bible before she died. He didn't read German very well, but enough to get the gist. "Maybe I don't need one."

"Knowing how and why you left home, I'm thinking you didn't bring it with you." Smiling, she held out the package. "And you always need one. Always. Happy birthday."

He accepted her offering. Her eyes were full of something he couldn't identify, something he hadn't seen there before. They were big and blue and clear as sky. She looked so sweet.

For one horrifying second, he thought he would lean down and kiss her.

No. No. No. He backed away. The smile on her face faded and her forehead wrinkled in puzzlement. "Michael? What's wrong? You look like you don't feel good."

They were friends. She'd befriended a complete stranger, alone in a strange city. He was thankful for her. What was wrong with him? Look where kissing a girl had gotten him in the past.

Phoebe. He wanted Phoebe. Sophie, he loved. He was sure of that. But he wasn't in lieb with her. So why had his thoughts gone there? Was that the only way he knew to express his feelings to a girl he liked? His stomach churned and a wave of nausea made him put his hand to his mouth. What was wrong with him?

"Thank you." He choked out the words, whirled, and almost ran across the parking lot.

"You're welcome." Sophie hollered. "I don't know what your big hurry is. Whatever's chasing you can't be left behind. It won't stop bothering you. Not until you stop running and face it."

He wanted to yell at her that she didn't know what she was talking about, but he was afraid he'd vomit. Mostly because she was right. And it wasn't nice. And because he was too busy walking away.

He kept going until he reached the bus stop. He knew he'd been mean to Sophie, but he couldn't help it. She had him all mixed up. Out of breath, he eased on to the bench and turned her package over and over in his hands. Finally, he ripped off the brown wrapping paper fast, in one swoop, like ripping a bandage from a wound. As he had suspected, the gold lettering on the outside read *Holy Bible*. An Englisch translation. Little yellow sticky notes stuck out the top, marking pages. He opened the book and found a note from Sophie. "Start anywhere you like. You can't go wrong. But I like Micah 7:18-20."

Not able to resist, he turned to the page and began to read. He read it over and over again. Then closed the book and closed his eyes.

Thank You, God, for being faithful despite how often I mess up. You never fail. You forgive. Your grace never ends. Help me to help myself. To forgive myself. Show me the road. I feel like I'm walking around blind, bumping into things and people and hurting everyone in my path. Help me.

That was a new one. He'd moved on from *sorry* to asking for help. Some might call that progress. He called it desperation.

Chapter 31

Her hands damp with perspiration despite a brisk breeze that held a strong hint of the winter to come, Phoebe stuck her head through the doorway of Elijah and Bethel's house. It had been a long, brisk walk up the hill and across the creek from her house to her onkel's. It seemed they would skip fall and jump right into winter this year. After the heat of the summer, it felt good. Still, she'd worried the entire walk about what she was doing here. Was something wrong with the baby? Why would they want her? "Aenti Bethel? Onkel Elijah?"

She'd knocked on the screen door frame, but no one had answered. Probably because of the high-pitched caterwauling that carried from the back of the house. Baby John did not sound happy. Poor baby. What was going on?

"Bethel!" The baby's crying propelled her forward. Daed had stopped by the house to tell her Elijah wanted her to come over this afternoon. Something about helping with the baby. Why her of all people?

"There you are." Onkel Elijah strode from the long hallway that led to the bedrooms of this one-story house he'd built for his bride who needed crutches to get around. He had John on his chest, his huge hand covering most of the baby's body. He had to shout to be heard over the screams. "Glad you could make it."

"Daed said you wanted me." Phoebe hollered. "What's wrong with John?"

"I don't know. Bethel says maybe colic or just a plain old stomach-ache. It's not like he can tell us." Spoken like a man out of his element. His shirt was wrinkled and stained and he looked as if he hadn't slept in several days. "We need help."

That he put it so bluntly spoke to her onkel's state of mind. Elijah was the helper. He helped her learn to skate. He taught Elam to throw a baseball. He took care of groosdaadi and groosmammi when they were sick before they passed. He helped everyone.

"What can I do?"

Elijah gingerly held the baby out to her. John's red face scrunched up and his mouth widened as he bellowed. What lungs for a newborn. Quite strong. "Take him. He won't stop crying and now Bethel's sick and I need to go to town for a part. I need to get one more round of hay while I can. We need at least one more to make it through the winter. Plus the fence around the chicken yard needs work and we need to get ready to butcher the fryers…"

Phoebe hesitated. Elijah's beseeching look would almost be funny if he hadn't been intending to entrust her with the safekeeping of his only child. Why not Rachel or Molly or one of the aenties?

"What's wrong with Aenti Bethel?"

"Flu, I guess, or she ate something that didn't agree with her. She was up all night." The worry in Elijah's voice spoke to his feelings for his wife. They'd been married a little more than a year and still had that newlywed eyes-only-for-each-other look about them. "She doesn't want to get close to the baby and give it to him. She's so tired—she fell asleep a few minutes ago despite all this screaming. Take him, will you?"

"Are you sure you want me to do this?"

"What? I asked for you, didn't I? You came. You're standing here." He definitely needed to get some sleep. "Will you help or not?"

His determination to leave the baby with her might be the result of his inability to think straight in his state of sleep deprivation. Or else he trusted her. Phoebe didn't want to examine this possibility too much.

She held out her arms and Elijah plopped his firstborn into them. She began to rock him back and forth in her arms. "When did he last eat? Could he be hungry?"

"She fed him before she went to sleep. We thought that would make him happy, but it only seemed to make it worse."

"I'll see what I can do."

"I'll be back as soon as I take care of the chores." He fairly fled toward the door.

"Is there anything else I should..."

The screen door slammed.

Phoebe looked down at the crying baby. "Well, it's you and me. Let's see what we can do to get you settled down." She checked the diaper first. Dry. Not the problem. She settled into the rocking chair and began to rock, John's writhing body tense against her chest. "Come on, little one, hush, shush, shush, it's all right."

She cooed sweet nothings in his ear, but she doubted he could hear them over the sound of his own shrieks. "What's the matter, sweet pea, what's wrong?"

Rocking didn't seemed to be working. She laid him on her lap facedown and began to pat his back. Pat, pat, rub, rub, in a circular motion, like she'd seen her mudder do with Sarah when she had a tummy ache. All the while she hummed—soft, tuneless, humming.

The volume of the shrieking died down a little. Even when her arm began to tire, she kept up the *pat, pat, rub, rub* routine, letting her humming increase in volume ever so slightly.

John burped, a burp so loud it couldn't possibly have come from such a small bundle of bones. She giggled. She couldn't help it. He hiccupped another sob and fell silent.

"Oh, my. Oh, my."

She'd done it. She'd soothed the child. She looked around, wanting affirmation for her victory and finding none. No one had witnessed her conquering of a little baby's cries. No matter; she knew.

"You are a big boy with a big appetite." She slipped him from her lap to her shoulder and continued to pat as she wiped at the spit-up that soaked a growing spot on her apron. "What do we do now? You want to go outside for a walk? How about that? A little fresh air? A little sunshine?"

He grunted. The clean diaper probably wouldn't remain clean much longer. She hugged him to her chest and used her free hand to push through the screen door. Then she shifted him into the crook of her arm so he could look up at her. "Hi there, John. I'm your Cousin Phoebe. I'm the black sheep of the family so do as I say and not as I do, you hear?"

He babbled something, little bubbles of spit-up floating on his pink rosebud lips. "You look just like your daed, did you know that? You've got his chin and his nose and his hair. But you have your mudder's eyes."

She walked him out to the corral, introduced him to the horses, and then showed him the batch of kittens snuggled into a corner in the barn. By now, he'd grown heavy in her arms and she suspected he'd made a nice deposit in his sagging cloth diaper. "Time to go in and get you cleaned up, little one."

As she trotted up the steps to the door, it occurred to her she hadn't thought about anything else, anyone else, for more than an hour. Just her and little John in their small little world. She smiled at him. He smiled back, she was certain of it. "You are so sweet. You are a looker, little one."

She'd heard Bethel tell Elijah that once when she hadn't known Phoebe could hear. She figured if Elijah was a looker, so was his son. She pushed through the door to find Bethel shuffling on her crutches into the front room. "You're up? Are you feeling better?"

"How's the baby? Is he better?" Her face pale, hair straggling from her prayer kapp, Bethel eased into a chair at the table. She put a hand to her mouth and swallowed. "I woke up and didn't hear him crying. I was hoping he was asleep."

"He had a nice burp and now it smells like he needs his diaper changed." Phoebe pinched her nose with two fingers to emphasize the smell part. She kept her distance from her aenti. "How about you? How are you feeling?"

"A little rugged, but I'll live." She wiped at her face with a crumpled hankie. "It's already starting to pass."

"I'll change this diaper and then get you some hot tea and toast. It'll help settle your stomach."

"You're good at this, you know?"

Phoebe felt her body stiffen. John gazed up at her, his blue eyes sleepy. Despite the terrible smell emanating from his lower region—how could someone so cute and small smell so bad?—she leaned in to kiss feather-soft hairs the color of corn silk. "I don't know about that."

"I do. That's why I told Elijah to fetch you. Because I knew you would be able to settle him down."

"He just needed a good burp."

"You're good with babies."

"Not with every baby."

Bethel leaned back in the chair, looking wan. "You made a mistake. Something any of us could do. None of us is perfect. God loves us anyway."

Phoebe went to the cradle in the corner of the room and grabbed a diaper from a stack on the table next to it, along with a washcloth and towel. "Time to get you cleaned up, little one, before I pass out from the smell." She laid him on the couch, sat down at his feet, and went to work. She kept her gaze on his feet, no longer than her pinkie.

"Phoebe, when will you forgive yourself?"

"Did you…did you ever do something when you were courting Elijah that you knew you shouldn't have?"

"Like kiss him?"

Phoebe swiveled to look at her aunt. "You kissed Elijah?"

"He kissed me in your father's barn." She chuckled, the sound weak. "We weren't even courting, exactly. I mean, we mostly bickered and picked at each other. I think he was so fed up with me he did the only thing he could. He kissed me."

"Did you…I mean…what did you…what did you do?"

"Nothing. There was nothing to do. I could tell from the look on his face he was mortified. I thought he might never show his face again. But he did. He proposed to me at the clinic in town. He was near frozen to death from wandering around looking for me, thinking I was lost, but I wasn't. He was so shaken up, he asked me to marry him.

Then he kissed me again for good measure. By that time, I figured it was about to become a habit so I said yes."

"That's why you didn't want to wait until November."

"Phoebe!"

They both laughed, a sheepish-sounding laugh.

Silence prevailed except for the sound of John sucking on his fist when he could find it. Phoebe wiped down his bottom, dried him off well, and then tugged his legs up and planted a soft, clean diaper under him.

"You look like you're exactly where you should be," Bethel observed.

"The problem is…" She couldn't give voice to her fear. Mudder and Daed still hadn't given her permission to go to Springfield. If she didn't talk to Michael, she might never have this. She'd never want it with anyone else. Of that, she was certain. She fastened the diaper with long diaper pins and tugged John's shirt down over his potbelly. He gazed up at her with the most trusting look in his eyes.

"The problem is you've lost your assurance."

"Jah, that's it." Nodding, she lifted John into her lap. "My assurance."

"You silly goose."

"Hey!"

"Does your daed still love you despite what you think you did?"

There was no doubt about what she'd done. Lydia's death ensured that. "What I did."

"Purely by accident, with no bad intent."

Intent didn't matter. Consequences did. Even so, Bethel had a point. Her father had not abandoned or forsaken her, as hard as it must be for him. "Jah, he loves me. At least I think he does. He hasn't tossed me from the house. He looks at me when he talks to me."

"He loves you like a good father. God loves you with a father's love. He gave His Son for you. He's not going to stop loving you now."

"I know." She did know, but she didn't see how it helped.

"Have faith. God will give you what you need, even if it isn't what you want." Bethel straightened. "Look at me. I thought I had to conquer these crutches and stand on my own two feet to have the happiness that was right in front of me. It turns out that God holds me up, not the crutches. God provides for me what I can't provide for myself. He gave me Elijah, who sees to my every want and need. He gave me a son. He gives me what I need, not what I want."

Phoebe opened her mouth and then shut it. She hugged John to her chest and breathed in his sweet, sweet baby smell. She not only wanted Michael, she needed him. As much as she needed the air she breathed. "I'll get you some tea and toast."

"I know you want babies of your own."

"I do, but how do I know I'll be a good mother? I have bad instincts."

"No, you don't. You proved that to yourself today, with John. You just need to get things in the right order, that's all."

She was right. Phoebe knew she was right. "I told my mudder I need to go to Springfield."

"To talk to Michael."

"Jah."

"You do need to go."

"Problem is Daed doesn't think it's right." Mudder had tried, but Daed was as stubborn as an old tree stump refusing to be pulled from the ground. "He says it's not right for a girl to go to the city for a man."

"Convince him."

"You know my daed."

"What does Katie say?"

"She says she's working on it." Phoebe blew out a sigh. "She says I need to go."

"Then you'll go. When the time is right."

Right. "Look at me, sitting here gabbing on about my problems." Phoebe popped to her feet. "You need the tea. And the toast."

"I keep a bassinet in the kitchen. Makes it easier for me. You can tuck John in there and we'll have a nice visit." Bethel grabbed her crutches from the floor and hoisted herself from the rocking chair. "It's the coziest place in the house, anyway."

Phoebe nodded and kept her suspicions to herself. Bethel undoubtedly had a little flu, but she also had a hankering for a visit. She wanted to set Phoebe straight. No matter. She wanted to know more about that kiss in the barn.

"So when do you start teaching?"

Phoebe hunched her shoulders. Another topic she'd rather avoid. Bethel certainly knew how to stir the pot.

Chapter 32

Inhaling the scent of soap and clean air that emanated from the sheets, Katie shoved the pillows aside on the bed she shared with Silas, tugged back the top quilt, and smoothed the sheets. Blowing out a sigh, she turned to face her husband. He glowered at her, his skin darkening under his tan. They'd had this discussion three nights running now and he still hadn't come around to her way of thinking. Sometimes, it took him a while. She slapped both hands, fingers splayed on his chest. "She needs to go. I know you don't agree with me, but I'm asking you to please let her go. At least talk to Luke about it. Let him and Thomas guide us."

"It's not proper for a young girl to go into the city with a young boy, looking for one who's run away from his responsibilities." Silas backed away from her touch and pulled his nightshirt over his head. He stood in the middle of the room as if he couldn't decide where to go. "That's what Luke will say and Thomas will agree and they'll be right. Michael's family should go."

Katie had heard this argument before. She knew her daughter and she knew Daniel. They were good kinner. They'd known each other all their lives. They would take care of each other and keep each other safe and they would do the right thing. She had to trust them. If she put her trust in God, so did she have to trust that she'd done her best to raise Phoebe right. Her daughter had made a terrible mistake. She had learned from it. Katie trusted in that. She trusted God. Now, she just had to get Silas to see it her way. She rubbed his back in a widening circular motion, soft, gentle. "Phoebe will never move forward in her life if she doesn't have the chance to make things right with this boy."

"He's not a boy. He's a man. And he made his choice. He ran away instead of being baptized and committing to his community and his faith." Silas whirled and faced her. The pulse jumped in his temple and his eyes blazed with a fury she'd not seen there before. "There's no making things right with Michael Daugherty. Not for her. Not for us."

"You haven't forgiven him, have you?" Dumbstruck, she stared up at his face, at once more familiar than her own and yet one belonging to a stranger. She tugged at the collar on her nightgown, suddenly feeling exposed. "You said you did. I thought you did."

"I'm working on it."

He sank on to the bed. She hesitated for a second or two. He was her husband. He'd been her strength all these years, like an oak tree unbending in a furious wind. Now he needed her to be the strong one. She joined him, leaning close to inhale his comforting man scent.

"In my head, I know I need to do it. I have to do it." He thumped his fist against his chest. "It's here I'm having a bit of a struggle."

She covered his hand with her own. "I understand that. Believe me, I do. But your struggle is yours. Phoebe has her own." Katie swallowed against the nausea in her stomach. A bitter metallic taste filled the back of her throat. *Relax.* Had the doctor really told her to relax? "I don't want her to miss what we have because she can't move on."

Silas lowered his head into his big hands. "I know. It's not just her or Michael. It's what the doctor told you. I'm having a hard time with it."

She couldn't begin to tell him how hard it was for her too. A woman her age with small children. Wasn't it enough that she had the arthritis—a disease of older folks? Wasn't it enough that she'd lost Lydia? Now she had heart disease. Her mudder and daed had died of this disease. The doctor said it passed to each generation. It wasn't unexpected, he said. It certainly was unexpected to her. "Me too. But there's nothing we can do but make the best of it."

"You seem so calm. I feel ashamed." He raised his head and looked at her. To her astonishment, he had tears in his eyes. "The thought of you going on ahead of me—I never contemplated that. I always figured I'd go first. I trusted God's plan for us. He's blessed us over the years."

So had she. Then Lydia died. Now the road crumbled under her feet and she feared she would fall to her knees with each step. Somehow it wasn't surprising that this new challenge had followed on the heels of the loss of a child. Her world had tilted and would never be the same. Why should she be surprised? "I'm not going anywhere yet. The doctor said if I took the medicine, watched what I ate, and took it easy, I'd be fine."

"He doesn't know you. He doesn't understand our life." Silas's voice rose. It was so unlike him. Her steady partner also walked this crumbling road. "There's no taking it easy. Even if there was, you wouldn't know how."

He only spoke aloud what she had been thinking in her head. He had to have faith. If it were God's will that she go on without him, he would raise Elam, Hannah, and Sarah. Phoebe and their boys, now men, would help. "That's why we have to give it up to God. His plan. He's in control." Her words shook, not sounding nearly as certain and convincing as she had hoped. "That's what you've always told me all these years."

He snorted, a half laugh, half groan. "And now my faith is being tested. I'm to put my faith where my mouth is. As if losing Lydia wasn't enough."

"Something like that." She tried a smile on for size. It felt small and tight. "Have you prayed?"

"Jah. But mostly I want to shake my fist at God. He should strike me dead for being so…angry. I've never felt this way before."

"Pray some more." She scooted closer and laid her head against his chest. "For both of us. That we find our faith and our joy in the Lord again. Whatever happens, we will need it. And pray for Phoebe. And Michael. They need our prayers more than ever."

He slipped his arm around her and hugged her tight. "I'll talk to Luke and Thomas. They'll need a say in whether Phoebe goes to talk to Michael."

Her husband, the strong one, the certain one, had returned. Katie stifled a sigh of relief and huddled against him. They prayed.

Chapter 33

Phoebe had forgotten how noisy the city could be. Were they all like this or only Springfield? Cars honked, people yelled, music blared. And it smelled. Some good smells like the aroma of meat grilling that wafted from a food cart on the corner, but mostly exhaust fumes and nasty smells she didn't want to think about too much. She scurried faster, trying to keep up with Daniel. He set a determined pace, dodging in and out between the people coming toward them on the narrow sidewalk. She sidestepped a chunk of pink bubble-gum and nearly stepped on dog droppings. Daniel slowed, his gaze on the street map in his hand. He glanced up at a sign on the corner and veered left, nearly running her over.

"Are you sure this is the way to the diner?" She did a two-step and avoided getting her black sneaker stepped on by his heavy work boot. "I think we're lost. We should've hired a driver."

"The bus was cheaper. We're not lost. The guy in the convenience store said to go two blocks east and then three blocks south and take a left turn." Daniel sounded more confident than he looked. He pointed to the street sign. "See, this is Dexter Street."

"Do you think he'll be glad to see us?"

Daniel studied the map some more. "I don't know. In his letters, he always says he's doing fine, he's working, he's making a living."

Daniel had offered to let her read the handful of letters he'd received from Michael, but she'd declined. It felt like going where she wasn't wanted. If Michael wanted to talk to her, he'd write to her. Fat chance of that, it seemed. "Does he say he's happy?" Happy might not be the right word for a Plain man. "Is he content?"

"Can't say."

"What do you mean, you can't say?"

Daniel shoved his good Sunday service hat back on his head, his gaze on the map. "I don't know. Let's just worry about finding him for now."

That was the closest to angry she'd ever heard Daniel sound. This was hard for him too. Coming to the city. Looking for his friend. "Sorry."

"No need to be sorry." His tone softened. "I want him to come home too."

"For your wedding."

"Because he needs his community and his church."

"He does." She glanced around, determined to find this place, this diner with the funny name. Park Corner Diner. "Look there—across the park. See that sign flashing?"

Daniel swerved and they stepped into the street. A horn blared and a driver yelled dirty words at them. Daniel grabbed her arm and yanked her back to the curb.

"Oops." Daniel grinned at her. Despite herself she grinned back, albeit a shaky grin born of part hysteria, part relief. "Okay, that was close."

"We need to get a grip before we go in there." Daniel led the way toward the crosswalk. They waited for the light to change and the little walk sign people to show up below it. Then they marched into the park.

"Let's sit down for a minute." Daniel pointed to a bench. "Think about what we'll say."

"Think? I know what we'll say. I thought about it all the way here on the bus. We'll tell him it's time to come home."

"Will you tell him you've forgiven him?" Daniel plopped down on the bench. "He'll want to know."

Phoebe wavered. This question had pricked at her brain the entire bus ride, keeping her awake, giving her a headache. "I'll ask him if he's forgiven me."

"For what?"

"For being a temptation that caused him to do something that meant a little girl would die." To her surprise, her voice didn't quiver. "For turning away from him after it happened. That's why he left."

"He left because he couldn't face the consequences of his actions." Daniel's anger had returned. "He left because he let his family down and I let him down and you didn't stand by him. We all have blame."

"Sounds like you've learned something in all this." Much as she had. "It's changed you too. You should tell him that."

"He never said a word. He could've pointed the finger of blame at me, but he never did." Daniel folded the map into smaller and smaller squares. "Michael was always so quiet. He always let me do the talking. I should've shut up and listened when he said he just wanted to go fishing. He didn't want to take that walk."

"He wanted to do the right thing."

"He let me talk him into doing the wrong thing."

"Michael has a strong will. He doesn't do things he doesn't want to do. I've learned that just by watching him over the years." The meaning behind those words hit her square in the face. "He really wanted to spend time with me."

"He really did."

"And then it blew up in his face."

"And yours."

"It's time for all of us to move on from our mistakes. We're a small community, just getting started, and this thing has made it hard for us to be that community."

Daniel slapped the map against his thigh and stood. "Let's get Michael and go home. Together."

Daniel had grown up too. So wrapped up in her own misery and consequences, Phoebe hadn't even begun to look at the bigger consequences. "You really think he'll grab his bag and come home on the bus with us?"

"Depends on how good you are at picking your words."

"Me? I thought you were going to do the talking."

They trotted across the park, across the street, and came to the diner, still bickering.

Daniel put his hand on the door. Phoebe glanced in the long window. There Michael stood. Plain as day. Not so Plain anymore. Sporting a smile that showed his dimples and blue eyes under a red baseball cap, he braced an enormous plastic tub on the corner of a booth table. He picked up tea glasses and a coffee cup along with plates bearing the remains of eggs and hash browns and slung them into the tub. He didn't look up.

Daniel followed her gaze. "There he is."

"There he is."

"Let's go in."

Something in Phoebe balked. "Nee. Wait."

His back turned to the window now, Michael slid the tub on a metal cart. Then he turned around so she could see his face again. Still smiling. He enjoyed this job, clearing tables and washing dishes. He wiped his hands on his red apron and then he slid into the booth.

Phoebe opened her mouth and then closed it. She'd been so intent on drinking in the sight of him that she hadn't looked to see who sat in the booth. Now, she couldn't bear it. She swung her gaze to the other side. A girl—a woman really, about Phoebe's age—sat in the booth, her hands clasped in front of her on the table. She wore a blue flowered dress and a kapp. The Mennonite girl. She smiled at Michael. He smiled back and pushed a napkin toward her. She picked it up and dabbed at her lips, laughing.

Phoebe backed away from the window. Someone behind her grunted. "Hey, girlie, watch where you're going." A grimy hand shoved her forward.

Daniel caught her before she hit the window.

Michael swiveled and looked out. Their gazes met. The smile drained from his face, like a light suddenly extinguished.

The girl across from him glanced toward the window, her face puzzled. She said something. Michael shook his head, but he slid from the booth.

Phoebe backed away a second time. "Nee." She whirled and headed toward the street.

"Where are you going?" Daniel took a swipe at her arm and missed. "You wanted to talk to him."

"I changed my mind."

She raced into the park, seeking shelter. Seeking a place to hide. She ran past the vendor hawking fresh popcorn that smelled so good and the hot dog cart and two ladies each pushing double strollers. Michael had moved on. He didn't need her forgiveness. He didn't want it. He had made a life without her. Daniel would have to convince Michael to come back to his family and community. His faith. She wasn't needed. Maybe he would bring his new friend the Mennonite girl with him.

Out of breath, her stomach heaving, she sank onto an empty bench by the playground. Only a few children played on its slides, towers, and turrets. A little girl with blond hair in long pigtails skipped across the shredded rubber fill around the playscape, a teddy bear in her arms. She sang the ABC song at the top of her lungs, urging the bear to join in every now and then. Phoebe tried to look away from her shiny, happy face. She couldn't. The girl's chubby cheeks and carefree smile mesmerized her.

God, will this ever be over? Will I ever feel happy again? Do I have a right to be happy? Michael is happy. He's washing dishes and he's happy. What's wrong with me? Please, God, give me another chance to be happy.

How could she be happy without Michael in her life? She'd tried so hard to convince herself that she could. She could be good and content and be a teacher, lead a good life. But one second of seeing Michael with another girl and she was right back where she'd started.

The road in front of her stood empty and silent and she couldn't fathom where it led. Should she go left or right? Stay the course? No one could give her a map or point to street signs to show her the way.

"Phoebe."

Her heart jerked and banged against her rib cage. She closed her eyes, willing him to go away. She breathed in and out.

"Phoebe."

She opened her eyes.

"I can't believe you're here. I've had dreams about you coming here and now you're here."

"I can't believe it either."

"Do your parents know?"

"Jah. They asked Luke and Thomas for permission. I don't sneak around anymore. I've learned from my mistakes."

"My mistakes, you mean."

"I don't blame you for what happened." Not much. Not anymore.

"Jah, you do."

She wiggled in the seat, wishing she'd never come, wishing she could jump into a buggy and be gone. The image of a horse and buggy on the clogged streets of Springfield almost made her smile. Almost. "Where's Daniel?"

"I left him talking to Sophie."

The girl in the blue flowered dress had a name. Sophie. "So she's your new friend."

"She's a friend."

"Didn't take long."

Michael sat down on the bench. She slid farther away. "It's not like that."

She sideswiped him with a glance. He still had those same blue eyes, the same dimples, the same face, yet he looked so different in blue jeans and a T-shirt with the diner's name on the front. He still wore the cap and tufts of his hair stuck out around the bottom. He looked Englisch, and yet she could still see the Plain man she loved in those bottomless blue eyes. She gritted her teeth and looked away. "What is it like then?"

"Her dad has a ministry to help runaways."

"You're a runaway?"

"Nee. I'm a grown man who came here to start over. But sometimes he helps Plain kids and Sophie thought I might need some help."

"Helps them how?"

"Helps them find a way to go home."

"Is he going to help you go home?"

"Nee. I don't need his help." Michael used a fingernail to scrape dried food—ketchup maybe—from his jeans. "He's been a friend. Like Sophie's a friend."

"A special friend?"

"Why do you care? You didn't want anything to do with me after what happened."

Not true. Not true at all. "I was baptized."

"Daniel told me in his last letter."

"You need to come back. You need to be baptized too." She drew a shuddering breath and tried to calm her roiling stomach. If he came back, she'd have to face him at prayer services and she'd run into him in town. She'd have to face her mistake over and over again. "You can't let what happened come between you and God."

"But it can come between you and me."

"You have Sophie."

"I don't."

Phoebe stood. "Your parents and your brothers and sisters—all the families in New Hope want you to come home. They're worried for you. They're praying for you."

"And you?"

"I need to go home."

She began to retrace her steps to the diner. Michael kept pace, but he didn't speak, for which she was grateful. Everything had been said.

When they stood at the diner door, he caught her elbow and made her turn to face him. "Come inside. Get something to eat. The food is good. Meet Sophie. You'll like her. She actually reminds me of you." He stopped and his face turned a deep shade of red akin to roses in the spring. "Come inside."

"Nee. I did what I came to do. Tell Daniel to come outside. Please." She turned her back and pretended to watch the cars that raced by. "Please."

"I tried to call you."

Her heart picked up speed, slamming against her ribs again and again in a painful thud that increased in speed and intensity until she thought she would pass out. *Stop it. Stop it. Be good. Be good. Be good.*

"Phoebe." His voice was closer now. She looked up to find him bearing down on her, his face close to hers. She could smell his familiar woodsy scent and see the tiny scar on his chin where he'd jumped off the swings in the fourth grade and landed on his face. "I tried to call you and you didn't answer."

"I buried the phone."

"When?"

"Right after Lydia died."

"You wanted a fresh start."

"I want to be good."

"You are good."

"Nee."

"I will come home, Phoebe, if you want me to."

Phoebe made herself look at him. "You have to come home because you want to do it. Not because of me."

He stared at her, his eyes mesmerizing. Finally, he nodded. "I understand."

Phoebe was glad he understood, because she certainly didn't.

≈≋≋≋≋≈

"Where are you?"

Startled, Michael looked up from the mop he pushed across the floor in a steady, wet *slap, slap*. Someone had spilled syrup and let it dry, making his job that much harder at the end of a day that couldn't end soon enough. Oscar had gone to run an errand, but he would be back later to check to make sure everything in his restaurant was spotless. "What?"

"You're a thousand miles away." Crystal snapped her gum and applied elbow grease to some equally dry mustard on one of the tables. She grinned. "On a deserted island with Miss Sophie, eh?"

"Nee. No."

"Does it have something to do with the Amish girl who showed up here earlier today?"

He pushed the mop harder, focusing on the back and forth, back and forth motion. He didn't mind hard work, but he hated cleaning. It only turned up dirty again the next day. The monotony tore at him.

"Giving me the silent treatment, huh?" Crystal tossed the dish-rag into a sink behind the counter and picked up a bottle of cleanser. "Come on, you're looking at a twenty-two-year-old woman with two kids. I've been married twice, divorced twice. No one knows more about love than I do."

"You're twenty-two, you've been divorced twice. What you meant to say is no one knows less about love than you do."

"Ouch. Harsh." She blew a bubble that popped all over her lips, laughed, and began to pick it off. "Maybe I've learned from my mistakes."

Learned from her mistakes. That's what Phoebe was trying to do. The unending good in her wanted to do the right thing. Wanted to say all the right things. She wanted him to come home because she didn't want his eternal salvation on her conscience. Well, it wasn't. He'd led her down the path to temptation. Not vice versa. He understood that now. No one was to blame except him.

"You look so sad."

He glanced up. Crystal stood on the edge of the wet floor, her white sneakers not quite touching what he'd mopped. She knew better. She tilted her head. "Come on, spill the beans. How bad can it be?"

Seeing Phoebe again had brought it all back. The day at the lake. The look on her face after the funeral. The guilt. The rejection. The emptiness. He couldn't help himself. He wanted it out of his head.

By the time he finished the story, Crystal had tears in her eyes.

"You have to go home. Now."

"I can't."

"She's right." Sophie strolled through the diner. He'd been so intent on his story and Crystal's reaction, he hadn't heard her come in. "You have to go home."

"I thought we agreed you shouldn't be riding that scooter around after dark."

"Leo brought me in his car."

She'd been so anxious to talk to him, she'd been willing to owe her big brother a favor. "Fine. You know Crystal. Sit." He was tired of mopping and cleaning. He was tired of washing dishes. He hadn't known how tired until today. "I'll get us some iced tea."

She sat. "We're in agreement here. You have to go home."

"I'm done in here. I'll finish up in the kitchen." Crystal flashed her usual grin and laid a wad of bills on the table. "Your tips. Add them to your kitty and buy a bus ticket. Don't worry about Oscar. He can get another dishwasher in about five seconds."

"Why does everyone get to tell me what to do?" He set the glasses on the table and plopped down across from Sophie. "I moved to the city to be my own boss."

"You moved to the city to run away from your problems." Sophie waved to Crystal as she pushed through the kitchen door and disappeared. "You're a coward."

"I am not." Anger roared through him. Their friendship didn't give her the right to call him such a thing. "I didn't run away. I started over."

"You ran away. Phoebe needed you and you left her in the lurch after you got her in trouble."

The words hurt. It surprised him that he was able to feel any more hurt. It surprised him that Sophie would want to inflict that kind of hurt. "You don't know anything." His voice sounded rough, hoarse, in his own ears. "You don't know her. You weren't there."

"I'm your friend." Sophie spread her long, thin fingers on the table and studied them as if looking for an answer there. "That's why I'm telling you the truth. I'm telling you what you need to hear, not what you want to hear. Go home. Get back to your life before it's too late. That girl Phoebe is pretty and sweet and smart and another guy will come along and snatch her up once she gets over you."

"She's not interested in me anymore."

"She came all the way to town on a bus to tell you to come home. Does that sound like a girl who's over you?"

"She's worried about my eternal salvation."

"So am I. Again, that's why I want you to go home and live happily ever after."

"Plain folks don't live happily ever after."

"They come as close as anyone in this world because they choose to be content with what God gives them. Go. Be content."

"You really want to get rid of me that bad?"

Her smile disappeared. "I learned how to do this from my dad. He's the best."

A slight tremble in her voice gave her away. Michael pushed his advantage. "You really want me to go?"

"I've learned not to get attached to the runaways." Her gaze dropped to the table and her fingers began to draw circles in the condensation on her tea glass. "To care, but not to get so attached I can't see what's best for them."

"I'm not a runaway. So you don't care if I go?"

"I care. If you stay much longer, I won't be able to hold out." Her gaze came up. Her blue eyes were troubled. "I'll start to care and then you'll break my heart *and* Phoebe's heart. Tell me you don't want to go two-for-two?"

That he had the ability to do such a thing confounded him. He sought the words to answer, but his thoughts scattered in all directions, like trees tossed into the sky by a tornado.

Trying to buy time, he dumped toothpicks from the jar and began stacking them in two separate, neat piles. Sophie ran a finger through them so they mixed together, his pattern gone. "Go home."

The lump in his throat surprised him. "It almost sounds like you're telling me to stay."

"I'm not." But her face said differently. Her face said she really wanted him to stay. "Go."

"I'm sorry." The realization struck him with the force of a hammer. He didn't know if he was ready to go home, but he couldn't stay here. She was right. He had to go before he made it worse. "I didn't mean for this to happen."

"You didn't do anything."

He examined the painful fluttering in his chest. It came from the realization that he was about to hurt her. "I wish I felt what you feel."

"You can't. I've always known that. Your heart is already taken."

"Timothy likes you." He made the words an offering. "Did you know that?"

"I do."

"But you don't care for him?"

"Maybe someday. With time."

If Michael stepped back. "Me not being around would help."

"I don't know. Maybe."

Michael slid from the booth and removed his apron. "Crystal!"

She stuck her head through the double doors that led to the kitchen. "Yep?"

"Tell Oscar I'm sorry. I can't give two weeks' notice. He can keep my last paycheck."

"No way. I'll tell him to mail it to you." She snapped her gum. "Good luck."

He didn't believe in luck. "Thanks."

He didn't look back at Sophie as he strode to the front door. He didn't want to see the face of another friend left behind, but he heard her words just the same.

"Godspeed, Michael."

As always, the good friend. The words of her father sang in his ears. *God sets people in your path for a reason.* He'd needed a friend and God had given him Sophie. God gave Sophie a calling. Michael couldn't abuse her calling. Sophie was a smart girl. His heart was already taken. He couldn't get it back so he'd have to figure out how to go forward.

From her lips to God's ears.

Chapter 34

Michael climbed down from the truck cab, pulled his duffel bag from the bed, and waved at the farmer. The old man touched a finger to his dirty sweat-stained cowboy hat and put the rusted gray Ford in gear. Michael slammed the door and waited for the billowing dust to settle before beginning his trek up the dirt road leading to his parents' home. It had taken him three days to get up the nerve to buy the bus ticket. Three days sitting in his room while his head and his heart wrestled. He didn't know which one overcame, but here he stood.

Hitching a ride to the farm had been easy. Now came the hard part. Talking to his daed. Michael took his time walking the winding dirt road past fields of winter wheat and rye, rolling around the words in his head. How could he explain to his daed that washing dishes and talking to a Mennonite girl had given him a certain bit of peace? Life did go on. He couldn't undo what he'd done, but he could make peace with it and try to learn from it. He could stop blaming God for what he had done and start taking responsibility for it.

A brisk breeze drifted over him, bringing with it the smell of hay. A flock of birds flying south in formation passed overhead, slivers of gray against the fall sky. Quiet reigned, but if he listened hard enough he could hear his way of life approaching. No buses grinding gears. No taxi drivers honking horns. No brakes squealing. No men on street corners shaking their cups at him and demanding a dollar. No vendors luring him to their trailers with the aroma of roasting hotdogs. He had missed the quiet of the countryside. Even more, he'd missed his room and the smell of *kaffi* brewing on the stove and biscuits in the oven in the morning. He missed the sound of his mudder chattering with his sisters as she slapped a plate full of eggs and bacon on the table in front of his daed, who nodded and smiled at her, giving her that same look every day as if he couldn't imagine how he'd managed to marry her.

"Son."

He looked up from the rutted road to see his daed pulling up in the wagon. "Daed."

"You're back."

"Jah."

"Get in, then."

They rode in silence for several minutes. Michael could see his daed taking his measure with a series of sideways glances. He waited.

"They don't have food yonder?"

"They have plenty of food in Springfield, just none of it worth eating." That wasn't true. Oscar's chicken fried steak and gravy with mashed potatoes had been good grub. Mrs. Weaver's brownies had been good too. "Leastways not like Mudder's."

"You look like a scarecrow."

When he'd pulled his pants and blue shirt on that morning, he'd noticed they were more ample than before, but he hadn't given it much thought. "No one to cook and it cost too much to eat out."

"You can't cook?"

Mostly he hadn't had the desire or the appetite. "Not much."

"Me neither." His daed snapped the reins, his expression thoughtful. "So you decided to come home to your Mudder's cooking before you starved to death."

"Nee."

"You got everything figured out then?"

"Nee."

Daed snorted. He drove on a while, the silence between them full of unspoken words milling around all tangled up like fishing wire.

"I'm sorry for everything."

"Your apology is accepted, but it's your mudder you need to be talking to." Daed's voice, always low, sounded even more husky. He cleared his throat. "She missed you something fierce. Womenfolk, you know how they are, they worry."

"I know."

"I heard your friends paid you a visit."

"You heard?"

"Thomas, Silas, and Luke came by. They felt we ought to know they'd given Phoebe permission to go with Daniel to the city. I didn't abide much by the idea of sending the girl, but Silas is her daed. It was up to him."

"Silas came here?"

"He did."

"How is he?"

"Fair to middling, I'd say." Daed brought the buggy to a halt in front of the house. "His fraa needs some doctoring for her heart. Even when you put such things in God's hands, they can take a toll."

"There's something wrong with her heart?"

"Don't got nothing to do with what happened. Katie's parents both died of heart attacks."

"I didn't know that."

"You were young. People with bad tickers go earlier than most, but they have more treatments for it than they used to."

So now Phoebe's family would walk that road on top of everything else.

"You need to stay away from the girl."

His daed had always been good at reading his face.

"She came to see me."

"The way Silas and Luke explained it, Daniel and Phoebe were sent to remind you of what the cost would be if you didn't come home. They came for your sake, not theirs. That's the only reason a bishop would let such a thing happen. A girl and a boy traveling to the city like that. You need to get yourself baptized. You need to get right with God."

"I know."

"Phoebe got baptized. She's helping out at the school and fixing to be the new teacher."

"I know."

"So let it be. Let her be."

He couldn't do that. As much as his head said his daed was right, his heart couldn't let her go. "The day that—the day everything happened—I was thinking of courting her, serious like. Serious."

"I know."

"You know? How could you know?"

"I'm not blind, son."

"I kept thinking if I stayed away long enough, the feeling would go away."

"It doesn't work that way," Daed grunted. "'Course, what I know about such foolishness would fit on the end of a straight pin."

"I know that now. I just don't know what to do about it."

"Stay away from her until you get yourself right with the Lord."

"How do I do that?"

"Spend some time with Thomas. He'll counsel you." Daed climbed down and tied the reins to the hitching post. "In the meantime, leave her alone. She's making her own way. Let her be."

"I need—"

"Michael! Michael, you're home!" His mudder burst out the front door, both hands in the air as if hugging him from afar. "You're here!"

"I'm here."

"Well, get out of that wagon, then, and get over here and give your mudder a hug." She flapped her arms as if she would fly. "Tobias, food is on the table. Get the boys. I have to set another place."

Michael hopped from the wagon and strode toward her. She enveloped him in a hug, smelling of vanilla and sugar and cinnamon. Smelling of home.

"It's good you're here." She smiled, but tears brightened her faded blue eyes. "Things haven't been the same without you."

Nothing had changed here. He reveled in that thought for a moment. Then another thought reared up. They hadn't changed, but he had. He wasn't the same person who had courted Phoebe at the lake. He wasn't the same person who ran away.

So who was he now?

Chapter 35

The wedding season should be a time of great joy. Phoebe knew that. Her heart needed to get with the program. Another thing she hoped God wouldn't hold against her. Today, Abel and Deborah would start their married life together. It was a day of great celebration and it meant Phoebe would start her new job as teacher at the school. She shoved the thought away and focused on Luke, standing at the front of the Daugherty barn. The space was crowded with family, friends, and visitors. He was an old hand at it now, conducting these wedding ceremonies. Tomorrow, in deference to all the families who had traveled from Bliss Creek, he would lead the service for Rachel and Daniel. That way everyone could attend both services. Many would stay on for Thanksgiving the following week. The thought should cheer Phoebe. It did cheer her. It did. Didn't it? All the company and the cooking and the chatting. The blessings of family together during the holidays. She had so much for which to be thankful.

How many more times would she sit through this service and watch a man and a woman join hands and have their union blessed by God? How many times, knowing it would never be her? It couldn't be. The man she loved didn't love her back. It had been four days and Michael hadn't returned. A woman named Sophie surely kept him in Springfield.

Somehow, she'd convinced herself that Michael would come home. Not for her, but for his family and his community. He'd never been a selfish person and he knew what his absence did to his family. He knew what it meant not to be baptized. Still, with each day, she became less sure that he would do the right thing. The love of another woman was that strong.

She had to move on. Her mudder said so. Rachel said so. Only her heart refused to do it.

She wiggled. Mudder elbowed her and gave her the usual look. *Sit still.* Some things, at least, didn't change. Hannah sat on the other side, mollifying a grumpy Sarah with a cookie. Mudder had charged her with taking care of Sarah today. She'd been doing that a lot. Phoebe couldn't decide if it was to help Hannah get over her fears of losing another child in her charge, or if it was because Mudder seemed to be worn out all the time. She did look better today. Less drawn and pale. Like all the other New Hope women, she'd been baking and cooking for two days for the wedding feast that would follow today's service. A good wedding feast always perked her up.

Finally, Luke called Abel and Deborah's names. Deborah, her face flushed, eyes shining, almost ran to the front of the barn. Her friend Joanna Glick, serving as her second, scurried to keep up with her. Abel, looking as nervous as a chicken on a chopping block, followed more slowly. Deborah answered the questions so fast, she talked over Luke. She'd waited a long time for this moment; she obviously didn't want to wait any longer. Tears crowded Phoebe. She pushed them away. *Thank You, Gott, for blessing these two people. They are faithful followers.*

Why can't I have this?

The selfish questions shamed her. *I'm sorry. Please forgive me.*

That was all she did lately. Ask for forgiveness. God must be tired of it. She bowed her head and prayed He would forgive her weakness and make her stronger.

The two clasped hands. Luke's hand covered theirs. He spoke the final words.

Each word felt like a stab to Phoebe's heart.

"So then I may say with Raguel, the God of Abraham, the God of

Isaac, and the God of Jacob be with you and help you together and fulfill His blessing abundantly upon you, through Jesus Christ. Amen."

She wanted those words. She wanted everything that came with them. Husband. Kinner. Home. A family of her own.

Smiling, hands clasped, people began to stand. Sniffing hinted at happy tears shed. Handkerchiefs appeared. A swell of talking broke around her in a wave. Still, Phoebe couldn't move, she was so caught in the agony of wanting something she couldn't have, might never have.

Another elbow to the ribs. "It's time," Mudder whispered. "We'd best get to the kitchen and help with the serving."

Silas and Thomas shoved open the barn doors and the crowd poured into the yard. Phoebe forced herself to stand on legs that felt a hundred years old. She needed a minute. She couldn't walk into the sunlight. Mudder would see her selfishness written all over her face. "I'm right behind you. I want to congratulate Deborah."

Her mudder was already carried away in the crush of people wanting to say hello and ask her how she was doing. She would be stopped a dozen times or more between the barn and the house, by all the friends and family happy to be here for a joyful occasion. Their last trip to New Hope had been for a funeral.

Phoebe braced herself and tried to squeeze her way toward the cluster of people who stood around Deborah and Abel. No use. She couldn't get close. Better she should wait in the yard. She might be able to walk with them into the house.

She put her head down and made her own path toward the yard.

"Hey. Long time no see."

She looked up. Richard Bontrager loomed over her. "Good service, eh?"

"Jah." She'd been rude to Richard the last time he offered to take her for a ride. Why did he bother with her? Because he was a nice man who liked her. She could at least be nice back. "Deborah and Abel make a good couple."

"Smells like there will be some good food too." He jerked his head toward the house. "You have to help with the serving?"

Of course she did. *Be nice.* "Jah. I'll take a shift in a few minutes."
She struggled for something to say. Anything. "A lot of work right
now?"

"Plenty to keep a man busy." He snapped his fingers as if eager to
get to it. "Plenty."

This was awful.

"You want to take a walk?"

"What?"

"Truth be told, I'm not that hungry and I'm tired of sitting. I'd like
to stretch my legs."

Her mind froze. She wasn't hungry either, but she'd just said she
had to help with the serving. There were at least three or four dozen
women to do the serving. They would do it in shifts. Nothing said she
couldn't take a later shift.

Was she really considering doing this? It wasn't bad. She was moving on. Trying to move on.

The image of Sophie sitting in the booth smiling up at Michael
played in a continuous loop in her head, keeping her awake at night.
Her throat closed up. She glanced around. No one would notice. They
were too busy visiting. She had no responsibilities in this moment.
Hannah had been charged with watching Sarah, along with the other
girls who would mind the kinner while the older girls helped with the
serving.

Anything to get out of this crush of people. Anything to get away
from the words of the wedding ceremony still ringing in her ears. Anything to blot out the image of Michael smiling down at Sophie. She
had to move on, whether she liked it or not. God's plan. "Truth be told,
I'm not that hungry either."

Richard's grin stretched across his face. He had that nice smile. No
dimples. Just a solid jaw and full lips. Dark brown eyes.

"This way." He angled toward the road and the long line of buggies
that stretched endlessly ahead of them. "You seem better."

"I am better."

"I'm glad."

They walked in silence past horses that nickered and went back to eating grass in the meadow across from the buggies. The wind whistled out of the north and she shivered.

"Winter's here."

"It is."

"I should've waited while you went in to get your shawl."

"I'm fine."

They continued to walk, the only sound the horses and the squawk of birds arguing in the trees over head.

"I've never found this to be so hard." He doffed his hat and scratched at his thick brown hair. "Talking to a girl, I mean."

"Me either." She chuckled, in spite of herself. "I mean, it's not usually this hard for me to talk to a man. Not that I talk to a lot of them."

He laughed outright. "I knew what you meant. I moved to Bliss Creek later. We didn't have all that time growing up together. Makes it harder, I expect."

"But your aunt and uncle have lived in Bliss Creek forever. Michael's your cousin; that makes you one of us."

"I'm related…" His gaze drifted ahead of them. "Someone's coming."

She followed his gaze. A horse and buggy came toward them at a pretty good clip. Who was it? The entire New Hope Plain community, along with their visitors from Bliss Creek, had already gathered at Peter's farm. She strained to see who was driving. Was that Daniel? No, he'd been in the barn for the wedding.

"Is that…" Richard frowned. "It's Michael. I guess he came home. Onkel Peter didn't mention it."

Phoebe stopped in the middle of the road. The buggy gained on them quickly. It was Michael, indeed. He'd missed the wedding, but still, here he was. Finally.

Michael pulled up on the reins and the buggy slowed. It slowed some more as it reached them until it stopped in front of them, blocking the road. Richard spoke first. "Welcome back, cousin."

Michael didn't answer, but he nodded, his gaze on Phoebe, his expression bleak. She stared back at him. She didn't owe him any explanations. It was broad daylight on a dirt road on his cousin's farm. He'd been gone almost five months.

"I'm late for the wedding." His tone revealed nothing. "I best get on up to the house."

Richard stepped aside. She should move too, but she couldn't seem to lift her feet. "Michael."

"Move." Michael snapped the reins as if for punctuation. The pulse in his jaw leaped. His gaze roved beyond her, never connecting. It was as if she'd been grazed by the blade of a newly sharpened knife, passing so near it drew blood. "Please."

She managed to pick up her feet. They felt as if they weighed ten pounds each. Moving like an old woman, she trudged to the side of the road. Richard followed. The buggy moved past them. "I'm glad you're back." She whispered the words. "Finally."

The buggy rocked and whipped forward as if pushed by a violent wind. Her words were lost in the clatter of the wheels and the clip-clop of the hooves. Dust whipped up and clouded the back of the buggy, making it seem as if it disappeared into a fog.

"Seems my cousin is in a hurry." Richard's tone was soft. It reminded her of the way her daed talked to the horses when something spooked them. "I imagine he feels he has amends to make with quite a few folks. Especially you."

"Nee." A shiver wracked her. Michael was the one who'd started up with another. Not her. She only wanted to take a walk, breathe the fresh air. And not be so alone for a few minutes. "It's fine."

"It's not fine. You don't deserve it."

"I don't know." She glanced back at the buggy moving away at a fast clip, dust billowing behind it. "I should probably go back and help with the serving."

"You will." His hand touched her arm and drew her back into the road, gently, but with determination. "First we walk and you talk."

The sad tale of her trip with Daniel to Springfield became no less dreary with the telling. Richard didn't say anything after she finished. He veered toward the tree line and the creek. She kept up easily with his smooth stride, as if he tailored his steps to hers. Heated by her exertion, she now welcomed the northerly breeze. Richard ducked under

a tree branch and then held it up for her. The stream gurgled ahead of
them. "Aren't you going to say something?"

"I imagine you've had your fill of people telling you what you should
feel and how you should act. Truth is there's nothing I can say to make
it better." He weaved between two oaks and trudged ahead. "Truth be
told, I'm not sure I want to make it better."

It might be the truth, but somehow she wished he would try harder.
"What do you mean?"

"It's not like I'm out here tramping around in the cold for my health."

The truth of his words—the obviousness of it—hit her. "*Ach*,
Richard."

He tramped ahead of her, not looking back.

"You knew I went to Springfield."

"Jah."

"Yet you asked me to take a walk."

"You went to bring a friend back to his faith and his community."
He paused on the banks of the creek, staring down at the rush of water,
its burbling loud in the quiet. "That's what I heard."

"That's true. But there's more." She followed him down to the edge,
close enough that her Sunday service shoes sank in the mud. "I wanted
to…there was more to it. You knew what was between Michael and me.
What happened to us and why."

"I know." He cut across the creek bank and headed for some rocks
that made a natural bridge. "I hoped maybe you got your answer and
were ready to go on with your life as he has done."

"Seeing him with someone else only made me feel…more."

Richard's gaze traveled beyond her, looking back as if seeking something. "I reckon that's how Michael feels about now."

His point pierced her to the bone. "I don't think so. He has her."

"He came back, didn't he?"

So he had. "He did, but I don't know why or for how long."

"We'd best get back to the house."

"Why?"

"You know why."

She did know why. Her walk with Richard Bontrager needed to end. For his sake as much as hers.

✤✤✤

Michael strode between the clusters of people visiting outside the house. He needed to find Deborah and Abel, offer his congratulations, and then go. He couldn't be here. It had been a mistake to come. His father's words of advice rang in his head. *Leave her be.* He'd had every intention of following Daed's command. It wasn't his fault she'd been right there on the road, between the wedding celebration and him.

She and Richard. A good man. His cousin. A man Michael respected and liked. She would be better off with a man like Richard.

He wanted to talk to her. He wanted to walk around the creek with her. He wanted to inhale the scent of her. He wanted to know everything about her.

It had been a mistake to come back. If he'd stayed in Springfield, he might have been able to build something new with Sophie. He liked her. He could've learned to love her. Nee, not fair to her. She deserved a man who loved her first, loved her only.

Besides, he couldn't give up his faith and his family and his community. That would be a terrible price to pay in order to distance himself from a woman he loved. One he would come to regret—and a marriage could not be built on regret.

He squeezed through the tables in the front room of Onkel Peter's house. Aenti Helen rushed by him, a platter of roast and stuffing in her hands. Emma Shirack followed behind, carrying mashed potatoes and a basket of rolls. He trailed after them until they arrived at the wedding table. Deborah and Abel were seated among friends, laughing and eating but looking dazed.

"You're here." Deborah clapped her hands. "You made it. I'm so glad. It's so good to see you."

"I'm not staying."

"You're leaving town again?"

"Nee, nee," he stammered. "I mean, I wanted to tell you and Abel congratulations. I'm not feeling well, so I'm going to head out."

"*Ach*, sit a bit. Have some food, you'll feel better. You have to have cake. There's going to be singing and games and more food."

"Enjoy. It's your day. I mean that." He patted his nonexistent belly. "Something didn't sit right. I don't want to spoil the day."

She tilted her head and frowned. "You do look a little peaked, now that I look at you."

"Sorry. I'll see you when you come visiting. I know Mudder has a nice little surprise for you—for your new house in Bliss Creek."

"That's so nice. We'll be visiting until after Thanksgiving, and then we'll head to Bliss Creek." Her smile disappeared. "I'll miss you, Daniel, Rachel, Molly…"

"And Phoebe. You can say her name, you know."

"I didn't know if you were still…"

"This is your day. I won't spoil it."

"Nothing could." She slid back into her seat next to Abel, who looked at her with puppy dog eyes. Did all men in love look like that on their wedding day? Most likely he would never know. "You'll see. You'll find out for yourself some day."

He didn't want to argue with the bride on her wedding day. "We'll see."

"Michael."

He turned at the sound of his name. Thomas waved his big hand. "Come."

It wasn't a request. He said his goodbyes and followed Thomas through the kitchen and out the back door. Fewer folks congregated in this area. Thomas headed for a picnic table beyond a massive barbecue grill. "Sit."

He sat. What else could he do? Thomas was not only a good friend to his daed, but the community's deacon. "I'm glad you're back." Thomas flattened both big hands on the weather-beaten, graying wooden table. "Tobias came by this morning and told me. He asked me to speak with you."

"Jah."

Thomas didn't say anything. The silence stretched, making the skin on the back of Michael's neck prickle. He shifted in his seat. The sun dipped behind clouds scudding across the sky. The wind picked up, sending a shiver through him. Hard to believe Thanksgiving would be next week. Winter. They might get snow by then.

He glanced at Thomas. The man's dark eyes were warm behind his gold-rimmed glasses. "What did you want to talk about?"

"I think you know."

"My daed wants me to leave Phoebe alone."

"This isn't about Phoebe."

He chewed the inside of his lip. "Baptism, then."

"Jah, and whether you think the months you spent in the city changed the way you feel about baptism."

The memories of Sophie's smiling face and Timothy in the batter's box and Crystal sipping from her Kansas City Chiefs cup and grimacing at the thick, black sludge her uncle called coffee warred with the dark nights and the smell of garbage in the motel parking lot and the incessant noise. "If anything, the things that happened to me—the things I did or didn't do—those things made me more sure."

Thomas's face broke into a broad grin. "Good to hear. Very good."

"It's too late for this year, isn't it? You've already had the baptisms and communion."

"We can consider baptisms for spring communion, before Easter."

That gave him four months to figure out if he could do it. Could he commit himself to a God who didn't answer his prayers the way he wanted them—needed them—to be answered? Could he live here within a stone's throw of the girl he loved, knowing she'd moved on? Why had she come to Springfield to convince him to return, if she really had moved on? And why didn't Daniel tell him? Why would his best friend let him walk—drive—into the most awkward and hurtful of situations without saying a word?

The questions pummeled him. He felt like a punching bag for question marks.

The hardest-hitting question smacked him between the eyes. Could he live with the constant reminders of what he'd done here?

"Michael?" Thomas's grin had faded. "Something you want to tell me?"

"Nee. I just need time to think."

"Don't worry. I'm not asking for a commitment now." Thomas smoothed his beard, his expression somber. "You and I need to do some talking first. And then you need to do some thinking."

"That's all I do it seems. Think. I'm sick of thinking."

Thomas chuckled and swung his legs over the bench so he could stand. "If it makes your head hurt, that's a good sign your brain's working. You'll figure it out. Just don't give up." He grinned down at Michael. "You came home for a reason. Don't lose sight of what it was—or who it was."

What did Thomas know? Everything, it seemed. "I won't."

"*Gut.*" Thomas tipped his hat and ambled away. "Be at my house Monday night after chores," he tossed the words over his shoulder. "Don't be late. I'm getting old. I go to bed early."

"Right." He would go home and help his daed with chores and learn to live with what he'd done.

The bleak thought made him roll up from his seat. First order of business was to figure out how to get Phoebe back. He'd returned for her. It had been a mistake to leave her. It wasn't his first and it wouldn't be his last. Richard would have to understand.

He'd taken the first step by returning home. He wasn't a coward. He'd come home to be baptized, to be with his family and his community. He'd come home for Phoebe.

After everything that had been lost through their mistakes, he wouldn't allow their future to be lost too.

Chapter 36

The temperatures had done that sudden autumn drop that always surprised people and reminded them that winter stood on the horizon, waiting impatiently to make an appearance. Phoebe leaned against the porch railing, her shawl wrapped over her shoulders, wishing she had her wool bonnet. The kinner, full of wedding feast for the second day in a row, were running off the excess energy with an exuberant game of kickball. Eli belted the ball over his sister's head and it sailed into a piercing sky so blue it hurt to look up. He whooped and lit out for first base. Phoebe clapped. "Good one!"

Grumbling, Rebecca chased the ball out to the corral while her brother zoomed around the makeshift bases that consisted of old floor rugs destined for secondhand use of some sort in the barn. Eli made it to third before Rebecca could toss the ball to Elam, who stood between second and third.

"We need a new pitcher," Lillie called from first base. "Come on, Phoebe, be the pitcher."

"Hey, I'm not doing so bad," William pouted. "I can't help it Eli has such big feet he can't miss."

Everyone whooped and hollered at William's teasing. Phoebe shook her head, but she moved from the porch to the steps, squeezing past her brothers who sat on the steps discussing the price of hay or some such thing that ought to be left for a work day, not the day of Daniel and

Rachel's wedding. Determined to see joy in this day, Phoebe smiled down at them. Today's service had been easier than that of the previous day. Practice made perfect? No, she saw the joy in her friend's face and could only feel joy in return. Daniel and Rachel were in love and this was their special day. "This is a day of celebration." She thunked Simon on his hat with her thumb and middle finger. He ducked. "Leave the talk of work for tomorrow."

Simon tugged at her skirt and smiled up at her. "I could say the same to you. Go play. Everyone knows you're the best kickball player around."

She had been pretty good once. She hesitated. She had vowed to set aside childish play.

"Go on," Martin chimed in. "Enjoy the day."

It meant so much to her that her brothers had gone back to treating her like the old Phoebe, the sister they liked to tease, the sister who hadn't yet disappointed them. They were two branches from the same sturdy tree. Broad shoulders, blond hair, blue eyes. Simple men content with their simple lives. Encouraged by their grins, she shrugged off the shawl, laid it on the railing, and trotted into the yard.

"Hand it over!" She crooked a finger at William. "Let me give it a shot."

Her first roll of the ball was dead center on the plate. Helen's daughter Betty whacked it a good one, but it came right back at Phoebe. She scampered forward, scooped up the ball, and slung it to Lillie at first base. "You're out of here! That's three outs."

The team behind her cheered and ran off the makeshift field.

"You're up first." Mary and Lillie, so alike in features she couldn't tell them apart, grabbed her hands and propelled her to home plate. "You first, teacher."

They'd been the first to call her that. Teacher. Monday would be her first day. A short week because of the Thanksgiving holiday on Thursday, but enough to get her feet wet. She shoved the thought aside. Today was for visiting and celebrating the union of her good friends.

She focused on Nathan's throw. The ball came right at her. She swung her foot out and met the ball square-on.

"Go, go, go!" Lillie and Mary screamed from the sideline. "Go, teacher, go!"

The rest of the kinner jumped up and down and yelled encouragement. She lifted her skirt and ran toward first base ahead of the throw from Jonathan at second base. Laughing, breathless, she careened around the corner and then backed up, foot squarely on the rug that marked the base. "I made it!"

"You made it."

That voice. She'd been avoiding it all day. She glanced back. Michael stood in the shade of the oak near the corner of the house. He stepped into the sun. His black pants, suspenders, and blue shirt were back. In honor of the wedding service, he wore his black jacket and black hat. He looked as Plain as ever. They both knew he wasn't. He couldn't be, not after his time away.

It didn't matter. Today was Daniel and Rachel's day. A day to celebrate.

"You should be with Daniel. You're his second."

She kept one foot on the rug, waiting for Nathan to throw the ball to Mary, who had both hands in fists at her sides, sneakers at the ready, a look of fierce determination on her freckled face. The twins were the spitting image of their sister Emma. And just as sweet and fun.

"He's fine."

She had been glad Rachel had chosen Molly to be her second. It saved her from standing in front of their community only a few feet from Michael. "This is one of the most important days of his life."

A day she'd once hoped they would also enjoy together.

"I needed a breath of fresh air. They're still going strong inside. The singing has started."

"Michael, play with us!" Eli shouted from behind home plate. "We need another player."

"No more big people," Lillie argued. "They kick too hard."

"Nee, no more." Elam stood behind home plate, arms crossed, no longer smiling. "We've got enough players."

"That's okay." Michael's gaze stayed on Phoebe. Her chest tightened at the sight of those dark blue eyes, so somber. The light once there had been extinguished. No more dimples, either. He looked older. "I'm more in the mood for can jam."

"We couldn't find the Frisbee." Eli's grin said he didn't mind. "Besides, all the trash cans are being used for the wedding."

Michael shrugged. "I have to get back inside to the *eck*, anyway. As Phoebe has said, I can't shirk my duties as Daniel's second on a day like today."

So why had he come out here? He should be sitting at the corner table with the wedding party. Had he been looking for her? Phoebe didn't dare ask. *Be good. Be good.* She was a teacher now. All grown up. *Be good. Be good.*

Nathan rolled the ball to Mary. She kicked wildly, missed, and sat down hard on her behind. The kinner roared. "It's not funny." She scrambled to her feet, rubbing her backside. "Give me another."

"That's strike one," Nathan yelled. "Here comes another."

"Richard paid me a visit last night." Michael took a step closer to first base. He kept his voice low. Phoebe had to strain to hear over the chatter on the field. "He said I shouldn't worry about what I saw yesterday. Is he right?"

Richard had gone to speak with Michael. Why in the world would he do that? Richard shouldn't have stuck his nose where it didn't belong. She crept off the base as Nathan wound up and tossed the ball. Lillie missed again. Phoebe rushed back to her base. This was no place for this conversation. Betty Crouch, the first baseman, had curiosity written all over her face. She would surely report everything to her mudder Helen.

"Go away, Michael."

"Richard meant well. He wanted me to know that he laid no claim."

Laid no claim. The sheer audacity of such a conversation bowled her over. She forgot about the game and the big ears on little girls. "He never even shone his flashlight in my window. He has no right to even—"

"Sometimes, it's not what you think."

Richard meant well. He'd let her go with grace. "He has no claim on me." The words came out louder than she intended. Betty scooted closer to the base, eying them both with obvious interest. Phoebe forced the volume down. "No one does. Now go away."

"Because I came back you've decided to stop seeing him?" He sounded mad. He had no right to be mad. She hadn't been courting with Richard, but even if she had, Michael had no claim on her. Not since he rushed off to Springfield and started hanging around a girl called Sophie.

"I'm not interested in more problems." She dusted her hands on her apron and prepared to dash to second base. *Be good. Be good.* "Please go inside. Now."

Simon and Martin stood. Even after five years of marriage for Simon and three for Martin, they seemed to move as a unit. Elam strode from the field and joined them. "You're back." The three of them stopped within a few yards of Michael. "We heard you'd turned Englisch."

"You heard wrong." Michael took a step back and leaned against the tree. His tone was calm but firm. Still, tension radiated in the set of his shoulders and the grip of his hand on his knee on the leg he propped against the trunk. "I came back to finish my classes, get on with my baptism."

"Your parents must be real happy about that." Simon chewed on a long blade of grass. "They've got some mighty fine cake in there. You might want to get some before it's all gone."

Michael straightened. His gaze brushed against Phoebe's. "I was just leaving." He made a wide berth around her brothers. "See you, Phoebe."

What could she say to that? Mary connected with Nathan's next pitch and the ball rocketed across the yard. It smacked Michael in the back of the head, saving Phoebe from having to answer.

"Ouch. Hey!"

Mary hopped up and down and then took off for first base. "Sorry, Michael, sorry!" she yelled, but didn't slow. The others clapped and hooted. Especially Elam, who looked tickled. "Wahoo!"

Phoebe couldn't help it. She giggled and raced toward second. Michael whirled and scooped up the ball. His face had turned red, but he grinned. "I'll get you, Mary Shirack. My throwing arm is rusty, but I still got it."

He loped across the yard, the ball in hand. Mary shrieked and headed for second. Phoebe raced for third. Michael's throw went wide, but Naomi raced forward to snag it and tag Mary, who made the mistake of taking her foot off the rug as if to try for third right as Phoebe headed for home plate.

"Gotcha! You're out, Mary." Naomi whirled and hurled the ball to home plate, giggling all the while. "Thanks, Michael!"

"I told you I still got it." His gaze collided with Phoebe's. He looked so wistful. "Some things, anyway."

"Play with us, Michael, come on!" Eli and Rebecca joined in the chorus with Lillie, Mary, Joseph, and William. "Come on. It'll be fun."

Michael glanced at Phoebe's brothers, who still stood side by side on the edge of the field as if they were watching the game. Their gazes were riveted to Michael. "I'd better get back."

Once again, he strode toward the house. This time, he didn't turn around. She considered hitting him with a ball herself, but the look on Simon's face as he walked around their makeshift field and made his way to home plate kept her glued to her spot.

"Mudder and Daed have been through enough." Simon twirled the blade of grass between two fingers. "You know what I mean."

"I know what you mean."

"*Gut.*"

"I'm grown up now. I'm a teacher."

"*Gut.*"

He didn't sound as if he believed her.

That didn't surprise Phoebe. She hardly believed it herself. It was all she could do to keep from dashing up the steps and into the house to find Michael.

Gott, forgive me.

Despite the pretty girl named Sophie, despite everything, she still loved him.

It didn't matter. Sometimes, love wasn't enough to fix things. If anyone knew that, she did.

Chapter 37

His bow heavy in his hands, Michael slowed and then stopped, not wanting his boots to make a crunching sound on the frosty crust of the snow. His daed and Silas did the same. The puffs of their breath hung suspended in the icy morning air and then dissipated. They hadn't even made it to the tree stand his daed built the previous week when they picked up the hoof prints in the freshly fallen snow—the first of the season. A regal buck, its antlers broad and heavy, stood on the edge of a small clearing, his nose close to the ground as if sniffing for leaves or grass under the blanket of snow. Michael caught his daed's slight nod in his peripheral vision. The need for silence kept him from deferring to the older men for the first shot. *Smell and sound, a hunter's biggest enemies.* The familiar refrain echoed in his memory from all the years his daed had taken him hunting as a boy. Daed even took a bath the night before, something that never ceased to amaze Michael. Tobias Daugherty hated bathing with a passion.

He liked hunting and he was giving Michael the first shot of the archery hunting season. That said something too. What, Michael couldn't be sure. Life returned to normal. It marched forward, surely and inexorably. A person either went with it or got left behind, doomed to live the same painful moment over and over again.

A simple invitation to hunt moved his life forward. His dad might not say it, but he meant it. Did Silas feel the same? How could he?

Focus.

Michael measured the distance. No more than thirty yards, well within range. Hand on the back end of the arrow, he inched his bow up and took aim. He pulled the string taut, feeling every bit of the fifty pounds of tension needed to pull it back twenty-eight inches. Carting around tubs of dirty dishes had served some better purpose.

Steady, steady.

The buck raised his head, his dark eyes bright in the dazzling sunlight. He danced on the shimmering snow and tossed his head, his neck long and graceful. Swinging around as if to bolt, he gave Michael the broadside target he sought.

Now.

A clean, sure shot, the sound a zing in the stillness. The deer snorted, bucked, and went down.

Michael let out his breath. Daed brushed past, his bow at the ready. "Good shot. Hit him right behind the elbow of his front leg."

A kill shot.

Michael was glad. He found no joy in taking the life of a magnificent creature such as this, one of God's creatures. Better he not suffer. Michael did take pleasure in knowing the venison would feed their family this winter. With the fryers that had been butchered during the frolic earlier in the week and the wild turkey and pheasant already hunted, they assured themselves that they would eat through the bitterest of cold winters.

He slotted another arrow in his bow. "Is he gone?"

Silas moved forward, his own bow still raised. After a few seconds, he snatched a branch from the ground, shook off the snow, and touched the animal's shoulder. "His eyes aren't moving."

Michael hung back, letting the older men take the buck's measure. He'd been surprised—shocked almost—when his daed suggested he accompany him on the first hunt of the season. He'd been even more surprised when Silas drove up to the house well before dawn. Daed could've mentioned he was coming, but chose not to. Michael still didn't know why.

Silas didn't have much to say. A nod of his head. Hand out to accept the cup of kaffi Mudder offered. An affirmative grunt that the weather was good for the first hunt. That had been the extent of their early morning conversation. Which suited Michael fine. Nothing left to say. Yet something still lingered in the air, something heavy and dark on his shoulders every time he looked at Silas and saw in his blue eyes, the shape of his mouth, and his high cheekbones the face of a little girl no longer with them.

The ride out to the meadow edged by a deep stand of trees had been equally quiet. Michael kept waiting for Silas to give him some hint of what went on in his mind. Nothing. An occasional grunt of *jah* or *nee* in response to Daed's conversation about hunting turkey after they bagged their limit on deer. That was it.

Silas slid his pack from his back and settled it on the ground next to the animal. "Let's get him dressed."

Daed chuckled, a deep, rumbling sound in the stillness of the morning. His laugh always made Michael want to laugh. For a minute, Michael had that feeling, that feeling that life could maybe get back to normal. It could be like it once was when he was a boy, hunting with his father.

Silas looked up from pulling his knife from the pack on his shoulder. "What's so funny?"

Daed slapped Michael on the back. "I was just remembering the first time I took this boy hunting. You were what? Five, six?"

"Six." Michael knew what was coming. His daed loved to tell this story. "We were hunting deer with rifles then."

"You didn't have the strength yet to use a bow." Daed leaned his bow against a nearby spruce and shed his gloves. "Anyway, I told him we needed to dress the deer. He wanted to know why a dead deer needed clothes."

The deep lines around Silas's mouth and eyes dissolved into a full-out grin. "Ain't nothing to be ashamed of. I think my brother Elijah might've asked the same question. My boys were too excited to give it much thought."

Michael let his gaze rove beyond the two men, trying to capture again the joy he'd felt in those days, the abiding joy of being chosen to hunt with Daed. Daed had given him the gift of a day, just the two of them. Father and son gathering food for the family. A long, quiet day sitting in the stand with few words spoken, sharing a companionable silence. A good day, one of many he would share over the years with Daed.

"You handle the bow well." Silas wiped the blade of his knife against his leg and then crouched. "Clean, merciful shot. You like bow hunting better than rifle?"

Pleased at Silas's assessment of his skill, Michael considered the question as he squatted next to the deer and helped roll it on its back. "It seems fairer, I guess."

"You mean more sporting?"

"Jah, more sporting. The animal has more of a fighting chance."

"We don't hunt for sport."

"I know. We hunt to eat. But they are God's creatures and they're beautiful."

"They are." Silas stuck his knife under the hide and cut the deer in one long, straight slice across his belly. "All of God's creatures are beautiful."

He let one knee drop to the ground and looked up at Michael. "Ain't one of them perfect."

Michael froze, caught in the older man's piercing gaze. What was he saying? "Nee, not one."

"Not one."

Silas went back to the task at hand. Between the three of them, they made quick work of it. They'd done this hundreds of times, but it never ceased to amaze Michael how quickly a living, breathing animal could become food on their table.

"Help me get him situated." Daed cocked his head toward the spruce. "Let's string him up there."

Once that was accomplished, they had to pass the time for about an hour before carting the animal back to the wagon. Daed announced his intention to walk back to it and bring it up farther along the road so they wouldn't have so far to carry the deer. Before Michael could offer to do it himself, his father stalked away, leaving Michael alone with Silas.

The older man brushed snow from a fallen tree trunk and plopped down on it. He tugged a thermos from his pack and gestured toward Michael. "Kaffi?"

"I have some." He pulled out his own thermos, prepared by Mudder, her face bright with anticipation of the work they would do later today should the men have success. "I hope it's still hot."

What else could he say? He poured kaffi into the cup and watched the steam rise and curl in the air over his hand. He pulled it closer to his face and let it warm his lips and cheeks.

"It's good you came home."

Silas's gruff words couldn't have surprised Michael more. "You think so?"

"I do." Silas slurped his coffee and gazed out at the meadow, glistening in the sun. "You need to finish the baptism classes."

Michael leaned against a tree, one boot propped against its trunk. He tried to understand what Silas really wanted to say. "I will."

"You can't marry or start a family in your community until you do."

"I know."

"Do you believe?"

"I do."

"I'll get with Luke and Thomas about starting another class so you can be baptized before Easter."

Michael struggled for words, found none. "Danki."

"Don't thank me. It's what's right."

"I know, but it must be hard. For you. How can you do it…do this?"

Silas's head came up at that. He stared into Michael's face. "It's what is right. Whether I like it or not. Sometimes it feels like a test. You made a mistake. Will I compound it and lose my own salvation by failing to forgive?"

"Nee." He didn't dare say more. His voice would crack and he would be mortified. "Nee."

"We both have to bend to the will of God."

"I'm trying."

"That's the thing. You best try harder. My girl is waiting. Her heart is sore."

Michael tried to sort through befuddled thoughts. "You would still have me court Phoebe?"

"Ain't up to me. It's up to the girl, I reckon." Silas tossed the dregs of his coffee and snapped the cup back on the thermos. "When you lose a child, you figure some things out. I want Phoebe to marry and have a family. It seems she's picked you."

Silas often gave long-winded sermons, but it was rare for him to put so many words back to back on a day not meant for a prayer service. Michael contemplated the love of a father for his wayward daughter, his daughter who had strayed and caused him such pain. How great must the love of a father for his child be? He hoped to have that experience one day.

Soon.

"You think she'd still have me?"

"I may be old, but I recognize the look on her face."

"Jah."

"Don't fiddle faddle around, either, or it'll be too late."

"I won't."

Silas didn't say anything else. He sat sipping his coffee and staring at the meadow, his face hidden in the shadows of the branches that bobbed in a chilly northern wind. Not talking. For that, Michael was glad. He had enough to chew on.

✾✾✾

"They're here! They're here!" Phoebe dashed from the screen door through the front room to the kitchen. They'd been waiting all day to see if Daed and Tobias would bring home a buck. Now there was work to be done. They had to butcher, cook, and can the meat before it spoiled. "The wagon's coming up the road."

Mudder stood in the kitchen talking to Edna and Irene. They'd spent the morning inspecting the canning jars for cracks and chips and washing them with hot, soapy water while Phoebe cleaned the pressure cooker. Cleanliness was important when canning anything, but especially meat, Mudder liked to point out every time they canned. Their small refrigerator would not hold such a bounty of meat and Daed preferred it canned, anyway. Edna clapped her dishwater-red hands together and smiled. "If they're back already, they bagged a deer. I wonder who got the shot."

"I imagine your Tobias did. He's the best shot. That's what Silas said last night." Mudder dipped a jar in hot, clear rinse water and set it on a towel spread out on the counter. "They'll want to go back out tomorrow for another one."

"I know Ben wants to go later in the week when he's done fixing the roof." Irene handed Mudder another jar. "He hated missing out today, but we can't have snow coming in through the ceiling."

"We'll have canning frolics all week long." Phoebe liked canning. Not the heat of the work so much, but the chattering that went on as they trimmed and chopped and cooked the meat before filling the jars and placing them in the pressure cooker. She liked the aroma of the meat cooking. It smelled like autumn and the promise of meals around the family table. She liked carting the jars into the cellar and filling the shelves. It felt like contentment and security. "We'd better get the pressure cooker ready."

"No rush." Mudder sharpened a butcher knife on the whetstone and touched her thumb to the blade with great care. "They still have to butcher it. Bring in the pants off the clothesline and hang them next to the woodstove to finish drying. They'll be frozen stiff as a board. Check to see if the men need anything while you're out there."

Feeling almost lighthearted, Phoebe grabbed her woolen bonnet from the hook by the back door, put it on over her kapp, and then shrugged her shawl over her shoulders. Doing laundry in the snow was not high on her list of favorite things, but it had to be done. She traipsed through the backdoor and down the steps and ducked between the pants on the clotheslines. Her brothers had gathered around the wagon to help Daed and Tobias carry the carcass from the back of the wagon and string it up on the elm next to the corral. Simon stood sharpening long carving knives at the wooden table they wheeled from the barn each time they butchered an animal. "Hey, Simon, Mudder wants to know if you need anything before you get started."

"Nee. We'll have meat for you to start trimming in about an hour, tops."

They'd done this many times and would make quick work of it. "I'll tell her…"

Michael strode into view at the front end of the long pole. The buck hung, swaying, between him and Tobias. A beauty from the looks of it. Phoebe's gaze strayed back to Michael. He looked up. They stared at each other. "Phoebe—"

"Over here. We'll string it up here," Simon interrupted. "Let's get started. The sooner we get it butchered, the sooner the women can start canning. Phoebe, tell Mudder we could use some kaffi."

"But you said—"

"Go."

Simon loved to tell her what to do. He took after Daed. Without looking at Michael again, she whirled and flounced back in the house. Why hadn't Edna told her Michael had gone with Tobias and Daed this morning? Every time she thought she might get back on an even keel, she saw him again. She would continue to see him at church, in town, at frolics. She had to learn not to feel as if her world tilted sideways every time he walked into view. She had to stop it from tilting, period.

"Where are the pants?" Mudder took a step back to let her pass. "What did Daed say?"

"Michael's out there." Phoebe grabbed a hot pad and picked up the coffeepot from the stove. "I didn't know he was out there. Anyway, they want kaffi."

Edna pulled mugs from the shelf and lined them up on the counter. "I'm sorry. I didn't want to spoil the morning." She clinked two of the mugs together hard. Her hands shook. "I know you're trying to move on and I didn't want to make it harder. Silas knew. Tobias told him when he invited him to hunt today."

"I know." Mudder took the coffeepot from Phoebe. "Silas told me. He bears no ill feelings toward Michael."

"No one told me." Phoebe considered running upstairs. Her apron bore stains from the breakfast dishes and her hair straggled around her kapp. "Don't you think I should have been told?"

"The world doesn't revolve around you." Mudder's gentle tone softened the words. "This is your community. Michael is part of your community. Our community. You'll see him."

"He's moved on. I've moved on. I'm teaching tomorrow. I'm helping Bethel with baby John. I'm moving on."

She didn't know if the words convinced the other women. They didn't convince her.

"What do you mean, he's moved on?'" Edna's eyebrows cocked. "I have the impression he still cares for you."

"There's another girl." Her voice cracked. Phoebe stopped. This was private. She had no right to mention anything that happened in Springfield to Michael's mother. "I mean, he's not meant for me. Things changed in Springfield."

"If there were another, I'd know." Edna shook her finger at Phoebe. "A mother knows these things. Besides, there've been no letters."

"It doesn't matter. I've moved on."

Irene put an arm around Phoebe's shoulders and squeezed. "You have indeed, and that's good, but sometimes you have to stop and face your fears. You can't run away from them."

If anyone knew how she felt, Irene did, but she'd had years to recover from the tragedy of losing her baby. Phoebe used her apron to wipe her face. She wasn't crying. The cold northern wind made her congested—that was all. She wiggled from Irene's grasp. "My apron's dirty. I'll be back in a minute."

"Phoebe…"

She flung herself up the stairs and into her room. Breathing hard, she peeked from her window overlooking the yard. Michael was handing a knife to her daed. Daed said something. Michael nodded and laughed.

Her father and Michael talking and laughing. Life moving on. Marching forward. When would he tell them about the girl in Springfield? A girl named Sophie. Would she visit? Or would Michael go back?

Michael turned away from Daed. He glanced up, squinting against the sun. After a second, he placed one hand to his forehead and waved with the other.

Phoebe jerked from window and hid in the shadows. She wanted to see him. She wanted to talk to him. She peeked out again. He stood looking up as if transfixed.

He was taken, wasn't he? He courted another.

So why was he here?

But the fact remained: He was here, not in Springfield. Not with Sophie.

She waved, a small quick flap of her hand.

He waved again, a big, floppy, exaggerated wave, and then turned and went back to work.

A start?

A start of what she couldn't be sure. Friendship? A Plain man and a Plain woman of their age could never be friends.

What then?

"Phoebe, get down here. We need you to start trimming the fat and chopping the meat." Her mudder's voice carried up the stairs. "There's work to be done. Stop mooning around and get down here."

If she stayed in the kitchen she wouldn't see him. She couldn't see him. Not until she could be sure she would be able to maintain her composure.

That might be never.

Chapter 38

Phoebe slid the eraser across the blackboard, back and forth, back and forth. Chalk dust flew. She coughed and ducked her face away from the board. Not her favorite part of the day. She should've assigned a scholar to do it, and in the future she would. But today had been her first day and she'd watched the students trot out the door, relieved and satisfied and uncertain all at the same time. She would do it all again tomorrow and do it better.

It still surprised her to think that this would be her future. This she could do. She could still have a place in this community. Here she stood on her own two feet, still going forward.

God had given her this second chance. She'd made it through her first day at the front of the classroom. No major disasters. Not even any minor ones. The scholars had been on their best behavior, it seemed, giving the new teacher a small reprieve before settling into their regular antics. Not that there were any problem children. Not during Deborah's tenure, anyway. It remained to be seen how well Phoebe handled the classroom on her own. Some of the oldest scholars probably remembered when she had been a student. She dropped the eraser on the rack under the chalkboard and picked up a piece of chalk. She glanced at the tablet on her desk. Algebra, English, Geography. Tomorrow's assignments.

Carefully, in her best penmanship—the teacher had to set the example, after all—she began to write the assignments in the upper right hand corner.

"You spelled *geography* wrong."

She jumped and dropped the chalk. It broke into three pieces at her feet. She whirled. "Michael! You scared me. What are you doing here?"

He stood at the back of the classroom, his hat clutched in fingers that curled, then loosened, then curled again. Something about his bare head made him look younger. "I came to talk to you. We didn't get to talk at the butchering frolic last week. Every time I tried to find you, you were gone."

She'd managed to avoid him throughout the frolic. An entire day at her house and she hadn't run into him a second time. Now here he was in her school. She raised shaking hands to brush tendrils of hair from her face and said the first thing that came to her mind. "*Geography* is not misspelled."

"I could be mistaken. It's been awhile since I've been in a classroom."

"Not that long."

His expression tentative, he rolled the brim of the hat in his hands as he inched forward between the rows of desks, his work boots smacking on the bare wood. In his black pants and his blue work shirt and his suspenders, he gave the outward appearance of being the same Plain man, but his hair was cut differently. Englisch, and his hands were raw and red-looking. He didn't have that tanned outdoor look anymore. But mostly his expression was different, more closed, subdued, wary. Before he'd been quiet, but there had been a certain assuredness in that quiet. As if he knew his place and felt comfortable in it. This man didn't know what to expect from her or from the world.

Needing a chance to collect her thoughts and steady her breath, she knelt and picked up the chalk. With deliberation, she stood and placed the pieces on the rack, her back to him.

"Phoebe, please."

His voice had a husky timbre she didn't recognize. It sounded rusty, as if he hadn't used it in a while. She dusted her hands and turned to face him.

"I wanted to talk to you."

"Here? When there's no one about but us?" She couldn't keep the sarcasm from her voice. "You don't learn, do you?"

"We could've talked at your house. Your daed wouldn't have minded. Instead, you did everything you could to avoid me."

"He told you that?"

"He did. He told me not to wait too long." He took another step toward her. "You came for me in Springfield. Why?"

"It doesn't matter now." She wanted to take a step back, but she was wedged against the chalkboard. "None of it matters."

"It matters to me."

"Why? You have your friend Sophie." She put her hand to her mouth. She sounded jealous. She had no right to be jealous. "You've moved on."

"Moved on?" He snorted in a half laugh that held no mirth. "Sophie was a friend when I needed a friend. She could never be more than that because my heart is already taken."

Dangerous grounds. Sinking, shifting sands. "I went to Springfield because you needed to come home to your community, your people. Your eternal life was at stake."

"But it had nothing to do with what you want?"

"What I want or need isn't important. If I learned anything from what happened, it's that."

"That day in the park, I felt…It seemed that you cared for me."

"I don't just kiss anyone." What was wrong with her? She couldn't get a grip on her raging emotions. So much sarcasm. She'd wanted Michael back and now he was here. He was trying. "I've never kissed anyone but you."

"You don't have feelings for Richard?"

"Richard already told you he has no claim on me."

"I wanted to hear it from you." His voice gained strength. "Do you feel something for him?"

Her throat felt so dry she couldn't form the words. She went to the pitcher and poured herself a glass of water. Cool, sweet water. Her back still to him, she spoke. "There is no one else. My heart's already taken also."

Much as she wished she could be freed of this bond between them, she knew, seeing him now, that it could never be. She loved Michael Daugherty and nothing could change that.

She felt rather than heard his approach.

"I came to say something. I'll say it and then I'll go."

Straightening her spine and lifting her shoulders so she stood as tall as a five-foot-three girl could, she faced him. "Say what you have to say."

He met her gaze squarely, his blue eyes somber, the eyes of an older, wiser man. "It's not about the kiss. It was never about the kiss. The physical part that happened between us. I know that's what you think about and what you remember from that afternoon. We were doing that when you should've been watching Lydia."

"That's right."

"Let me talk. I'm not good at it so let me get it done." He held up his hands, palms out. They were steady. "I've had months to think about this. So let me talk and then you can send me away, if that's what you want."

She nodded. She had no choice. Her voice had stopped working. He motioned with his hat toward her chair. "Sit. It might take me a minute or two. It's been building up a while."

Phoebe understood, having practiced her own speeches in the dark of night when sleep wouldn't come. Now that Michael was here, she couldn't remember a single word.

"All this time I've been away, I've been missing you something awful." There was a catch in his voice she hadn't heard before. "Like an arm or a leg had been cut off. Or both."

He cleared his throat, his gaze on the hat in his hands. "I didn't dream about kissing you. I didn't dream about touching you. I dreamed about hearing your voice. I'd wake up in middle of the night, sure I'd heard you say my name. Nobody says my name like you do."

Phoebe's cheeks burned. She wanted to bury her face in her hands, but she couldn't look away. She was caught by the sight of him, wanting to drink him in, to slake a desperate thirst. His words were like a page from her life, her nights, since Lydia's death and his departure. "Michael—"

"I missed you. I missed seeing you. If I could never touch you again, I would still want to be right here where I can see you." He gritted his teeth, his breathing ragged. "I'm not much of a talker, so I never talked to you. About all the things I think about. I never heard what you think about. I'm sorry I left. Forgive me. I want you to always be where I can see you. Every day. Please."

He ducked his head, his broad shoulders bowed, and took a long, deep breath as if the words had drained him. "I won't lie to you. I liked kissing you—"

"Michael—"

"We did something at the wrong time, but what we did wasn't wrong." He met her gaze. "I want to marry you. After I'm baptized. I'm planning to ask you. Then. Not now."

His skin darkened, but his gaze didn't waver. "That's all. That's it. All I have to say." His Adam's apple bobbed. "Do you have anything to say?"

"You're going to ask me to marry you?" She knew she sounded stupid. "You already know what the answer to that question will be."

"A fellow doesn't take anything for granted when it comes to the woman he plans to have as his fraa."

Phoebe rose, her legs unsteady, and met him halfway down the aisle. "Your fraa?"

"Jah." He took a few more steps in her direction. She stopped out of arms' reach, yet she felt as if their hands touched. More than that, she felt his heart beat the same rapid staccato as her own. She put her hand on her heart as if she could steady it. His gaze followed her movement. "If you'll have me."

"You know I will." Her voice sounded husky but steady in her ears. "I've been waiting for you."

"This time we have to do it the right way." He laid his hat on the desk, his face steeped in sadness intertwined with a determination that told her how much he meant these words. "Do you think we can do it differently? Is it too late?"

"I don't know." She wanted to say they could, she wanted it so badly, but she honestly didn't know the answer to that question. "I don't know if we *can* go back."

"Not back." His features softened. "We go forward, doing it better. God forgives. He doesn't just forgive—He throws our sin away; He crushes it under His feet and it's gone. That's how big His grace is. If He does that, shouldn't the rest of us do the same?"

The strength of his words—the fierce belief in his voice—lifted her. She rushed to match his candle of hope with her own. "We can go forward. We can try again, only try harder to do it better."

"Would people accept this effort, this wanting to change, do you think?"

"I wouldn't." The high, tight voice behind them held disbelief and contempt. "I can't believe you're in here, the two of you, doing who knows what after what happened to Lydia."

Phoebe looked beyond Michael, who stood frozen to the spot, toward the source of that sharp, angry voice. Hannah's voice. She stood in the doorway, hands on her hips, her face scarlet with fury.

"We're just talking."

"Talking about…I can't even say it. I'm out here in the buggy, waiting for you, ready to go, and you're in here with the man who caused our sister to die." Her voice cracked as tears began to course down her pinched face. "You're both terrible, horrible, awful people."

She whirled and slammed through the door, gone in an instant.

Chapter 39

By the time Phoebe raced to the school door and out onto the small porch, Hannah had disappeared. She'd left the buggy, the horse tethered to the railing next to Michael's, and run away on foot. "Hannah! Hannah, come back," Phoebe shouted, knowing her sister wouldn't obey. Hannah had been the one dark spot in an otherwise good day. She sat in her row a silent, yet condemning reminder that the past had accompanied Phoebe through the door at the beginning of this day, this new start. She'd answered questions when called upon to do so but had volunteered nothing. At recess she'd sat on a swing, not moving, not talking, her gaze on something no one else could see.

"*Ach*, Hannah. Come back! Please come back."

Nothing.

Phoebe bent over, hands on her knees, trying to get a breath. She stared at the wood under her feet and tried to understand how such sturdy construction could rock. Her whole world rocked.

The sound of Michael's boots on the porch behind her brought her upright. He cleared his throat. She faced him.

"If that's any sign of how folks will react, we're in deep, muddy waters." His face bleak, he slapped his hat on his head and started to duck around her. "I shouldn't have come."

"Nee." She put out her hand to stop him. What was she doing? She pulled it back. Their gazes connected. He opened his mouth. She rushed to speak first. "Hannah is hurting, maybe even more than Daed and Mudder. She feels responsible. And it's our fault. I know it's our fault. We need to find a way to reach her so she can heal and begin to move on."

"The way we have?"

"We're beginning to."

He nodded, his gaze locked with hers. "You're right. Hannah's too young to understand that life does go on. That mistakes don't have to define your whole life."

"God forgives and gives a person a second chance."

"God forgives and so do we."

"Hannah's not too young to understand God's grace."

"We have to tell her. I have to tell her." She brushed past him and paused in the doorway. "I'll close up and take the buggy after her. It's a long walk, too long. And the days are only getting shorter."

He took the porch steps two at a time, then turned back. "I'm sorry if I've caused you more trouble by being here."

"I'm glad you came." The words came as a surprise, even as she said them. "We will figure out a way back."

"We will, won't we?" His wonderment at the thought lighted his face and Phoebe saw an inkling of the man he would become. The man who would be her husband someday. The thought lifted her up until she felt as if her body floated off the ground. "We'll do it together."

"We'll figure it out."

He climbed on to his horse, reins in his hands, then looked down at her. "Talk to you later then."

It was a promise. "Talk to you later."

She made quick work of closing the school, hopped in the buggy, and headed for home, sure she would see Hannah along the road. The sun hung on the horizon, forcing her to shade her eyes with her hand as she scoured the countryside for the dark blue of her sister's dress.

Nothing. Where had she gone? Phoebe slowed her pace even more until Roscoe whinnied in an aggravated complaint. He surely wanted to be home in the corral enjoying his oats as much as she wanted to be eating her supper, finishing her chores, and climbing into her bed.

"Hannah, where are you?" A chill climbed Phoebe's spine and

tickled her neck. Her sister hadn't been herself for so long, but surely she wouldn't do anything to upset Mudder. "Hannah, come on, let me give you a ride!"

No high, childish voice called back to her. Dread coursing through her, Phoebe shouted her sister's name louder and louder. She didn't want to return home—couldn't return home—without her sister. Mudder would worry and Daed would want to know why she'd done this again. She'd have to tell them what had happened. She bowed her head. *God, not again. This is different. It is. It's different. Please help me find Hannah.*

She pulled the buggy to a halt and squeezed in front of its roof so she could stand. Nothing but brush and trees and then fields of winter wheat and rye. "Hannah!" She wanted to stomp her foot and scream. But she didn't. Grown women didn't do that. "Hannah, please come out and we'll ride home together. Please!"

Michael's horse trotted into view. He waved at her and waited until he was close enough for her to hear before he spoke. "She's not on the road. She's not at the house."

"You went to my house?"

"I did." He slowed and pulled up next to her buggy, then halted. "I spoke with your daed."

"You did?"

"I told you, I've changed. I'm not letting you go through anything by yourself anymore." He turned the horse so he faced the same direction as the buggy. "You're in this predicament because of me."

"What did Daed say?"

"He said to come home. Your mudder wants you with her. Your daed and I will look for Hannah."

She found it hard to comprehend. He had changed. So had her Daed. They'd been honed by the events of the past summer, their character burnished to a smooth golden sheen by tragedy. They'd gone through the fire and emerged on the other side.

Phoebe snapped the reins and followed Michael home.

Chapter 40

Her stomach roiling, head aching, Katie stared out the door, her hand on the screen, waiting. She peered out at the yard and the meadow beyond, her hand up to shield her eyes from the sun now waning in the west. No Hannah trudged along the road toward the house. How could she do this to them? The child was selfish. No, she was hurting. Katie wanted to scream. She wanted to cry. She did neither. She waited, her back to Silas and to Elam. She could hear her youngest son's boots smacking on the wood floor as he paced. Elam never said much. He reminded her so much of Silas. Solid, steady, unflinching. Yet he paced. Hannah's decision to run off now, after all that had happened, was getting to him too.

"You might as well sit. You're doing no good standing there." Silas touched her arm. She turned to look up at him, led by his tender tone. A tone he reserved for her only. He tucked his arm into a coat and pulled it on. "Hannah's fine. She's a stubborn girl who needs to grow up."

Careful to keep her aching arm close to her side, Katie nodded. "You think that's so easy to do?"

"I know it's not. For none of us. But Phoebe is doing her best to make amends. Even I can see that." Taking advantage of Elam's turned back as he paced toward the kitchen, Silas placed his rough, callused hand on her cheek. His eyes were blue pools of emotion. "You were right."

"About what?' She put a hand to her mouth, afraid she'd lose her lunch right there in the front room. The bitter, metallic taste was back. "I haven't been right about anything in a long time."

"I want Phoebe to have a chance at what we've had—what we have." He tugged her against him in a quick, fierce hug. "If that means Michael, so be it."

"So be it." She nodded, aware of a familiar tingling sensation working its way up her arm and into her chest. Fatigue threatened to overwhelm her. "Right now, I just want my girls home."

"Michael is bringing Phoebe here. I'm headed out to find Hannah. I'll give her a good talking to when I find her. Don't you worry about that."

"I want to come too." Elam spoke up, his teenage voice cracking. "I'll take the sorrel."

"Nee, you should get back in the field."

"With Hannah out there—"

"If we don't get that fence mended, we'll lose the hogs to coyotes for sure. I'll not let this foolishness cause us more problems. I'll deal with Hannah."

Katie had no doubt. She wouldn't want to be in Hannah's shoes when Silas found her. A curious weakness invaded her body. She tottered to the chair and eased into it, glad Sarah was taking an unusual late afternoon nap. She wouldn't want to sleep tonight, but right now, Katie needed a minute to rest.

"They're here." Silas opened the screen door and bounded out. "Stay where you are. I'll send Phoebe in."

Ignoring her husband's words, Katie struggled to her feet and trudged to the door. Phoebe slipped up the steps and strode across the porch. "I can't believe she didn't come home. How could she do this to you and Daed?"

His expression dark, Elam slapped his hat on his head and barged through the door. "I'll be in the hog pen."

"Elam!" Phoebe whirled as if to follow him. "I had no idea she'd run off."

"Some of us are still grieving." He let the door slam.

"Hannah's not herself. Don't worry about Elam. He's just like your Daed." Katie backed away.

Phoebe took Elam's place in the pacing department. She seemed beside herself with pent-up energy. "Michael said she heard the two of you talking."

"Jah. She did. She was angry."

"Are you…Did you and Michael work things out?"

"Hannah's gone and you're thinking of me and Michael."

"Hannah will be found. I have faith in that." As she said the words, Katie realized they were true. God would not do this to her again. Not so soon after Lydia. And Hannah wasn't four. She was twelve, with a good head on her shoulders when she chose to use it. She'd lived here long enough to know her way around. She'd be fine—until Silas got ahold of her. "She'll be found, and your father will deal with her."

"Michael and I talked. He talked mostly and I listened."

"And?"

"And we'll be all right. God willing."

"I'm glad for that."

So was she. Glad and grateful and yet uncertain. Katie took a breath, fighting the trembling that shook her. The air around her seemed to heat up despite the cold wind that wafted through the open door. The furniture blurred. Phoebe's face blurred, her features dissolving as if she'd walked into a fog or a sudden cloud of smoke. A terrible pain shot through Katie's arm and drilled its way into her chest. In agony, she wrapped herself in her arms and doubled over. "*Ach, ach*, Phoebe, I can't…"

Her legs gave out and she collapsed. She rolled into a tight ball, aware only of the pain.

Phoebe's mouth moved, but Katie could hear nothing. Her daughter's voice receded into the distance, growing further and further away. She tried to reach for it, to grasp it in her hand, to pull herself toward it, but to no avail.

Gott, have mercy.

Phoebe rushed forward and sank to her knees. Her mudder's face had gone white. She curled into a tight ball, one hand gripping her upper arm. She moaned.

"What hurts?"

Mudder gasped and then went limp.

"Mudder? Mudder!"

No response.

Phoebe scrambled to her feet and raced out the front door, pounded down the steps, and hurled herself across the expanse of yard that went on and on. "Elam! Elam!"

Her bruder, clad in tall, black rubber boots, sloshed his way through the pen. "What are you hollering about? Did they find Hannah?"

"It's Mudder. She collapsed on the floor." Phoebe fought for air, her words coming out in a stuttering mess. "Something's wrong. I think it's her heart."

He broke into a run. One of the boots slipped off as he struggled across ground slick with mud from melting snow. He floundered, went down, and then pulled himself up.

"What do we do?" He threw himself over the fence and landed on one knee in front of her. "Do I find Daed?"

"No time. Go to the phone shack. Call for an ambulance. Go. Hurry."

Her mind flung itself about, doing mental jumping jacks and back-flips as she tried to recall what Bethel had taught her about first aid. Every teacher needed to know about first aid. Teachers should be pre-pared for all things. The scholars were entrusted to them.

Phoebe whirled and raced back to the house. She took the steps in one giant leap, skidded across the porch, and slammed open the door.

Seconds later she was on her knees, applying pressure to Mudder's chest with the palms of her hands. One-two-three-four-five-six-seven-eight…She counted aloud, to one hundred, and then leaned her head close to her mother's open mouth. Nothing.

Nothing.

She heard no breaths. Bethel said to keep going. Not to worry about trying to breathe life into the scholar. Leave it to the people who knew how. The paramedics who would come with the ambulance. She didn't know how.

Rescue breathing, Bethel had called it. She wanted to rescue her mother.

Push. Push.

She started over. She kept going and going and going. Her shoulders ached and her own heart seemed to be a train careening off the track. "Come on, come on, come on. Please, Mudder, please."

Stirring in the nearby playpen told her Sarah had awakened. *Not now. Please not now.*

The little girl began to fuss. Phoebe allowed herself one second to look up. Sarah's face, puffy with sleep, peeked over the edge of the playpen. "Mudder, Mudder, Mudder!" she called, and then began to cry in earnest.

Phoebe wanted to do the same. "It's okay, Sarah, Mudder is fine. Hush now, hush now."

She began to pray, the words flowing from her mouth in a steady, unceasing stream. "Gott, please. Thy will be done, but if it's Your will, please give her body strength. Be her strength. Make her heart beat for her. Take me. Don't take her. Take me. I'll gladly go for her. Hannah needs her. Daed needs her. Sarah and Elam need her. They'll do fine without me. They'll go on without me, but they need Mudder. Take me. Take me."

Sarah stopped crying. She stuck a fist in her mouth and sat down with a plop.

Mudder moaned.

Phoebe stopped, her hands poised in midair.

"Mudder?"

A faint moan came in response. Mudder breathed.

Phoebe stared down at the face that she knew as well as her own. She touched her forehead to her mudder's. "Please don't go. Please don't go. Please don't go. I need you. I'm not ready."

"Jah, you are," Mudder whispered. "You *are* ready."

Chapter 41

Michael's horse picked its way along the bank of the creek, its hooves moving without hesitation, finding the nooks and crannies, stepping almost daintily. Michael let him find his way, focusing instead on searching for the blue of Hannah's dress in the drab browns and grays of the winter landscape. The trees were barren, allowing him to see through naked branches into the far reaches of the tree stands that hugged the creek. Nothing. Dusk began to settle around him as the sun floated on the horizon, preparing to slip away. He shivered, the cold wind biting at his chapped skin. He couldn't believe this was happening again.

It's not happening again.

Hannah was old enough to know better. She had chosen to be willful. It was one thing to punish him and Phoebe with her absence. Quite another to punish Katie Christner, who'd been through so much already. He'd been shocked at her appearance during the deer butchering frolic. Always rather round and plump, she now looked gaunt. The smooth skin of her face bore lines around the mouth and eyes. She'd moved as if her joints hurt. She moved like an old woman.

He'd done that to her.

Yet today, as last week, she'd greeted him with kind words of welcome. Nodding, looking intent as he explained what happened. Silas had been there to put an arm around her when she faltered over the fact that Hannah had apparently run away. Katie's face had taken on a stoic expression he'd seen before. At Stockton Lake. At the funeral. She'd nodded and accepted Silas's order that she stay and wait for Hannah should the wayward child decide to return.

He had to bring Hannah home to Katie. This couldn't happen again. He wouldn't let it. Ignoring the still agonizing memories of the hours he'd spent stumbling around in the woods of Stockton Lake Park, he tugged at the reins and forced the horse away from the creek and into the woods.

Where would she go? This wasn't a situation involving a lost four-year-old in unfamiliar surroundings. This was a girl nearly in her teens who'd lived in this countryside for more than a year. Hannah had run away to nurse her wounds, to cry in private, maybe even to punish them. To be alone with her outrage and her guilt.

Where would she go? An instant later, he knew. She would go where she didn't feel alone. She would go to offer her remorse and to seek forgiveness from the one person who could never give it. She'd want to punish herself some more with that very thought. She was a child picking at a scab so it couldn't heal.

Michael made his way up the steep slope from the creek to the open pasture that separated Silas Christner's property from Onkel Peter's homestead. In between lay a chunk of land the community had joined together to purchase, each family giving what they could, each knowing eventually they would partake of this place, when their time came. He urged the horse forward, anxious now to arrive at his destination, hoping he was right.

It took almost fifteen minutes, but he made his way up over the rise and cantered through the open gate of a fence that had been erected and painted white by the men of the community. Inside that fence was one short row of headstones amid a pasture of neatly cut grass. They hadn't been in New Hope long enough to need more. By God's grace they hadn't needed more.

Dusk made long shadows of the trees that shaded these resting places. Michael struggled to make out the shapes hidden in the darkness of those shadows. Was that her, huddled on the ground by the last headstone?

Her face stained with tears, Hannah looked up. "It's you? Go away! Go away!"

Michael dismounted and tied the reins to the fence, taking his time. All the while, Hannah took turns glaring at him and scrubbing her face with the back of her hands. He strode toward her, finally halting on the other side of that small mound of dirt that hadn't yet begun to settle in. Soon it would be covered by snow and then in the spring, plants would start to grow.

"Your mudder is worried about you."

"Mudder?" She frowned as if it just now occurred to her that her actions might cause another pain. She really was too young to see the world through the eyes of another instead of focusing inward on her own hurt. "I didn't mean to worry her. I was just so mad."

"At me."

"Jah. You. And at Phoebe." She scowled. "Both of you. You were selfish. It was your fault."

"You have a right to be mad." Michael squatted across from her. "At us, but you need to stop being mad at yourself."

"I'm not mad at myself."

"Jah, you are."

"I'm supposed to forgive you."

"You are, and you're also to forgive yourself. That's what God expects. The Bible says so."

"How can I do that?" She pointed her finger at Lydia's grave. "How can I? Lydia died."

"I know. I think about it every night and every day." He plucked a few weeds that had begun to sprout in the dirt. "You know God's already forgiven you. Not only has He forgiven you, He's taken your puny little sin and smashed it under His foot and tossed it in the ocean. It's gone."

"How do you know?"

"It's in the Holy Scripture."

"You read it?"

"A friend gave me an English Bible. She said reading it would help me understand God's will for me."

"Did it?"

"It made me understand that God's grace covers me and you and Phoebe and everyone else in this world."

Hannah wiped her dirty hands on her apron. She raised her face to the setting sun. "I'm tired." Her voice was so slight he leaned forward to hear her words. "So tired."

"Me too. Let me give you a ride home."

"Not that kind of tired. I'm tired of feeling this way." Her nose ran. She sniffed, but it didn't help so she swiped at her face with her sleeve again. "Is it ever going to be better?"

"They tell me it will."

"I don't think you should get to feel better."

"I know that's how you feel, but you only make yourself feel bad by hanging on to this anger. It hurts you more than it hurts me. Let it go for your own sake, not for mine." Michael struggled for the words. He let his knees sink into the dirt, shaking hands on his thighs. He wanted to give Hannah her peace back. She deserved it. Despite what she thought, she'd done no wrong. She didn't deserve this. "God is giving us another chance to do things the right way, to be better people than we were before."

"You and Phoebe?" She sighed, a long, sad sound. "How do I know you won't mess up again?"

"You don't. We're not perfect. None of us is." He tried a smile. Hannah didn't smile back. "Not even you, and God doesn't expect you to be. He only expects you to try to learn from your mistakes. That's what I'm doing. That's what Phoebe's doing."

Turning to the grave, Hannah ran her fingers through the dirt and let them close around a loose clod. It crumbled in her hand. "I'm so sorry. Lydia, I'm so sorry." She hung her head and sobbed. "Do you hear me? I'm sorry."

Her words of anguish ripped the still-tender skin from Michael's own wounds. He brushed his own hands through the dirt, cool and damp under his fingers, and closed his eyes, trying to absorb her pain. It soaked everything around him. The air, the trees, the dirt. The entire earth.

"I'm sorry too," he whispered. "So sorry."

Silence descended. He let the peace of this place soak through him. He inhaled the cool air. The tension seeped away. God, in His goodness, would take care of them. He had a plan. Michael only had to wait.

Hannah crawled around the grave on her hands and knees, her skirt tangling around her. She halted on her haunches a foot or so from Michael. "Pray," she begged. "Pray for me and you and Phoebe. Please."

He nodded and he prayed. Silently at first, then aloud. "Forgive us, Lord, for falling short. For disappointing You. Help us to do better. Help us to forgive each other. Thy will be done. Show us what to do next. Amen."

"Amen."

They stared at each other. Michael needed to get her home so that Katie could breathe again. And Phoebe. He rose. "Your mudder is waiting for you."

"And Daed will be angry with—"

The shriek of a siren drowned out her high voice. An ambulance roared past them on the road Michael had just traveled, dirt billowing behind it.

"An ambulance?" Hannah scrambled to her feet. "An ambulance going to my house?"

"There are other farms in that direction." Michael rose as well. His skin prickled up and down his arms. "Could be one of several others."

But it wasn't. Somehow Michael knew that.

Chapter 42

Thankful the horrible shrieking of the siren had finally been silenced, Phoebe scrambled from the ambulance, Sarah on her hip this time, instead of on the stretcher. Phoebe tried to cling to Mudder's limp hand, but the paramedics moved too quickly, ripping them apart. The sound of Elam's boots scraping on the floor of the ambulance said her brother followed, but she didn't look back. She couldn't take her gaze from the faces of the paramedics. She wanted to read something there. Hope. Assurance. Peace. But their faces told her nothing as they popped the stretcher up on its metal legs and wheeled it into the New Hope Medical Center emergency room. They rushed past rows of chairs, mostly empty, toward double doors that led to those same small rooms created with curtains where Sarah had been taken when she suffered the bee sting. A nurse, overly plump and pink in her matching pants and smock, stepped in front of them. "Stay here, folks. This is far as you go."

"She's our mudder—our mother."

"We'll take good care of her." The nurse patted Phoebe's shoulder, her expression kind but firm. "Take a seat and we'll be right with you."

Take a seat. The curious rush of energy that had propelled her through the ministrations that had kept her mudder alive and breathing continued to pour through her wave after wave, pounding at her temples and the base of her throat. Her arms and legs hummed with it.

She opened her mouth, but the nurse did an about-face, her sneakers squeaking on the shiny tile floor, and disappeared through the swinging double doors.

"But…"

She stood at the doors, not moving, waiting. Elam cleared his throat. "Maybe we should…"

She didn't hear the rest of his sentence. The pounding in her ears swallowed it up. Sarah began to fuss. "Take her." She handed the girl over to her bruder. "You can sit."

"You don't want to sit?"

She shook her head.

"I want to stay with you."

At the tremor in her little bruder's voice, cracking with the sound of being caught between child and man, she turned. "It's all right, Elam. She'll be fine."

He hunched skinny shoulders. "She didn't look fine. Her face looked kind of…purple."

"Her heart needs help."

"How did you know what to do?"

"Bethel showed Deborah and me when we were getting ready to teach." Phoebe flinched inwardly at the memory of how lighthearted she'd been about those instructions, not even taking note of how difficult it was for Bethel to crouch on the floor, her crutches at her side, using Molly as the patient. "She said we needed to know about first aid if we were going to be responsible for the scholars."

"How did you know it was her heart?" He hitched Sarah up on his hip. She hiccupped and began to fuss. "She never said anything."

"She told me." Phoebe fished a bag of oatmeal cookies from Mudder's canvas bag. She knew they would be there. Mudder never went anywhere without snacks for her little ones. "Take these and sit down with Sarah. Break it into little pieces and give them to her one at a time. She missed her supper."

"So did you."

"Who could think of food now? I'm not hungry."

Not looking convinced, Elam glanced around the room and up at the TV blaring overhead. Phoebe followed his gaze. "Pay no attention. Just sit and rest."

His skinny frame rigid in protest, he went. Phoebe remained standing. Time passed, but she couldn't say how much.

A doctor in a white coat, stethoscope dangling from his neck, jostled her as he rushed past. "Sorry. You need to move," he called over his shoulder as the double doors clanged shut with a definitive bang. She tried to imagine what was happening to keep Mudder alive. Machines? Medicine? More banging on her chest, bruising her fragile bones that already ached from arthritis?

Gott, help them. Guide them. Guide their hands and their heads and their hearts.

It was the best she could do, so muddled was her mind.

"Phoebe."

Thank You, Gott.

She whirled and ran smack into Daed's outstretched arms, burying her head against his solid chest. He pushed her back, his hands gripping her arms. "Where is she?"

"In there." She jabbed a thumb over her shoulder. "I don't know what—"

He lifted her into the air and set her to one side in a seemingly effortless move. A second later he disappeared through the double doors, looking neither left nor right.

"Daed, you can't—"

The doors clanged shut again.

✦✦✦

Katie struggled to open heavy eyelids. They wouldn't cooperate. They were so heavy. She wanted to raise her hand to her face, but it had a mind of its own. Too heavy. She inhaled and willed herself awake. Her eyelids fluttered. Bright light overhead. Far too bright. She let them close again. The darkness felt better. She wrapped it around her against the unknown that awaited her out there. Noise. So much noise. People talking and talking. Words she couldn't understand. People she didn't know. Voices she didn't recognize. A cold, bright place not like home. She'd been home, hadn't she? With Sarah and Elam.

Hannah. Hannah had run away. Silas looking for her. "Silas… Silas…Silas." The sound coming from her mouth bore little resemblance to speech. More of a cry mixed with a groan. "Silas?"

A hand—his hand—grasped hers. "Katie, are you there?"

"I'm here."

She forced her eyes to open once again. This time his head bobbed over her, blocking the awful light. "I'm right here, fraa. You're all right. You're fine."

"Hannah?"

"She's fine. Michael found her. She'll not do such a thing again, not when I get done with her."

"Easy."

"Nee. No easy. Do what's hard now, for her sake." Silas's hand caressed her cheek. She wanted to lean into it, but the wires and tubes and machines held her fast. Her sight adjusted and she could see his features now. White lines around his mouth, eyes red, teeth gritted. He cleared his throat. "You didn't need this. The doctor told you to take it easy."

"It was coming anyway."

"What do you mean?"

"I haven't felt good in a while."

"You didn't say anything."

"Didn't want to worry you."

Silas leaned down, his face bobbing about her. "And this doesn't worry me?"

"I know." She licked dry, cracked lips. "How did I get here?"

"Phoebe and Elam. The paramedics told the doctor Phoebe saved your life."

"Saved my life?"

"She gave you CPR."

"I…I remember her praying. She prayed and prayed aloud. I could hear her, but I didn't feel anything."

"She kept you alive until the ambulance got there."

"Gott kept me alive."

"Jah."

"But Phoebe helped. Phoebe knows what to do. She's grown now."

"She is."

A voice belonging to someone she couldn't see spoke.

Silas turned away, then looked back. "I have to go now. They're going to get you ready for a procedure. The doctor will explain."

She gripped his hand, unwilling to let go.

He touched her cheek. "You're fine."

"Phoebe's in charge. Tell her I said she's in charge." She tried to get her lips to turn up into a smile. "You silly men don't know anything. Phoebe's in charge."

He kissed her forehead. His lips were cool and dry. "I'll tell her. I'll be right back. I'll be with you every step of the way."

To the end. He didn't say those words, but she knew he thought them. Their vows were such. *Until death do us part.*

But not today. Today, by God's grace and with the help of her oldest daughter, she would live.

❦

Phoebe touched the double doors. Daed had gone in. Why couldn't she? No one stood on the other side, barring entrance. Her daed's disappearance proved that.

"Stay here, Phoebe. Leave it to your daed. He's her husband." Michael strode toward her, Hannah trailing behind, her dirty face red and puffy with tears. "There's no keeping him from his fraa. They'll know that."

"How did you get here?"

"Jake gave us a ride into town in the back of his pickup truck."

That accounted for their red cheeks and Hannah's wind-whipped hair tumbling from her kapp. Phoebe nodded, unable to speak over the enormous stony lump in her throat.

"What did they say?"

She cleared her throat. "They said to sit and wait."

The words came out in a croak.

"Then that's what we'll do."

"I can't." Her feet were glued to the floor, it seemed. "I'll stay here."

"Come on." Without touching her, he guided her to the row of chairs closest to the double doors. "You look like you're about to collapse. Sit."

Hannah plopped into a chair next to Elam and took Sarah from him. The toddler wiped grubby, slobbery cookie hands on her big sister's dress, wrapped her chubby arms around Hannah's neck, and laid her head on her shoulder, almost instantly asleep.

"You have a way with her." Michael smiled at Hannah as he dropped into a chair across from her and Elam. "I expect she'll be following you around for the next several years."

To Phoebe's amazement, Hannah's lips turned up in a quivering attempt at a smile. "I expect you're right." She huddled the little girl close and laid her cheek on Sarah's head. "She's my schweschder."

After that they were quiet. Not many people waited in the ER this evening. A quiet day in New Hope. A good day for most, if they weren't in a hospital emergency room. Phoebe tried to sit still, but she fidgeted, leaning forward on her knees, then back against the uncomfortable, plastic of the chair. "Why is it taking so long?"

"Because they're doing everything they can for her."

The statement took its time sinking in.

"I need water." Elam stood. "I'll be back."

"Try around the bathrooms." Michael pointed toward a hallway with a sign hanging at the corner featuring a stick man and a stick woman. "The fountain's usually in the same place."

He would know, having spent months in the city. The thought barely penetrated. Phoebe watched, mesmerized, as Hannah's head began to nod, then jerk up as she tried to stay awake. The emotion of the day taking its toll. Phoebe couldn't imagine sleeping now. Not now, while Mudder's life hung by a God-spun thread.

"Are you all right?" Michael whispered, apparently also aware of Hannah's desperate attempt to avoid slumber. "What are you thinking?"

"When Mudder told me about her heart problems, she said I might have to step in and take care of the family if something happened to her."

"And that scares you?"

She studied Hannah's dirty, tear-streaked face. "Not anymore." The answer surprised her. "I lived through Lydia's death. I lived through you leaving. I took care of Sarah when the bee stung her. And now I've done everything I can to help Mudder live. The rest is in God's hands. I've weathered the storm as best I can. I expect that's what God wants of me."

His hand crept across the arm of the chair that separated them. His fingers touched hers, a light, tentative touch. She held herself still, waiting. His hand withdrew. "Do you forgive me?"

"I do. Do you forgive me?"

"Jah."

"You did good, Phoebe," he whispered. "I love you."

She swallowed tears, fighting for her composure. She wanted to say the words to him, but she didn't want her voice to sound weak. She was strong. Together they would be strong.

He stood and moved into the chair next to her. Now she could smell his woodsy scent, hear his breathing, light and quick. He removed his hat and ran his hand over his hair in a futile attempt to make it lie flat. She found herself gazing at his face, tracing the familiar features with her eyes. The schoolhouse boy had disappeared, leaving behind a man who had weathered a storm so like her own. "Phoebe?"

She ducked her head, wanting to think without looking into those probing eyes.

"Phoebe, do you love me?"

No coward, she raised her head and nodded.

His hand covered hers in a tight, sure grip. "I want to spend the rest of my life with you at my side, as my fraa. No more wasted days apart."

She placed her free hand over his. "Me too."

He leaned back into his chair. "Now we wait."

She settled into her own chair. At long last, she felt at peace. "Now we wait."

The double doors banged open and Daed strode into the waiting room. His face didn't look quite as grim as it had an hour earlier. They all arose at the same time, talking over each other, asking questions.

He held up a hand. "They're admitting her, but she's stable. She's awake."

"Admitting her—"

"When can we see her—"

"When will she get out—"

"Quiet! Everyone quiet." Silas raised his voice only a little, but they all fell silent. "They're doing something called an angioplasty. You don't want to know what that is. She's sleeping now. They'll do this thing in a few hours and if all goes well, she'll come home in a few days. In the meantime, she says to tell you Phoebe's in charge."

They all turned to look at Phoebe. Her cheeks heated up, but the serenity of the past few moments didn't flee. "Well, you heard Daed. Hannah, we best get Sarah home and get supper started."

She started toward the door and then stopped, aware none followed. "What is it?"

"How are we getting home?" Elam asked, his freckled face perplexed. "You plan to steal an ambulance?"

"Don't be silly."

Daed chuckled, a sound that told Phoebe more than words that her mudder really would be all right. "I called Mr. Cooper from the nurses' station. He's bringing his van by to pick you up."

"You're not coming."

Daed shook his head. "I'm staying with your mudder. You take care of them."

She went to stand next to Michael. "We'll take care of them. Together." Michael slapped his hat on his head. "You can count on that."

Daed nodded at him. Michael returned the nod and Phoebe knew some unspoken message had passed between the two most important men in her life. Daed slipped through the double doors, letting them swing shut with a bang.

Phoebe slipped her hand into Michael's and squeezed. "Let's go home."

Michael's fingers entwined in hers and tightened. "Let's go home."

Epilogue

Phoebe's heart stopped. She couldn't feel it beating anymore. Maybe it had broken from her chest out of the sheer joy of this moment. She stole a glance at Michael. His dimples were out in full force and the fire in his blue eyes leapt and danced. Phoebe managed another breath. Her heart beat after all. She forced herself to focus on Luke's words. The final words that would make her Michael Daugherty's fraa. Every man, woman, and child in their small community, along with several loads of friends and family who'd traveled from Bliss Creek, gazed upon this wedding ceremony, but she and Michael might as well have been alone. She saw no one but him. Finally, the long, treacherous, pit filled road they'd traveled together—and apart—had led them here to this moment where they dedicated themselves to each other before God.

His gaze somber, Luke took Phoebe's hand and laid it in Michael's. He then placed his own hand over theirs. *"So then I may say with Raguel, the God of Abraham, the God of Isaac, and the God of Jacob be with you and help you together and fulfill his blessing abundantly upon you, through Jesus Christ. Amen."*

The words she'd heard said so many times for her friends as they married. A sob caught in her throat. She forced it back. No tears today. Only unrepentant joy. She looked out at the sea of faces. Mudder with a handkerchief dabbing at her face. Deborah and Rachel, both big with child. Molly, her plain face made beautiful by the joy she felt for her friend's good fortune. Even Hannah smiled, one arm around Sarah. Her family and her friends praying for her and Michael, that their union be blessed.

The moment passed and it was done. They were wed before God and their community. Michael clutched her hand and they moved into the crowd of well wishers. So many hugs for her and slaps to the back for Michael. Tears and handkerchiefs and good wishes. It took half an hour to make their way to the barn doors. To her surprise, Michael tugged her in a direction away from the house. "Where are we going? The meal is about to begin."

"In a few minutes." Michael guided her in the opposite direction, toward the meadow half hidden in snow that had been melting under an unseasonably warm November sun. "I want you all to myself for just a few minutes."

She glanced back and saw Daniel grinning as he watched them make their getaway. "Rachel and I will cover for you," he called. "Don't be long."

She waved with her free hand and allowed her husband—her husband!—to pull her toward some unknown destination. "Where are we going?"

"You're my wife." He pulled her closer and then let her hand drop. His arm went around her shoulder. "Now I have a right to take you anywhere I want anytime I want."

"Oh, you do, do you?" She laughed, the sound bright and airy in the clean, cool air. "Don't I have a say in any of this?"

"Nee." Despite the answer, he slowed a little, allowing her to keep up without running. "You will obey."

"I guess you don't know me all that well, after all."

They both laughed.

"Oh, believe me, I know exactly what I'm getting into. Your brothers bent my ear about you for a good hour and then your daed added his two cents' worth." Michael shoved back some branches and made room for her to slip by. "Simon and Martin are sure I'm daft to think you can be a good fraa."

"They're just giving you a hard time."

"Jah. But they learned quickly that my mind was made up. No going back."

"No going back."

They trotted down the path until they reached the stream that burbled in the depths of a stand of spruce trees. Michael stopped abruptly and turned to her. "Now there is nothing between us. Nothing." He took both her hands in his and lifted them to his face, kissing each one, his lips brushing them. "This is our new start, fraa. From this day on. We start fresh and new as husband and wife."

"Jah." She found it almost impossible to utter that one word, much as she wanted to pour out her feelings. A shyness she didn't recognize gripped her. "This day on."

"We won't forget what happened before." A touch of sadness softened his voice. "Nee, we'll always remember because we must learn from our mistakes. We'll remember Lydia and we'll remember the lake."

"We'll honor those memories." Her voice cracked. "Always."

"Always."

He let her hands drop and cupped her face instead. Bending his head, he brought her closer until his lips touched hers. Words might have deserted her, but nothing could keep her from responding to his touch. Her arms went around his neck without hesitation. He stooped and lifted her off her feet and swung her around. The kiss deepened until she felt her heart truly would stop beating. Finally, breath gone, dizzy, she found herself back on her own two feet on solid ground.

"I've been wanting to do that again since that day at the lake." His Adam's apple bobbed. "Now I have the right to do it. Now is the time."

"Now is the time." She leaned her forehead against his chest and hid her face, not wanting him to see the rush of emotion. "Every day for the rest of our lives."

He touched his fingers to her chin, forcing her to lift her head and look at him. "For the rest of our lives."

Together, arms entwined, they walked the path that would lead them home.

Discussion Questions

1. Michael and Phoebe wanted to spend a few moments alone on a family vacation, getting to know each other. They knew they were doing something they shouldn't, but they did it anyway. Does that make them responsible for Lydia's death?

2. Amish faith demands forgiveness in every situation, as does the Holy Bible. If you were in Katie and Silas's shoes, could you forgive them?

3. Phoebe rationalized that Hannah was better with children and could take care of them on their own. Her decision changed Hannah's life forever, as well as her own. Does Hannah bear any responsibility for what happened? Have you ever rationalized your behavior, knowing you were doing something wrong? How did it make you feel?

4. At four, Lydia already had chores and responsibilities around the house. How do you feel about the Amish practice of giving much greater responsibility to young children than *Englisch* folks do?

5. Katie and Silas both feel guilty for not reining Phoebe in more. Compared to *Englisch* society, Plain youngsters are bound by much stricter rules regarding how they are to

behave in almost every facet of their lives. Do you think Katie and Silas have any blame in what happened to Lydia? Are parents responsible when their children make mistakes that have serious repercussions?

6. After Lydia's death, Phoebe decides she is going to be "good" from now on. She's not going to get into trouble ever again in hopes that God will forgive her and extend His grace to her once again. Is it possible to be "good enough" to earn God's grace? What does the Bible say about how we receive God's grace?

7. What does the term "Friend Evangelism" mean to you? Have you ever experienced it or offered it to another person? If so, what did you gain from those experiences?

8. Sophie's father asks Michael if he's ever noticed that God places people in his life to help him exactly when he's desperate for help? Like the woman on the train. Like Sophie. Like Oscar, the restaurant owner. Can you identify times in your life that you've been the recipient of this kind of help? Can you identify times when God has put people in your life to help you through a difficult situation? How did that make you feel?

9. Michael can't understand why God would ignore prayers for the safe return of a four-year-old girl. Do you think God answers some prayers and not others? What do you say to people who ask how can God "let" bad things happen to children? Is there an answer in Scripture?

10. Has there ever been a time in your life when you felt God didn't answer a prayer the way you wanted it answered? How did you react?

11. Have you ever done something you feel is too terrible to be forgiven by God? Is there anything God can't forgive? What does Scripture say about His forgiveness?

Kelly Irvin is a Kansas native and has been writing professionally for 30 years. She and her husband, Tim, make their home in Texas. They have two children, three cats, and a tankful of fish. A public relations professional, Kelly is also the author of two romantic suspense novels and writes short stories in her spare time.

To learn more about her work,
visit **www.kellyirvin.com**.

To learn more about books by Kelly Irvin
or to read sample chapters, log on to our website:
www.harvesthousepublishers.com